A CONFLICT OF CLASS

Joanna Joslin

authorHOUSE®

AuthorHouse™ UK Ltd.
500 Avebury Boulevard
Central Milton Keynes, MK9 2BE
www.authorhouse.co.uk
Phone: 08001974150

First published by AuthorHouse 2/17/2010

ISBN: 978-1-4490-7490-6 (sc)

Printed in the United States of America
Bloomington, Indiana

This book is printed on acid-free paper.

This book is dedicated to the memory of my late mother, Winifred North, who gave me the inspiration for writing it.

Grateful thanks must also go to my husband Brian, and to my agent, Darin Jewell, for their support and encouragement.

"Oh, what a tangled web we weave,
When first we practise to deceive."

Sir Walter Scott (1771 – 1832).

CHAPTER ONE

The purposeful gait of the woman and child caused many heads to turn that afternoon. Annie Ledgard was not the focus of their attention but rather the small girl at her side, desperately clutching her hand as they rounded the corner of the street and passed by the enquiring glances. The small brown suitcase which Annie carried confirmed their suspicions. Surreptitiously the eyes of both young and old of each sex keenly followed their progress. The footsteps of the woman and child continued to resound past each humble house before dying away as the pair turned through a passageway and finally disappeared from view.

Beckston was a northern town which by 1919 was just beginning to recover from the trauma of the Great War and the loss of many of its young menfolk. Neighbours genuinely cared for each other, living and working in close proximity, but at times this interested concern could result in unwanted attention. Of all the inhabitants just two elderly women had remained in the street to witness the arrival of the young girl, the others preferring to retreat into their own homes and watch from their windows.

'I didn't think that Annie would want to take on another child. Not somebody else's.'

This remark promptly caused the woman's companion to remind her of another fact.

'Aye and this won't be the first child she's had to rear for somebody else. Thomas may be her husband's, but he's not her flesh and blood. You can't quite feel the same when they're not your own.'

Annie and her charge continued their way through the passage, rounded the corner and found themselves standing at the base of two

1

steps leading to a rather drab, brown door. The Ledgards inhabited a 'back' house of a northern type of terracing, locally referred to as 'back to backs'. As the door opened the little girl peered with both inquisitiveness and caution into a dark interior. This was the living room which proved to be not quite as dark as first anticipated. The sun rarely touched these back houses and a permanent dullness about them at first conferred darkness, which later gave way to a lighter vision as the eyes became accustomed to the internal surroundings. The walls were distempered in a colour of pale green which somewhat helped to lighten the drabness of the heavy and solid furniture. Built-in cupboards and a black-leaded fireplace, the latter having a large overmantle shelf festooned with ornaments and tins above and washing below, seemed to dominate the room. They were permanent fixtures and remained with the house as solid unmoveable items, unlike many of the tenants of these properties who came and went as finances dictated. A table and chairs stood in the middle of the room whilst the remaining walls played host to a sideboard complete with large pillars and a mirror, an upright piano, a wringing machine triumphant in a corner, a settee and a matching chair. Sitting in this chair was a man of around fifty years of age. His face wore a tired and exhausted look, his eyes quite expressionless, his skin white in pallor with an afternoon growth of bristle; all serving as signs of age in a man who could have looked younger, if only the inclination had existed. This was his house. There was little need for formalities. Displaying an air of total disapproval and disinterest towards the young visitor, he remained seated in a rather slumped position, moving only once to gain a slightly more comfortable angle in his chair by the side of the fireplace.

'Go and say hello to your uncle,' prompted Annie who was not indifferent to her husband's moody behaviour. A scowl flashed across her countenance as she emotionally pleaded for him to accept the girl. The child, however, was reluctant and preferred to remain at the side of her aunt, a woman with whom she at least felt at ease with, unlike her host.

'Come along Helen, don't be shy. He's not going to bite you.'

Annie tried with a light-hearted approach in her persuasion but caution once again intercepted. Remaining firmly by her aunt, Helen refused to be coaxed to either move nearer or speak to this man.

'What's the matter lass, cat got your tongue? Perhaps our 'elen is too set in her fine ways to let on to the likes of us.'

This gruff and offhand remark from the man only served to confirm Helen's suspicion that she was not wanted in this household, at least not by her uncle. Brushing Helen and her aunt aside he abruptly slammed the outside door behind him, leaving the pair alone to contemplate the household readjustment. Annie was unable to hide her relief at his departure, albeit a temporary one, and allowed a warm smile to penetrate across her face.

'When you get to know him he's not so bad. He's just not used to having a young girl in the family,' remarked Annie trying hard once again to make light of a situation which was well rooted with problems. Attempting to smooth over the differences which existed she placed her hand on the child's head, pulling her towards her and tried to reassure Helen that stability would return to her little life. The maternal instincts at least existed and Helen revelled in the warmth and security of her aunt's embrace. It was not her mother's arms around her, but nevertheless the little girl felt a genuine fondness for her aunt. The feelings were mutual.

The afternoon had been extraordinarily long for Helen as she had been subjected to many new experiences and a stifled little yawn signalled to her aunt that it was time that she rested. On mounting the top of the staircase they turned left into a small bedroom which boasted two beds set closely together, owing to the lack of space in the room. Helen removed her coat and shoes herself, in a very independent manner, whilst her aunt drew the curtains and pulled down the top cover on one of the beds. Helen's tiredness quickly overwhelmed her and, before her aunt had covered her and left the room, she was already falling into sleep with its accompanying dreams of her mother, a distant father, and a life completely different to the one downstairs.

When she awoke she did so to sounds of an argumentative nature arising from below. The words were not clearly audible, presumably because the door at the bottom of the staircase was closed. Feeling refreshed from her slumber she arose, drew back the curtains and gingerly crept down the stairs until she reached the closed door dividing her from the living room. Instinct told her not to progress any further. She sank down on the bottom step and listened to the gruff tones of her uncle, which from time to time were peppered with the gentler voice of her aunt.

'Another child means another mouth to feed. Things are hard enough as it is. Good God woman, we just haven't got the room here,' snarled her uncle.

Her aunt prepared to retaliate.

'All you think of is yourself. That little lass lost her father in the war, now her mother's gone.
All she has is us. Would you really turn her away?'

Before the last word had been uttered something prompted him to burst out:

'All she has is us! That's bloody fine. What about her grandfather? He's made plenty money out of the likes of us and has a bloody big house to show for it. He could take her and never know she was there. But he wouldn't, would he? And we all know why. His precious daughter married beneath her when she married your brother.'

The man curtailed his onslaught and all that Helen could hear was her aunt sobbing. The cessation of the argument, however momentary, indicated that a raw nerve had definitely been exposed.

Although only seven years of age Helen possessed a bright intellect outshining many of her contemporaries. Her mother, a well-educated woman, had seized any available time to mould and fashion her daughter into an individual who would inquire, rather than accept, the nuances of life.

4

Some of the facts of this argument Helen clearly understood. Money was in short supply and another child would place an even greater burden upon any family of this ilk. Her uncle's earlier reaction to her had already confirmed this particular point. However the references made to her grandfather appeared somewhat groundless. Her parents had never spoken of grandparents and indeed the fact that her only living relative was her aunt had until this point determined the reason for her habitation under their roof.

Musing upon these points her mind momentarily drifted from the argumentative tones of the couple in the downstairs room, preferring to engage itself with an enigma devoid of an apparent solution, until the resounding of yet further voices brought everything to an abrupt halt. The voices, for indeed there was more than one newcomer, were male with distinctive childlike inflections. Suddenly the door that had provided a safe haven for Helen, separating her from the emotional outbursts, opened and she found herself staring at two small boys and an older youth, who perhaps was almost on the verge of entering manhood. As an eavesdropper the girl was neither embarrassed nor eager to retreat, age and innocence prevented either.

Annie quickly scurried across, obviously having forgotten about Helen, even though ironically the argument had instated her as the central character. She pushed herself in front of the boys, smoothing away any creases in her apron with one hand, and took the girl's hand with the other.

'Now Helen, this is my little boy Henry who everybody calls 'Harry'. He can be a right little demon when he wants, can't you?' At this point Annie stopped her introduction and tweaked the boy's right ear in an affectionate gesture. He appeared to grimace and made more of the situation than was needed, pretending to writhe in pain and shrink from the hold.

'Stop being daft, Harry. Anybody would think I was hurting you!' snapped his mother.

Only two years separated Helen from Harry in age. At nine years old he was the senior and no doubt would endeavour in the future to remind her of this fact. However Helen was not one to be intimidated. Standing erect to clearly show herself to be the taller of the pair, she stared at the boy with some disdain. The assembled party then turned their attention to the little boy at the side of Harry.

'Now this is Harry's pal, Arnold, who lives further down the street,' remarked Annie. 'I think your mother will be wondering what's happened to you.'

Annie's remark served not so much as an introduction but as a reminder to the little boy that as Saturday teatime appeared he had outstayed his welcome. Another mouth to feed was not to be encouraged, as Annie knew to her cost. Therefore Arnold duly complied, being of a malleable nature, and quickly left. Helen wondered whether his pliable nature and gentleness were in themselves major attractions to Harry, a boy who would clearly want to make the decisions and expect others to conform.

The final introduction had been reserved for the older boy. Stepping forward he crouched to a position which enabled Helen's eyes and his to be equally aligned, and warmly introduced himself without Annie's intervention. His name was Thomas and, being neither quite boy nor man at fourteen years of age, he unleashed a type of respect in Helen by his behaviour towards her that no one else in that household had succeeded in doing. Naturally Helen respected her aunt but here was someone who was young enough to understand the traumas of youth but old enough to be considerate and protective towards her. A curious inconsistency was laid bare. His manner exuded an empathic gentleness whilst his dark features and solid body frame denoted a developing masculinity traditionally unassociated with tenderness and feeling. His hands were already beginning to show signs of roughness even though his working days had only recently begun in one of the nearby textile mills. The voice, combined with his dialect, likewise communicated hard sounds as harsh and unbecoming as the windswept moors to the west of Beckston, along the Pennine backbone. His face, however, was different. Dark eyes sparkled with interest but a depth of penetration conveyed a feeling that he had experienced losing someone close. There was a kindred spirit here, the bond being grief.

Thomas's father Tom had married Annie shortly after his wife Edna had died. Never a well woman Edna's constitution had finally become wearied through winter chills and the final onslaught of pneumonia took a toll which the poor creature had no resistance to fight. Life with Thomas's father had no doubt contributed to her decline. Years of being lambasted for alleged petty misdemeanours, which in themselves presented no grounds for arguments, had erased any self-esteem the woman might have had. The nearby community spoke of her as a gentle rather self-effacing individual, who blended into any background when in the company of others. Rather plain in looks and always agreeable in temperament to anyone around her, she would have appeared very bland and unremarkable had it not been for one distinctive quality: the possession of a fine voice.

Hours had been spent by many, listening to the beautiful melodies which Edna had transformed into reality. The piano in the living room had been hers, and in the early days of their marriage it had been played upon Sunday evenings to accompany her whilst she entertained family and friends. Sadly the pianist had been an elderly but nimble weaver and not Tom for he possessed no musical inclination. other than in his courting days, to listen to this songstress; captivated he had certainly been by someone so outstanding in an ordinary street, in an ordinary town, to own something so remarkable which claimed the envy of every man and woman. Keen to be associated with such a talent, irrespective of the lack of physical attraction for him, he had persuaded her to marry him, not because he loved her but because she was different. This difference had quickly soured into indifference, the catalyst being Tom's lack of appreciation for his wife. Initially flattered by his sensuous dark features and attentive manner she had unwittingly been lured into a marriage of misconception. They tolerated one another, conceived a child, and lived as man and wife, but the marriage lurched from day-to-day and year-to-year without mutual affection, until Edna's voice became extinct. Upon being told of his wife's death after his day's work, Tom shrugged his shoulders, left his small son in the care of a neighbour and accordingly went to the nearest public house to drown his sorrows. This was the closest Tom ever came to grieving for his first wife.

If the seeds for the first marriage had been sown in a bed of novel dalliance, those of the second one grew out of convenience. Only a year separated Edna's death before Tom exchanged his vows, this time with Annie Siddall. Now cold and indifferent in affairs of the heart Tom Ledgard, although recognised for his disparagement of women often labelling females as 'expensive liabilities' and 'empty headed hussies', could not manage to live without a wife. This time he chose a mother for his son and a housekeeper for himself by combining the maternal qualities inherent in many women with the Victorian beliefs of ordered cleanliness, now found wanting in some since the Great War had emancipated females from the drudgery of the sink to the expanded horizons offered through employment on the trams and in the munitions factories. Compliance to a husband's needs had distinctly lost its shine. The band of females, known collectively as the Suffragettes, were to Tom, and many of his male contemporaries, a bunch of upper class women who were sadly in need of a 'damn good hiding' to bring them back to their senses. Campaigning for 'Votes for all Women' since the turn of the century, the Suffragettes had not been deterred or deflected by the events of the war; their involvement in employment had only served to increase their determination. Fortunately for Tom, Annie did not share their enthusiasm or beliefs.

Annie possessed a fine culinary ability which kept the family free from debt. Her mother had possessed the same quality of 'making something out of nothing'. Vegetables usually accompanied meat but on the few occasions when the meat was conspicuously absent Annie was able to turn the bubbling contents of her black enamel pot into a myriad of sustaining but tempting delights. The versatility root vegetables possessed in the hands of Annie reminded one of a conjuror with his illusions, everyone knows that the effect is not quite what it seems, but are more than happy to accept the brilliance of the delivery and overlook the intention to deceive.

As teatime approached the mastery of the pot revealed that the pecuniary position of the household was in credit and had afforded a large rabbit, which had obligingly simmered on the stove for the past few hours. Once the lid was lifted steam escaped and an intensified array of smells wafted across the room, beguiling Helen with richness so unlikely in a home in stark contrast. The propensity of the situation created confusion rather than ease in her mind. Her mother's cooking had never produced aromas with such impact, the truth being that her mother had known little about cooking as there was no real necessity for that until her marriage.

Suddenly the room became a hive of domesticity which Helen herself was sucked into. A drawer opened and a cloth appeared which Thomas threw gracefully up into the air enabling it to unfurl like a flag in the breeze, before it descended to cover an unattractive oilcloth on the family's table. Crockery and cutlery chinked and clanked as Harry reluctantly set the table being firstly admonished by his mother to do so. In an effort to repay their hospitality Helen offered to help but was directed to the small cellar head and told to wash her hands. Harry threw a penetrating look of disdain indicating that chores were not excluded for some. Jealousy had already reared its head.

Seated around the table with Tom at the end, assuming his headship of the household in a hierachial setting, the five quickly wiped away any trace of the rabbit stew. Tom sliced a loaf for those with appetites who desired more, namely the boys and himself, before reclining back in his chair, satisfied and full. The meal had been a true example of the family's diet; the setting with the cloth and extras had not. In an effort to welcome Helen Annie had brought out her best linen and table accessories, an act that was only to be repeated on special occasions. Never one to let a situation get the better of him, even at his modest age, Harry seized upon this and brought his self-interest out into the open with a rather spiteful display.

'Why 'ave you got your best things out on the table? It's not Christmas and nobody's got married. Nobody special has come for tea.'

'Harry!' snapped his mother, once again embarrassed by his behaviour but this time unable to hide it with good-humoured gestures, particularly as his last sentence had been deliberately loaded to sting in its attack.

'Helen has come to live with us. This is going to be her new home and we're her new family.' Annie had tried to smooth the animosity away and felt that she had succeeded until her son retaliated.

'Does that mean I'll have to share my bedroom with Thomas and now a girl? There isn't enough room. She'll have to sleep down here.'

'That's enough lad,' snarled Tom.

This was the first occasion that he had rebuked his son in defence of Helen. The boy knew he had gone far enough. Further goading would be foolish for his father's temper, once aroused, could be frightful.

Tom stood up, pushing the chair behind him as if to further reinforce his role of patriarch, staring at each individual in an effort to challenge his dominance.

'I'll have none of it. The house may be small but we'll just have to manage the best we can.'

Only a few hours earlier Tom had argued the reverse of this point with Annie. His change of policy may have been down to the contentment his stomach enjoyed or to a stoic realisation that even though he didn't welcome the girl into his home, the fact remained that without anyone else willing to have her, he would have to put up with an extra mouth to feed. Further his decisions were absolute and were not to be questioned by anyone else, as Harry was evidently aware. Life was never fair but as long as Tom's portions were not reduced, Helen could remain at his table.

Throughout that evening one person who had failed to participate in the taking of sides was Thomas. As a mere spectator he knew he would not run the risk of blame by remaining silent. He knew too well the course of events which could be unleashed if his father's temper was provoked. Verbal outbursts always led to a climatic furore which had to be quelled with disciplinarian force: the fist or the belt exacted obedience. Thomas had now left childhood behind him and could expect the unrestrained impact of his father's force. That night he had decided it was better for silence to prevail.

In spite of Harry's protestations that the boys' bedroom could not adequately accommodate another person Helen was given one of the beds for her sole use, the other bed had to be occupied by the brothers. This arrangement inevitably angered Harry whilst Thomas seemed content to oblige. The two younger children were always in bed before Thomas and remained there after he had risen and gone to work, thereby apportioning him a little freedom and privacy for his additional years.

Thomas, along with his father, left the house early each morning for Padgett's mill. As work began at 6am a solitary figure prior to this time was often seen walking down the street, winding in and out of the passageways. A long stick tapped mercilessly at Tom's bedroom window, a privilege he paid for, before progressing to a neighbour's window. The knocker-up, who was also a lamplighter, always prompt and reliable, came through every season and never allowed an excuse to deter him from his job. The Ledgards likewise could afford no excuses for lateness to work. Docked wages meant avoiding the rent man or walking past the butchers for that week for the loss of a quarter of a day's wages could not easily be made up.

Mills and their workers coexisted in an almost symbiotic relationship, neither being able to continue without the other. Beckston had been well-established since the Middle Ages, even the Domesday book had accorded it some reference. As a market town its fortune had rested on wool and this one ingredient became the catalyst for its transition. The sylvan scene of rural life began to evaporate around 1799 when the first mill appeared and domestic hand production was replaced with mechanised factory production. Victorian England saw Beckston's population rise to over 100,000 by 1850 as hopeful workers travelled from the surrounding countryside to find employment in its 129 mills. The creation of wealth laid further foundations for more mills and by 1900 the landscape had been irretrievably altered by 350 grim structures. Adjacent rural hamlets became encompassed to collectively produce a sombre and haphazard series of streets and homes punctuated by mills, warehouses and chimneys. Beckston's attraction lay not in gentility or greenery, for neither of these were evident, but it clearly had an attraction for a population which had increased by fifty per cent each decade since 1800. The people had squeezed themselves into cramped houses, backing onto others known as 'back-to-backs' crowded around the mills.

Beckston's fortune as a large woollen textiles town was based upon its tenacity to be part of the West Riding textile industry. This factor alone had made it the worsted capital of the world. Success indeed rested upon the geological basis of Beckston being blessed with minerals around the area ensuring a supply of soft water, an ingredient integral when washing wool. The other element of success lay in the fact that the worsted industry could only thrive on the availability of capital. Entrepreneurs were also evident in the town as an increasing carriage trade, later being replaced by automobiles, plied its way back and forth along the more fashionable lanes from mansion to workplace. These were the men of means who carefully organised the work and traded it but were not necessarily involved in the exact process of production. Vast fortunes were made for them to spend but those that made it for them were never as fortunate themselves.

Living in the shadow of the mill Thomas and his father felt its direct pull each morning as they routinely rounded the passageway into the street, before crossing the main road at the end and then descending down another street to Padgett's mill. Slowly the gates gaped open and allowed a pulsating throng of workers to bring daily life to the stone inhabitant.

Having only just begun his working life in a spinning mill Thomas was a bobbin ligger and it was his job to put empty bobbins onto the spinning frames whilst his father had progressed and was an overlooker.

His seniority, afforded by age and experience, allowed him to supervise the workforce under him and keep them busy for his job also entailed maintaining the machinery. He was quite aware that inactive machinery meant an idle workforce and a presiding horror of being laid off or replaced. Here in the workplace, like his home, Tom wielded some authority and anyone caught 'laiking abaht' would find their wages lighter, or an enhancement of enforced leisure time.

Every wage counted and as Tom had so bluntly pointed out, 'another child means another mouth to feed,' was an adage all too clearly understood. Winter was beginning to slowly creep up on Beckston and its arrival meant that Helen had been in the Ledgard household for almost six months. She loved her aunt and looked forward to Thomas's company, albeit as infrequent as it was, but her uncle, she was aware, tolerated her presence whilst Harry had a vindictive streak in him that constantly made her wary. Continually rebuffing her attempts to befriend him, he would positively refuse to walk with her to school. Moody and manipulative he was a child who seemed to have inherited none of his mother's qualities. Helen at last gave up her will to please him and began to ignore him. Indifference, however, stirred something within him.

Harry, as always, was the first one home. He would run all the way home from school knocking on people's doors, especially those he knew could not get to the threshold straight away and chide him. He would set the dogs off barking by imitating feline sounds and chase the cats away with pretentious hound like noises. Eventually the neighbourhood knew who it was but as few could match his boundless energy they, like Helen, ignored his schoolboy pranks. As Helen walked through the passageway one teatime she was about to round the corner and shout out her cheery greeting to her aunt, as she did each school day, 'Aunt Annie, its Helen!' when the sound of indignant voices stopped her.

'Why do I have to wait for her? That bread has just come out of the oven, it's warm and if I have to wait for her, it'll be cold. I'm always having to wait for her. I didn't have to before she came here.'

'Harry! Harry! That is enough!' snapped Annie. 'You're not a baby now and I expect you to act your age. I want you to be nice to Helen.'

'Why should I? She's nothing to me. I wish she wasn't here.'

'Any more talk like that and you'll get something you didn't wish for. I've had enough Harry and I shan't tell you again.'

Annie rarely lost her temper but her voice was beginning to apply a staccato delivery of short bursts.

'It's not fair, Helen never gets told off because she's a girl. I bet you don't tell her off because her mother was a fancy lady. I've heard you and my dad talking. Her mother's dead and I wish she was as well.'

Harry suddenly burst into tears as Annie hit him across the face.

'I hate you and I hate her and I'm going to tell my dad what you've done to me,' snarled Harry as he ran from the house, pushing Helen aside before disappearing through the passageway.

Inside Helen tried to comfort her aunt who was sitting with her head in her hands, crying uncontrollably. The sight of a grown-up behaving in this manner made her feel uncomfortable. In her world only the children cried and it was the adults who offered comfort and reassurance.

'Don't cry. Please don't cry auntie.' Helen cradled her small arms around Annie in an affectionate gesture.

'I'm alright lass,' came the reply as Annie dabbed at the corners of her eyes with her apron. She sat up and carefully looked at Helen, smoothing her fine hair away from her face. They gazed at one another, neither knowing how to react in front of the other.

Holding Helen by the shoulders, Annie clutched the child to her.

'I wish you were mine Helen, then it would all be so easy. But you're not and I can't make it any different. What's done is done and we must all just live with it.'

Annie wanted to relinquish the past. The small girl in front of her knew nothing of the divisions which had imparted misery and questioned loyalties. It would be better to forget it, except that the proverbial eavesdropper was always there. Like unexpected guests they appeared at inopportune moments to gather titbits to be stored and bargained with later. Harry was quite a professional eavesdropper and one who could not be ignored.

'Why does Harry hate me?' questioned Helen, her eyes carefully focusing on her aunt's face in close proximity.

'Of course he doesn't hate you.'

'Yes he does. I heard him say that he hates us both. Why? I haven't done anything to him.'

'Helen, I know that you've done nothing to cause him to say that, but I'm afraid that his problem with you is jealousy. He thinks that I'm favouring you over him. You see, until now he's been the baby in the family and when you arrived he found he had to grow up a little. He doesn't like it because he's used to being made a fuss of, but he'll come round, you'll see.' Annie tried valiantly to persuade Helen of this fact, even if she herself did not believe it.

Winter was often a grim reminder that the transitory delights of sun-filled days had deserted Beckston for darkening humourless skies. The season reflected the atmosphere of the Ledgard household. Thomas and his father returned home from work with Harry following the latter, having enlightened his father over his unprovoked treatment. Fortunately for Helen Tom had refused to take sides and for once chose to believe that his son had warranted being struck.

Little conversation passed that night, but Helen felt Harry's eyes burning into her with extreme hatred. The usual bedtime routine occurred. Helen, followed by Harry, was the first to go to bed. Hours appeared to have passed, for Helen had fallen into such a deep slumber that the sudden presence of Thomas in the room convinced her that morning had arrived and he was rising for work. For a few minutes she watched him removing his shirt in the dim light, undressing instead of dressing; he was oblivious to her gaze. Content that the night had not fully passed she closed her eyes and turned her body away from the two boys. Something slithered across her face, being loose it covered her nostrils and her mouth. Feeling that she was being smothered she pushed it away, only to find it separate and fragment into slivers of a fine, silken nature.

Suddenly crying out, Thomas was next to her, holding her small frame close to him, in an effort to comfort her.

'Helen, you're alright now. You must have had a bad dream. Come on, that's all it was, go back to sleep. Oh my God, your hair, it's... it's all over the bed.'

Long tresses lay strewn amongst the sheets. The remaining tufts of hair, which had been left after the hacking, jutted out in ill-defined bristly shapes from Helen's head. She sobbed, touching her hair left on the pillow, wanting to believe that it was nothing more than a nightmare. Quite oblivious to Thomas's actions, her attention was overtaken by a deep feeling of sickness in her stomach. Her mother had often meticulously brushed her long hair. In her mind she pictured her mother's face, gentle and reassuring, a beautiful woman, a lady of distinction. Why had she been taken from her, why had death intervened?

'You little bastard, Harry. I knew that you were capable of somethings but to cut Helen's hair off is just the end.'

Thomas's calm composure had evaporated. Dragging the younger boy out of bed he punched him in the stomach and, although winded, the lad attempted to pull himself up as Thomas hit him across the face. Blood trickled down from his nose as he slumped to the floor.

Thomas had gone too far. Almost a man himself he had exacted a brutal retribution on Harry and knew now he must expect the same from his father. Annie ran to her son whilst Tom stood calmly in silence at the bedroom door. The inertia was terror in itself. Relief came as Harry sat up, coughed and Tom beckoned to Thomas to follow him downstairs. Helen sat unblinking, not daring to move. She dreaded what might come next. The silence continued, only to be punctuated by the slamming of the outside door. Running to the window she saw Thomas alone outside. As ice glinted everywhere in the moon's light, she knew it was a penetratingly cold night.

When Tom returned he did so calmly which in itself triggered Annie to react with anxiety.

'Where's Thomas, what have you done to him?' she asked with unease.

'Nothing, I haven't so much as laid a finger on him, if that's what you mean,' declared Tom seemingly quite detached and undisturbed by the night's events.

'You've not hit him, have you? You're a lot stronger than he is.'

'Like he is than Harry?' Tom quickly glanced at his younger son who was sitting quietly, recovering from a nosebleed and a sore abdomen, before he continued.

'I said I haven't. He's spending the night out of my sight, which I think is best for all of us.'

'What do you mean by that?' puzzled Annie, agonising now not just over one son but two. Thomas had always been a kind boy and one she had taken to her heart with motherly affection.

'For God's sake Tom, where is he?'

'He's spending the night in the closet.'

The reply seemed cold and cruel. Annie began to sob with pity.

'Please Tom, you can't do that to him. It's freezing cold out there, he'll die. Please Tom, let him come back in, he'll know he's done wrong. I'd rather you have walloped him one than this. Let me go and tell him to come back in.'

Annie went quickly to the bedroom door but Tom intervened, positioning himself in her way.

'You'll do no such thing. Take one more step and I'll not be responsible for my actions. He's out there to be taught a lesson One, he'll not forget in a hurry. I could have hit him, but I know that this way he'll remember not to start throwing his weight about whilst I'm here.'

Annie sank onto Helen's bed. Physically and emotionally she was drained and thereby unable to offer any morsel of resistance to her husband. He prevented her taking any bedding out, remaining resolute in his dictatorial stance.

Throughout all the proceedings Helen had patiently sat on her bed without being spoken to or indeed noticed at all. Her appearance was frightful and even when Annie finally looked at her she showed no surprise or shock on her face. The truth was she could no longer summon the required energy to display compassion; weariness had simply usurped it. Helen slept with her aunt whilst Tom joined Harry in his room. Annie had suggested these arrangements in an effort to avoid a surge of arguments. The night stretched ahead with infinite hours as bodies tossed and turned, their minds consciously enacting the preceding trauma and its culmination. Annie finally began to doze but awoke startled as an image of a corpse wrapped in white presented itself; the shroud being not material but ice.

Exhausted through worry and sleeplessness Annie crept quietly down the stairs ahead of the household, in order to prepare breakfast as well as to convince herself that Thomas was still alive. Frost had covered the windows hindering any clear visibility of the backyard. Tentatively she opened the outer door and immediately sensed a presence behind her. Turning round she saw Helen staring up at her.

'He will be alright, won't he?' demanded Helen.

'Yes, of course he will,' came the firm reply executed with the maximum of assertion which masked a degree of doubt.

A terrible thought suddenly filtered into Annie's mind. What was the worst possible thing which could happen now? She had already had several images of part of it: Thomas, frozen to death, but to compound that she pictured Helen's inquisitive little face peering at the point of discovery. She had already lost her mother and father but had at least been spared the sight of them when dead. The child could not be party to this. She had to think quickly, give herself time to open the closet door and look inside without a spectator at her side.

'Helen, will you go upstairs and bring me the blanket from my bed? I think Thomas will be glad for a bit of warmth.' She tried to deliver the request in as light-hearted a manner as possible.

Opening the closet door was as difficult as she had imagined. Every conceivable emotion transgressed from her to its servile body, until finding the inner strength, she flung back the door and stood in disbelief. Thomas smiled, stretched his arms and yawned before rising to his feet.

'Don't look so worried, Annie. It'll take more than a lack of leg room and a cold night to finish me off.' The remarks were delivered with a nonchalant air.

'Oh, thank God you're alright lad. I've kept thinking the worst all night long. I couldn't sleep with wondering about you. How did you survive? You don't even look half-starved to death.'

'Come on Annie, that's enough about last night. I wouldn't say no to something to eat.' Thomas placed a kiss on her cheek as a mark of gratitude. Looking uncomfortable and perplexed she motioned for them to return to the house.

Upon seeing Thomas Helen skipped lightly into the yard, thrusting the blanket upon him.

'Oh Thomas, I'm so pleased you're alright. We all thought you were going to die.' Helen, forthright in her speech as always, tried neither to conceal nor embroider upon the facts. Age and innocence contributed to that.

'No, it'll take more than that to carry me off. Anyway look at you.' At that point he ran his hand through her untidy, spiky hair. She was not normally given to looking dishevelled. 'Is this the new fashion?'

Suddenly the austerity of the moment evaporated as the pair giggled. Holding her close to him she felt happy, cocooned in protection.

'I think we'd better go in or else I'll be in trouble with Annie as well,' laughed Thomas.

'Aren't you scared?' enquired Helen.

'Scared of what?'

'Of him. I mean Uncle Tom.'

'It's no good being scared Helen. Life is too short to live in fear. I've been frightened of him in the past but that's all behind me now. Besides, what is done is done. Oh, he blows hot and cold sometimes, but I know what he's really like. He thinks he's taught me a lesson and that'll be enough for him.'

Helen's lack of years did not prevent her from sifting through the arguments to return to the cause of them. The motive which had initially caused the upset had been her presence.

'Thomas, I'm very sorry for all the trouble I've caused you.' Her gentle little face began to distort as her eyes filled with tears.

'Trouble? You haven't caused me any trouble. It was Harry who caused that. He always does. Besides I'd do it all again for you.'

'It was horrible you having to sleep out here.' Thomas smiled and catching her little hand he pulled her towards him, crouching to her level.

'If I tell you a secret, will you promise to keep it? You mustn't tell anyone else.'

Helen's eyes grew large as the iris in each emitted a beguiling blue as the pupils dilated. No one had ever favoured her with such a demand. Excitement was something which she always seemed excluded from. Lowered voices and whispers abounded but who could tell what riddles they held when she was not permitted to hear them.

'I promise I won't tell anyone,' came the reply.

'Well, I didn't sleep in the closet all night. Old Mrs Shackleton next door took me in and gave me a bed. She might be slightly deaf but she doesn't miss much, especially when she's putting her cat out at night.'

Helen's mind raced ahead. 'But Auntie found you in the closet.'

'I know she did. That's because I got up early this morning and sneaked across to make everyone think I'd slept there all night.'

A look of relief filtered across Helen's face. 'I'm pleased you're alright. Can't we tell Auntie? She's been worried about you,' asked Helen.

'No, especially not Annie. If we do she'll tell my dad. Oh she won't mean to, but if I know Annie it'll slip out somehow. It's a secret just between the two of us Helen, isn't it?'

'Yes. I promise I won't tell anyone,' came the excited reply. She was determined to maintain this bond of trust, revelling in the delicious feeling of being a chosen confidant. This was a new feeling for Helen to experience and one which she was pleased to share with Thomas. She was quite sure that she would never let him down for a promise was a promise and she would keep it forever. She was also sure that she would never do anything to hurt Thomas. He was her special friend.

CHAPTER TWO

The new decade introduced contrasts of far reaching consequence, more than any that had gone before it. Victorian and Edwardian propriety had at times been broken behind closed doors, but the 1920s flung back those doors to expose a habitual excess of frivolity and liberation which before the world had barely glimpsed. Sombre browns of traditional responsibility inherent in life's canvas were painted over with vibrant shades of gaiety by the nouveau riche. Centuries of careful practice were swept aside by a young generation, exuberant to be alive after the carnage of war, their egomania turned them into exhibitionists.

Codes of deeds and dress confirmed this. American fever arrived to ensnare both the minds and bodies of the young whose extremities gyrated to the heady rhythms of the Charleston and Foxtrot whilst any thought of morality became abandoned in the face of the Tango, as cheeks touched together in tantalising displays. Women's bodies, no longer imprisoned in tightened whalebone corsets, enjoyed a relaxed state of shapeless indulgence. Gathers and tucks were abandoned and garments falling from the shoulders gave not a hint of feminine form. Ankles and calves were no longer concealed as hemlines rose considerably and men became accustomed to a pair of shapely legs, rather than the desires of an hourglass figure.

Life's familiar 'tried and trusted' conventions paled into the background as new crazes landed into the laps of those with both the time and money to dabble. They initiated the sensation of change in an effort to free themselves from the turbulent aftermath of war, but at a speed that was too frantic to take account of the pull of the direction and therefore the consequences. Yesterdays were forgotten and tomorrows had not yet begun. Only the todays had any true meaning.

It seemed Beckston had been exclusively bypassed by this masquerade of enjoyment which manifested itself continually at every cocktail and fancy dress party given. The larger houses lying in elevated positions above the town no doubt concealed the whims and fantasies of their households whilst the parallel streets, lined with families, played host to the mills and not to distractions. Plenty of ex-servicemen had returned to their wives and children but not to employment and with only medals to wear and signs to carry, they reminded others that their sacrifices needed supporting.

The world had changed, whether for the better was a question posed by many a philosopher who would have to be content with waiting before exacting a judgement. A topsy-turvy state of confusion seemed to prevail with women emulating masculinity, sporting short-cropped hairstyles, voluminous trousers and illicitly sampling the challenge of cigarettes in public. All this against a backcloth of what a few years previously would have seemed an impossibility: the dawning of the first Labour government, bringing with it a glint of hope amidst the despair of drudgery and deprivation. Ramsey Macdonald was indeed welcomed by those with a heart for change. Being the first Labour Prime Minister he presided over the hopes inspired by socialist policies and, like Lord Caernarvon who had recently opened Tutankhamen's tomb, the population were waiting to see the hidden treasures which the government would unearth to fight unemployment with. 1923 was for many the year which would bring about those long awaited changes.

Beckston continued to pulsate as a microcosm of British daily life, as did the Ledgard household. The new crazes of the age had not arrived at this doorstep but the day-to-day arrangements of domesticity had somewhat shifted, owing to individual convenience. Thomas, now unquestionably a man at eighteen, was lodging at the adjoining house over the passage with Mrs Shackleton, the neighbour who had given him refuge four years before during a penetratingly cold night. Thereafter it had seemed the most sensible thing to do. Alice Shackleton, an elderly widow with a vacant room, had readily warmed to the idea of company with the added attraction of board and keep, whilst the Ledgard household spread themselves a little more comfortably with four rather than five bodies at bedtime. Annie's evening meal, however, was strongly held in preference to anything that Alice Shackleton could produce and Thomas always eagerly used the chance to see his family as the reason for returning home at that particular time.

Harry had learned to avoid confronting Thomas and appeared to tolerate him as he did Helen, except that he afforded Thomas a little more respect, possibly a legacy that night had fashioned upon his soul. No longer did Helen share a room with Harry. The sting in that tail had been unquestionably removed by Annie who quickly suggested that Tom should share with Harry whilst Helen remained in her room. The speed at which the suggestion came was sufficient to smack of an ulterior motive. Only Annie was keenly aware of the opportunity offered to her, which she executed with her own brand of manipulative innocence. No longer would she face the insulting and undignified fumblings of Tom's lovemaking, his breath always strong from beer, his mind unable to concentrate and his body uncoordinated. There had been too many occasions when he had repeatedly tried but had reluctantly conceded to defeat in an exhausted stupor. Lying next to him she had again and again found his touch repugnant. Physical requirements and the fear of losing his manly reputation governed his need of her. Her need of him was as a father and provider who had long ceased the role of fulfilment as a lover. She no longer cared if he looked elsewhere and for this reason had swiftly installed Helen as her insurance against such demands.

Helen was also beginning to change. No longer the little girl her mind and body were beginning to make preparations for another stage of her life, but without her knowledge or consent. She had known nothing of the menstrual cycle until its alarming appearance convinced her that there was something wrong with her. Only the ashen colouring of her normally rosy complexion had made Annie concerned, believing that she was sickening for some ailment. The truth of the matter was that Annie had failed to prepare the girl. Having raised two boys, and Helen only eleven years old, Annie had simply put the matter to one side, believing that the time would come in the future. But the time had come as the incident had painfully proved. Annie for once looked carefully at Helen, taking time to scrutinise her. Aunt and niece were close but being constantly busy with household chores Annie had failed to see the changes taking place. The caterpillar was becoming a butterfly and Annie had never noticed the metamorphosis. She rebuked herself for being so blind for the signs were there. Slight curves around the breasts and the hips had already begun to transpire which in themselves had given emphasis to a waist, as well as the fact that she had grown rapidly over the last few months, causing Annie to unpick hems for an extra inch of decency. All the signs of approaching womanhood had been there but Helen had been left in a state of ignorance.

One aspect of her development which had not been overlooked was her beauty. Adjectives such as 'bonny' and 'pretty' had always been attributed to her, but now she was on the verge of becoming beautiful. Her blue eyes were offset by long, thick, dark eyelashes, which seemed to intensify the eye colour every time she blinked. Dimples would appear in her cheeks every time she smiled. Even an ordinary bland hairstyle fell into a teasing bob around her face. Helen was no ordinary girl.

A difference of seven years separated Thomas from this girl. Although now a man he still sought her friendship with its fine brand of innocence and undemanding loyalty. The relationship was mutual for she craved the reliability of protection and the bond of affection which he generously provided. Neither quite a father figure nor an idol, he managed to unleash feelings in her which had they been left to anyone else, would have remained dormant.

She waited for him each evening as he routinely made his way along the street before turning into the passageway. Tom on some occasions walked with him but his presence never deterred her from running to Thomas's side to accompany him home. Sometimes she would slip her hand into his as she skipped alongside him, endeavouring to match his long strides. Tired and hungry Thomas always found the little ritual quite refreshing. Together they would return to the Ledgard household and enjoy Annie's cooking.

One evening their routine was interrupted as Alice Shackleton called to her lodger.

'Thomas, can you come and lend me a hand?'

Perpetually obliging Thomas followed her into the house with Helen in his wake.

'That window up in my bedroom is so stiff I just can't manage to shift it. I opened it this morning to let a bit of fresh air in and now the thing's refusing to budge.' Suddenly aware of Helen's presence Alice turned to her and knowingly remarked, 'That's the price you pay for getting old lass.'

With youth on his side Thomas bounded with repetitive ease up the staircase leaving the woman and girl downstairs.

Everything about the room appeared haphazard and cluttered. A large sideboard held court at the back of the room, its intricate, inanimate carvings of flowers entwined with fruits began to take on human forms, the hollows between the wooden blossoms emerged into eyes and mouths and entire faces that stared blankly back at Helen. She blinked and the carpenter's skills returned to their original designs, enabling her transfixed glare to be broken. Pottery and glass competed for attention in an excessive show of clutter on the sideboard and around the room in general. The difficulty of removing all those items was clear enough for layers of dust had gathered to produce a dull covering on the furniture, evidence enough to support Annie's theory that her 'next-door neighbour was non-too-house-proud'. A curious array of ribbons and lace lay strewn on the horsehair sofa. They had obviously lain there dormant for some time until the unexpected chimes from the wall clock activated the cat snoozing next to them, to stretch and jump to the floor, pulling many of them with him as a party goer collecting streamers.

'Now then Lloyd just look at the mess you're making,' came the timely warning.

Helen smiled to herself, wondering if the cat usually received the blame. Dark and sleek he approached Helen, purring at her side, whilst she stroked his back and helped Alice wind the narrow lengths of adornment into order. She was a milliner by trade who also turned her hand to dressmaking.

'That's a funny name for a cat,' enquired Helen.

'You might think so but to me it was a logical choice. I've had my Dizzy and my Gladstone and now my own Lloyd George. The next one no doubt I think will be a Baldwin. It could even be a Ramsey or a Macdonald.'

Helen stared puzzled with the origins of such names. 'Ramsey or Macdonald?' she muttered.

'Yes, you know the new prime minister. I always call 'em after prime ministers. It doesn't matter which party they stand for. I think if the names good enough for 'em, it's good enough for my little companion.'

As she spoke her dark eyes sparkled. They were not the eyes of an old lady but more like those of a blackbird, bright and intense.

It seemed rather appropriate that this spirited little lady should have a cat, especially if Harry's description of her was true. Her cat was black and didn't they always have a black cat? But surely witches were just a figment of the imagination. Harry didn't think so. How many times had he said, 'I dare you to go in there, where it's dark and she's waiting,' but Helen had never had the courage to until now. The large aspidistra appeared threatening as it waited near the door, like a huge spider ready to devour its prey. It waited, but Helen could not move. Why were her thoughts so terrible? The answer no doubt lay with Harry. Subconsciously her actions were being governed by an infiltration of hearsay and emotion, compounded out of all proportion.

'Helen, what's the matter with you?' came the familiar reassuring voice.

Everything had become obliterated in that room, including Thomas's return. Suddenly the darkness of the moment passed as the demons in her mind vanished and Helen became aware of Thomas and the old lady staring at her.

'I'm sorry, I suddenly felt frightened. I don't know why, I just did.' The reply seemed feeble and embarrassed Helen, causing her to slightly blush as she voiced it.

'Come on lass, come and sit over by the fire and have a cup of tea. Thomas certainly deserves one for doing what he has done for me and you look as though you could do with the colour putting back in your cheeks. Now a few more minutes won't harm will they? Thomas, just pop next door and let 'em know what's happening, will you?'

Such kindness quickly dispelled any former unease and Helen now felt ashamed by her behaviour. Her manners were usually unquestionable, setting her apart from others of her age. Alice Shackleton had for a long time sensed that there was something very different about her. Until now she had never had an opportunity to study her closely, but the time was ripe for an inquiring mind to be laid to rest. The girl had arrived at the Ledgard household with characteristics true of upper class breeding. Alice had mixed sufficiently with the echelons of high society, albeit only as a milliner who served attention to their headstrong fancies, but nevertheless she recognised gentility in its purest form. This child had not learned such genetic secrets from Tom or any of his household, including Annie's brother. The poise, the walk, the entire disposition had been inherited rather than created. Therefore if the past held intrigue the future would surely predict fascination.

'Give me your hand Helen.'

The girl's face took on a state of perplexion as Thomas entered the room.

'Annie says tea'll be ready in quarter of an hour,' Thomas breezily announced.
Silence prevailed momentarily as the trio stared at one another.

'Alice, come off it, you're not trying that one with Helen are you? Just because I won't have any part of it, you're going to get round her and tell her that she'll marry a rich man and travel the world.'

'There's no harm in it. There are lots of people who believe in my powers and seek me out. Why be frightened of what the future has in store for you. You can't completely change it but you can prepare for it. Anyway I can also see the past which can often have a bearing on the future.' Alice reclined back in her chair in a triumphant mood and waited for Helen to make her decision.

'Come on Helen, I think we'd better go back to Annie's,' Thomas intervened with decisive haste, offering an outstretched hand as a tangible inducement of motion.

The girl, however, was unwavering, her thoughts having been teased away from the routine sequence of daily life.

'You can see both the past and the future, just by looking at my hand?' enquired Helen.

Perhaps Harry had been right all the time. If she was a witch she would be able to unlock a door in Helen's life that hitherto had remained strictly out of bounds to her. There was nothing to be frightened of,, the only unnerving aspect here was ignorance, a state that Helen was continually wrapped in.

The past and the future unlocked in the space of just a few minutes. Curiosity had no boundary. The old lady had anticipated well Helen's curiosity and had used the time to brew the tea and pour it out whilst the girl resolved her inner dilemma.

'Will you do it please, I want to know?' came the anxious reply.

'Give me both your hands then.' Alice carefully examined each hand in turn, touching and turning them before focusing entirely upon the right one. She stroked each crevice on the fleshy mounts of her palm and carefully followed the deeply defined lines of heart, head, life and fate. Occasionally she gripped the hand and attempted to bunch the fleshy protuberances, so as to further define the markings of the lines and their subsequent branches and deviations. A pensive air of anguish began to slowly form on Alice's face.

'Well lass, you have very soft hands, just like those of a lady. You can always tell breeding.'

The pair looked at one another, Helen reluctant to utter a word in case Alice became distracted from her reading.

'I can definitely see that money surrounds you but you cannot touch it. Not at the moment, in any case. One day you will. However you will have to right the wrongs that have gone ahead of you and in so doing, you will bring unhappiness to others.'

'Come on now, that's enough!' declared Thomas. 'I knew that all of this would end in tears.'

The girl looked confused and upset. 'I don't want to hurt anyone, why should I?'

Alice tried to offer comfort to a situation which she herself had not hitherto predicted. In truth the lines on this hand held a future of turmoil and trouble, offset by a past of conflict. The girl held an inheritance of sorrow in her hands as well as prospective wealth.

'Don't look so worried lass, you're going to be a very rich woman.' Alice attempted to alter the atmosphere with uplifting conviction. 'There's a man in your life that you don't know about. But he's there, waiting for you. His house stands high above everyone and everything else and one day he'll welcome you.' Despondency, once again closed-in, Alice allowed her young companion's hand to drop loose from her grip.

'I think that you'd better go home for your tea now Helen, as Annie will be wondering what's happened to you.' The old lady felt tired and exhausted and was no longer able to conceal the future's bare facts with intrigue, as apprehension had already taken a firm hold.

The pair left quietly and Alice was at ~~last~~ left alone to contemplate her thoughts. Lloyd curled up with contentment at her side as she stroked him, indifferent to the proceedings that had taken place unlike his companion who could not erase the turbulence from her mind. Many would laugh with mockery at the supposed powers of palmists, but few had had cause over the years to question hers. She played no part of a charlatan and yet in this case was beginning to regret her integrity to relay a truthful interpretation. Not that she had completely divulged everything that had been apparent, but the child was as yet too young and naïve to fully appreciate the consequences of a predestined future. Her childhood was almost at an end and no doubt she would be longing to fill her adult life with stability and love. The future it seemed would be as unreliable and conflicting as her past.

An atmosphere of muted expectation surrounded the table that night. Tom was a man unaccustomed to waiting and Harry a lad who feasted on adversity. Only Annie as a woman had sympathetically tried to contain the situation but the emotions, like her dinner, had simmered for too long.

'Where the bloody hell have you been?' came the volcanic surge. Tom seemed almost in danger of exacting a thrombosis in front of the assembled party. The rage had surfaced to his face which resolutely reddened as his eyes narrowed.

'When I've been at work all day, I expect to come home to my dinner. I don't expect to have to wait for you to play nursemaid to some old biddy.'

The strain of remaining quiet in order to lessen the provoked attack began to show uncomfortably on Thomas's face. 'To be fair Tom, I did say that the meal would be ready in fifteen minutes,' Annie intervened meekly.

'You may have said that, but I didn't. Besides your fifteen minutes turned into forty-five bloody minutes. What's the matter son, can't you tell the time?' Father and son glowered at one another. Only Harry sat at ease, seemingly enjoying the lively remarks.

'It wasn't Thomas's fault. It was me who wanted to stay,' Helen quietly intercepted. The girl's admission momentarily diffused the situation, but unwittingly she had placed herself directly in front of the firing line.

Slowly Tom pushed his chair back and rose to his feet. Silence prevailed as the patriarch made his way towards Helen, causing fear to tingle down her spine as he stooped behind her. She felt his hot breath burn into the flesh of her neck. The silent seconds seemed like minutes before he made his attack using soft sarcasm.

'So it was you who wanted to stay. I didn't realise that we were waiting for you. If only I'd known, I wouldn't have been so impatient.' A leering grin flashed across his face as he straightened his posture to tower above the girl.

'Thomas you should have said that we were waiting for her ladyship here, for then I wouldn't 'ave minded my dinner burnt to a cinder.'

His right hand rose with the final word before being wielded down and across the right side of Helen's head. The sudden unexpected blow made the girl topple from her chair, causing her to bang her left cheekbone on the table corner before reaching the floor.

'The next time the little bitch might remember that there's a set time for meals in this house and that we all sit down to 'em together.'

Completely devoid of any remorse Tom left the table and the household, slamming the outside door behind him. Only Harry sat at ease, clearly having enjoyed the distasteful scenario.

Dazed and sore, Helen was carried upstairs by Thomas whilst Annie anxiously collected a bottle of iodine and lint. A small cut on the left cheekbone had acted as an open floodgate to incessant bleeding whilst an enlarging swelling on the side of her head was beginning to give cause for concern. Cautiously and gently Annie tried to minimise the sting of the antiseptic, but Helen stoically refused to wince for to have done so would have been an admission that she was in pain. At that moment she felt nothing. Emotionally her feelings had drained away leaving her tired, listless, and totally disinterested in the care being afforded to her injuries. Neither Annie nor Thomas appeared in normal form to her, their shapes slowly blurring into incandescent vapours, as consciousness finally gave way to the obscurity of darkness.

Neither Annie nor Thomas had much sleep that night. Dividing the time they each in turn took their place at Helen's bedside, remaining vigilant and hopeful that she might need them. As daylight slowly began to penetrate through the chinks of the curtain's sides, Thomas realised that he would shortly have to leave his patient and begin his toil for another day. She was so still, so unlike the girl he knew, vivaciousness had been replaced with silent vulnerability. He wanted to hold her close to him and wrap his strength around her. He imagined what it would be like to stroke her hair and caress the fine soft skin of her face, neck and shoulders. He also imagined what it would be like to feel the curves of her lips against his own. Suddenly his imagination began to disgust him. How could he allow his thoughts to turn to this? Neither fear nor exhaustion was an adequate excuse. Helen was certainly a beautiful girl.

That salient thought remained with him even as Annie took charge and reminded him that if he was late to the mill he would find the gates closed and his wage 'quartered', factors which would do no one any good. Obligingly he left Helen in the care of her aunt, but as he closed the outside door he paused for a moment in the cold morning air, willing her to recover, and wondered if the friendship could ever be the same.

Helen quickly regained consciousness, much to Annie's relief, but found herself relegated to bed and rest. Even the chores of the day were swept aside as the girl was pampered and fussed over with an abundance of charm and care. Nothing was too much trouble. Helen had only to ask and the favour would be granted. The mind was alert and the moment was ripe as Helen summoned up the courage and asked what she had wanted to know for so long.

'Will you tell me about my parents?' Annie looked aghast as the request was made, fearing that the blow to the head was beginning to incur serious repercussions.

'Now then, what's brought all this on? We'll talk when you're feeling better.'

'But I want to know now. Everyone else knows. Even Mrs Shackleton could see more than she was prepared to tell me about. I'm not stupid and I'm no longer a child. I think I have a right to know.' Helen was in a defiant mood, one that Annie could not deflect from.

'Are you saying Mrs Shackleton read your hand Helen?'

'Yes, she did. She told me I'd be a very rich woman but that I'd hurt others, which I don't want to do. That's why I want to know about my parents and my past. Please Auntie, I need to know.'

'Did she tell you anything else?'

'She just said that there is a man waiting for me in a house high above everything else.'

The reputation which went before Alice Shackleton was richly deserved. On occasions she had prophesied events in Annie's life which had occurred with a routine expectancy in the life of the millworker's wife. Only now it was clear that she had excelled herself.

Drawing up a chair to the side of the bed Annie settled herself, earnestly trying to wear the look of composure.

'There's not a lot to tell. Your mother, Arabella, married my brother Robert. I think it was love at first sight for him. I can remember him coming home all excited on Sunday teatime to tell us that he'd met a beautiful girl in the park. They'd spent the whole afternoon together, just talking and listening to the band playing. We all knew that he was really smitten. Each Sunday they used to meet and then one time he brought her back for tea. She was lovely with big blue eyes and a gorgeous smile. In many ways a lot like you.'

Helen began to blush being unused to compliments. A moment elapsed as Annie carefully studied the girl's face and began to recognise a younger version of Arabella.

'They were married in 1911. It was a gloriously hot day in June. The butter was melting as we made the sandwiches. Even the jellies couldn't hold their shapes. I can't remember a hotter day than that. And then a year later you were born, which made their happiness complete.'

Annie slowly walked over to the window in a subconscious attempt to distance herself from Helen and the more unsavoury parts of the past. She stood for a moment gazing down onto the backyard. The words were there but the will to disclose them was lacking. Suddenly the awesome responsibility evaporated.

'It's alright Auntie, I know that father was killed in the war and that mother died in an accident at the munitions factory.' The child was remarkable. She calmly announced what Annie had evaded. Relief filtered through momentarily until Helen's curiosity surfaced with inquisitive precision.

'You haven't told me about my grandfather.' The words had been delivered with innocence but they struck with compelling force.

'Your grandfather,' Annie hesitated, 'I know nothing of him.'

'I know I have a grandfather,' Helen persisted, 'I heard you and Uncle Tom talking about him.'

The deception was laid bare as Annie's composure disappeared leaving her cornered with no leave to escape.

William Fawcett, Helen's grandfather, had been born into the comfortable surroundings of Mount Hall, a large prestigious house erected high above the smoke filled air of Beckston's mills, as a testament to the entrepreneurial foresight of his ancestors. Business acumen was a distinct hereditary trait of the Fawcett men and William was no exception. Born in 1864, the second child of James Fawcett, the first infant having the unfortunate fate of being born a girl, William proved himself to be both sharp and shrewd, earning his fathers trust and securing his right to succeed him in running Fawcett's mill a quarter of a century later.

Such men, the Textile Elite, belonged to a distinct class that met regularly through business and social connections and further compounded these links through marriage. Hence there was a close and reciprocal protection within this web of relationships. William himself belonged to such a group having married into a family of like-minded individuals, the purpose of which was to combine the strengths of two aspiring businesses into the ultimate strength, a business concern so large in a district without any viable competitors.

Helena Ingham, William's wife, dutifully bore him one child, a daughter, before childbirth exerted its price and demanded her life. He was left with the responsibility of a small, helpless infant whose upbringing he eagerly relegated to a nurse. Retaining the child at a suitable distance afforded him the strength to maintain his powerful leadership in the textile community without jeopardising his hard bargaining reputation. There was no place for soft sentiment in his life. His workers relied upon him for their daily employment and their daily bread and money was there to be made. A daughter was, after all, a financial liability until marriage.

He used his mind with sharp discernment and penetration so that business dealings always followed his direction. His household was likewise tempered and moulded to his exact requirements of a hierarchy, consisting of himself at the pinnacle and any relations and staff filtering below in a rank organised by age and status. Only one unforeseen weakness threatened the Fawcett domain and that lay in

Arabella's emotional strength to defy her father and fall in love with a man without money or class, a worker at the mill. Arabella would see no reason, to her father's eyes, and no amount of threats could persuade her to adopt an alternative course. Consequently she left Mount Hall and her father's wealth with a few portable possessions and married Robert Siddall.

One year later, on the 4th of August 1912, Helen Siddall was born. Her initiation into the world was not wrapped in upper class style, or middle class comfort, but instead lay with insecurity in working class fashion. Arabella recalled her father's words as she glanced across to the tiny bundle, wriggling helplessly in a drawer from the sideboard, 'Marry that lad and I'll wash my hands of you!' Those words had been uttered with reproach in an attempt to dissuade his daughter from marrying without his consent. No amount of advice or threats would have done that then, but the difference that a year had made rested entirely upon a baby whose future had been predestined by her mother. There was no nursery, no proud grandfather, not even a cot to herald her arrival. Arabella had sunk back into the bed finally aware of her actions and that the only legacy to the mammoth fortune was a name. Her mother's name had been Helena; her daughter would be christened Helen.

Although William Fawcett's granddaughter grew up devoid of her true family connections and all the comfortable possessions accredited accordingly, she did have compensations in the way of parents who genuinely loved not only her, but each other. Family life however soon began to fragment and eventually shattered in a world convulsed with war. Beckston was not exempt from the patriotic excitement, which swept through the entire country on August 4th 1914 when the declaration of war was proclaimed. The regular troops marched out of the town on August 10th and a short time later were followed by the Naval Reserves amidst renditions of 'God save the King', and 'Rule Britannia.'

Recruiting started early in one of the most prominent places in the town, on the steps in front of the town hall. Business and trade union leaders, prominent thespians, members of parliament and soldiers flanked the Lord Mayor as he encouraged all young men to volunteer for

'King and Country'. The momentum of war continued to be stepped up as official and precautionary announcements were made, including one advising the public on how to react to air raid danger as it was strongly believed that Zeppelins would appear in the vicinity. The fields of war and death were miles away, but the furore of action manifested itself in Beckston as recruiting increased, encouraged by determined marches through the town by local battalions.

As much as Robert wanted to remain with his family he also had a desire to perform his duty and was convinced that the recruiting posters claiming that:

'Yorkshire, with its broad acres, dense population and strapping sons, must not lag behind in this life and death struggle against the German military despot,'

were aimed to encourage decent men to fight for home and country. Not to do so would have exposed a coward. Robert was not that.

Amidst the furore and passion of marching battalions, resolved with enthusiasm to fight the enemy and return back to their loved ones, came a debt to the nation. Death and injury abounded and those young men who were fortunate enough to survive and return home on leave found their relatives examining the horrors of war in faces which had aged witnessing suffering. Some of these men, including Robert, returned home on leave in 1915. Arabella saw a husband traumatised who wished not to talk of the trenches or of the war but who preferred to wander round the park, go to the music hall and superficially block out the thought of ever returning to France. A few days later he left his hometown and family, afraid to return but equally afraid to desert. Within the year he had been killed in the Battle of the Somme.

Robert's battalion had left their trenches at Serre in Picardy on the Western front, made their way precariously across no-man's-land, only to be confronted by German machine-gunners who fired with deadly accuracy. Lloyd George spoke of 'the choicest and best of our manhood' slaughtered, but the exhortations of bravery did little to improve the fact that women were left without husbands and children without fathers. The *Beckston Daily Telegraph* nightly carried lists of killed and missing men. In total 2000 Beckston men failed to return; statistics which completely obliterated any proud memory of men marching to defend their homeland.

Prosperity did not accompany the peace of 1918 for poverty spread through the northern towns like an incurable disease. Despite this malady a community spirit survived sufficiently enough to enable the population to rejoice. Machinery in the mills ceased to run and the trimmings and decorations normally reserved exclusively for Christmas celebrations adorned the silent looms. The people of Beckston sang, danced and talked as they had never done before. A war which had had such a direct effect upon them had to be laid to rest; like a wake, this was their way of doing just that.

It was inconceivable how four years could disproportionately affect a lifetime. The Victorian and Edwardian values which had dominated in 1914, along with their staunch class distinctions, had given way to a new era of independence and, to some degree, feelings of freedom for women. The war had been a leveller in households, both rich and poor. The menfolk had been gone and the women had had to take the place of those men.

Arabella, like many women, had supported her child and herself by working in a munitions factory. However fate unkindly decreed that on one of the few night shifts that she happened to undertake a shell exploded in a fusing room killing thirty-eight people, herself included. It was believed that pressure had been applied upon the workforce to ensure a more sustainable output, but this had been at the expense of safety precautions. Undue regard for this factor gave rise to thirty-eight corpses, sixty injured and considerable damage to surrounding homes, as an unparalleled sequence of explosions gave vent to the short measures of the war effort. The tragedy of this event was doubly enforced as the war finally came to an end a short time later. Helen was left with neither parent, and briefly resided with a neighbour until Annie persuaded her husband that the little girl should live with them. The persuasion factor was of little revelation to Helen for she was quite aware of Tom's resentment of her. There were now no more secrets left. Events of the past could in no way be altered. Facts which had to be faced. In the course of one afternoon Helen had grown up, enriched by her aunt's trust and disclosure.

If the past was over, the future was still to arrive and in Helen's mind she began to conjure up the image of an elderly grandfather, waiting for her in a house high above everything else. Only the future could confirm Mrs Shackleton's revelations.

CHAPTER THREE

Miss Frood's fingers tapped on the desk with increasing impatience.

'Come along girl there must be an answer in your head. Have you really spent the last year soaking up everything and absorbing nothing? Perhaps you really are an empty vessel!'

The class was careful to avert their eyes from Miss Frood's unrelenting stare, as each individual tried with great resolve to suppress any induced humour from such a remark. Ironically the lesson was a science one and only the teacher appeared indifferent to the use of her own puns.

'Diana, am I to understand that your inability to voice an answer is the ultimate result of abject ignorance?' bellowed the contemptuous articulate tones of Miss Frood.

Daringly the class fixed their eyes upon Diana who seemed quite oblivious to their attention, unlike Helen who sat beside her with her head bowed in condescending fashion.

'It's 212 F,' whispered Helen.

'Who cares if that's her age?' came the retort.

'Do you think she's ever had a man?'

Helen blushed as Diana tried to shock, albeit in a whisper, and only wished that her friend would act sensibly instead of foolishly prolonging the inevitable.

'For the last time, can you enlighten us to the boiling point of water?' came the final taunt.

'No, I don't usually bother testing the temperature when my mother makes the tea,' came the defiant reply.

Bubbling to the boil Miss Frood's anger surfaced with thunderous effect as she ordered the girl to the headmaster's study. The entire charade had been manipulated with calculated accuracy so as to provide the audience with a modicum of enjoyment at the expense of their teacher's authority.

Diana endured the cane with stoic determination rather than masochistic derision. Strong-willed and at times temperamental, she often allowed herself to be swept into situations which were entirely off course for her and therefore had to accept the ensuing consequences of her actions. As a friend to Helen she provided inspiration, challenge and a complete belief that nothing in life was insurmountable. Far from being a fool, which she regularly enacted during lessons, she had a sharp intelligence which she saw little value in blighting with academic trivia; not that the Bell School could be haled as a great institute of wisdom, but it performed its task of educating the masses with decorum if not gentile refinement.

Helen had never encountered anyone quite like Diana. The enticement of danger constantly prevailed, drawing those around her like a moth to the flame, ever conscious of the resultant perils but eager to savour the transitory delights. An only child, she extracted from the situation her full entitlement to a pampered life on the very stretched wages of her father's bank clerk position. Her mother had already worn the poor man out with her incessant demands for a lifestyle that outstripped her husband's potential and now his daughter had a craving for the same aphrodisiac. Although plain in looks Diana, with her mother's assistance, capitalised upon every little marketable nuance. A new plain coat instantly became transformed with a fur collar and cuffs, and suitable matching accessories of felt hat and gloves would be sought. Whilst most children thought themselves lucky if their feet were covered at all, Diana, with her mother's persuasion, regularly added to her footwear and every other collection. She attended dancing lessons to master the waltz, foxtrot and tango in an effort to become nimble and poised. In truth the girl was spoiled but her mother viewed it as an investment for her daughter's future happiness. How else would she appreciate and attain the finer things in life? And attract the calibre of husband to pay for it all?

At first Helen had seemed insignificant in Mrs Wilkinson's plans, living in a millworker's home her humble upbringing was hardly likely to penetrate her into the higher social strata. First impressions, however, had perhaps been misguided interpretations which were sorely in need of being revised.

'Are you sure Helen's telling the truth? She might be making up a few white lies just to impress you.'

'No she's not, I know she's not like that!' Diana seemed indignant that anyone, least of all honest Helen, would attempt to pull the wool over her eyes.

'But after all Diana, if her grandfather is William Fawcett do you really think that she'd be living in a little back-to- back? I don't really think so!'

It was on occasions like these that Diana's mother was keen to assume precedence, giving herself inflated airs and graces. They lived in a large through end terrace which immediately elevated her and her family from the squalid poverty indured in a back-to-back.

'However, if what you're saying is right, perhaps she ought to go and see him. In fact we could all go and call at Mount Hall. You never know, we might get asked to stay for tea.'

The notion of polite conversation in an elegant drawing room, where silver sparkled and china chinked as tea and cakes were consumed, was a hope which was too much for Mrs Wilkinson to abandon.

'Why don't you ask Helen to come to tea? She's just the sort of girl you should have as a friend.'

****

With regret Helen wished that she had been less hasty in her disclosure to her friend as she sat at the table and listened to Diana's mother talking about William Fawcett as though she knew him well, or even at all. The woman had never spoken to him but she possessed sufficient bluff to dominate the conversation.

'Mrs Hargreaves, who lives just three doors down the road, was telling me that her youngest used to work for Mr Fawcett before she married. She's now got a little boy and her husband's doing ever so well. He's in insurance you know.'

It totally amazed Helen how every passing acquaintance mentioned was successful and accomplished, leaving no room for failure or struggle. Momentarily the flow of conversation ceased as the woman passed round a plate of shortbread and silence longingly prevailed. It was not etiquette to talk and eat at the same time.

'Anyway as I was saying, Mrs Hargreaves's daughter used to help out at the hall. She did very well there for herself; being a maid she obviously had the full run of the house. You should have heard about the things that he has there, they're beyond belief. It's obviously good taste but then of course money always breeds that. Well you should see his bed, a proper full-tester with heavy drapes. It's so big that his staff often joke that he'd be able to fit all of his millworkers into it!'

The conversation was becoming more absurd by the minute. Like a storyteller the supplier of this information was relying upon make-believe and an incongruous base of second-hand experience.

'And the gardens are absolutely breathtaking. Do you know that he employed nine Italian workmen for four months to lay mosaic paths? It's all very classical. He even has a hanging garden, where plants hang down from rocks, and at the bottom there's a walkway around a large ornamental pond. He even has a billiard room which leads out to the garden and on summer evenings they throw open all the French windows and he entertains on the terrace. I've heard in the main it's business associates but he always moves in the right circles. Well a man like that won't put up with anything less than the best.'

'Best' was a word which Helen had rarely experienced if one related it to the material goods of this world. To relate it to people was but a relative exercise. How could one human being be measured against another human being? Hadn't Annie always said that 'there's good and bad in everyone', even taking into account the fact that Harry could be most objectionable, he was still Annie's son and the recipient of her love. To counterbalance individuals' human characteristics and then place them in some form of pecking order was surely an impossible exercise, unless the scales became heavily stacked with the weight of gold. Helen's father would never have had a hope. He would have been far from the best in Fawcett's eyes, who was nothing more than a bigot. To care more for money than love had left the man inferior in Helen's eyes and at the bottom of the scale.

Soon Helen began to tire of the elongated descriptions of the elaborate embroideries, the plethora of paintings by celebrated artists and the adornment of carved panelling, entirely encapsulated in a mausoleum of wealth. She had also become weary of hearing the woman's pretentious voice and her intrusion, albeit based on hearsay, into the house which at one time had been her mother's home. Diana evidently felt the same and seized upon her father's arrival from work as a chance to go for a walk.

'Mother does tend to go on a bit. I bet she's bored you rigid, she does me. The thing is nothing's ever good enough for her. She always wants more. I know I like to have nice things but I don't think I'm a snob, do you Helen?'

There was no reply. Helen's mind was preoccupied.

'Helen! What's the point of me talking to you if you're not going to listen? I might as well go for a walk on my own.'

'I'm sorry I wasn't ignoring you on purpose.'

A smile suddenly became transfixed on Diana's face.

'I can read your mind Helen Siddall. You want to go and have a look at Mount Hall. My mother has already had that idea along with tea and cakes there. Oh, don't look so worried, you don't think I'd let her come with us, do you? She'd spoil all the fun. Have you any money with you?'

Helen shook her head. Alone she would not have had the courage to embark on such an adventure, but her companion could mastermind the plan without effort.

'Stay there. I'm just going to my grandma's. She always offers me money for sweets. I'll try and get enough for there and back on the tram. If I don't we'll just have to walk back.'

Helen did as she was told and waited with anticipation.

As Highbury came into view the tram made a vigorous attempt to complete its journey over the final steep gradient, almost emitting a sigh of relief as the terminus was reached. This wealthy district of Beckston was aptly named for it stood proudly in an elevated and privileged position well away from the polluted air, suspended above the town. Beckston itself had settled and sprawled with haphazard irregularity out of a valley which could no longer be classed as beautiful. Even though industry had darkened and smudged the land, defiling its natural allure, there still remained an attraction. The area was a natural amphitheatre which had been fashioned by glacial lakes thousands of years previously and now man, in his unique, selfish way, was adding his own insignificant markings to the terrain. These could not eclipse the northern exposed moorlands, or the solid Pennine backbone to the west, eternally hostile to the transitory threats of man-made structures.

Gigantic and awesome, the true land dwarfed any intruder, as did the waning July sun whose rays filtered and fanned down, producing a canopy of incandescent magnitude.

Helen had never viewed Beckston from this vantage point as she had never visited Highbury before. For a while the girls wandered around unsure of the location of their destination until Diana took the initiative and asked for directions to Mount Hall, whereupon they found themselves meandering down a wide tree-lined avenue. A varied assortment of foliage, including those of copper beech, yew and oak, provided a degree of privacy to the large houses behind them. At every entrance the house name was scrutinised, often the stone gateposts bore the inscription, but the true interest lay in the individual facades. In the main the houses were detached, but there the similarity ended as each one boasted a unique quality of style, further compounded through the choice of conservatory, balcony and bay window, each one vying for position with its neighbour. The time had passed quickly but still Mount Hall had not been found. The avenue seemed to be of infinite length as it stretched into the distance until the road unexpectedly curved. At this point there were no houses to be seen or driveways, only thickly wooded trees and a high stone wall. No conversation passed between Helen and her friend as they followed the wall with parallel precision until it revealed a large open drive, offset by large ornately carved stone gateposts, on which each held the name, Mount Hall. The house itself was not visible from this point as a sweeping drive and further trees obliterated any possible sighting but both girls knew that this residence possessed a grandeur found wanting in those they had just passed.

'Come on Helen, we haven't come all this way to look at a couple of gateposts!' Diana's confidence was to be found wanting in her companion.

'I can't go in there! I just can't. You don't understand what it's like for me.' At this point tears began to trickle down Helen's face and the pallor of her face highlighted her distress.

'Alright, perhaps we can't just march up the drive and knock on the door asking to see your grandfather, but there might just be another way to get asked in.'

'But I don't want to see him. He doesn't want to see me. And besides I don't want to be caught trespassing on his land. That's what it would be. Annie would never forgive me.'

'I'm not talking about trying to see him, but it would be nice to take a peek at the house and gardens. I doubt you can deny that.'

A plan needed to be seized upon and put into action quickly. Left to Helen they would now have been returning to the tram but Diana was tenacious, stubborn and frightened of nothing.

'Wait here, I won't be long.' Again Diana left her friend alone, returning within a very short time. She had continued down the avenue past the grounds of Mount Hall until she had reached the entrance to a farm beyond which only verdant fields dotted with docile, content cattle could be seen. She noted the farm's name and returned quickly to Helen.

'Where have you been? What are you up to?' Helen enquired anxiously.

'I wanted to find out if there were any more houses past the Hall. There's only a farm.'

'What on earth do you want to know that for?'

'Because Helen if our plan is going to be swallowed at all we need to have our story straight. We were walking down past Mount Hall to Ingham's Farm, that's why I had to find the name out, and we need to be going this way because past that place there's nothing to be seen as far as the eye can see.'

'But why would we be going to the farm in the first place?'

'Oh to collect some milk, to meet your dad who's just started working there, who cares? No perhaps we'd better forget the milk idea, we haven't brought a container.   Anyway here we are walking down the road when you suddenly feel faint and pass out. You come round but are too weak to walk to the farm so we have to get some help at the Hall. Brilliant don't you think?'

Helen was amazed at the ingenuity of her friend and at the choice of role she had been given.

'Why does it have to be me who faints? I think you'd be much better acting out the injured person.'

'Because ever since I suggested going in there you've looked pale. Anyway, might as well make use of any props that we have.'

Diana chuckled with delight. She was most adept at improvisation and was a difficult character to sway with conformity. Besides which Helen had never been party to such an adventure. She even recalled that delicious feeling of sharing a secret with Thomas, the night he had supposedly spent in the outside closet. To this day she had divulged nothing to the contrary and hoped that the enticement of this situation would be as emotionally fulfilling as that. Her friendship with Thomas though had noticeably changed of late, not in any instigated move on her part, but he had become less tactile, choosing not to hold hands or touch her as he had once done, with his hand around her waist or resting on her shoulder. At times now he appeared distant and cool. The vacuum slowly beginning to form between them had gradually been filled by Diana's effervescence. A new chapter had begun in Helen's life with her friend stage managing the entire plot.

Winding around well-established rhododendron banks, the approach to the hall was further shaded by a number of finely grown trees whose exact arrangement contributed to the climax of anticipation any visitor might have upon first visiting this residence. Precisely when one least expected an opening the Hall majestically appeared, large and well-proportioned, its opposing turrets presiding over a predominantly Scottish style of architecture. Facing towards the east the principal façade, being screened by trees of ample girth and stature, would be sheltered from the bitter blasting winds of winter whilst extensive views of the northern moors ensured an excellent vista of brown and purple hues of the heather-clad hills in summer. Constructed from mellow Yorkshire stone, whose gentle colouring belied its inherent strength, the present hall was a comparatively modern building having been completed in 1856, replacing a dwelling of a much older date, which had served as an isolated manor house to the numerous sheep and dairy farms of the surrounding hills. The site itself obviously had had an attraction for centuries to those with wealth and dominating power.

A large portico shielded the main entrance, its dense coping stones being supported at each of the free corners by stone columns, the whole effect adding to the grandeur of the building. Parked to one side of this was a dark blue and black Armstrong Siddeley automobile, its distinctive sphinx mascot positioned with full aggressive splendour above the radiator. Such a motor car epitomised wealth. Its sleek elongated running boards, spacious interior and uneconomical consumption of fuel, guaranteed a vehicle which at 1000 pounds only the privileged could ride in. The Duke of York had himself given the royal seal of approval to it when he had taken delivery of one in 1920 with a second one in 1921, and evidently William Fawcett had bestowed the same honour by selecting one for himself.

Walking out into the open, away from the cover of the trees, Helen at least felt uneasy. Her feelings were not without substance as the sound of twigs and leaves rustling underfoot made both girls turn with some alarm. A man in a black chauffeur's uniform stepped from the bushes, unaware of their presence, having just relieved himself he was struggling to fasten his buttons.

'That's why those trees are so big. You wouldn't think they'd do that sort of thing here,' whispered Diana, giggling with delight.

Helen, clearly embarrassed, gestured to her friend to remain quiet in the hope that she would refrain from further faux pas. If they were going to offer a convincing act it had to be realistic and free from fickle behaviour.

'Do you two want something?' the man questioned with a disapproving look.

'My friend's just fainted. We were on our way to Ingham's farm to meet her dad who's working there now and it just happened. I didn't think she'd be able to make it as far as there so I wondered if anyone here could help. All she needs is a little rest.'

Diana had performed her part well, so much so that the man began to show concern.

'Come to think of it she does look a bit peaky. Yes, she certainly looks pale. Are you alright walking?' Helen slowly nodded and the man intimated to them to follow him. Ignoring the extensive terrace, which seemed to encircle the hall, they followed a lower pathway down the side before turning into a doorway situated on a lower level. Even from this angle it was possible to glimpse the smooth lawns intercepted by winding walks and enjoy the feeling of space which several open acres of land bestows.

The eminent exterior did not extend to the basic interior. A large, scrubbed white-wood table took the place of pride before walls filled with shelves of crockery meticulously arranged, pans that gleamed, always with their handles positioned to the right paying tribute to the large Victorian range and a large wall clock that served as a reminder that as one meal neared its completion another was yet to begin. As the heart of any home the kitchen maintained a circulatory service to the rest of the household and it was therefore an important place to be.

'Mrs Bentley, could you spare me a moment of your precious time?' came the well-rehearsed but perfectly delivered request. At mealtimes a cook needed to be approached with almost sycophantic reverence.

'You always want something when I'm up to my eyes in it. There'll be hell to pay if I don't get his sauce just right. I've only one pair of hands and I'm behind hand as it is. It's been like this all day. If you want to make yourself useful pass me that sauceboat.'

The chauffeur sprang with alacrity to the side of his ill-tempered colleague whilst a butler flanked her at the opposite side with demands of haste.

'I can't go any faster. If Mr Fawcett doesn't like it, he can come down and do it himself!' snapped the irate woman.

The two girls had remained at the far end of the kitchen, just inside the doorway, and with the atmosphere as it was they felt reluctant to venture any further and draw attention to themselves. Within seconds the drama had subsided as the butler and the sauceboat hastily retreated.

'I won't be rushed in my own kitchen. He wouldn't be rushed when he's making business deals. It's always the same, there's one law for them and another for us. And it doesn't help when there isn't a mistress in the house. Women have some understanding and some patience, but men don't. Especially him. He thinks I can just conjure something up out of thin air whenever he wants. He should've told me this morning that he wanted his meal earlier instead of having me rush like this. If he finds a lump in that sauce he's only got himself to blame.'

Being agreeable to everything that was said the chauffeur finally calmed the woman down with his own brand of home based psychology, before raising the issue of some maternal care and attention for his companions. Everyone including the pseudo 'patient' for a time forgot their immediate business, withdrawing like understudies to the wings of the stage.

Showing some alarm the corpulent frame suddenly swung around and moved with the kind of urgency not normally associated with those of ample flesh. There was no time for stage fright as Helen's pale complexion whitened as her heart palpitated with an irregular rhythm. Diana fussed with feigned concern as her friend was seated before her head was unceremoniously bent low between her knees. Later smelling salts were held to her nose, the stimulating effects of which caused her to cough with compelling force, enough to put some colour into her cheeks.

'That's my girl!' The chauffeur's anguish turned to relief.

'You always know what to do Mrs Bentley, especially in a crisis.'

'I hope you do Mr Clough,' the cook retorted as the drawing room bell rang forcibly, summoning the staff's attention to the ever-present needs of their employer.

'I'd better look sharp, it'll be me he wants outside. Is it seven o'clock already?' The chauffeur instantly disappeared.

'You jump to it lad. I just hope that you've put enough spit and polish on it, otherwise you'll be for the high jump.' The woman sniggered to herself as she publicly voiced her thoughts.

'Don't you like working here?' Helen enquired hesitantly.

'It's not that, goodness I've worked here long enough to be used to his awkward ways and he knows it. He'll not boss me around for there's no one to hold a candle to my cooking and he knows that. But the others aren't as indispensable. Like the workers in his mill there are always plenty more to step into their shoes.'

If the woman had a penchant for indiscretion and self-importance it seemed excusable whilst in the employment of such a man. Wealth was not an excuse for the ill-mannered or unfeeling and Helen often questioned how it was that her maternal grandfather had fathered a loving and generous daughter, her mother Arabella. Perhaps the error of his ways was responsible. He had steadfastly taught his daughter a lesson, paying for it with loneliness and perhaps bitterness. The question was, would he have done the same again or had regret soured the old man to such a degree that he was incapable of feeling anything but cold indifference to others?

The standard of hospitality below stairs, if not grand, was warm and friendly as the girls welcomed the invitation of tea and cakes. The rich plum cake and individual ground rice cakes were, according to their hostess, a speciality requested throughout the household. She regaled how she had won her late husband's heart, before her waist had spread from an enviable twenty inches, with the tempting delights of the table. Entertaining and at times whimsical she peppered her tales with proverbial wisdom's; encouragement to take another piece of cake was instilled with 'Better wait on cook than doctor;' replenishing the teapot exacted 'Tea seldom spoils when water boils;' at this point the two girls swiftly exchanged glances repressing any laughter as Miss Frood's science lesson surfaced in their memories. That seemed such a long time ago and almost another world away as did the frugality of the Ledgard household. Relaxed and happy Helen was oblivious to the attention being paid to her by Mrs Bentley until she caught the woman's penetrating stare out of the corner of her eye. The moment suddenly became uncomfortable as guilt threatened to usurp the entire enterprise and expose their charade. Helen averted her gaze, cast her eyes downwards, blushing under the intense scrutiny and waited for the accusations to begin. Ingham's farm was too close an alibi for comfort.

'It's a funny thing, but ever since I set eyes on you, I've been trying to think who you remind me of.'

The woman pitched the remark with some certainty in her voice, implying that she had solved the conundrum.

Ingenuity was Diana's strength and she delivered her trademark with intervening swiftness.

'That's what everyone says about you, don't they Connie? She's a marvellous mimic, always clowning about. You wouldn't think it, but she is.'

Diana had tried to lighten the situation and further the anonymity by selecting the first girl's name she could think of. There were in fact two Connies in her class at school whose names were constantly used in reprimands for misbehaviour, so a familiar name became a logical choice.

'No, it's definitely the eyes and the smile. You remind me of Miss Arabella, Mr Fawcett's daughter,' came the unwelcome remark.

Helen fidgeted and felt decidedly hot.

'That is a compliment Connie. Fancy likening you to somebody like that!' Diana was still trying to play the game but her remark had strayed outside the rules of convention, serving only to embarrass and hurt her friend, whilst Mrs Bentley unreservedly disclosed more.

'What a tragedy that was. And they say 'Children are poor men's riches.' If that were true Mr Fawcett would have lost his fortune a long time ago. By now he'd be the poorest man on earth. He can be an awkward devil with the best of 'em but he didn't deserve to lose his wife, daughter and granddaughter. How unlucky can a man be?' The woman dabbed at the corner of each eye with her finger.

'They were so young for death to creep up on them. It was a tragedy that's what it was,' continued the woman.

'Death,' repeated Helen. 'When you say he lost them you mean that they all died?'

'Yes, just that. First his wife in childbirth and then his daughter in an accident.'

'And his granddaughter?' demanded Helen.

'That's something that none of us know much about. He just said he'd lost the girl as well and muttered a common misery which had caused a great deal of pain to all. We think that it was diphtheria as there was plenty around at the time. He doesn't want to be reminded of his losses and that's probably the reason for the way he is. You know it's just as well that he didn't set eyes on you tonight for I'm sure that you would have reminded him of the past.'

Helen felt sure that there was a great deal of truth in that. Annie had once said that she possessed her mother's eyes and smile, which had now been confirmed by a stranger. Why should William Fawcett not see the same with his own eyes? Of course he would not choose to for the common misery he had referred to was a potent and infective cocktail of poverty inseparably mixed with the working class. One sip and it would slowly take its degenerate hold, inflicting a low life with no escape. Under such circumstances quarantine could only be assured by absolute destruction. To him everything connected with that humiliating part of his life had died. Helen felt nothing, there was no sadness, no hurt, no resentment, no longing for bloodline affection. How could there be, when she had never even seen the man? Her emotions, like the situation, were non-existent.

Mrs Bentley had been preoccupied for too long with her own microcosm of events that she had failed to direct her inquisitive nature to scour the recesses of her visitor's lives. At this point Diana intervened and fended off the questions with contrived credibility, revelling with impromptu importance as the sole performer in a finale of deceit. The performance was over as they left the hall and followed the serpentine windings of the drive. Only once did Helen look back at the imposing structure bathed from behind by the light of a setting sun. The desire for an improved lifestyle had been kindled but there was not a thought of what might have been but what could be. That thought did not include Mount Hall or her grandfather. She was totally unsure of what it did include except for the fact that any success in her life would be her own doing. Coldness and indifference had taught her that. The visit had also taught her that whilst death destroys and obliterates memories, birth can create the growth of a new beginning. Within her determination had already begun to grow.

The return journey passed quickly. Whether the adventure had been successful was still in the balance. To Diana it had fulfilled her need to perform, but even she recognised the fun had now evaporated and would not sustain a sequel. Helen, quiet and reflective, preferred to gaze at the panorama of difference which the changing landscape provided as the tram left Highbury and descended to the vicinity of her home in Milldyke. A stench of unwashed wool filled their nostrils as they passed the numerous mills before the tram stopped by a collection of shops, a tripe shop, confectioners, butchers and drapers. Familiar territory, this was home to the populace of Beckston and the end of their journey.

The friends parted and Helen made her way to Paradise Street. This, like hundreds more, was the haunt of the rent man who would consider himself fortunate if the money was there. Many husbands claimed it as beer money before his arrival and thereby pre-empted a chain of events involving the womenfolk, the pawnbrokers and anything which could be deemed as being worthy of being pawned. Money, or rather the lack of it, kept these streets aired and alive and for this reason alone to equate the word 'paradise' with a working class street was an antithesis of belief. For those who knew nothing else, however, contentment reigned supreme. A group of children amused themselves with an old clothes line, one at either end twining the rope, often vigorously, as the skippers jumped gleefully in response to the tunes.

'All in, a bottle of gin,
All out, a bottle of stout.'

'Raspberry, strawberry, gooseberry jam,
Tell me the name of your young man,
A, B, C, D, E, F...'

Helen watched with envy as the collective group laughed and giggled until exhaustion took its toll. They seemed happy, not wanting anything else except a make-do rope and each person to play their part. As Helen turned and walked through the passageway to the Ledgard's home she wondered if that symbolised life: making do with what you have been given or was that simply what the working class had to believe? A little voice within said that paradise is what you make it, and having seen the Highbury paradise she knew that everyone's standards were different. She was determined that one day she would leave Milldyke and set her own standards.

CHAPTER FOUR

The office reverberated with an inexhaustible pounding of typist's fingers which failed to perform in unison and thereby created a continuous metallic clatter of alphabetical keys. Helen watched in awe as each member of the organised and meticulous workforce performed individually but with collective orchestral ease. A girl of fourteen was indeed fortunate to be given the chance to work in such an establishment, a piece of advice which Helen was instilled never to forget: far better to earn one's daily crust here rather than behind a loom. Tetlow Brothers was an established and well-respected clothing manufacturer supplying in the main, high quality overcoats for gentlemen. A term used broadly to describe that part of the social echelon who could afford the high prices of these quality garments. Money, as always, remained the deciding factor.

The firm, a family one, operated with organised precision under the steely guise of Mr Edward Tetlow, a somewhat hard-faced character, stout in build, whose reputation frequently preceded him with new business contracts as that of a 'rough diamond' who had ascended to his position by working hard under his father, the initial founder of the firm. A hard task master he contented himself with being in charge of the cutting room where his aptitude for shirt sleeves and profanities declared him more at ease with the workforce, unlike his reserved and respected brother Richard who acted with quiet decorum to secure the new orders which the business existed upon. Each brother, totally different in temperament and outlook, played his role unquestionably well. Neither one could have stepped into the shoes of the other without exacting a loss of success. The phrase 'each to his own' was especially suited to this partnership, like worsted and shoddy, each a fabric in its own right but easily discernible in its appearance and performance.

Each individual in the firm co-existed only with the mutual assistance of the next. Therefore the precision of the cutter's skill was essential for the expertise of the machinists, in particular the buttonhole machinists, who handed their garments over with pride to the finishers, pressers and buttoners before having their work subjected to the unrelenting and intense examination of the faultless passers. Careless work was always exhibited with disapproval and returned to the unfortunate individual with a severe reprimand that not only would a repeat performance result in the wrath of Mr Edward, but in a nonnegotiable invitation to seek work elsewhere. As employment was fast becoming an endangered occupation it was considered wise not to tempt providence in the first place.

The same steely rod of management equally applied to the running of the office, an internal microcosmic organisation that lived and breathed at the side of the manufacturing element. Each one reliant upon the other, like the action of the heart ever reliant upon the arteries and veins and they in turn rendered lifeless without its sequential pumping. Helen was both impressed and a little frightened by the unknown expectations which awaited her. Mr Booth, a rather dour faced and exacting little man, motioned for her to follow him through the office. He was the senior in charge of this administrative realm and commanded with ultimate precision exactness in the standards of bookkeeping with the ever-accompanying columns of debits and credits. Not one head was raised from its paper as the exactor and his protégé walked through the desk-lined room.

'Come along young woman, time is money, an important factor to remember in business. Ah Miss Walker please let me introduce Miss Siddall, Miss Helen Siddall to you. She will be joining us and I trust you'll find her eager to fulfil her obligations in meeting your high standards.'

Although Mr Booth was senior in position, at that moment he almost appeared to withdraw backwards and assume a lowering sycophantic gesture towards this woman.

'As you well know Mr Booth, anyone who doesn't, is of no use to me.'

The words had such venom in them that it was fitting that this tall thin spinster should feature in Helen's mind as a cold-blooded viper. The eyes seemed small and the lips thin and unappealing, possibly never having been touched with a smile.

'I take it this is your first position? Yes I'm sure it must be.'

The girl nodded without uttering a word, waiting anxiously to be given her instructions.

'All the ladies here are experienced typists, a position that someday even you may rise to. For the time being however, as Mr Booth has possibly told you, we need an office junior. Someone who can make the tea, collect the post, file and undertake the general duties as and when needed. Do you think you have the necessary attributes for such a position?'

'I hope so, I will try and do my best,' uttered the perplexed girl. 'I would like to… '

'Never mind, what you would like! I need someone who can do as they are instructed. Just remember that your first priority is to me. The typing section is my domain and so you will take your orders from me. Is that clear?'

'Yes Miss Walker. Very clear.' A succinct answer was more than adequate.

The days linked together slowly to become weeks and they in turn faded into oblivion as the months passed by. Even an office junior did not remain an office junior, especially when they had taken the initiative to enrol on a secretarial course at nightschool for shorthand and typing.

Richard Tetlow, regarded by some as a dandy, a perfect gentleman, always immaculately dressed and groomed with his neat little moustache, had a propensity whilst talking to finger the large heavy ring on his small finger, thereby drawing attention to it. Such habits in a softly spoken man could have been misconstrued by some as the actions of a soft and easily led man. Nothing could have been further from the truth. A quiet and cautious man he missed nothing and noticed everything, including the existence of potential in his workforce. Helen was a bright girl who with a little encouragement could go far.

'Come in Helen. Please take a seat.'

As always Helen entered Mr Richard's office with propriety as demanded of her situation, but at the same time a natural ease wafted over her as she entered his domain. He was fastidious in his dealings with others thereby earning him the reputation of being a hard man to please; the office cleaner was routinely subjected to scrutiny of the highest level as he produced an immaculate white handkerchief and proceeded to run his finger wrapped inside it around the dado rail in pursuit of neglected, but unwanted, dust. Brass was there to shine, windows had to sparkle and wood needed to show the effects of polish, otherwise business contacts would assume that attention to detail was lacking and take their custom elsewhere. That was the key to success. A customer who felt nothing had been overlooked, would relax in those leather bound chairs and unwittingly be persuaded to increase their initial order, knowing that they could rely upon the quality of the merchandise for their impressive London stores.

Neatly efficient as always, Helen walked to one of those leather-clad chairs and seated herself, before realising that her employer was not immediately ready to test the skills of her shorthand.

'What do you think uncle, isn't it just the fastest thing you've ever seen? If you'd like I'll give you a spin in it right now. I'll open her up and show you what she can really do.'

'Oh, I don't know about that just now. If you've nothing requiring your attention, perhaps later this afternoon? Yes. Let me see I should be free from two-thirty. I have a round of golf booked for three. Yes, let's make it then.'

The two men, seemingly oblivious to Helen's presence, continued to peer through the window with decided interest and with their backs to the girl whilst she slowly examined the silhouette of the taller and younger man. His was a striking posture enhanced by the detailed cut of a no doubt expensive but fashionable suit.

Until now Helen had failed to find herself in the company of smart, advantaged young men. Richard Tetlow, ever keen to wear his attire with certain aplomb found wanting in his coarser brother, did not draw the interest of this sixteen-year-old. Turning suddenly from the window he subconsciously reminded himself that there was work to do.

'Well Denis as attractive as your new acquisition is I need to submit that quotation to Bradys for their approval. I must get on with it if we are to secure that new order. Miss Siddall, are you ready?'

Helen coyly shuffled in her seat at this point, in an attempt to arrange her skirt and enable it to be tugged to an even more demure length, whilst signalling with an obliging smile and nod that she was ready to commence.

The young man swung around on his heels and immediately Helen felt his gaze upon her. Casting her eyes downwards she felt embarrassed to return the glance and tried to effect an all-consuming involvement in her work, albeit no dictation had been uttered. That momentary gaze became one of infinite length until the spell snapped as the older man collected his thoughts.

'Begin as we usually do, Miss Siddall, with the aforesaid formalities.'

'Don't forget uncle, I'll be back to collect you and just you see if I don't get the old girl up to forty.'

'Forty!' You mean forty miles per hour? You'll kill us both Denis. Are you mad?'

'Totally. As mad as a hatter. But what's life without a few risks?'

Quietly amused by this outburst, Helen revelled in the witticism as her eyes met those of her employer's nephew. He was blonde and sun-tanned and the possessor of eyes that laughingly longed to tease. A smile spread from his lips and his eyes appeared to totally bestow such individual attention that Helen felt as if she was the only person in the room, beside himself. He was without question handsome in his looks but it was the roguish and boyish personality shining from those eyes that was the captivating force.

'A few risks! Where would we be if we all took that attitude?'

Richard Tetlow was still airing his concerns as the door clicked with the disappearance of his visitor.

'We'd better get on with that letter Miss Siddall, for who knows whether I'll live to dictate another day!'

****

Helen's time spent between the domains of home and work contrasted sharply. Annie appeared more careworn with the demands of a family and housework, a point noted markedly as Helen compared the anguished look of struggle found in her aunt's face, as opposed to the relief of liberation worn proudly on the faces of the young and not so young women, in particular spinsters, at Tetlows. Helen had broached the subject of Annie earning a little independence for herself with paid employment but Tom had quickly snuffed out that enlightened idea, preferring to dictate to his family, aware of his invincible position, where his residing spouse waited for him to bring home the money. Money that put food on the table, a roof over their heads and clothes on their backs. Surely all of this was enough for any woman to want; the only trouble being that emancipation and votes for women had swept aside convention and complacency, to replace them with awareness that life could be improved.

Helen, however, was more aware than ever that changes were needed and with quiet persistency she once more tried with her delicate art of persuasion.

'They're needing some more packers at Tetlows. I know the money's not wonderful but…'

'Don't start that again lass. Tom just won't hear of it.'

'Why should you be beholden to him, auntie? He doesn't own you. You should have a life of your own before it's too late.'

'Too late! Don't you see Helen, it already is for me. But you deserve better. You always did.'

Annie withdrew to a chair and tried to suppress her tears whilst her niece placed her arms around her shoulders, totally aware that she had exposed a raw nerve.

'I'm sorry auntie, I didn't mean to upset you, only I do think you should have a life of your own. Thomas, Harry and I are all in paid employment. We don't need you to be a drudge at home. You've looked after all of us and now it's time you thought about yourself.'

'Aye, I know lass, but Tom isn't the sort of fellow to come home to an empty house and no dinner ready for him. When I married him I realised I'd made my bed and now I have to lie in it whether I like it or not. But life's not going to be like that for you. Enjoy it whilst you can and don't take second best. Just look at you, there's no need for that. You're quite a stunner Helen. You'll be able to attract anyone you want. Just don't fall for the first man around.'

'Oh, auntie I'm not ready for any of that. Besides which I'm quite happy just being here with you.'

'Well you might say that now but life has a funny way of catching up on you. Perhaps your life's all mapped out for you at the time of birth. Some say it is, some say it isn't. But all I'm saying is there must be more to life than this. I'm sure there is for you. Just don't settle for second best. Look further afield than these streets. If I had my time over again I know I would, and that's without your looks and your breeding. You come from a different stock to us. Remember, don't waste it.'

****

Fate, consequence or scheming manipulation could have triggered the initial meeting. Helen would never know. The end of every working day saw the young typist walk up Brereton Street before turning left along Mannville Parade to catch a tram into Beckston and then another up to Milldyke. That routine had never been broken until the unmistakable lines of a 4.5 litre Bentley drew alongside her. Helen continued to walk briskly to ignore the opulence at her side but a sudden toot from the horn commandeered her attention. She instantly recognised the tease of the eyes and the dedicated interest which they lavished upon her. They belonged to a rogue and a gentleman masquerading as Mr Richard Tetlow's nephew.

'Hello, I thought I knew that captivating little walk. It's Helen isn't it? I'm usually pretty good with faces, or do I mean a shapely pair of legs? Well, whatever, I don't forget a pretty girl in a hurry.'

Helen felt herself blush vehemently. Ashamed and rather bewildered she struggled to offer a suitable reply. No one had ever spoken to her in this way.

'Don't look so worried. I haven't come to drag you back to work and into the clutches of that old dragon, Walker. In fact, just the reverse.' The eyes began to intensify their tantalising appeal as Denis leaned towards the passenger door luring the girl with his smile. 'I bet you've never travelled home in a Bentley before.' The spell was set and the temptation was too great to resist.

As the car turned into Paradise Street Helen began to feel very tense. She felt uncomfortable at the thought of privilege encountering poverty as she was driven home to this habitat of drabness. The thought indeed disgusted her. How could she be ashamed of the only home that she had been offered? Indeed without Annie's kindness even this would have been unattainable. Suddenly a worse scenario faced her. The inhabitants of the street had suddenly curtailed their activities as woman ceased their gossiping and children allowed their skipping ropes to dangle from their hands. For a moment the street was frozen with interest.

Once again Helen was the focus of their attention, like the day she had first walked into their lives holding Annie's hand. Whispering and nudging, some craned for a better view as Helen hurriedly got out of the car.

'You're in a mighty big hurry. I thought I was the one for speeding! You're not ashamed of me are you?' The question almost appeared absurd in the circumstances.

'Of course not,' came the servile little reply.

'Well then, have you any plans for next Saturday?'

'Any plans?' The response was a vague repeat.

'How do you fancy a drive out to the country and a nice meal afterwards?'

Helen found the question bewildering. 'I don't know, would it be right for me to... '

'For you to come out with me? Do we need your father's permission first? I'm not offering a proposal of marriage, well not yet anyway.'

Helen blushed as Denis roared with laughter. The silence of the street had been broken with that laughter. Helen almost thought that she could still hear it as she closed the Ledgard's door.

The week passed slowly, each day filled with the irksome prospect of habitual work and Tom's infuriating table manners. Carefully scrutinising every aspect of this man Helen repeatedly questioned how her aunt had ever been duped into walking out with him, irrespective of marrying him. His eloquence and charm were decidedly lacking, his financial appeal had been totally spent and any future prospects would be a potential liability. This description fitted as well now as it would have done on the eve of their marriage. The attraction must have been a physical one. Like Thomas he was tall and swarthy in looks and with fewer years must have had attraction for Annie. There the comparison ended. Thomas was now a man and one who possessed looks, charm and a string of admirers. Although Helen knew she was attracted to him he never reciprocated with a hint of affection other than that of a caring member of the family. The days when she had held his hand and delighted in his secrets were long gone and instead he seemed to deliberately avoid her gaze and the chance of being alone with her.

How different Denis was. Blonde and suntanned, the purveyor of wealth, he could indulge in idle pursuits and pastimes with alacrity. He didn't possess the sombre colouring of Thomas, nature had found it unnecessary for such a hedonistic lifestyle.

Helen was not a fool and knew that she could expect nothing more than a nice afternoon drive and a meal from this acquaintanceship. She doubted that the experience would ever be repeated and resolved as a result to tell no one of the plan. A falsehood used once, even to Annie, would surely do no harm. As a result everyone was under the illusion that she was spending some time with Diana. Working until midday on Saturday Helen delayed leaving the office until the other staff had done so as to avoid being seen. In the ladies she was unfortunate enough for Miss Walker to catch her applying some makeup but quickly left for now the time was her own and she was obligated to no one in either thought or deed.

Turning from Brereton Street into Mannville Parade her heart slightly skipped as she instantly recognised the waiting car and its driver. Both were fuelled with charisma. Denis excelled in charm. His face exuded a captivating expression which would reassuringly guarantee acceptance of his desires. Helen did wonder if it was possible for any woman to defy him or maintain their conviction without being melted by that smile into submission.

'Helen, you look marvellous. Stunning is surely the word I'm stumbling for.' A remark of this kind enhanced by the smile and the body gestures ensured that the prey would be ensnared.

An open topped Bentley could not fail to attract attention. Its size and power commanded approving glances as pedestrians turned and watched its sturdy chassis speed past them with solid reliability. Persons travelling in such a mode of transport had to be wealthy, worthy of respect and naturally deserved a second glance.

'Sit back and enjoy the drive and the envious looks, Helen. This is a showpiece of perfection, a little like you.' The remark rather than leading to reassurance served only to embarrass. Helen cast her eyes downwards until the busy streets were passed by.

Beckston finally gave way to quiet lanes as the car climbed away from the smoky inhabited town and exchanged a vista of pollution for a panoramic view of pastoral pleasure. Backdrops of rolling moor land beauty, utterly awe-inspiring in their magnitude, gave way to meadows and sweeping pastures, peppered with irregular shaped dots of limestone surrounded by herds of sheep. Numerous quaint little villages harbouring weathered stone cottages snuggled into land packed with history and interest. Helen marvelled at the unspoilt beauty around her.

'I never knew places like this existed, well not so close to Beckston. Do you think the people who live here have any idea of what it's like to live in a town?'

Denis was quite amazed by the naïve but thought provoking remark. His usual female companions normally boasted only beauty rather than brains. 'Possibly not. Generations upon generations here have farmed these slopes and produced the wool which the Beckston mills have prospered upon. Some of the original mill workers came to find work from the countryside in the last century, but I expect their families wished they'd not done so.'

Helen looked perplexed. 'Why do you say that? Do you mean because of the freedom and solitary beauty here instead of the pollution and cramped living conditions in the town?'

'Those are certainly factors to consider, however I mean that you've got more space out here to park your automobiles!'

The remark served as an instant icebreaker. Denis was incorrigible and refused to be taken seriously. How different he was to Thomas.

An expectation of complete enjoyment seemed to be the only prerequisite of the day. How easy it was for Helen to indulge in laughter, both at and with her companion.

Quite unexpectedly Denis changed the course of conversation with a direct question. 'Feeling hungry yet?' Helen had completely lost account of time and had failed to realise the necessity of mealtimes. 'Now that you mention it, I am absolutely starving,' came the reply.

'I thought you might be. Will this view suffice for Madame as she savours her culinary delights?' Denis slowed to a halt before turning down a rather over-grown track which he had to negotiate with caution instead of speed. The lane wound down into a secluded opening, fringed by a wooded bank overlooking a picturesque stream. Helen remained still and silent as she gazed at the calm and surreal beauty of the scene. She failed to notice that Denis had suddenly produced a large wicker basket from the rear of the car and was proceeding to set out a picnic on a large rug by the edge of the bank. The now familiar tones of his voice awakened her from her unconscious indulgence. 'Come and help me. There'll be plenty of time for daydreaming later.'

Helen continued to remain silent as she knelt on the rug and watched in disbelief as Denis laid out a luncheon feast. The majority of dishes were totally unrecognisable.

'Champagne or Chablis, which do you prefer?'

'I don't know. I've never tried either one.'

'Well now's your chance. Let's begin with the Chablis.'

Their feast had been prepared by the family's cook under the auspices of the housekeeper who all too well understood Mr Denis's requirements. They lunched on salmon tartlets and lobster in aspic jelly to begin with, followed by small moulds of chicken, pigeon pie, plover's eggs and bean salad and then sampled the delights of small apricot creams, meringues, Neapolitan oranges and a selection of biscuits and cheeses. All of which was regularly moistened with ample glassfuls of the chosen Chablis and later the Champagne.

Relaxed and sleepy, Helen began to feel the allure of the recumbent state and willingly succumbed to the idea. She was blissfully oblivious to the actions of her companion, preferring to allow sleep to take its toll. Quite startled she awoke from a brief slumber to find Denis kissing her lightly on the lips. Initially the action seemed inappropriate, but the warmth and sensitivity of his touch persuaded her not to resist. Quickly, the frequency and intensity of his affections increased. She felt his hot breath descend down her neck and his fingers brush across her blouse. The swiftness of his next action both alarmed and embarrassed her. She felt the wetness of his tongue and the softness of his lips guiding him to her breasts, her blouse buttons were totally undone. He began to pull her brassiere down against her own efforts to pull the garment up. Lying on top of her his own body weight gave him the advantage. Suddenly his fingers were stroking and teasing her exposed nipples until each one became prominently erect, before licking his tongue around each areola and engulfing them with his mouth in satisfaction.

Helen had never before experienced such physical sensations. These feelings of pleasure were totally indescribable. Aroused by his touch and the knowledge that what was occurring was extremely intimate she found it difficult to deprive either of them of further excitement. Burrowing his head between her breasts he kissed the soft white skin in delicate recognition. She groaned as a wave of sensuous enjoyment journeyed down her body. He in return grasped her to him tightly and she felt his face and hair brush against her own, exuding a distinctive masculine scent. Suddenly his fingers travelled with alarming speed down her body until they began to make grasping gestures towards her skirt which was tugged at as his hand slithered against her stockings rising to her thigh.

'No! We mustn't go any further.' Helen summoned up the courage to push Denis away from her before bursting into tears. 'I'm sorry, I just can't do this.'

'It's alright, you don't need to explain.' This time his arms enveloped her with protection rather than desire as he pulled her towards him and allowed her to sob.

'I'm not a tease, you know, I wasn't leading you on.'

'I know you're not, Helen. I can wait.'

Helen's understanding of sexual matters was extremely limited. Both Annie and Miss Frood had failed to prepare her for any such experience. Presumably it was felt that that was only necessary on the eve of marriage. However times were changing and women were now more liberated than ever, the universal right to vote had secured that. It was Diana who had been the font of all knowledge where sex was concerned. Helen remembered the tale of Diana's aunt who finding herself pregnant had naively questioned how her baby would come out only to be told 'the same way it had gone in!'

The remainder of the afternoon was spent quietly coasting along the tranquil lanes of the Yorkshire Dales. The peace was only shattered by an occasional gamekeeper's gun as the couple drove around the periphery of some of Britain's sprawling estates and through their dependent timeless villages. The allure of an old coaching inn in one village proved too persuasive to pass as its charms enticed once again. Authentic oak beams and panelling genuinely greeted the customer and served as a reminder of the quality one could expect.

'Good evening sir, what can I get for you?' A rounded red-faced man smiled with delight at the couple.

'A pint, landlord! And for you Helen?' The man's reference to time abruptly startled Helen. She had been oblivious to the passing of time.

'Nothing, thank you. I need to go home.'

'Is this a pumpkin I can see? Umm, they don't know you're with me? Well the way I look at it is you might as well be hung for a sheep as a lamb! I've always found that to be true.' The smirk on Denis's face coincided with a knowing wink from the landlord and both men laughed heartily.
'Come along Helen, one drink and then we'll make tracks.'

A singular drink was not surprisingly a rarity in Denis's experience and on this occasion nothing but the usual prevailed. Helen was now anxious to be home and feared that the intoxicating allure of the liquor and the surroundings would persuade Denis to linger longer than was advantageous.

'Helen, you don't need to worry, the car knows its own way home,' came the far from reassuring remark.

The drive home was a troubled anticipation of tragedy on the part of Helen whilst Denis rose to the challenge with speed fuelled by adrenalin. Oblivious to danger Denis confidently persisted testing the bends and sharp corners of the country lanes until he approached the inhabited roads of Beckston. Triumphantly he began to slow the Bentley down as the end of Paradise Street came into view.

'What's the hurry? Are you not going to ask me in then?'

'It's very late. Thank you for a lovely day.' In order to avoid further embarrassment Helen quickly kissed him on the cheek and left him alone before running along the pavement only to disappear through one of the many passageways. Denis was too drunk to argue and decided to let the car take him home, as was often the case.

As Helen's hand reached out to open the door a wave of foreboding paralysed her. The outside door was slightly open and she could hear unfamiliar voices speaking in hushed tones. Tom's voice was evident but unusually soft. Summoning a degree of courage Helen opened the door further and entered. Tom was unsurprisingly seated in his normal chair. Thomas and Harry were also present. There the normality ended.

The Ledgard household were not renowned for entertaining and Helen was rather surprised to find a small gathering of neighbours, mainly female, in the house. Harry looked up at Helen and she could clearly see that, unusually for him, he had been crying.

Complete silence prevailed as everyone in that room turned and stared at Helen.

'What's the matter? Where's Auntie?'

'You may well ask!' came the all too familiar response. 'Somewhere where she won't have to put up with the lies from the likes of you! Diana might be your friend but even she couldn't lie for you this afternoon. Wherever you were it certainly wasn't in her company.'

The whole scenario was a nightmare and one being performed in front of both family and strangers. Helen admitted to herself that she had told them a little white lie, but could not understand why it had had to unravel itself to such scrutiny.

'I'm... I'm so sorry.'

'You certainly will be you little bitch. Well you might as well know. Annie died this afternoon. They said it was a heart attack. More than likely died from a broken heart, probably caused by you!'

Helen was numb. Her only thought was that at the moment she was experiencing those totally indescribable feelings of pleasure, Annie was probably dead.

CHAPTER FIVE

The weather epitomised the feeling of the day: damp, grey and lifeless. Expressionless eyes stared from forlorn faces as Annie's body was lowered into the ground. Death had certainly thrown its mantle around the gathered crowd as each individual silently paid their last respects. Afterwards the funeral tea was eaten by those who had lived alongside Annie for many years and, as dependable neighbours, were well aware of the type of life she had had.

'Expect you'll now take over from Annie?' a lone voice enquired. Helen suddenly found herself the centre of attention.

'I... I suppose so.' Unconsciously Helen replied first and thought later.

Recollections of Annie and domesticity involved hours spent black leading. This had been a Friday ritual of applying black lead, commercially termed Zebo, to the black parts of the fireplace with one brush, then brushing it up with another brush. The 'end irons' also had to be black leaded but as they were put into the sides of the fire itself, in order to save coal, the black lead soon burned off which made it a useless exercise. Nonetheless it had to be done regardless. The same sentiment applied to the laundry of the household. Every Sunday night the weekly ritual began. Items would be mended and linens would be categorised into 'whites' or 'coloureds'. Dirty garments would be steeped in water and wrung out early the next morning. Water was then ladled from the side pan into the peggy tub before Annie spent backbreaking hours with a posser, rubbing board, large bar of soap and a scrubbing brush. Collars and cuffs were always the worst as they demanded excessive scrubbing. The 'whites' such as towels, pillowcases and sheets always had to be boiled in the wash boiler and some articles also had to be starched. Everything then had to wind its way through the wringer before being twined. The water was then emptied and replaced with rinsing water and a dolly blue, before all items were sent through the wringer twice more, before being put out on the line to dry. Finally the only chore left was the ironing and that was done with a pair of flat irons which were systematically heated over the fire. Housewifery was not a simple task. Any self-respecting woman would also bake her own bread. Mealtimes had not even been contemplated. Helen began to wonder with dismay where she would find the time to work and run the home.

Life was to alter quite dramatically in the Ledgard household, but in a totally unexpected way. Within a short time Tom had installed his new companion, whom he introduced as his 'housekeeper', a pretentious description in view of the humble surroundings. Mary Brooke was the type of character one could best describe as 'warm hearted', totally the opposite of Tom. Corpulent in frame and devoid of any good taste in life's attributes, particularly men, she had first entered the house proudly linked on his arm. Being neither sentimental nor perceptive to the thoughts of others, Tom had seen nothing wrong with this arrangement. Clearly he was a man who could not exist without a woman, but the need was not dominated by desire. Initially the sleeping arrangements remained the same: Tom and Harry sharing the large bedroom whilst the smaller room was deemed adequate for the women. However Mary quickly began to question these plans, realising that as an unpaid 'housekeeper,' she had surely been duped into believing that Tom held affection for her. The threat of departure pressurised Tom into installing Mary as his new bed mate. Helen could not help but feel that Mary had secured an even worse deal for herself. The phrase 'there's no fool like an old fool' came to mind.

The new domestic arrangements now demanded further changes. A two bed-roomed house was clearly inadequate. Harry, resolutely stubborn as always, refused to move, much to Helen's relief. The solution was to come from Thomas. That day Thomas moved back to the Ledgard house whilst Helen moved in with Mrs Shackleton.

The eyes shone with a bright intensity from a face unable to conceal its octogenarian origin.

'Come in, come on in lass. It's going to be wonderful to have some female company. Not that I've minded having Thomas here! He's a fine fellow but you're a little different.' Alice Shackleton's welcome was unpretentious, warm and generous. It also held a hint of future fulfilment.

Alice Shackleton was definitely a woman who could be described as 'one of a kind'. Although elderly she was swiftly perceptive and resolutely unshakeable from pursuing the facts. Her undisputed 'gift' was the indefatigable catalyst.

'You are definitely surrounded by men and money.' The reading was the same each time.

'The only money I'm surrounded by is the wage packets once a week at Tetlows.' Helen nonchalantly tossed back the same sentiment each time.

'No not that,' came the familiar reply, 'I mean your own money.' Mrs Shackleton would not be dissuaded from her interpretation of these innermost secrets, etched finely into Helen's palms. Each time Helen would find herself bemused by these revelations. The frequent occasions that she had longingly admired the tantalising displays of ladies footwear in Busbys' and Brown Muffs' windows, only to be reminded that her pay packet would not stretch that far, was unlikely to convince her that she was stepping into wealth. Likewise the distinct absence of love struck male suitors also seemed to invalidate these startling claims. Denis Tetlow was a slight possibility but even his interest seemed to have waned of late. Perhaps the office gossips were right in that his money and position enabled him to philander with any girl of his choice, any willing girl of course.

Helen often noticed an anxious look pass fleetingly across the old lady's countenance whenever she undertook these readings. She would never divulge her thoughts at these times. On one occasion Helen pressed her to voice what she had seen. 'Oh, it's nothing to worry about.' However the reassurance failed to work as Helen reflected upon the number of times she had witnessed that look.

The readings were always exactly the same: men and money. Helen tried to press for further details, but invariably was unsuccessful until one evening.

'Surely you must be able to tell me a little more.'

'Yes, but will it be the little more that you want to hear?' Helen wondered why a question had to be answered with a riddle.

'Well I won't know until you tell me.'

'Have you ever heard the saying that a little knowledge can be a dangerous thing?' came the teasing remark.

'Yes I have. I've also heard that ignorance is bliss and having lived for too long in that state I'm now willing to take a chance and find out for myself.'

The old lady's eyes scrutinised Helen's face. Profile to profile these two women searched for the answer in the opposite one's eyes.

'Very well. Every time I see the same thing. There is always a fair-haired man and a dark haired man. You will become involved with each of them and they will cause you to be unhappy. Be careful as the dark one is not all that he seems whilst the fair one is. Each one will shape and change your life forever. The hardest thing for you is making the right choice.'

Silence prevailed as Helen watched Alice slump back into her chair. Tired and drained she welcomed no further questions that night which Helen was perceptive enough to understand. Her future seemed nothing more than a riddle and one that would test her ingenuity for its reply.

As the months passed by Helen seriously began to feel that her life would remain the same forever: her working hours in the office and her limited spare time with Alice Shackleton. Very little remained of her previous life. All too frequently did she hear the outbursts of anger between Tom and his new wife. Harmony had failed to survive, even with another partner. Harry rarely appeared, particularly during the daylight hours. It was assumed that he spent his days sleeping off the excesses of nocturnal drinking bouts following evenings of hidden shady deals. The way he made a living was far from conventional, but Helen cared little for she was content to distance herself from any dealings with Harry. The only persons she truly missed were Annie and Thomas. The death of this gentle woman had had a profound effect upon Helen and on occasions she would find herself sobbing for no recognisable reason. Thomas also seemed to have distanced himself from her company. He was always content to return a smile and a brief pleasantry but reluctant to offer more.

Unexpectedly one evening as Helen walked her usual route after work along Mannville Parade to catch her nightly tram ride home, she suddenly recognised the familiar tones of a female voice calling out her name. Unmistakably they belonged to Diana. Giggling and excited the pair hugged one another. Although they had once been very close friends at school, they had lost contact once work intervened.

'Look at you! Quite the office fixture I would say.' Diana was irrepressible.

'Why do you say that? How do you know that I work in an office?' Helen's response was a naïve contrast to her friend's outburst.

'Because you blend in with the furniture.'

Momentarily Helen was stunned with disbelief. The person she had regarded as a friend had humiliated her within minutes of their reacquaintance. The tears fleetingly dissipated into anger, which in turn melted into humility. Once more in control of her emotions Helen calmly began to notice her companion. The wayward schoolgirl had changed quite dramatically. Daring alacrity had become potent sophistication. The eyes and mouth were heavily defined with noticeable makeup, the clothing swirled with expensive design whilst the air carried a scent of sensuality. Diana was a woman and one who wanted everyone to notice her.

'What do you say Helen, to catching up on old times? Shall we go to Paterson's for a pot of tea?'

The idea was appealing and before Helen could muster up affirmation or refusal for the plan Diana had linked arms and was leading her to the tearooms.

Helen had never ventured inside a tearoom before. There had been many occasions when she had glimpsed elderly matriarchs or frivolous young ladies emerging from Paterson's doorway, engrossed in dedicated gossip which had initially commenced with the pouring of the tea. As the door opened and the bell tinkled a new experience unfolded before Helen's eyes. White heavily starched tablecloths covered neat little tables. Chairs were precisely positioned around the unoccupied tables unlike those with seated customers whose corpulent frames and shopping parcels over spilled with indulgence. The slim frames of the waitresses darted around with graceful servitude supplying temptingly filled cake stands to beguiled eyes and above this scene, seated at her own rostrum, was the establishment's equivalent of Miss Walker.

'Yes,' snapped the businesslike voice.

'We would like a table for two.' Diana appeared totally unaffected by the woman's disapproving expression. With a simple gesture of her hand a waitress appeared and showed them to a table.

'God, fancy having to work for an old battle-axe like her. I thought for a moment that they'd dug old Frood up there.' Diana may have matured but she had not mellowed with her comments.

'Ssh. Be quiet she might hear you.'

'So what! She can't send me to the head's office. I'm the customer here and my money is as good as anyone else's. I think it's just as well we met up again Helen. You definitely need taking in hand and I'm just the sort of person to do it.'

The two women chattered incessantly over endless bone china cups of tea, pausing only momentarily to choose their next confectionery temptation. Since leaving school Diana had flitted between several employment venues, notably within the retail sector of ladies fashions. She was currently engaged at Brown Muffs but, as she so forcefully pointed out, only as a stopgap measure. Her true calling lay on the stage of the theatre. It was little wonder that Helen showed little surprise at this revelation when she recalled her friend's antics of improvisation at school. Diana now possessed an aura of worldliness quite evidently lacking in her companion. She also possessed jewellery of the authentic kind, genuine and expensive. As Helen's eyes became fixated upon the dazzling brooch and splendiferous sparkling earrings Diana appeared to resent the momentary lapse of concentration from her friend, adamantly waving her hands across them whilst describing the 'baubles' dismissively as 'tokens of affection from a friend'. It was at this point that Helen wondered what sort of friends Diana now had.

In the true spirit of the modern woman Diana insisted upon taking care of the bill. Helen had thoroughly enjoyed the company of her friend and daringly suggested that they meet for tea again. Diana's immediate response was for Helen to come to the next stage production of the play that she was starring in. As always, Diana was content to take charge of the arrangements. Helen was promised a ticket for one of the best seats in the house and the chance to mingle with the 'stars' backstage after the show. It would definitely be an evening to remember.

CHAPTER SIX

The long awaited invitation failed to transpire in the short term. As Diana failed to appear the expectations of excitement gradually began to wane. Helen had rather relished the prospect of sampling a little frivolity but thought it inappropriate to approach Diana. No doubt there would be a perfectly good explanation for the delay and Diana would be in touch in due course. The daily working pattern continued to prevail. That was until one evening when the feeling of deja vue intervened. Walking briskly along Mannville Parade Helen's attention was suddenly drawn to the unmistakable sleek lines of a 4.5 litre Bentley at her side. She continued walking with purpose, adamant in her mind not to fall prey to the charms of the driver but she had not reckoned upon the continued persistence that she now faced.

'Helen. Wait a minute. I need to talk to you.'

Defying his request the pace became faster until Helen found herself running away. Oblivious to any thought of her pursuer being more agile than herself, she continued to ignore his shouts until the next little intervening road enabled him to swing his chassis into her path and wait for his prey to be cornered. The momentum of her movement propelled her directly up to his car.

'My, we are in a big hurry. Perhaps I can give you a lift somewhere?'

'No. Thank you. I don't take lifts from strangers!' Helen wondered where she had summoned up the courage to deliver that sentence. She was innately proud of herself.

'Point taken! Please just get in. I really do need to talk to you.' Sincerity suddenly pervaded across the face and Helen duly complied.

'I'm sorry Helen if you think I've let you down. Of course I have but it was not of my own choosing.'

'Not of your own choosing! Do you really expect me to believe that? You were quite happy to try and seduce me but when you found out that I wasn't prepared for that, you simply lost interest and no doubt looked elsewhere.' Unable to hide her emotions any longer Helen suddenly found herself weeping. Her priority was to get out of the car and away from Denis but his arms around her provided too much comfort: a feeling she had rarely known.

'I don't blame you for feeling this way. Everyone, including my father, thinks of me as just a goodtime playboy. The truth is that when he asked me to meet with some prospective clients on the continent I saw it as a way to prove my worth. That's exactly what I managed to do. I charmed them with our products and as a result have increased the order books. Well that's enough talk of work. I don't want to be sounding like father now, all profit and loss. What's the good of making money if you never have the time to enjoy it?' He was totally incorrigible and without doubt a rogue, but a loveable one. The tantalising smile and the tease of the ice blue eyes were certain to uplift the most dejected of spirits, Helen's being no exception.

'That's better; at least we have a smile back on that pretty face. To make sure that it remains there would you do me the honour of accompanying me to the Ickringill's Ball?'

Helen found herself momentarily unable to answer. She stared for some time in disbelief.

'Is that a no or a "I'll just have to consult my diary" reply?' It seemed that Denis was incapable of taking anything serious.

'Are you mocking me?' Helen enquired calmly.

'Good God no! Just trying to lighten the situation somewhat. You look rather disturbed about my invitation. Thought you might have had a better offer.'

'A better offer! Do you really suppose that I get asked to go to balls? I've never been to one in my life. That's the reason I'm looking worried, as well as the fact that I've absolutely nothing I could wear for it.'

'Not a problem Helen. Allow me to treat you.'

'I couldn't, that wouldn't be right.'

'Just think of it as an early Christmas present. Shall I pick you up after work on Saturday? We'll have lunch first and then find you a beautiful evening dress. I hear that Brown and Muffs have a good reputation for ladies fashions.' Helen recalled little of the journey home in the imposing Bentley. Her mind was no longer preoccupied with the ball but of the unbelievable expression on Diana's face which would ensue when they asked to look over the eveningwear. Helen dreaded the thought of the situation and preyed for an excuse to avoid entering the store.

****

A true gentleman was always recognisable in the manner of his dress, conduct and general demeanour. Denis Tetlow proved no exception to the rule. An added attraction lay in the fact that he could charm any female of any age and this was evident with the manageress of the ladies fashion section at Brown Muffs who had become completely snared. She simply fawned with servility in front of her male customer whilst reserving full judgement upon his attractive companion. At the same time she issued urgent demands upon her younger assistants. Helen was slightly bemused at the prospect of this chatelaine and her followers engaging their services upon an office girl. Offset against this was the relief of not finding Diana amongst them. As Helen began to relax a little she suddenly recognised a familiar voice quietly whispering into her ear, 'Seen anything you fancy yet? I certainly have!'

'Diana!' Helen mouthed anxiously.

'He's an absolute dish and a rich one at that. You sly old thing! You never mentioned your conquest.'

Helen found it difficult to defend herself without blushing. 'He's my boss's son.'

'Oh Helen, I think he's a little more than that.' As Diana winked with a knowing smile her superior quickly demanded, 'Miss Wilkinson, there you are. Will you kindly bring out the latest Paris collection for this lady to peruse? Quickly, our customers are important people and do not wish to be kept waiting.' Diana responded with unusual haste but Helen could not help wondering what thoughts were presently going through her friend's mind.

Helen's curvaceous figure became enhanced by each creation. A little routine soon began, as Helen felt impelled to parade from the changing room to where Denis was seated so that he could make the ultimate decision. The problem was that it became increasingly difficult with each sumptuous design. The sensuous mix of exposed youthful skin draped in an allure of decided femininity only served to confuse, titivate and tantalise. Alarmingly he realised that he had to capture her heart and her body. He needed to make love to her. Damn it, no other woman had held out and resisted his advances as she was doing. That of course made everything more importunate. Denis was completely smitten and was prepared to settle the bill for the most expensive creation in the store.

The final choice was settled upon. It had been a difficult decision to make, particularly between the pale green georgette dress adorned in rich embroidery of silver and gold thread or the duck-egg blue chiffon one with fine embroidery accentuated with minuscule silver beads. Each one had been cut on the bias and possessed long skirts which swirled with flared panels as the wearer moved inside them. Neither of these were the most expensive gowns in the store. Helen's appearance in them persuaded Denis that the best did not always have to cost the most.

Ultimately Helen chose the blue chiffon one as Denis persuaded her that it accentuated the colour of her eyes. However he insisted that a silver sequinned evening purse and silver kid shoes were absolutely necessary to complete the transformation. Helen was gratefully agreeable to such suggestions for she had little in accessories herself.

The most surprising fact of all was that throughout all of these proceedings Diana had remained silent until Helen returned to the changing room to dress and collect her belongings. Diana quickly followed, closing the door swiftly.

'I cannot believe that you just did that.'

Helen looked perplexed. 'I'm sorry, I don't know what you mean.'

'You're so naive Helen! He was prepared to splash out and buy you the most expensive dress we have here and you turned him down. If it had been me I would have snapped his hand off.'

'But you're not me and that's the point. I don't want something just because it's expensive.'

Diana found it difficult to understand such logic, she had been schooled under her mother's tutorage and firmly believed in having the best at all times.

Helen began to notice how different her friend looked and behaved compared with the previous time they had met. The strong self-assured young woman complete with expensive jewellery was a toned down underling. Diana instantly perceived her friend's thoughts.

'You don't need to look at me like that,' snapped Diana.

'Like what?' Helen was beginning to become annoyed.

'As though I've just crawled out from under a stone.'

'I'm not! If you must know Diana, I was wondering why I hadn't heard from you as you promised. You said that you would get me a ticket for your next production.'

Diana appeared slightly taken back by this remark. Her normal cool resolve in all matters appeared to have momentarily vanished.

'Auditions and rehearsals are just under way. I haven't forgotten you. I tell you what, meet me after work next Friday at Paterson's and I'll have a ticket waiting for you.' The simple solution instantly transformed the atmosphere between the two women causing a smile to appear on each of their faces. Helen felt it would be an opportunity for her to find out more about Diana's ability to work as a shop girl and afford expensive jewellery. Diana's motive was not dissimilar from that of her friend. How could an office girl interest the boss's son? Knowing Helen she suspected little in the way of intimate favours.

As agreed the two women met at Paterson's for tea. Unlike the previous occasion Helen took little notice of the waitresses, the surroundings or indeed the other customers. This time all of her attention was spent upon her companion.

As was customary Diana took the lead, delving into how and when Helen had first met Denis Tetlow. She seized every opportunity to establish how far the relationship had gone which in the end only confirmed her earlier thoughts.

'So you've never let him... ?'

'No, certainly not,' came the enforced quietly spoken reply. Helen perceived that everyone in the room had ceased speaking in an effort to hear her answer. Shocked and embarrassed she hoped to divert the topic of conversation, but to no avail.

'It's a good thing we've met up again Helen. I think you need to be made aware of the ways of the world and I'm just the person to teach you.' The waitress suddenly placed a tiered cake stand of mouth-watering delicacies between them which abruptly interrupted the flow of the conversation.

Finally Helen managed to summon up the courage to ask Diana the seemingly unresolved question. She wondered whether the enquiry might prove impertinent, but instead provided the perfect stage for disclosure.

'Oh Helen I wondered how long it would take you! If it had been me I would have asked you long before now.' Diana appeared to revel in obscurity. 'Well the truth is I don't earn enough in the fashion department or indeed on the stage put together to afford these little gems. Oh and by the way they are real. I happen to have caught the eye of an influential patron of the theatre. I'm doubly blessed as he's incredibly wealthy.'

'And doubtless married and old enough to be your father!' snapped Helen.

'Jealousy doesn't become you but you are correct on both counts.'

'Diana! What do your parents think about this?'

'Nothing, because they don't know. Father never takes any notice of me and mother is too wrapped up in her world of social coffee mornings and little soirees to see me coming and going.'

It was one of those rare occasions when Helen actually felt sympathy for Diana. In fact it was impossible to recall a single moment when she had experienced this feeling before, with the exception of Diana's regular visits to the headmaster's study for the endurance of the cane. Even then these visits had been self-imposed as Diana had deviously stage-managed the entertainment within the classroom which had ultimately concluded with the same penalty. Helen now wondered if the delights and trappings enjoyed from this admirer were worth the underlying investment. That was the problem. She decided not to ask any further questions for she feared that Diana would answer them.

****

Throughout the following week Helen kept looking at the two tickets which Diana had given her. The fact that there were two implied that she was expected to take someone with her. Momentarily her choice had been Denis but she had dismissed that in case it appeared she was being too forward. Always better for the man to do the chasing Annie had repeatedly said. Alice Shackleton thanked Helen for her kind invitation but declined for not favouring leaving her home on a night. In reality Helen felt it was a polite way of saying that it would be better for her to have company of a similar age. The other younger women at Tetlows seemed to spend their free time with their boyfriends, especially if their conversations were to be believed. There was no one, Helen thought, except Thomas. She wondered why she had not thought of him before and then realised that she had. The decision was made, she would go alone.

CHAPTER SEVEN

A ticket for the entertainment industry was a way of securing escapism. The humdrum existence of working class families in 1930 momentarily became transformed as drabness gave way to unprecedented luxury. The start of this decade had already witnessed the collapse of the American stock market, which had heralded the wake of the Great Depression, bringing mass unemployment and unbelievable financial hardship to millions. Provincial theatres, therefore, were guaranteed to promise transportation to a carefree oasis of enjoyment far away from the troubles of reality. This was accentuated by the traditional densely woven carpet which guided each member of the audience to the auditorium of pleasure. Here the overwhelming feeling was of sophistication. Heavily encrusted plaster ornamentation on the proscenium and on the boxes had been deliberately designed to convince the spectator of assured satisfaction. The nation now had a choice of entertainment in the form of live stage shows or, by the technological advances of the theatre's rival, the cinema screen. Silent films had entertained for some time but the introduction of the first 'talkies' in 1928 ensured that cinema going would become even more popular. These glittering new 'picture palaces' introduced reels of film direct from Hollywood which consequently affected the speech patterns of the population. Children in particular relied upon 'OK' as a figure of acceptance, or 'No Kidding' for exclamations.

Helen had been to neither the theatre nor the cinema. She had frequently overheard animated descriptions of both the shows and the movies from the girls in the office, always envious of their outings. For the first time in her life she was about to embark upon her own magical adventure. Throughout the week, she found it difficult to concentrate upon her work, willing the days to pass. Finally the night arrived and Helen found herself entering Beckston's Theatre Royale being instantly overawed by the sumptuous interior design. The foyer made the first impression with its tessellated marble and daintily decorated panels of ornamental plaster. Helen's shoes seemed to sink into the rich carpet, which had been specially manufactured, whilst her eyes were drawn to the walls and ceilings heavily decorated in Louis XVI style. Inside the auditorium consisted of orchestra stalls and pit stalls on the ground floor, dress circle and eight boxes on the first tier and a large balcony on the second tier. Dominating all this opulence was the stage, enticingly concealed with heavy ruby red curtains. Helen found her seat at the centre front of the dress circle realising that she would have a full-uninterrupted view of all proceedings. Her attention was drawn to other fellow spectators as they filed in searching for their seats, the more corpulent drawing their garments around them in an attempt to squeeze along the seating aisles. Silence pervaded as the lighting dimmed gradually and an air of expectancy filtered through as the curtains rose and the stage revealed itself.

The amateur production was Beckston's interpretation of the musical *No! No! Nanette!* which had opened to rave revues in 1925 on Broadway and later in London. Anyone who had seen it instantly became infatuated with its hit songs, 'I want to be Happy' and 'Tea for two' and preceded to infuriate those who had not with their own performances.

Helen found the whole spectacle lavish. The costumes, the scenery, the vivid makeup and the entire choreographic production were so wonderful that Helen felt that she was witnessing the Broadway debut. However, as this was only her first visit, Helen could not be classed as a connoisseur of the arts. The rose tinted spectacles only allowed the spectator to see what she wanted to see.

Diana appeared to revel in the ardent interest shown to her by the male performers, irrespective of whether it was feigned or genuine. She used every opportunity whilst on stage to push herself harder than any other girl so that she would be noticed. Ever a true professional in this she sang with far more gusto, danced with more stamina, smiled with more feeling and revealed more thigh and cleavage than any other girl. Helen was quietly amused. Diana would never change. She could always manipulate the situation to her own advantage. The time at

Highbury had certainly displayed her inventiveness. She was a girl who knew what she wanted out of life and no doubt would attain it. Helen on the other hand was uncertain on both counts.

Throughout the evening Helen had continually scanned the stage for appearances of Diana. Although she had not been cast as the leading lady she continued to figure predominately. Helen put that down to two reasons: her natural talent to entertain and her ability to persuade. The latter had been confirmed with that expensive jewellery. An influential patron of the theatre would always get his way, especially if he was assured of certain favours. Diana no doubt would soon be the star of the show. Preoccupied with such thoughts Helen had failed to notice a familiar figure in the background chorus. Similarly dressed males who did not dance and only appeared to move with slight hand or limited body gestures flanked him. Perhaps that was one reason why Helen had not noticed him. It could have been the fact that this was the last place she would have expected to witness him singing. Staring in total bewilderment Helen unconsciously mouthed his name, 'Thomas'. No one heard her or noticed that she ceased to look with anticipation for her friend Diana.

Tall and slightly swarthy his appearance had been enhanced by his garments, albeit a cheap theatrical suit, white shirt and cravat. His hair seemed to glisten and his features were no doubt emphasised with stage makeup. However, the most outstanding difference was the expression on his face. Normally quite serious and reserved, his eyes positively shone with radiance. His performance was unreservedly extroverted, fuelled by internal enjoyment and satisfaction. It was obvious that singing here provided him with a contentment that was found lacking in the rest of his life.

The surprise of the evening made Helen question why she had failed to notice Thomas's interest. She vaguely remembered Annie recalling how Edna, Thomas's mother, had entertained family and friends with her fine voice. Indeed Tom had presumably only married her because she was blessed with such a talent and envied by others. Helen now wondered how much of this talent had been passed to Thomas. As the final curtain came down Helen had already vacated her seat and left the auditorium and the appreciative applause behind her.

Life behind the stage curtain was far less attractive. Following Diana's directions Helen had managed to surreptitiously slip through one of the staff doors and found herself following a brick lined corridor completely devoid of decoration or attraction. High-pitched chatter and giggling at the end of the corridor served as a navigational aid. Momentarily she hesitated before knocking on the door. Shrieks of laughter from within shrouded her raps for attention into oblivion. Cautiously she turned the handle, pushing the door aside until she was just able to peer through the opening. Girls, many of them naked or semi-naked laughing and talking, filled the room with high spirits. One of them turned towards Helen and instead of displaying embarrassment she encouraged the stranger into their midst.

'I'm sorry to disturb you,' muttered Helen, casting her eyes downwards as the girl in question made no attempt to cover herself up, 'I'm looking for Diana, Diana Wilkinson.'

'Helen, I'm over here.' The familiar voice was reassurance in this alien environment.

Although still in her undergarments Helen was thankful that Diana was partially clothed.

'What did you think of the show? Was your seat all right? 'Aren't the costumes just heavenly?' Diana bombarded her with question after question, but resisted waiting for any replies. Feeling like stars the adrenalin levels had accelerated so much that everyone in that dressing room was excited and it appeared it would take some time before they descended back to earth. That was of course with the exception of Helen who, standing in their midst, felt completely alone. This feeling became even more enforced as one of the girls called out to Diana, that Mr Godwin was currently waiting outside the dressing room door. Diana quickly finished dressing and grasping Helen's arm propelled her to the door where she promptly introduced her friend to her ardent admirer. Firstly he fawned his affection on Diana with a huge hug and an expedient, surreptitious squeeze of her bottom, before pressing into her arms a bouquet of tightly closed red roses. Having performed what was clearly an accepted routine he then proceeded to turn his attentions to Helen. If Helen had known the meaning of the word she would no doubt have described him as an ageing Lothario. Evidently approaching sixty, his frame slightly stooped and his face wrinkled with time, it was his manner that served as his most objectionable trait. Peppering every sentence with 'my dear,' and caressing Helen's arm with a fondling touch may not have disturbed Diana's sense of propriety, but it did that of Helen's. Having endured the necessary introduction Helen resisted the invitation to dine with the doting couple, feigned her excuses and promptly left.

Reflecting upon the evening Helen began to realise how unusual the proceedings had been. Walking quickly in order to catch the last tram home, her mind tossed the revelations around with unease. She recoiled at the thought of Diana and that obsequious man and moreover of any expectations he had of her. It was certain that those jewels were not just tokens of affection, but rather payment in kind. How could she do it? Allow herself to be mauled by a disgusting old lecher. Diana had always been the controlling force, the one who planned and made events happen, contrived with improvisation. She had always been the strong one, but now seemed to yield to his beckoning. However important it was to better oneself, Helen instinctively knew that she would never use this method. Money would never dominate her life.

The thoughts of poverty and hard work made her think of Thomas. She could not resist the urge to think of him and as she did so her eyes brightened and a smile played across her countenance. Warm feelings pervaded through her body as she recalled his appearance on stage. Dark and swarthy, strong and distant, Thomas possessed the exact catalyst of sexual desire. His performance on stage had been totally unexpected and no doubt held in secret from his acquaintances and family. Helen suddenly felt privileged that once again she was privy to his secret. Her mind drifted back many years before when she had promised that his secret of spending the night at Mrs Shackletons rather than in the outside closet had been safe with her. She also recalled that the reason for his banishment from the house that night had been in her defence. His words the following morning of 'I'd do it all again for you,' now more than ever seemed so poignant. Why after so many years had she suddenly brought them back into her thoughts?

The coincidence of these thoughts and feelings unexpectedly manifested itself when a familiar voice broke Helen's preoccupation.

'I thought it was you. You're out late on your own.'

Helen was stunned into silence as she turned and looked at Thomas.

'I didn't know I had such an effect upon women.' His teasing remark was more akin to one of Denis's.

'You don't,' came the awkward reply, which only served to make Helen more embarrassed. 'I'm sorry; I didn't mean that to sound as it did. What I really meant was… I'm sorry I don't know how to put what I'm trying to say into words.'

Thomas smiled and said 'You don't have to.'

As silence prevailed momentarily, each one smiled with a look of embarrassment, neither one aware of the underlying reason.

'I take it you're waiting for the tram home then?'

'Yes,' came Helen's reply. She declined to give any further information.

'So you haven't said what brought you down here late at night, all alone.'
'Nor have you!' Helen's reply served to remind Thomas that she was no longer a little girl.

'I asked for that, didn't I?' Thomas stared downwards with unease.

'Actually, I've just been to see *No! No! Nanette!* at the Theatre Royale. My friend Diana Wilkinson managed to get a ticket for me.' Helen persevered with the final sentence looking elsewhere before facing Thomas. The lack of reaction and response was marked.

'Thomas, I'm so proud of you.' Helen produced such a captivating smile with this sentiment, stirring Thomas to reply.

'I suppose sooner or later someone was bound to find out. For goodness sake just don't let on to the likes of Father or Harry, otherwise I would be a laughing stock to them all.'

'Why? Because you want to use your talent and do something more than just going back and forwards to work everyday.'

'It's not exactly seen as a manly thing to do, is it?' Helen outwardly chose not to contradict or agree with this response, preferring to remind herself how Thomas had appeared on that stage. Dark and swarthy, strong and distant: the antithesis of effeminacy.

The journey home on the tram was quiet. Tension lurked in the surrounding silence, neither one wishing to release its absolute effect upon the other. Upon reaching Paradise Street the pair walked side by side conditionally before turning through the passageway and were about to depart to their respective homes when Thomas reached for Helen's hand without warning. He tightened his grasp and pulled her towards him.

'I don't want you to think badly of me. I'm not a theatrical person; it's just that I enjoy singing and doing something different to work. I mean there has to be more to life than going to the mill everyday. Don't you agree?'

'Definitely!' Helen moved closer to him and smiled her captivating smile once more.

'I knew you would understand. Thank you Helen.' He waited until she had entered Mrs Shackletons before entering his own home. Helen suddenly began to realise that her earlier feelings of tension had now turned into disappointment and frustration.

CHAPTER EIGHT

They made a handsome couple as they emerged from the 4.5 litre Bentley. Many heads turned initially to survey the splendid sight of a variety of automobiles, including Bentleys, parked next to one another. A number of owners keenly swapped accounts of their motoring exploits and were only too happy to show off the contents of their bonnets to fellow enthusiasts, much to the annoyance of their wives and girlfriends who remained totally oblivious to the talk of valves and cylinders. Denis and Helen strode past the admiring glances of the men who surveyed Helen's curvaceous female form and the women who coyly pretended not to notice Denis's endearing smile. No one appeared to notice the look of unease on Helen's face.

Westleigh House stood as testament to the success of Ickringill's Textile empire. A plain but substantially built residence of the 1860s, its sweeping entrance by means of a broad flight of steps led each guest through double doors into a central hall. There Helen gazed with bewilderment at the internal features of the house. She had never seen such opulence in a private house before. Momentarily the experience reminded her of the theatre, the difference being that this was someone's home. The entrance hall was a large square in the centre of the house and afforded direct access, by means of a magnificent arched staircase, to the upper storey as well as all the reception rooms. An oak parquetry floor contrasted beautifully with the walls, which were wainscoted in American walnut and had inserts of delicately carved oak panels. Quite unexpectedly a white-gloved hand appeared and a monotone voice enquired politely if he could be permitted to take charge of the lady's coat. Helen offered no response until Denis whispered that she was the lady in question.

They were directed into a large reception room on the right, where sheer crepes and chiffons draped themselves alluringly over nubile young female bodies that attracted the attention of immaculately turned out gentlemen in dinner suits. Helen froze and felt immediately overtly conspicuous. Drawing her upon his arm Denis prepared to greet the Ickringills, a portly-bodied gentleman and his matronly figured wife.

'So pleased you could make it Denis. Who's the delightful lady?' Both Denis and Helen's attention was drawn to the childish sniggers that emulated from the two young women standing next to the couple.

'You of course remember our two daughters, Constance and Violet?'

'Yes of course. Who could forget such beauty?' Denis's reply was so typical of him. Helen, however, did notice that even this compliment did not attract the two young women's gaze towards him. Instead they scrutinised and stared with derision at Helen.

'Please feel free to make yourself at home, my dear.' Helen began to feel reassured as Mrs Ickringill uttered these words with sincerity.

'Thank you very much for your kindness. I'm so looking forward to the ball.' Helen was desperate to convey her feelings of gratitude that she failed to notice the initial half suppressed laughter emulating from the two daughters.

'Oh, I wouldn't go so far as to describe tonight's proceedings as a ball. We used to host them here, but the craze these days, especially for the young, is that of the party, wouldn't you say girls? However I may add that that description will in no way detract from the fact that we want everyone here to... Oh, what was it that Noel Coward said? Yes, yes I remember, we want everyone to 'have themselves a ball'!' A smile of pride beamed across the hostess's face. The matronly figure was clearly incompatible with the modern liberated mind.

Denis, who had been busily engaged in conversation with Mr Ickringill, began to lead Helen towards an enticing tray of cocktails, totally oblivious to the muffled giggles behind them. Helen was not and heard every syllable distinctly.

'There goes another one of his women. This year's model. Used and soon to be replaced. Where does he get them from? I mean the poor little thing doesn't even know what a party is. She's still living in the last century. It's time that Denis was married. Quite a wealthy catch for one of us, don't you think?' The two sisters broke into unashamed laughter as Helen slumped onto a chair for support. Shocked and sickened she had little appetite for either the Martini cocktail or the delicate canapés, which Denis placed into her hands.

Furtive exchanges of flirtatious conversations abounded between the young whilst the elders were more predisposed to discussions of a more sombre note. The collapse of the American stock market in 1929 had been the start of the Great Depression, unleashing in its wake a vulnerability of economic hardship and uncertainty. Some lamented tales of friends and family who had recently suffered the loss of investments and also of those who could stand the indignity no longer and ended their misery. Heads shook with such thoughts of brittle dependency in monetary terms. The men proudly displayed their amply proportioned abdomens as a sign of their healthy bank balances whilst their wives affectionately fingered the precious jewels adorning their bodies. The facets of large diamonds, rubies, emeralds and sapphires sparkled with colour and perfect clarity as an indication of their worth, whilst ropes of pearls hung in abundant strands. Financial hardship seemed to be absent from this gathering. A few moments of transitory contemplation quickly gave way to boisterous agility as someone wound up the gramophone encouraging all 'the bright young things' in the room to indulge in the Charleston and the new jazz rhythms from America.

Helen declined Denis's offer 'to party' but watched with quiet resentment as the two Ickringill daughters used the opportunity to concurrently partner Denis. They maximised the occasion by requesting the foxtrot and then the tango, allowing each one to entwine Denis alone. Their triumphant smiles thrown back to Helen only seemed to reinforce their earlier prediction of regular replacements. Constantly Helen questioned why Denis had brought her here. There was no shortage of heiresses here. Money and beauty were in abundance and therefore only reckless dalliance could exist with an office girl. 'This year's model. Used and soon to be replaced.' Regrettably Helen realised this was the only deliberation.

The guests were requested to enter the dining room as folded doors were drawn back to reveal another room of substantial proportion. A handsome fireplace of Italian statuary marble, inlaid with curiously variegated Brocatella marble, caught the eye immediately. The ceilings were panelled and richly moulded with beautiful flowers and tendrils of the trumpet-shaped convolvulus which were gently entwined with the thoroughly English honeysuckle. Cut glass chandeliers hung from the ceiling casting their illumination over a heavily laden table below. Gentlemen and ladies were seated alternatively round the table. A glazed damask linen tablecloth lay underneath an attractive epergne displaying flowers and fruit. Gleaming cutlery, pristine crockery, elaborately folded damask napkins and crystal glasses completed the setting.

A fine menu then ensued:
<u>Hot Dishes.</u>
Clear soup.
Devilled Lobster.
Pigeons stewed in Casserole.
<u>Cold Dishes.</u>
Oyster Patties.
Fillets of Sole in Aspic.
Partridges masked with sauce.
Galantine of Turkey.
Game Pie.
Pressed Beef.
Salad.
Oranges in Jelly.
Russian Charlotte.

Stewed Pears and Cream.
Meringues with Vanilla Cream.

For the exact order for the use of the cutlery, Helen relied upon Denis's instruction. He appeared sensitive to her needs of etiquette and subtlety indicated the correct choice. Picking up an inappropriate utensil could have had catastrophic consequences for Helen in front of twenty-three diners. Much to Denis's relief, she was an astute and willing student.

The dining room seemed to echo the Victorian age in terms of decoration, formalities of dining and expectations, whilst the drawing room had adhered to the requirements of the young, gaiety and 'modernity'. As the meal progressed Helen began to feel more at ease. This she accredited to her confidence in mastering the cutlery and Denis's attentiveness. The young men around her had been assiduously polite and appeared genuinely beguiled by her beauty. Denis was not ignorant of this fact.

'Have I told you how beautiful you look tonight?' Helen could feel Denis's hot breath upon her neck as he whispered these words. Momentarily it felt as though everyone in the room was staring at them and her face spontaneously warmed as she blushed with embarrassment.

'I would even go so far as to say that you are the most beautiful girl here tonight!' Denis's hand clutched her inner thigh and once more she felt a facial glow of intensity. Offering an irrepressible smile and a momentary wink he then proceeded to indulge in the principal table talk of automobiles. Much to Helen's relief the female conversation was less focussed and flitted between fashion and films. Afternoon and evening wear with the appropriate accessories tended to be the dominant topic. Compliments were traded around the table, and Helen's blue chiffon dress was even admired by these followers of fashion. Everyone agreed that Al Jolson's spoken words in *The Jazz Singer* were purely magical. Everyone that was, except Helen, because she had never been to the cinema. Unheard of films and theatre productions were discussed which emphasised to Helen her ignorance of the entertainments business. She imagined if only Diana had been with her, her friend would have revelled in this discourse. Suddenly someone mentioned *No No Nanette!* and Helen found herself commenting on the performance.

'Did you attend its opening on Broadway, or was it in London?'

'It was just a local performance,' Helen quietly admitted.

'Oh, an amateur one. Well there's nothing quite like the real thing.'

Once more Helen felt embarrassed and declined to look at the Ickringill sisters for she felt sure they must have been aware of her faux pas. The incident did bring back recollections of a happier nature, as she remembered the thrill of discovering Thomas in that production and of her meeting with him afterwards. She also recalled Diana and Mr Godwin. That relationship, like the topic of conversation around the table, was solely driven by money. She also thought of Annie and the numerous occasions she had witnessed her producing a meal out of nothing. Contrasting that thought with the sumptuous choices of courses they had just enjoyed emphasised the fact that life was far from fair. Indeed fate was always responsible for dealing the cards. She had often heard it said that luck depended upon which side of the blanket you were born on. Judging by the conversation Helen realised she had been born on the opposite side to everyone else in the room. This sentiment did not imply illegitimacy, just inferiority.

At the end of the meal the ladies, as was customary, withdrew to the more comfortable drawing room, leaving the men to enjoy the private pleasures of port, cigars and manly conversation. Helen was beginning to tire of the superficial content of the ladies' conversation and found herself longing to be with the men. Her mind drifted and she found herself once more thinking about Thomas. Eventually approaching male voices broke her indulgent reverie as the men joined the ladies. A mixture of pastimes ensued. Those, whose constitutions allowed following the culinary delights, wound up the gramophone and danced.

Those who were not so inclined chatted and observed, or indulged their competitive streak in games such as bridge or mah-jong. Curiously Denis continued to be most attentive. Helen's glass was perpetually filled and refilled until she declined any further indulgence. Her head was beginning to spin and for the first time in her life she was starting to feel drunk. Denis was concerned and led her to a French window where he stepped outside with her into the chilling but sobering November air. He threw a protective arm around her shoulders and walked with her until she felt better. They then returned to the house and Denis thanked their hosts before making an early and unexpected departure with Helen from the Ickringills.

Helen felt the momentum of the car as it left Westleigh House and travelled back towards Beckston. She began to doze as an overwhelming tiredness swept through her body. Oblivious to their exact location, she relied upon Denis to transport her home, and resisted the temptation to remain alert. She curled her body sideways almost into a foetal position, burrowing her head into the leather seat for support, before falling asleep.

The car turned down a quiet track before coming to a halt. The absence of any noise made Helen stir.

'Where are we?'

'We've just taken a slight detour.' Denis was most confident in his manner. He reached across and began to lightly kiss her on the face and neck. Startled Helen pushed him away.

'I want to go home. Please take me home.'

'Don't play games with me Helen. You know how I feel about you.' He began to repeatedly kiss her on the lips whilst his fingers touched the outline of her breasts before descending to her thighs. His hand slithered to the hemline before feeling its way upwards to her stocking tops.

'Don't! Please don't.' The crying made him stop.

'Oh Helen. If only you knew what you do to me. The effect that you have, then you might say 'yes'.'

'I don't want to be this year's model. Used and soon to be replaced!' The remark appeared to stun him.

'You think that I just want you for sex?'

'Well don't you?' The silence was sufficient confirmation.

'Helen, you deserve to be mistress of a house like that. You were by far the most beautiful girl there tonight. If things were different, you could be.'

'If things were different! You mean if I was one of those empty headed females with a fortune then you would do the honourable thing before seducing me. Whereas I'm only a paid employee at your firm and should be content to settle for what you want.'

'There's no denying that I want you. I also know that I have a reputation amongst the ladies.'

'Yes I overheard the Ickringill daughters discussing your conquests and your marital potential.' This remark also served to stun.

Denis smiled at Helen as he pulled her coat around her. 'Better cover you up or you'll catch your death.' They drove home in silence, each one reflecting upon the other one's words

****

Life once more settled into a humdrum existence. Helen repeatedly endured the critical disapproval of Miss Walker in the office. She was continually rebuked for typing too slowly and then for rushing her work. Nothing seemed to appease her demands. Denis had distanced himself from her environment, visiting European connections in a bid to swell the order books. A momentary pang of jealousy made Helen question whether the sales trip would apportion sufficient time for pleasure. There would no doubt be wealthy industrialists with strikingly beautiful daughters whose unfamiliar use of the English language and characteristic continental looks would attract Denis's attention.

Christmas passed quietly and seemed to be an anti-climax to the events preceding it. Diana had failed to keep in touch; presumably her time was pre-occupied with her wealthy admirer. Helen began to feel disconsolate and wondered whether her life would ever change. Almost accepting of her situation she suddenly found excitement in watching the Easter Fair arrive. The noise heralded its arrival. Large 'tide engines' arrived blowing out steam whilst their iron wheels rattled over the granite sets and tram lines pulling long trains of caravans and trucks. Behind them children followed, squealing with excitement. As Helen watched the passing scene at the end of her street, she was unaware of being watched.

'It's quite something when the fair comes to town.' Helen turned and found Thomas smiling at her.

'Yes it is. I should think it's quite remarkable when it's all set up.'

'Don't tell me that you've never been to the fair.' Thomas seemed to find her comment incredulous.

'Well, no I haven't.'

'I'll have to change that. Let's see it opens on Friday night. Would you like to come with me and try out the swings and rides? I'll treat you to a toffee apple and some candy floss.'

The invitation was too irresistible. Helen could already feel the excitement of the fair.

True to its word, the fair, or 'tide' as it was locally known, threw open its attractions to everyone on payday. The owners possessed sufficient business acumen to understand how to maximise profits.

Those magical sounds truly beckoned as the bells on the sideshows merrily rang alongside melodious notes bellowing from fairground organs. Smoke and steam rose into the sky as visual reminders that the fair was open. In the unlikely event that anyone had failed to realise this the proprietors relied upon one more tactic. The aroma of a fair is distinctly unmistakeable and unforgettable. Air currents carried sweet odours of candyfloss, toffee apples, brandy snaps and popcorn as well as savoury ones of pies and peas boiling over a coke fire. Resistance was a true test of willpower.

Helen had only just finished her meal with Alice Shackleton when Thomas arrived. Jokingly he admonished her for having eaten and trusted that she would not be too full to sample the culinary delights of the fair. Only a tram ride away, they quickly reached their destination. Helen was instantly mesmerised by the continual array of enticements and did not know in which direction to look. They strolled passed large fairground organs, which summoned their attention with bandmasters, and moving figures playing popular music. Turning their attention away they were suddenly beguiled by the big rides which were the unmistakeable prima donnas in the show. The carriages of each ride were adorned with beautiful unique paintings, gilded carved work, cut glass mirrors and rods of twisted brass. Stationary they were impressive, but the thrill was obviously in the ride. Speed and danger were always a potent and intoxicating mix. Screams of fear and excitement rang through the night as the little carriages careered with death-defying precision around the helter-skelter tracks, before delivering their charges to a swift and grateful end. With no time to be lost Thomas grasped Helen's hand and led her to one of the empty carriages. Protesting her indecision and airing her doubts about the likely risks only proved to be futile. Without notice the journey began. Fear of the unknown made her very wary. A sudden jerk and a drop caused her to scream in automatic response. Immediately she was cocooned in his arms, being drawn into the warmth and security of his body. Another turn and unexpected fall found her clinging to him. She closed her eyes, willing the nightmare to end, but at the same time also revelling in this first touch of intimacy. When the little carriage finally stopped the pair were still wrapped in one another's arms and only broke free as he kissed her forehead and smiled warmly into her eyes. After that the excitement was no longer just confined to the fairground attractions. Neither uttered a word but instead relied upon touch as the means of communication. It seemed natural for him to reach for her hand and walk together, pressing the sides of their bodies together as one. Each face showed a transition of relief to contentment as they strode passed the sideshows featuring a varied assortment of attractions, including boxing, freak animals, a fat lady and even a small circus. None of these could possibly interest them for they had just discovered a new experience.

Their laughter continued long into the evening as they enjoyed the delights of the galloping horses, steam swings and the roundabouts, particularly the cockerels which moved up and down and the waltzers or spew pans which spun around at the same time as the roundabout revolved. Screaming and giggling they held onto one another, to provide a mutual feeling of safety which also provided ample opportunities to embrace and cuddle. When they had saturated their thirst for excitement they then preceded to the refreshment stalls. Helen declined a pie and peas, wishing that she had not already eaten, but was tempted with candyfloss and a brandy snap. The fluffy mass of spun sugar caused Thomas to tease Helen as he provocatively tore thin shreds away from her stick. He danced around her threatening to remove more until she ran away causing him to follow. Inevitably they once more found themselves in a deeply held embrace. He lightly kissed her on the cheek and then more forcibly on the lips. She reciprocated by drawing his head towards her with her hands wrapped around the nape of his neck. They both wanted more.

The pleasures of the fair had begun to wane. It had provided the catalyst for emotional gratification but could no longer satisfy the physical desires. As they passed by the pot stalls and the smaller children's roundabouts, they were oblivious to their sights and sounds. A group of gypsies sitting on the steps of their caravans called to them to come and find out what the future held in store. Ignorant of their existence they passed them by. The group undaunted continued with their conversations in the Romany language. An old lady, probably the eldest of the group, maintained her gaze upon them until they were no longer in sight. She alone could foretell that this night would be portentous. In her long life she had known such omens before: thankfully, only on one occasion.

Riding high on the euphoria of life they rushed back to Thomas's house. The evening had unleashed a roller coaster of emotional turmoil. Neither could recall the journey back to Paradise Street as all events succumbed into a blur. The house was empty as Tom and Mary were frequenting the local public houses and Harry had left the house just before Thomas, stating that he would be back late. Thomas knew with certainty that they would not be disturbed. Helen had not entered the house for some time. She almost expected to see Annie but quickly realised that that could never be. The untidiness and dishevelment around the room confirmed her complete absence.

As the outside door was closed each one looked nervously at the other. It had not occurred to Helen that a man could be frightened of love but she witnessed apprehension and indecision in his eyes. In a bid to possibly summon up Dutch courage Thomas began searching for remnants of Christmas cheer. He found them in the guise of bottled beer for himself and port wine for Helen. With each drink they began to unwind. They kissed and touched with increasing fervour until Thomas pulled away abruptly.

'Helen, perhaps this is not a good idea. We could end up regretting our actions and I don't want to take advantage of you.'

'You wouldn't be. It's what I want as well. It's taken all this time for us both to admit how we feel about each other. Please don't stop now. It's you that I want.'

Further encouragement was not needed. Unbuttoning her blouse he began to undress her, sliding the straps of her undergarments over her shoulders, to expose her breasts, which he gently touched and kissed. Her body ached with desire as she suddenly began to feel wet and open. As he lay on top of her she could feel his hardness through his clothes and she knew that like her, he was aroused. She was therefore astonished when he suddenly stopped.

'It's not right Helen. Not here like this. We've no protection.'

'Go and get some. I'll wait for you in your bed.' The drink was now beginning to take effect. Helen began to stagger towards the door. She managed to climb the stairs and entered the smaller bedroom, which boasted two single beds. She remembered his instruction. 'The bed nearest the door is mine.' With that in mind she managed to remove her remaining garments, slid under the covers and waited.

She did not hear him come into the room, presumably because she had fallen asleep. As she opened her eyes a chink of outside light was being obliterated as he pulled a shabby piece of cloth across the window. The room was now in complete darkness. That seemed to only serve to heighten the senses. Each now relied upon touch. She suddenly felt his body upon her. Grasping him to her she began to kiss him. The moment was intoxicating. She had waited for this night for so long and that was the problem. She did not mind that the surroundings were less than glamorous or that there was no wedding ring upon her finger. Thomas had always been the one to whom she would give her virginity. However the effects of the drink were beginning to take their toll. The consequence of alcohol indulgence had seized the romance of the moment. Helen's head began to spin as she felt him thrust his hardness with ever increasing force into her body. Tenderness was absent as he stormed into her, ignoring her pleas for him to stop. To offer resistance only made it more painful. With reluctance she yielded to his demands until she felt a spasmodic reaction throughout his body, finally culminating in a climax of intense excitement. The enjoyment was not shared. Eventually it was over. She felt him leave the bed, dress and close the door.

Her feelings for Thomas had also left her.

CHAPTER NINE

The wedding had been of a smaller nature than anticipated. She wore white and looked absolutely beautiful and he instantly understood why he was marrying her as he gazed into her eyes. Innocent and virginal, she had managed to retain his interest in her for so long.

It had not at first been apparent to her that she was pregnant. In spite of everything she had trusted him to take precaution and make love to her both with passion and compassion. Anxiously awaiting the monthly sign that failed to show and secretly coping with nauseous bouts of sickness, only confirmed her suspicions. There was no one to confide in. If only Annie had been there for her. She could not tell Thomas. In fact she could not even bear to speak to him. On numerous occasions he had caught sight of her, but she had just ignored him. Ironically, he had always been the one with whom secrets had been shared, but not this secret. This one she would keep to herself.

Terrified and lonely, Fate intervened in the shape of Diana. Helen had considered seeking her out, but had refrained convinced that Diana would have no useful advice to impart. How wrong her judgement had been. Diana was a true advocate in the ways of the world.

It was one of those moments of coincidence when they met. Helen had at the last minute decided to miss her tram in order to make a purchase. As she crossed the road she suddenly saw a familiar face. They embraced and chatted, each one eager to learn of the other one's news. The regular meeting place was decided upon; Paterson's for tea and indulgent talk.

Diana, as before, sparkled with jewellery and tales of her enticing treats: trips to London, Paris and Rome, all paid for by Mr Godwin. It would have been easy now for Helen to be envious of her friend but she was not. She still found the thought of Mr Godwin unpleasant. She hoped that Diana understood the consequence of her actions. Society had always viewed adultery in a dim light, as indeed babies born out of wedlock. That thought brought home to her the reality of the situation. Diana was the first person to witness the tears in her eyes. She was also perceptive enough to know that Helen needed someone to talk to.

'Are you absolutely certain?'

'Yes. There is no doubt.'

'Well it might not have been planned Helen, but he's free to marry you. I know that you've always had a soft spot for him. I can remember at school you were always mentioning his name and telling me how he looked after you.' This remark only served to release the tears.

'I thought I loved him. But how can you love someone when they've raped you?' Diana stared in disbelief as the words fell from her lips.

'Rape... Helen I can't believe that Thomas is capable of that. He's always looked after you.'

'He didn't on that night. There was no tenderness, no love, only pain and now I'm carrying his child. I wanted him so much and that's what hurts even more. I don't think that I'll ever trust a man again.'

The time passed quickly as Helen unburdened herself to Diana. She had given herself freely to a man whom she had always loved, trusting him to be the same. She spoke of the times when ironically she had preserved her virginity, when Denis had tried to persuade her to do otherwise. Throughout all of this Diana remained silent. Finally the revelations were at an end and it was now Diana's turn to speak.

'Helen, it seems to me that you have four options. You could marry Thomas as the father of your child, but having told me what you have that is out of the question. You could have an abortion, but the look of horror on your face speaks for itself. You could of course have the baby and either bring it up on your own or let someone else bring it up as their child. You're far too sensitive for the latter and do you really want to spend your life in poverty? Helen, that's not you. I haven't forgotten about your grandfather. You don't think that there's any possibility of going to see him?'

'Certainly not! What makes you think he would warm to me with a bastard child when he wouldn't to his own daughter who was married? That isn't a proposition.'

'Well there is only one way left.' Diana's eyes sparkled as she spoke.

It would not be the first or the last time that this idea had been used. To Helen it appeared unethical and unjust. To Diana it was the perfect solution.

****

Dressed in an expensive wedding gown Helen became Mrs Tetlow. The train flowed effortlessly behind her as she emerged into the sunshine from Beckston church. At her side was Denis; together they made a handsome couple. All the arrangements had been expedited with the utmost haste. At five months pregnant, Helen was fortunate not to be showing, particularly as Denis believed that she was only four months with child. Initially Helen had abhorred the thought of duping Denis into fatherhood. Diana had played the card of reason well against the card of conscience.

'What choice have you got Helen?' Diana had repeatedly asked of her. Helen finally conceded.

Any distance between Helen and Denis was quickly transcended with an encouraging smile on her part and an invitation to dinner on his. At last he had achieved his ultimate desire, the opportunity to make love to her. He was without doubt a skilled lover and any apprehension Helen might have had following her last experience, quickly vanished. His readiness to accept his responsibility was at first lacking in enthusiasm, but he perhaps realised that his bachelor days had, as a matter of course, come to an end. There was only one way to do things and that was to do them well. Money secured the quality of the arrangements.

As established and wealthy clothing manufacturers, Tetlow Brothers had a number of well-known connections in the fashion industry. These were used to secure the urgent design and production of Helen's wedding dress. The main body of the garment was of silk which flowed out into a stylish train. A lace cape with rouleau bows and bindings covered the shoulders demurely; this was complemented by two overskirts, one of lace and one of crepe, which fell open in a gradual decline from the front to reveal the dress in full. A diamond-shaped panel with gathers for the bust in the bodice provided a perfect fit along with the rest of the dress for Helen's slightly 'blooming' figure. The couturier had produced a masterpiece of fashion for the late summer season of 1932, whilst avoiding highlighting any additional weight gains. The result was a total mix of style and taste which Helen carried with dignity as she did the headdress and accompanying fine chiffon veil. Diana, as her best friend, eagerly enjoyed the role of bridesmaid.

The 4.5 litre Bentley was the bridal car which transported them from the church to the reception at Horton House, the family home of the Tetlows. There they dined with their guests on a Wedding Breakfast:

Oyster Patties.

Salmon cutlets.
Lobster Salad.

Lamb Cutlets masked with Sauce.
Roast Chicken.
Salad Waldorf.

Mixed Fruit with Kirsch.
Meringues with cream.
Lemon Water Ice.

A selection of Fruits.
Coffee.

The table decorations were arranged entirely with white flowers and foliage whilst the cake was decorated with Helen's bouquet. Tradition had definitely been adhered to.

Their honeymoon took them to Italy, in particular Venice, where they stayed and visited the unique city set in its own lagoon, as well as the lesser known islands with magical sounding names such as Burano, Murano and Torcello. Helen found the whole experience breathtaking. Venice was a labyrinth where sinuous canals were used instead of streets, spanned by bridges and protected by the magnificent imposing buildings of St. Marks Basilica and the Doges Palace. Their hotel, the Danieli, lavishly furnished and decorated in true Venetian style, overlooked the lagoon. A former palace and home of Doge Dandolo, it maintained the feel and atmosphere of the once noble home that it had been. Amidst such opulent surroundings Helen at times found it difficult to believe that she was not dreaming. Life had suddenly become surreal amongst the plethora of gothic facades and elegant gondolas, plying their way back and forth across the waterways. Denis had been unquestionably attentive and loving and Helen had almost convinced herself that nothing could possibly alter that.

One evening sitting at one of the many little tables surrounding St. Marks Square, Denis asked a question that Helen was unprepared for.
'I wonder whether he or she will look more like you or me?'

'I'm sure there'll be aspects of both.' It was the only reply that Helen could manage. He was smiling at her and holding her hand, in the most acclaimed romantic city in the world and she instantly felt nauseous.

She slept little that night. Her mind drifted back to Annie and the conversation she had had with her, regarding life. 'Just don't settle for second best. Look further afield than these streets,' Annie had said. Helen thought that under the circumstances she had. The irony was that without her pregnancy she would not be married to Denis. If only the child had been his, but she had repeatedly resisted his advances, saving herself for

Thomas. God it was a mess! She closed her eyes hoping that the nightmare would pass. When she finally fell asleep it was not long before she began to dream. Denis was pushing a pram along Paradise Street, where she used to live. She called out to him but he did not answer. Finally she ran to him just as he had stopped to pick up the baby. He turned to face her with the child in his arms and said, 'Shall we call him Thomas?' Helen looked at the baby and saw dark hair surrounding Thomas's face. Snatching the child from Denis's arms she began to run until she stopped by a bridge overlooked by another bridge. The latter was the Bridge of Sighs. Throwing the child into the canal she then found herself falling after it. The fall finally stopped when she hit the floor. Alarmed, Denis swiftly ran to her side of the bed and carefully helped her back into bed.

'Helen, are you alright? Do you want me to get you a doctor?' Denis was clearly most anxious.

'No I'm perfectly alright.'

'Was it just a bad dream? Don't worry it's all over now.' Helen wished that she could share his conviction.

The dream or rather nightmare became a recurring event. They spent their days visiting the historical sights, escaping to miniature versions of Venice, in the form of the island of Burano, whose brightly painted houses were reflected in the waters of its own canals or relaxing upon the sands of the Lido. Helen tried very hard to reflect upon the beautiful sights of each day as she fell asleep but some nights brought back the unwelcome image of infanticide. It was only when they returned home that the nightmares ceased.

Horton house possessed neither the grandeur of Mount Hall nor the charm of Westleigh House, but it did have a presence of impressive solidity. Home to the Tetlow family for three generations it had been financed through the successive family business based on the manufacturing trade. The building, constructed of ashlar work, could scarcely be described as appertaining to any particular order of architecture except that it did possess the distinctive features of both

Italian and English schools. Although not impressively large in size, Horton House could eminently be described as a comfortable home.

As the family and staff greeted the newlyweds it became clear how different life would now be. Edward and his brother Richard had lived in the residence all their lives. It was here that Denis had been born and his mother had died. Helen did wonder whether the two brothers would resent her intrusion. On the contrary they appeared to genuinely welcome her. Richard Tetlow, a reserved and quiet man, had always treated Helen with complete respect and courtesy. Edward Tetlow, Denis's father, was more of an unknown quantity to Helen. In the workplace he appeared hard and defiant but in his home softness pervaded. He was the first one to stride across and kiss his daughter-in-law on the cheek.

'Welcome to the family Helen. You look stunning. Obviously the Venetian air has agreed with you. Or perhaps it was something else? You're a lucky devil, Denis, having a beauty like this on your arm. Don't you forget it!' The remark served to make Helen blush.

Richard's response was more reserved. Stepping forward he shook the hand first of Helen and then Denis, welcoming Helen into the family and wished them both happiness in the future. A bottle of champagne was opened and Edward made a toast to the young couple. Each person drank and then a further toast was made.

'Helen, this toast is to you. You are now a Tetlow and we welcome you as such. You are also carrying a Tetlow in your belly, and therefore we offer a toast to the young heir.' All in the room drank except Helen. The colour drained from her cheeks as she suddenly felt faint. Everyone offered concern as she was helped into a chair. She declined to be examined by a doctor allowing all those around her to believe that exhaustion from the travel had been the underlying cause. Retiring to their bedroom she closed her eyes until Denis had left and then lay awake pensively considering her future.

The trap that she had set had now unwittingly ensnared her. She felt totally helpless and in truth knew that she could not deviate from the course of her actions. It would have been easier if the family had been less agreeable to her but they had shown nothing but consideration. At times she wondered whether it stemmed from the belief that the wayward playboy had finally settled into domestic responsibility. Respectability was far more of an attractive trait than dalliance in the world of business where trust could secure a batch of orders. She allowed herself to believe that she had brought something worthwhile to the marriage.

Helen was now six months pregnant, although to everyone else she was five months and beginning to display a definite bulge. Her old life and work were now completely in the past. There were servants to carry out the household tasks who now looked to Helen as mistress of the household. Richard Tetlow was sufficiently astute to recognise her initial discomfort and spent time guiding her in such matters. She admired his patience and dedication and soon began to enjoy time in his company. A lifelong bachelor his passion was for works of art. He possessed a series of beautiful sketches by the late painter-poet, Dante Gabriel Rosetti, including, amongst others, the study for his famous work *Andromeda*. He also held an extensive and valuable collection of old Chinese and Japanese ware. Helen marvelled at his knowledge and listened intently as he explained that his collections were from the masters of Satsuma, Kaga, and Kioto who were skilled in the art of perfection at a time when their contempories in Europe were still in their infancy. In Helen he found a young mind with a thirst for knowledge which he duly replenished with anecdotes of his travels and an introduction to his library. Neither Denis nor Edward had ever shown interest in this room and therefore it was quite refreshing to be able to tutor a soul mate into the realms of literature. Shakespeare, Milton, Keats, Byron and Sir Walter Scott were but a few of the authors and poets who were introduced to his willing protégée. They all provided a safe haven for Helen to travel to when her mind wandered into dark thoughts. She increasingly found herself visiting the library more frequently in an effort to suppress her anguish and immerse herself in tales of the imagination.

As Helen began to acclimatize to her comfortable lifestyle and relinquish the past an unforeseen event occurred. A hand delivered envelope had been placed upon her breakfast tray. Of late she had yielded to Denis's persuasion of having breakfast brought to her in bed. Alone in the house with only the servants she examined the handwriting. Her name, 'MRS HELEN TETLOW' had been printed in capital letters and therefore afforded no clues to the sender's identity. With mounting curiosity she ripped the envelope open and pulled out a folded piece of paper. As she unfolded the paper she stared with shock and disbelief at the contents in the letter.

IT'S A WISE CHILD THAT KNOWS ITS OWN FATHER

PATERSONS   TUESDAY 4PM

The message like the name on the envelope had been printed in capital letters. There were grammatical errors with the absence of apostrophes. Whether the sender was aware of this, deliberately choosing not to use them in order to maintain anonymity or ignorant of their use, Helen could not tell. She continued to stare at the message, feeling nauseous and hot. It had to be Thomas. There was no one else. Was he now seeking revenge for her marital elevation in life? Did he really think that she could marry him after that night? How did he know that she was pregnant? Even if he had heard that she was pregnant, could he not accept that her husband was the father? She continued to interrogate herself until she felt faint and exhausted. There were no answers to these questions. None of the servants had seen the person who had delivered the letter. The only solution was to go to Paterson's the following Tuesday at 4pm.

****

As the day dawned, Helen dreaded the fateful meeting. She had already rehearsed the conversation a thousand times but knew that predictably when she faced him her repertoire would vaporise, leaving her tongue-tied and no doubt emotional. Pregnant ladies were always considered emotional due to their fluctuating hormones. Helen, however, needed to be strong.

Allowing herself plenty of time she arrived half an hour early, confident that by arriving first she would be in a stronger position psychologically. Every time the doorbell tinkled with a new arrival or departure she looked anxiously for Thomas. As the waitress returned to her table to enquire whether she was ready to order her attention had been momentarily diverted. Helen's heart began to beat erratically as she stared at him. Her initial thoughts had been to say that she was waiting for someone, but without hesitation he sat down opposite her. Where was Thomas?

'Have you ordered yet, or were you waiting for me?' A malevolent smile flashed across his face.

'No, not yet.' She continued to stare impassively.

'I take it that you weren't expecting me then?'

'No.'

'I always find a little of the unexpected makes life more interesting. What can I order for you?'

'Just tea.'

'What about something to eat? I'm sure you must be eating for two now. By the way when's the baby due?'

'Can we stop the pleasantries. What do you want, Harry?' This was the first time that she had managed to say his name.

'I think I'd like the same as you: a life of comfort. However for now I'll settle for afternoon tea.'

Helen felt decidedly uncomfortable in his company. They sat in silence as the waitress brought their order and only Harry appeared to enjoy the indulgence of cream cakes and tea, Helen merely sipped her tea having little appetite for anything else.

'What do you want?' Helen was determined not to prolong her time in his presence.

'What do you think I want?' Harry demanded.

'I don't know.'

'Well I'll tell you. I want to know why you're having one man's child and passing it off as someone else's. Let's put it this way, I don't suppose the Tetlow's expected damaged goods for their money. You certainly managed to convince Denis of your pure virginal state. But of course we both know the truth.'

Tears began to well in her eyes and she became unable to speak.

'You were always very good at using the feminine tricks, especially where Mum and Thomas were concerned. However they're not here. So, it's all a waste of time with me, because I don't fall for tears.'

'How did you find out? Did he tell you?'

'Good God no! Are you assuming that Thomas was so proud of his conquest with you that he had to brag about it? No, I'm sure that he wanted to keep quiet on that score, having had far better than you. He didn't need to tell me about it. I was there and witnessed all the sordid goings-on for myself. You're quite the little harlot. In fact, if ever your husband throws you out, I'm sure that you could earn a living on the streets. That is of course, once you've lost the bump!' He sat back in his chair and smirked with great contempt.

Helen understood totally that he held all the winning cards, and that she would have to yield to his proposition. The trouble was, as yet, she did not know what that would be.

He suddenly leaned closely to her.

'I'll put you out of your misery. I don't want anything for nothing. In fact I'm prepared to work for anything that I get. I can't say fairer than that. If you remember we took you into our family and gave you privileges and now its time for you to do the same for me. I'm relying on you to put a very good word in for me, so that I can be a part of the family firm. I've worked in insurance and could charm the birds out of the trees with my plausible ways. I'm sure I'd give Mr Denis a run for his money in the orders department. I quite fancy a job travelling abroad to secure the orders. Yes, we'd all be part of one big happy family.'

The words 'happy' and 'family' were ill-suited, especially when applied to Harry. He had always taken pleasure in her discomfort: he was a constant anathema to her. His delivery of poison had not, however, affected his appetite as he gorged on a large cream cake before draining the teapot dry.

'I'd better settle the bill, as I invited you here.' He rose from his chair and was about to leave when Helen abruptly confronted him.

'Is that it? Do you think that you can turn my world upside down, upset me and then just go? I'm sure there must me a concluding part to all of this. Tell me what comes next?'

'It's all down to you. I'm sure that you haven't forgotten where I live. I'll leave it up to you to come and find me, when you have some news.'

'What happens if I am unable to bring you that news?'

'Oh Helen, I don't think that it will come to that, do you? You're far too resourceful for that. Besides you and I are out of the same mould . We're survivors.' He grinned and once again was about to leave when a final question stopped him in his tracks.

'Did Thomas know that you were meeting me today?'

124

'Thomas. No! I haven't seen him for some time. He left Beckston, not long after that night. I've no idea where he's ended up.' Helen felt that this was the truth. Harry had no vested interest in Thomas's whereabouts as such information could not be used for profiteering purposes.

'I take it then that Thomas has no knowledge of my pregnancy?'

'No, as I said, he left quickly.' Harry likewise turned and left Helen to contemplate their conversation. There was a great deal for her to consider.

****

The pain was intense. Initially there had been painless bright red vaginal bleeding which Helen had tried to counteract by resting in bed. To begin with the loss had been slight and temporarily had ceased. She had stoically resisted being examined by the doctor but the onset of severe, incapacitating abdominal pain had prompted the servants to send for him. Her pleas to avoid doing so were ignored, for they feared for their livelihoods in the absence of the Tetlow men. Denis was away on business and his father and uncle were gainfully employed at the family business. The bleeding and the pain continued accompanied this time by griping pains in the lower part of the abdomen and back. The pain only ceased when the foetus, with its sac of membranes and placenta, had been expelled. The miscarriage had ended.

The doctor was unable to provide a satisfactory explanation. As Helen grew stronger and began to recover he explained that she had probably suffered a miscarriage due to an abnormality in the womb. It was likely that the placenta had grown inadequately, or become diseased and unable to maintain an adequate oxygen and food supply to the foetus. She recalled in her own mind how following her meeting with Harry she had suddenly begun to stop feeling pregnant. There had been a complete cessation of movement. That had been two weeks ago. She felt she was a murderess, as those dreams of infanticide returned to haunt her. She dreaded seeing Denis. Half of her was relieved that the pregnancy was over, but the other half could not help but feel that she had let her husband down. This sentiment seemed strange as the child was not her husband's, but the baby had been a boy. A son and heir was all that was needed despite the deception.

'Darling, we've all our lives ahead of us. Please don't cry. You'll conceive again. This one was just not meant to be.'

Denis's words were truly prophetic. Only Helen could understand their true value.

CHAPTER TEN

A definite air of uncertainty had begun to pervade throughout the Tetlow household. It was most likely that it had manifested itself from the contagious depression which seemed to be sweeping through the country. The thirties had evolved with a legacy of mass unemployment and a distinct vulnerability of fiscal disarray; 3 000 000 out of work was testament to this. Britain was still the ruler of a mighty empire but many recognised that the steadfast imperial hold was beginning to diminish. None more so than the Tetlow Brothers as their reliance upon overseas trade began to be affected.

Helen could never quite find the right time to enquire about a position for her cousin. Harry had made it extremely clear that he would not tolerate anything less than managerial. Feminine persuasion might have worked with Denis but she very much doubted its affect upon his father or uncle. Therefore she did nothing. The inertia however began to exact its own revenge. Every moment of every day she began to consider the consequences. Physically she was beginning to feel stronger after losing the baby but mentally she was drained with worry. The problem would never resolve itself but Helen was totally unprepared for Harry's plans.

He emerged from the office with a look of self-satisfaction across his face. At his side Denis was busily engaged in affable conversation with his new companion. Only the look on Helen's face curtailed the friendly banter.

'Helen, I didn't expect to see you here today. What's the matter, you look as though you've just seen a ghost?' Denis's question seemed to be naive.

'That's just it, I have.' Helen stared at Harry and pondered the numerous possibilities of his presence at Tetlows. Denis's affability affirmed that he had not divulged any indiscretions.

'Do I take it you know one another?' Denis enquired in his continual naïve fashion.

'Do we know one another? Helen is only my cousin. We'd lost touch and haven't set eyes on one another in ages' retorted Harry. It was quite evident from his little charade that he was a most accomplished liar. A true conman in every sense of the word, thought Helen.

Turning towards his wife Denis began to laugh and reminded her that during the preparations for the wedding she had steadfastly denied having any living family. Now Denis seemed bemused by his wife's reunion with her cousin.

'Helen, are you sure you're not holding back any little secrets from me? Are there any family skeletons in your cupboard which you haven't mentioned?' Helen immediately felt her face warming with blushing. This appealed to Denis as he kissed her on the cheek recognising that he had unleashed a feminine response. He perceived this to be innocence whereas Harry identified an emotional vulnerability.

'Well Mr Ledgard I'm sure we'll be able to do business with you. Send me the details and we'll see what we can do. For now I'll leave you with my wife. I'm sure you must have plenty to discuss.' The two men shook hands and Denis walked away, leaving the cousins together.

'I hope you'll sing my praises Helen. I'm angling for some insurance business with your husband.' Harry winked and added, 'I know you're very persuasive and am sure that you haven't forgotten our earlier conversation. This way I'm just making it easier for you. I'm sure that I can count on you.' The emphasis ended with the final word implying that Helen must now direct the next stage of events.

The next few days proved to Helen how instrumental Harry had been in determining his own destiny. Denis spoke of him with a certain admiration. It was undoubtedly clear that he would be given an insurance deal for the business. He had charmed and beguiled with total selfishness. However Helen knew that she needed to act as the provocateur in order to instigate the next stage of development with Denis's support.

'You seem to get on well with Harry,' Helen remarked casually.

'Yes, he's certainly a personable fellow.'

Helen took a deep breath and swallowed. 'Yes, he's always been the same. He's very good at his job.' Helen suddenly felt exposed as Denis looked at her. 'What I mean is, he's obviously done well for himself, which implies that he's good at the selling side. As you know I've not seen him for quite some time, but by the nature of what he's doing...' Helen was suddenly interrupted.

'I couldn't agree more. In fact I was so impressed by his sales technique and, notwithstanding that he's family now, I think he'd be a wonderful asset to the firm. It's good to have the family at the helm in a family firm, wouldn't you agree? Trust and reliability are not always true bedfellows in the eyes of a stranger.'

Helen was totally incapable of speaking. It had all been so easy, in fact, too easy. For weeks she had planned and contrived in her mind the opening lines for a scenario which had already been worked out. She had dreaded endorsing the false attributes of a rogue rather than a gentleman and was only too relieved to discover that she was no longer required to play the part.

'What position do you intend to offer him?' Helen tentatively enquired.

'That of Sales Manager. Initially in Britain but if he makes a go of things he could represent us on the continent.'

'That's your job surely?'

'Yes, but I'm hoping to have more time at home with my wife and family.' Denis grinned mischievously.

'Family?'

'Yes didn't I mention? We're going to need a future generation to carry on the good name and I can't think of a better time than now to begin.' Kissing her sensuously on the lips and around the neck he began to hurriedly undress her. They had not made love for months because of the pregnancy and the miscarriage. He had genuinely proved his love for her by being patient and now each one took delight in touching and exploring the other ones body. His fingers rolled each nipple before his tongue licked each one. The sensation aroused Helen into orgasmic pleasure, which instantly stimulated Denis to move sensuously down her body and find new experiences of mutual delight. He quickly entered her wet and open body and penetrated with a deep force in an effort to satisfy their needs. Helen frantically grasped him to her as she felt his body explode with sexual energy. Finally they lay together in one another's arms totally content and happy. Helen was secure in the knowledge that this child would be her husbands.

As the weeks and months passed Helen began to feel despondent. Eager to be able to inform her husband that she was pregnant, she awaited the telltale signs. However they failed to transpire. The unwanted monthly show never failed to appear and Helen could not understand the reason for it. Denis was a most caring and accomplished lover. Little excuse was needed to indulge in love making which they had enjoyed frequently in the privacy and confines of their bedroom, as well as in lesser-frequented rooms around the house. The result was always the same. Denis showed no anguish, believing that another pregnancy would surely follow the first one. Privately Helen was beginning to be less optimistic. Ironically, Thomas had slept with her but once and she had conceived an unwanted child, but now multiple occasions of amorous affection could not impregnate her with the child they both so desired. On occasions Helen did wonder whether her wickedness in deceiving her husband had returned to haunt her. She reflected upon Annie's words of wisdom: ' Be careful with what you wish for, it might just come true.' Helen had been so full of desire for Thomas and had wanted him so much. The trouble was that her passionate desire for him had resulted in a consequential string of events which were beginning to destroy her life. Everything was out of control and she dreaded any further repercussions. Fate was only dealing her loosing cards.

Those particular thoughts made her think of Mrs Shackleton, the old lady who had foretold her of her involvement with two men. She recalled her words of caution. 'Be careful, as the dark one is not all that he seems whilst the fair one is. Each one will shape and change your life forever. The hardest thing for you is making the right choice.' Thomas had certainly behaved despicably and not as she would ever have believed possible. He definitely was not all that he seemed. With that thought Helen decided that she would visit her old landlady.

Paradise Street remained untouched by time and modernity. The nostalgia awakened a number of feelings in Helen's heart as she remembered the first time she had walked down the street clutching Annie's hand, the numerous occasions she had waited for Thomas to return from work, and finally that fateful night when hope had disintegrated into despair. Helen turned and walked through the passageway and, without looking at the Ledgard house, knocked upon Alice Shackleton's door. Initially there was no response. Helen knocked again and this time she sensed a movement behind the door. Age had continued to wither the face and the frame but the eyes shone back with recognition and excitement.

'Helen, Helen, come in!' The welcome was warm and genuine.

Alice Shackleton was keen to hear Helen's news in its entirety. Helen, however, recounted details of her new life with a certain economy of the truth, wondering whether this clairvoyant could sense the slight deception. If she did she failed to show it.

'Do you remember Helen, I used to tell you that money surrounded you and that you would be rich one day?'

'Yes, I do, but you also told me about a fair-haired man and a dark haired man, each one causing me unhappiness. I presume my husband Denis is the fair-haired man that you mentioned. He is kind, gentle and loving and I cannot imagine him hurting me.'

Suddenly Mrs Shackleton reached for Helen's hands. As always she examined each one before displaying a look of anguish across her face.

'What is it? What do you see? Please tell me. I need to know.'

'I once told you that each man would shape and change your life forever. Do you remember?' Helen quickly nodded in agreement. 'I also told you that the hardest thing for you was to make the right choice. I'm so sorry Helen, but you made the wrong decision. Each one will cause you unhappiness because of this decision.'

Helen stared with disbelief at the old lady. It would have been easier for her to shrug the proceedings off with mere contempt for clairvoyance, but she respected Mrs Shackleton. Tears began to well in her eyes as the colour drained from her face. There was only one thing to do. She recounted the full and unabridged version of her recent life.

The old lady sat in complete silence and listened intently. At the end of it she made but one comment.

'Helen, you must remember that everything that has happened to you has been fate. When I said you had made the wrong decision what I failed to say was that you were meant to make that decision. In other words you had no choice in the matter. Everything in life is predestined for you. It is all in the stars.'

'There was no choice?' Helen enquired. Mrs Shackleton shook her head. It was at this point that Helen remembered a similar conversation that she had had with Annie. She recalled her advice 'Look further a field than these streets.' She also recalled her advice of not wasting her life. With these thoughts in mind she wiped away her tears, determined to fight back.

'Helen, I've never told you this before but you hold a considerable legacy in these hands. I'm not even talking about your lifetime but of those who have gone before you. There are traces of love, hatred, jealousy, pride and deception. You have the ability to unravel all of these to produce contentment.'

Helen sat quietly for a moment, contemplating these revelations.

'What you're trying to tell me is that my future has in some way already been predetermined by my parents and probably by their parents?'

'Everyone's future is initially shaped by the background into which they are born Helen. Yours however is a little different. Do you remember the very first time that you came in here? I told you about a man that you had no knowledge of. I can still see in your hand that he is still waiting for you. He is the one who holds the key to unleash any demons that you may have. Do you know who he is Helen?'

'Yes. He's my grandfather William Fawcett.' The words tumbled confidently out of Helen's mouth.

Alice Shackleton sank back into her chair, stunned into silence.

'You have heard of him?' enquired Helen.

'Oh yes I've heard of him. The whole of Beckston knows his name. How do you know he's your grandfather?'

'Annie told me. She wasn't going to at first, but eventually explained how his daughter, Arabella, who was my mother, had married my father Robert Siddall, Annie's brother. Apparently he disowned her for marrying beneath herself.'

'The legacy etched into the lines on your hands speaks volumes. A conflict of class has put it there. Helen, you've already had to cope with a great deal in your young life and will still have to overcome many more obstacles. But you can and will cope. Adversity will be overcome. Remember that Helen and you won't go far wrong.'

Helen left with apprehension. Her visit, instead of solving problems, had merely intensified them, but she took comfort in Alice's final words and was intent upon remaining strong. The old lady felt as though she had aged considerably throughout Helen's visit. She slumped back into the recognisable comfort of her favourite chair and closed her eyes, determined to obliterate the afternoon's events. Her mind still active refused to cooperate. All that Alice Shackleton could remember before she died that night was that death was etched deeply into Helen's hands.

CHAPTER ELEVEN

'The old witch is dead!'

These words continued to ring through Helen's head. No one else could inflict such pain with five small words. Harry, as ever, was the exception. He had managed to visit Horton house on the pretext of discussing business with Denis, when no doubt he was aware that Denis was in a meeting with a client at work. Helen tolerated him no longer than she had to, explaining that her husband was not there. As he turned to walk out of the door the words fell nonchalantly from the smirking face. The man was definitely poisoned with hatred.

Adversity surrounded Helen. Whilst her past had been troubled her future was uncertain. Alice Shackleton had been her link with these times and the one person who could offer guidance. The demise of this old lady was a devastating shock for Helen. She felt that all her benign links with the past had been severed, but she had overlooked one contact.

Her presence was almost a remedy for Helen's melancholy. Diana was as effervescent as ever.

'I hope you don't mind me calling to see you Helen, but I have been touring with the cast for some time and suddenly I just felt the urge to see you.'

Helen had written to her informing her of the miscarriage.

'Don't worry Helen, you just keep trying and I'm sure you'll soon be pregnant again. You lucky thing, he's rather a dish as I remember!'

The two friends chattered incessantly, recalling old times as well as catching up on gossip.

'Have you given up your job at Brown Muffs?' Helen enquired.

'Good God, yes! You know me; I just couldn't stand the old dragons there. In fact I've never been any good at being told what to do by someone else. Anyway my career in the theatre has taken off. I was offered a part with a reputable company Helen, before you ask, based upon my talents. My theatre talents.' Both women giggled.

'I didn't say a word,' muttered Helen.

'No, you didn't need to. The look on your face speaks for itself.' Suppressed laughter once again intervened.

'And, what about Mr Godwin, your, eh… '

'Lover?'

Helen blushed with embarrassment.

'No, I was going to say "admirer".'

'I'm afraid he's no more. He had a heart attack and died.' Diana appeared quite matter of fact in her delivery.

'I'm so sorry Diana, I had no idea.'

'Don't worry, it could have been worse. Just imagine if it had happened whilst he was on the job with me, that would have taken some explaining to his wife!' Diana was totally irrepressible.

'You must still miss him?' Helen enquired.

'Yes, of course I do. He was very kind to me and extremely generous. Did you know that he was a wealthy jeweller?' Helen shook her head. That explained why Diana had so many jewels given to her.

'Anyway, I'm no longer interested in men. Well, let's say just at the moment, I want to concentrate upon my career. And thanks to the generosity of Geoffrey Godwin, who had many of my pieces of jewellery specially commissioned, I do have a little bit to fall back on. Not that I intend to sell them, but it is nice to feel secure.' Helen smiled at her friend with both admiration and envy.

'Helen, before I forget, I happen to have two tickets here for Beckston's Theatre Royale. This time I'm the leading star, with my own dressing room. Do say you'll come and bring that delicious husband with you.'

Long after Diana had left Helen continued to look at the tickets. They were a welcome means of escapism into a world of excitement.

****

Helen tried very hard not to show her disappointment. Unusually for Denis he seemed to be diverting more and more of his time to the business. His apologies for being unable to accompany Helen to the theatre were of small comfort to her. The other problem of course was finding a replacement companion; someone she would feel at ease with and someone who would appreciate theatrical entertainment. The solution was far closer to home than she had realised.

'I don't suppose you would like to accompany me to the theatre on Tuesday evening. A friend of mine who is appearing in the performance has given me two tickets. Denis is unable to go and I wondered if... '

'Helen, I can think of nothing better than spending an evening in your company. I would definitely enjoy a visit to the theatre. Thank you.' Richard Tetlow epitomised the true meaning of the word 'gentleman'.

'Please don't feel under any obligation to... '

'Helen, I do not. In fact I was going to put forward a social proposal to you. I've received an invitation to the annual Beckston dinner dance. It is held each year in the town hall for local businessmen. Edward used to attend and so have I in the past. I would normally pass the invitation onto Denis but I have to attend this year as I am to be presented with an award.' Modesty prevailed as Richard cast his gaze downwards in an attempt to divert the conversation away from his glory.

'An award! Richard, I'm so pleased for you. Can I ask what it's for?'

'Oh, it is just a local award for service.' Richard was unreservedly modest and unassuming in his manner and Helen could not but wonder whether the choice of entertainment would prove too raucous for such a refined palette.

Knowing her companion to be punctilious Helen dressed with propriety and haste knowing Richard Tetlow's penchant for punctuality. Waiting in the drawing room he immediately rose to his feet as she entered the room and complimented her upon her appearance. Being an ambassador for style and attention to detail he was immaculate in his appearance.

They entered the foyer of Beckston's Theatre Royale with ease. This time the sumptuous surroundings failed to overawe Helen. They found their seats and waited with anticipation. Helen also waited in trepidation as she feared the production would be too licentious for Richard's taste. As the lighting gradually became subdued and the curtains rose she frantically wondered whether he would consider her uncultured. The dark profile of his face gave little indication of his opinion. She could do nothing other than hope that the production was more in tune with artistic culture than boisterous sensationalism.

The cast gave their own interpretation of 'My Baby just cares for me', 'Puttin' on the Ritz', 'Mad About the Boy' and 'Night and Day'. The compendium of songs was contemporary and allowed the performers to indulge the audience with new material. Diana was unquestionably the diva of the show. She danced and sang with graceful professionalism. Her figure was at its very best as she used her feminine contours adeptly to enhance the sensual undercurrents of the musical lyrics. Her long shapely legs teasingly provoked the testosterone levels within the auditorium as the slashed skirts of her rich outfits momentarily opened to reveal a significant glimpse of thigh. Helen shifted uncomfortably in her seat as she still agitated over her companion's enjoyment. The only time when her mind failed to dwell upon this matter was when she recalled her previous visit. A dancer on stage had instantly reminded her of him. The only similarity, in truth, was the man's build and dark hair, but it had been sufficient to resurrect those memories. She recalled her feelings for him, feelings of intensity that she had never experienced since, even with Denis. At that moment she realised how deeply she had loved him. She was totally oblivious to the applause as the curtain descended for the interval and only responded as Richard beamed with delight whilst applauding.

'Marvellous, absolutely marvellous! Did you see that girl? She is so talented. She absolutely makes the show.' Helen was left in no doubt that Richard was enjoying the performance.

The second half continued to beguile and entrance the audience as a choreographic spectacle. At the close of the show Helen found herself rather bemused by her companion's behaviour.

'Helen, I have so enjoyed tonight. In fact I cannot recall a time when I have felt so relaxed and happy. By the way I seem to remember you mentioning going backstage to see your friend. I was so enthralled with it all that I forget to ask you to point her out. Come along then, we do not want to miss her.' The excitement across his face reminded Helen of a little boy at Christmas who had just opened his favourite present and was now anxious to play with his toy.

'Come along, I am looking forward to meeting her.'

The introduction proved far from disappointing. Helen knocked hesitantly upon the door with the unmistakeable star.

'Helen, I feel you've stopped at the wrong door.' Richard's words had failed to leave his lips before Diana's laughter was heard behind them.

'I can assure you, that it is the right door sir!' Helen and Richard turned to find Diana looking radiant. The show had definitely been a success. Both women embraced enthusiastically.

'Diana! You look marvellous.'

'So do you. Did you enjoy the show?' At this moment Helen saw the curiosity in her friend's eyes as she glanced at Richard.

'Very much! Can I introduce my husband's uncle, Richard Tetlow? Denis was unable to make it tonight so Richard kindly agreed to accompany me.'

'I hope the evening wasn't disappointing for you?' Diana asked this question whilst casting an uncharacteristically reticent smile towards Richard as they shook hands.

'The entire evening has been marvellous. The show, the cast, and you. I will not forget any of it.'

The next few days proved this point avidly as Richard failed to speak of anything else. In fact he seemed totally preoccupied even when Edward or Denis was around. Normally totally focussed upon the business, he appeared somewhat distracted, a fact that had clearly not gone unnoticed. The problem was that Richard was not the only business associate with divided loyalties. Raised voices emulating from the drawing room one evening attracted Helen's attention.

'If things don't start to alter it won't be long before we'll be saying goodbye to the business. Richard seems to be in another world at the moment and all you can do is run up debts. I've had enough of your gambling. I'll not bail you out any longer. You've heard the old saying, 'clogs to clogs in three generations,' well that'll be us sooner rather than later.' The gruff tones were unmistakeably those of Edward Tetlow.

'You owe me father.'

'I owe you nothing and that'll be what you inherit unless you sort yourself out. Talking of which, it's about time that you went upstairs and did your duty as a man or are you no longer even capable of that?' The final remark seemed to act as a catalyst. Helen heard the drawing room door open, defiant steps crossed the hall floor and the moment culminated with the slamming of the outside door. Momentarily the events evoked recollections of the Ledgard household and Tom's hot temper. Helen shuddered as she recalled the oppression that she had once lived under. Thankfully those days were in the past.

Helen was unable however to forget the nature of the argument. Subconsciously she had been aware for some time that Denis had been spending more evenings, and even nights, away from the family home and her bed. The dark spectre of adultery began to formulate in her mind. She had been aware when she married him of his attraction to and for the fairer sex, but had genuinely felt that his attention in that quarter was now being lavished within matrimony. She began clutching at straws as her mind tried to reassure her that his nocturnal obsession was purely based on gambling. Calm and composed she allowed herself to believe this until she considered whether gambling debts were just a euphemistic concealment of the requirements of keeping a mistress.

The only person Helen could confide in was Diana. As always, Diana provided the perfect solution.

'Follow him, or have him followed. That way you'll know the truth.' Diana's pragmatic approach seemed harsh but necessary.

'I can't follow him. He'd recognise me immediately. Oh Diana, the thought of hiring someone privately appears somewhat tacky.'

'You don't need to. I'll do it for you. I've access to wigs and makeup. I could follow him without the least suspicion. Oh I'd love to do it. It would just be like old times.' Diana's increasing excitement finally persuaded Helen.

A week later Diana imparted the truth.

'Your rival is not another woman.' Diana appeared to deliver this remark with an underlying message.'

'I don't understand. What are you trying to say?'

'I've followed Denis on two occasions now. Each time the same thing happened. He had a drink with a friend at the Craven Heifer pub before disappearing to a room upstairs. The barman told me that a gambling party regularly uses the room. There are never any questions asked as a large deposit on the room acts as the sweetener for confidentiality.'

'You say he had a drink with a friend?'

'Perhaps I should call him an acquaintance.' Diana's reference to male company seemed to have a comforting effect upon Helen. 'What I mean to say is that he is an employee. He works with Denis.'

'Harry! You mean Harry! He's not a friend! Anything but.' Helen's outburst made Diana wonder whether Helen would have found the idea of another woman more appealing. 'He's up to something. He's managed to worm his way back into my life and I know he won't be content until he's brought me down. He's going to ruin all of our lives. I don't know how but I do know he's out to destroy me.'

'Come on Helen I think you're dramatising the whole thing. Denis is not the first man to succumb to bets...'

'I'm not concerned about the gambling. What I'm concerned about is the supposed friendship of Harry with my husband. You've no idea how cunning he is. That's what I'm afraid of. He has a hold over me.

He knows the child I was carrying wasn't Denis's but Thomas's. I've kept waiting for him to blackmail me but he hasn't. I'd even deluded myself into thinking that he was just content to have landed a job in the firm. But no, I should know better. He's got a plan. I know he's got a plan and that's the scary bit.'

For once Diana was the one who remained calm and tried to prevent her friend from succumbing to dramatic outbursts.

'Helen, he's probably just out for what he can get. A well paid job and a better lifestyle. If it means that he's used your connection with him, who can blame him? We'd all probably do exactly the same in his shoes. Everyone wants to better himself. Just try and put all of this out of your mind and be thankful that your husband isn't playing around.' Helen wished that she possessed Diana's optimism but sadly it lingered only momentarily before her friend left and once again she found herself contemplating dark thoughts.

****

Helen had been totally ignorant of Richard's attention. For some time he had noticed that she had lacked her usual sparkle.

'You haven't forgotten your promise to me I hope?' Richard enquired in a light- hearted manner.

'My promise?'

'I am referring to your agreement of accompanying me to the Beckston dinner dance.'

Helen feigned total recollection, but in truth she had completely forgotten about it.

'What is the matter Helen? A case of demons in the mind?' The remark caught Helen off balance and made her wonder how astute he really was.

'I myself have recently been afflicted with them. Troubles in the mind can sometimes make you oblivious to everything else. Thankfully I think that I have now laid mine to rest. I cannot promise that the evening will banish all of yours, but I am certain it will be one to remember.'

Helen little doubted his words. As always they were words of wisdom. She could not, however, help but wonder the nature of Richard's demons.

****

From the moment they entered the magnificent chamber his eyes became fixated upon them, in particular on her. Richard Tetlow had long been respected within the textile industry as a gentleman of trust. His word was his bond. His private life, like his business, was without redemption. Therefore the beautiful young woman on his arm was proving to be an enigma. Richard Tetlow had always invested his energies in trade and had consequently been seen to resist feminine temptation; a modest man both by nature and deed. The old saying 'still waters run deep' began to form in the observer's mind as a wry smile played across his lips. He purposely walked towards them.

'Good evening Richard.'

'Good evening William. Allow me to introduce Helen Tetlow, my nephew's wife, who has kindly agreed to accompany me here tonight. Helen, this is William Fawcett.' Helen was totally unprepared for the meeting.

Coyly casting her gaze downwards she suddenly felt undignified and exposed as she shook hands with him. Excusing herself she withdrew from their company, feigning a need to powder her nose. On her return he had thankfully taken his leave to the opposite side of the room. With Richard at her side she now began to make polite conversation with fellow guests around the room whilst simultaneously casting a furtive glance in her grandfather's direction.

The events of the evening began to be eclipsed by this encounter in Helen's mind. The formal dinner and the accompanying small talk were necessary requirements but totally unmemorable. However the after-dinner speeches were to secure Helen's attention. William Fawcett, the patriarch amidst the textile elite, delivered the presiding speech. It was now that Helen could legitimately observe him. A man of around seventy years, he possessed strength and proud determination, so prevalent in his oratory.

'Since the fourteenth century Yorkshire has been in the cloth and clothing industry. As every Yorkshire man knows, we are born with it in the blood. Up on the limestone fells and the sometimes inhospitable moor land, where the sheep graze before being sheared, that's where it all begins. Those surroundings have produced the wool and the soft water for which Beckston stands so proud today. It is quite rightly recognised as the Worsted Capital of the world. It has kept our families and those of our workers in comfort.' Helen little doubted that the beliefs of everyone else in the room were in tune with this orator. There was an enormous amount of wealth and power assembled. However, she could not help but wonder whether the workers of Fawcett's mill would describe their lives, or those of their families, as comfortable.' She also mused over the word 'family' and wondered what implications it held for William Fawcett. Her mother Arabella had been shown little understanding or comfort from this man.

'However it has not been an easy ride as the late years of the twenties and the early ones of this decade have shown. The economic depression has gripped the world and overwhelmed companies in all industries. As a result, between three to four million people are without work in Britain. But against all the odds, despite competition from overseas, it seems likely that there are signs of an improvement in trade. Ladies and gentlemen, if it were not for the likes of Richard Tetlow, the glimmer of hope would be non-existent.' William then proceeded to pay homage to Richard's dedication and selfless pursuit of trade for the Beckston community. In keeping with his character he quietly received a commerative-boxed medallion engraved with his name and responded with self-effacing gratitude.

The formalities now at an end, the evening gave way to entertainment in the form of a small orchestra. Couples danced in unison following the musical tempo of the waltz and the foxtrot. A number of gentlemen, including Richard, danced with Helen but it was not until the end of the evening that William decided to dance. He led her to the dance floor and together they began to waltz. The conversation was polite and centred mainly upon Richard's achievement. Helen tried to avoid direct eye-to-eye contact for she found his piercing blue eyes to be interrogating. Following the usual pleasantries they took leave of one another and Helen returned to Richard, feeling imbued with restored confidence. For the rest of the evening she felt relatively relaxed.

A number of people had congratulated Richard and so it continued until their departure. William Fawcett himself once more expressed his sentiments. He heartily conveyed his best wishes, shaking his hand firmly, before directing his gaze towards Helen.

'It has been a pleasure to meet you.'

'Likewise.' Suddenly Helen became aware that Richard was walking towards the door leaving her in this man's presence. He leaned closely towards her.

'Goodnight Helena.'

'My name is Helen.' The emphasis was placed upon the name.

'Yes, I do know that.'

The blue eyes continued to pierce into her soul long after that evening.

CHAPTER TWELVE

An air of change was in the wind as the old year gave way to the start of 1934. Ominously Nazi Germany had ceased to be a member of the League of Nations as well as announcing the intention to withdraw from the Geneva Disarmament Conference. Ironically only the previous year had witnessed Adolph Hitler rising to the position of Chancellor of the German Reich. European events, however, were far from many people's minds as the nation came to terms with the aftermath of the economic depression. Times were set to change with the consequential developments empowered through science and technology, and slowly working class people were beginning to enjoy a standard of living that would transform the inherent backbone of society.

Helen herself found that there was an atmosphere of change running throughout the Tetlow household. Denis had once more become an attentive loving husband, keen to provide an abundance of sexual interest in the bedroom, much to his father's evident relief. As a result the arguments seemed to subside. Even Richard Tetlow himself was not immune to the effects of change as his punctilious lifestyle began a transformation. Regular absences on certain evenings would normally have evoked interest but the other members of the household were too preoccupied with their own arrangements to warrant such curiosity.

Amidst all of these changes Helen continued to ponder over the meeting with her grandfather. She had confided in no one and therefore could only play out the scenario in her own mind. He had made no attempt to contact her but she was certain that he knew who she was. How that was possible she could not answer. The only place she could find solace was in the company of Richard's books. She regularly withdrew to his library and found herself returning again and again to one particular book. The play *Julius Caesar*, by William Shakespeare, held her attention each time with one quotation:

'There is a tide in the affairs of men,
Which, taken at the flood, leads on to fortune;
Omitted, all the voyage of their life
Is bound in shallows and in miseries.' Act 5, Sc 1.
The words were truly profound.

As tradition goes the early months of a new year are generally quiet and uneventful. 1934 was proving to be no exception. Helen had still not conceived and was beginning to consider seeking medical advice. She desperately craved feminine company and seemed perpetually unable to satisfy this longing with the one friend who understood her needs, Diana, it appeared, was completely elusive. The weeks were giving way to feelings of frustrated inertia. It was precisely at this point that fate intervened.

The letter possessed an air of old-fashioned quality which Helen attributed to the distinctive copperplate handwriting. It was addressed solely to her. She took time to read the contents and then further time to re-read them. She had never before seen a document from his hand.

Dear Helen,
May I firstly take this opportunity to wish you a Happy New Year? I trust that the events of 1934 will continue to make you content and prosperous. Please convey my sentiments to your family, including your husband.

I confess that my reason for writing to you is to enquire if we can meet at a mutually agreeable time. No doubt you are aware that I have cause to speak to you, perhaps now more than ever. I can understand that you may not wish to see me and that would be your prerogative. However Helen I hope you will find it in your heart to return your answer in a positive way. If you would be so kind as to contact me at Mount Hall, I would be most grateful.

Yours sincerely,
William Fawcett.

Contradictory qualities prevailed through these words. Whilst the letter was decidedly strong and resolute, having been penned by a patriarch, it also diffused feelings of humility and submission. Gratitude and kindness were also evident bedfellows; these were emotions which Helen had always believed her grandfather to be lacking in. As the days passed she began to find it increasingly difficult to make a decision. This was a man who had shunned his own daughter and granddaughter and perhaps now in his dotage was attempting to achieve forgiveness for his past misdemeanours. Reconciliation would of course exact its own price; decimation of the reasons for her mother's struggle. Acceptance would be morally wrong and yet a refusal established only an inconclusive result. Withdrawing to the library she finally made her decision as she read those words again:

'There is a tide in the affairs of men,
Which, taken at the flood, leads on to fortune;
Omitted, all the voyage of their life
Is bound in shallows and in miseries.'

The opportunity to have long awaited questions answered was one not to be missed.

The telephone call to Mount Hall was kept businesslike and purposefully short. Helen needed to look into his eyes, those windows of the soul, for a delicate tête-à-tête. Curt arrangements were therefore agreed upon: date, time and travel.

As promised the large car with its accompanying chauffeur transported Helen from the familiarity of Horton house to the grandeur of Mount Hall. As the car turned into the imposing driveway and meandered through the thickly wooded glade of trees and bushes, Helen's thoughts turned to that earlier escapade with Diana. The memory made her smile. This time the visit was legitimate but even so the outcome would still be unpredictable.

At the first sighting of the hall Helen felt overawed. Seeing it for the second time did not diminish its effect. Large and majestic with imposing Scottish style turrets, the hall was unquestionably unsurpassable. The question, of course: was its owner? Helen refused to be intimidated and therefore resolved to be indefatigable.

The car drew to a halt under the large portico. As the chauffeur opened the back door Helen nervously peered out at the surroundings. Instinctively she walked towards the impressively solid oak doors which ceremoniously opened to reveal an equally imposing interior. She had little time to look around her as the butler seemed predisposed to escort her swiftly to the drawing room. There she was left alone to collect her thoughts and take note of the surroundings. The walls were panelled in figured satin, complementing the drapery and the upholstered furniture. However the main item in the room, which utterly captivated Helen's attention, was the large portrait above the fireplace. Whilst the quality of the oil painting was exquisite, Helen was not a connoisseur of artists' skills and was more preoccupied by the choice of subject. The more she studied the painting, the more she felt as though she was staring into a mirror.

'Extraordinary! The likeness is definitely unmistakeable.' Helen had failed to notice that her grandfather had entered the room, until he spoke. His sudden presence broke her gaze.

'I'm sorry. Please forgive me,' Helen stammered.

'Forgive you, why? When your grandmother entered a room, every head turned, and so it still does, even with the portrait. She was so beautiful. You, my girl, are the spitting image of her.'

Helen began to feel herself blush and looked downwards in order to avert his gaze. Sensing her embarrassment William invited his guest to be seated and as he did so the butler entered the room carrying a large silver tray which he placed before them. China, silver and a tempting array of sandwiches and cakes, no doubt the specialities from Mrs Bentley's hands, were spread in front of their eyes. It was at that moment that Helen recalled the cook's words. 'So young for death to creep up on them... his wife in childbirth and then his daughter in an accident. He said he'd lost the girl as well and muttered a common misery... we think that it was diphtheria...'

'Helen, you seem to be deep in thought. Are you well?'

'Yes thank you,' came the reply. She only wished that she had had the courage to add, 'especially for someone who has died from diphtheria.'

The conversation flowed lightly as each one sipped tea and nibbled the delightful treats. Polite and informative, William spoke of the history of the house and its contents. He purposefully avoided referring to the residents who had resided there until he was asked.

'How do you know who I am?' The question stopped him in his tracks.

'I only had to gaze at your face, to know.'

'To know what?' The question seemed impertinent. 'The fact that I'm Arabella's daughter or Helena's granddaughter?' This time her question was double-edged and appeared to wound with calculated severity. The great patriarch gradually lost the amicable expression and aged quickly in front of his companion.

'I loved Arabella.'

'Despite the fact that your wife died in childbirth for her?'

'That was the very reason why she was so special. She was the only tangible memory that I had left of Helena. Helen, I never blamed Arabella for my loss. You must believe me.' There was no doubt in Helen's mind that he was speaking the truth.

'Why did you abandon her?'

'I didn't abandon her. She left of her own free will.'

'She married a man that she loved, but who was only a mill worker; not good enough for your daughter. As a result you missed out enjoying her happiness and seeing a granddaughter grow up. You also missed out seeing my mother lose a husband to the war and having to make do, working and bringing up a daughter on a meagre wage.' The words stung him without mercy. He clasped his hands over his face and began to sway back and forth.

'I deserve all of that. The old cliché of turning back the clock seems inappropriate. Oh Helen, I've been a misguided and bigoted old fool who does not deserve your forgiveness and will not ask for it.'

'I'm pleased about that, for I am not going to give it!' The woman was staunchly resolute and it was at this moment that she behaved exactly as her grandmother would have done. The temper was perhaps not as acidic, but it was non-the-less inherent.

'Over the years Helen I've cursed myself for these consequences, but I was powerless… '

'Powerless! That is hypocritical! You sit here surrounded by wealth and influence and dare to speak of being powerless. Were you powerless to prevent my mother from having to work in a munitions factory, where she was killed when a shell exploded? It was sweat labour. Safety precautions compromised for the sake of output. That's probably something you know all about. You're no doubt sitting here as a result of your workers toiling and grafting for little thought from yourself.' Her words were venomous as was the look of contempt across her face. William Fawcett had never before been spoken to in such a manner by anyone. His reputation had always guarded against that. His response was uncustomary for him: abstinence from speech or gesture. Instead he remained seated, stunned and stultified. Helen meanwhile rose to her feet and it was at this point that his silence affected her.

'Are you not going to say anything? Argue or defend yourself?'

'Helen, there is little that I can say. The truth is I could have done more. That I will bitterly regret until my dying day. However there are things that you know nothing about which were not of my making.'

'What things? What are you talking about?' Helen was perplexed.

'It is not for me to say. The time is not right.'

'How can you say that? I have spent my life trying to piece together some semblance of family connection. You at last invite me here to tell me that the time is not right and expect acceptance of everything, including a disassociation of your guilt.'

'I can see how it must appear to you Helen. However for the time being the past must remain undisturbed. One day you will understand why I acted as I did. Everything revolves around love. Remember that Helen. Don't lose sight of that fact.' Helen stared incredulously at her grandfather. He was a complete contradiction.

'You stare at me in bewilderment Helen. You think because I'm elderly that I've never experienced love. Well let me tell you that I have. Strong, burning love; the type that completely engulfs you with desire and makes you turn away from convention. That's the type of love I felt for Helena. It's because of that love that I acted as I did with your mother. I don't expect you to understand unless you've had such an experience in your life.' The words rang through her. She painfully realised that such emotions, whilst sadly lacking in her own marriage, were reminders of Thomas. Such thoughts made her blush.

'Have I made you blush or have I touched upon a memory?'

'Neither'. Helen quickly composed herself, returning to the issue in hand. 'If you place such value upon love why didn't you encourage my parent's love? That was genuine and true.'

'Helen, it is always easy to be wise after the event. Initially, perhaps, I deemed your father to be a gold-digger, a man from humble beginnings who saw the chance to better himself through involvement with your mother. It all now seems so long ago that my initial objections seem immaterial. What does matter is the fact, which you quite rightly point out, that I remained steadfastly obstinate and blind in my biased conviction. I chose to wash my hands from any family involvement. That is the most painful part of it all. That is the part which only I am responsible for, no one else. As I said before, I am not seeking forgiveness from you, merely the opportunity to become acquainted with you. Helen, you would be totally within your rights, morally and ethically, to simply walk away and never give me a second thought. I hope you won't take that course of action, but the future is now in your hands.'

The sentiments were strong and heartfelt. With his closing words, Helen stared at her own hands and ironically recalled Alice Shackleton's words: 'You hold a considerable legacy in these hands. There are traces of love, hatred, jealousy, pride and deception. You have the ability to unravel all of these to produce contentment.' As Helen began to muse over these words she also wondered how her mother would have reacted in her place. The truth was she did not know and finally concluded that the decision must be of her own making.

'I don't know what you want from me. Indeed I don't even know what I want from you. However the time has come to put aside recriminations and I agree that it would be nice to become acquainted.' William sprang to his feet and walked across to Helen before patting her gently upon the shoulder.

'Helen, thank you. It is far more than I deserve. I have dreamed of this moment for so long. You do not know what this means to me.'

William walked across to a bureau, opened the angled top and carefully pulled out a small drawer. Helen watched him produce a small leather-clad box from within which he then offered to her. The contents inside consisted of pearl drop earrings, plain and unadorned.

'I'd like you to take these and wear them.'

'No! This is not the reason for becoming acquainted with you.'

'Helen, these were the earrings which I gave your grandmother to wear on our wedding day. They are simple and not necessarily expensive. However she did wear them and I've always considered them to be a token of our love. I can think of no one else that I would like to have them more than you. Please take them.' The outstretched hand almost seemed to symbolise the olive branch and the gesture of reconciliation and friendship.

'If you put it like that, then I would be most happy to wear them. Thank you.'

'You don't need to thank me. Your presence here today is more than I deserve. Helen, you will come again, won't you?'

'If that is what you would like, then yes.'
Although not considered a demonstrative man, William could no longer conceal his emotions as he affectionately clasped her to him. Helen turned but once to glance at the house as the chauffeur drove her home. For the first time in her life she wondered what her grandmother had been like and slowly began to empathise with her death, from her grandfather's point of view.

✳✳

William watched the car until it was no longer in view. He understood that he had a responsibility to undertake. Better to dispense with it now than to delay. His business tactics were always in evidence. He still marvelled at the complexities of the telephone as he waited for the servant at the other end to inform the man of his call.

'Well?'

'I'm sure,' William replied.

'Sure?'

'Yes, without a doubt. The investigator had already produced the evidence but having met her there is no doubt in my mind.'

'Good.'

The call ended as the owner of the monosyllabic voice hung up.

****

The meeting had had a decidedly clandestine feel about it. Initially Helen had considered telling Denis about her grandfather, but refrained from doing so. The reason was for the purpose of anonymity. One whisper of her new connections would be used by Harry for his own advantage. Suddenly the mere thought of him made her realise that he had recently maintained a very low profile. Perhaps she had been wrong about him, however, subconsciously, she knew she hadn't. It was merely a matter of time before she knew he would strike his next move.

Desperate to confide in someone Helen had already decided that she would, as always, share her secret with Diana. Coincidence intervened as the recently elusive Diana suddenly visited Horton House. She appeared to call unexpectedly but had conveniently selected a time when Helen was alone, except for the maid and housekeeper. Her manner was quite unlike her; at times she babbled with confidence before lapsing into embarrassing silences. There was a definite purpose to her visit but one which did not include listening to Helen's news.

'Helen, we've known one another for many years, in fact we've been like sisters with no secrets between us. I've always been straight with you and I just can't bear to keep my news secret any longer. Helen, I'm getting married.' The disclosure seemed to somewhat momentarily alleviate her anxiety.

'Oh, Diana! Congratulations. Who is the lucky fellow?'

For the first time in her life Diana appeared to be speechless.

'We do love one another.'

'Well I hope you do! You're marrying him, so you should.'

'You don't understand. I am genuinely in love with him. It's not infatuation or the lure of his wallet. At long last I've found a man that I enjoy being with. He's a gentleman and makes me feel special. He treats me with respect like a lady.'

'You don't need to convince me; I can tell that you're head over heels. Do I know him?' enquired Helen.

'Yes, you know him. Oh Helen, please don't think badly of me. I'm in love with Richard.'

'Richard! Denis's uncle?' A nod of Diana's head affirmed Helen's surprise.

'He's... he's in his fifties. Diana, he must be more than thirty years older than you. It's like marrying your father.'

Helen's mind began to whirl with speculation, until it calmly rested upon the idea of it all being nothing more than a humorous deception, played out by Diana with theatrical aplomb. The look upon her friend's face however confirmed it was genuine.

'Please stop and think about what you're doing. The age gap is too wide. Just consider if you want a family. Knowing you Diana, you'll want to be out enjoying yourself, living your life to the full. As nice as Richard is, he's an old man and will become more so. Will you be content to stay in with him? Diana, this is madness.'

Diana stared impassively before retorting.

'I suppose if the truth be known, I didn't expect you to welcome this with open arms, but I had expected some flicker of support. After all Helen, it was me who offered you support in your hour of need, or have you forgotten that?'

'That was completely different,' snapped Helen.

'It certainly was. I want to marry for love whilst you married for convenience.'

'How dare you!' Helen was unable to refrain from holding back the tears any longer. The reminder of her position proved too much of a strain. The bond of friendship proved too strong a hold to be broken as the two women embraced one another, weeping in unison, until finally wiping one another's tears away.

'I take it you'll be needing a bridesmaid? Do I qualify,' enquired Helen.

'I wouldn't dream of asking anyone else.'

****

The prospect of finding herself alone with Richard made Helen wonder how she would react to him. The air of decorum would surely have evaporated from the aura of his presence. At the first opportunity he subtlety invited her into his study, being careful to close the door and graciously asked her to be seated, as only he could do in his elegant manner. He began the conversation immediately.

'Helen, what you must think of me, I dread to consider. How could I have ever thought that a young woman of your age would be interested in someone of my years? However the truth is she is and I must confess that I have never known such happiness. Is that wrong? I know that I will be castigated by everyone around me, no doubt as a cradle-snatcher. But if the truth be known, and I can only confess this to you and you alone, I am completely besotted by her and totally in love with her. Is that a crime?'

Helen shook her head. She possessed a great deal of empathy for this kind and gentle man who impressed her with the emotional intensity of his feelings and his divulgence of them. At the back of her mind a small thought began to gnaw away at her conscience, with increasing fervour it made her question whether this reserved gentleman was aware of his lady's past. Would it matter to him that she was already tarnished with experience and sullied by desire? Perceptively he studied her troubled face and answered her question.

'I am aware of Diana's past. She has been totally truthful with me. Her direct honesty is another reason for feeling the way I do about her. I wouldn't expect a free spirit like Diana to have a chaste history. Her magnetism on stage is so powerful that any man would find it difficult to resist. I certainly did. The important thing now is that her past is just that. I am quite content for her to continue enchanting every male whilst she sings and dances, safe in the knowledge that it will be me that she will come home to. Preventing her from performing would be cruel, it would be akin to locking up a precious bird in a gilded cage. Far better to allow her her freedom. That way I know she wants to be with me.'

Helen remained silent. She acknowledged that Richard was sufficiently astute to recognise the dangers in this relationship; his words were wise and profound. However philosophical, love was rarely allowed to be predetermined; erratic and uncontrollable but seldom predictable. That was the key. Richard had lived all his life cocooned and governed by convention. Diana had temptingly introduced him to rebellion.

Helen threw her arms around him and exuberantly declared her best wishes for the marriage. The pleasure on his face was sufficient for Helen to recognise that he was doing the right thing.

The wedding was a civil ceremony; businesslike and formal it lacked the essential trimmings and potential pageantry of a church wedding. The choice of venue had been a surprise to Helen as she had assumed that Diana would crave the ceremonial lime light of entering down the aisle amidst a congregational audience. The sheer plainness and lack of decadence seemed to emphasise Diana's commitment to the marriage. Nevertheless Beckston registry office provided a quiet dignity to the sincerity of the nuptials.

Diana's suit was eminently fitting for the occasion. The silk crepe dress and over jacket were afforded stylish elegance by both the cut and experience of the couturier's hand and the choice of colour. Pale green was perfect for it possessed a degree of decorum and class, which other areas of the spectrum could not even touch. In keeping with the virginal appearance of a bride Diana had also selected a style that managed to be both modest and slightly alluring at the same time. Helen began to smile as Diana made her appearance. Only she could present provocative purity and be admired. Curved seams ran from the high neckline downwards, sweeping around the breasts before reappearing on the hips and plunging together as a central seam down the skirt front, eventually ending in a long, tempting slit below the knee. The accompanying jacket, held together centrally by a single loop and button fastening, had been cut wide enough at the front to expose the artistry of the dress whilst tapering at the back to fall flatteringly over the hips. Finally a milliner's skills had emulated the outfit in the production of a matching green hat worn strikingly to the side of the head. Diana, as always, captivated the small audience by her presence. There was no requirement for a large conventional church wedding; additional props would have been a waste.

The invitations to the small gathering of family and friends had conveniently managed to exclude employees at any level. Diana had ensured for Helen's sake that Harry would not be on the guest list. Denis and Helen acted as witnesses to the proceedings in front of everyone, including the stern face of Edward Tetlow. Richard's brother had dismissed the whole affair as ludicrous, citing Diana as a gold-digger and her new husband as an old fool. He was adamant that his brother would be a lonely old man by Christmas whilst his new wealthy wife would be having the time of her life with any young man that she cared for. Helen prayed that Diana would prove him wrong as she waved goodbye to the happy couple as they departed for a honeymoon on the French Riviera.

Weddings, like funerals, always seem to nurture the primeval instincts of reproduction. Whether the proceedings of the wedding had unleashed strong sexual urges in Denis, Helen was uncertain, but she suddenly became his constant desire. His lovemaking became insatiable, constantly driven by the need to succeed, the need to father a child. Edward relentlessly reminded his son that the family business would not run itself. The future of the firm was at stake.

Helen continued to blame herself for failing to fall pregnant. She suggested that a medical examination might prove useful in an attempt to diffuse the agitated looks between father and son. They agreed that the miscarriage could hold the answer and encouraged her to book an appointment. The diagnosis was conclusive: there was no reason for Helen not to fall pregnant.

****

He was so angry, so very, very angry. At the root of this lurked embarrassment, a feeling of inadequacy as a man. His playboy days were behind him when he had relied upon his good looks and charm to woo the ladies. That had all been before his marriage. He had actually been faithful to her. The thing that hurt the most was that he was a cuckold. Him a cuckold! It had taken time for the doctor's words to sink in. 'I'm afraid Mr Tetlow, you have been, and always will be, incapable of ever fathering a child.' His secret visit to the clinic had meant to exonerate him not implicate him.

He drove aimlessly, not noticing where he was going. Faceless strangers walked by on the pavement and he sensed little movement. A voice shouted out to him but he chose not to hear. The man shouted again, waving his arms and Denis pulled over and stopped the car.

'You were miles away. I thought you'd never see me,' remarked Harry.

'Yes, that's me, blind to everything. I suppose you knew all along?'

'Knew what?' enquired Harry.

For a moment Denis remained silent. Staring at the steering wheel he appeared to be contemplating his next move.

'Tell me Harry, was Helen ever involved with anyone else?'

Harry could barely believe his luck. Thinking carefully before he replied, he instinctively knew that the propitious time had arrived, without any of his meddling.

'I do know that there has always been a strong mutual attraction between Helen and her cousin Thomas,' Harry replied naively.

'Enough of an attraction for them to have been lovers?'

'Well it's difficult for me to say, except they did spend a lot of time alone together. Come to think of it, they were exceptionally close, now that you mention it.' Harry excelled in his guise of the innocent bystander. He managed to implant subliminal messages without complicity.

'Why do you ask?' The final question reinforced his support and male bonding. It also allowed Denis to unburden himself. They sat together in the car for some time, before Denis declared his intentions.

'I'm going to confront her with this. I've decided that's what I'm going to do.'

'Just remember Denis that you can rely on me. I won't ever let you down.' The opportunity was too good to miss for Harry to ingratiate himself with a very useful ally. As Denis drove away Harry felt quietly confident that his star was about to ascend in the heavens, whilst Helen's was looming into disaster. He smiled at the impending prospect.

Denis had intended to drive home but his mind was not unnaturally predisposed with other thoughts. In conversation with Harry the scenario had appeared clear-cut, but alone the past, present and future began to entwine and confuse him more. Without knowing he drove to Highbury and then began to follow the road aimlessly to Haxton; a decidedly exacting route which tested the most assiduous drivers with its precipitous and demanding bends. This route was in the opposite direction to Horton House, a fact that he would not have been able to answer had he considered his course. The 4.5 litre Bentley continued to increase in speed, propelled by its undeniable weight, it careered wildly down the steep road with its driver oblivious to the possible danger.

The stonewall proved to be an inadequate restraint. A car with such momentum could not be held. Leaving the road it ploughed through the wall and continued down the sheer embankment, tumbling with inelegance until it reached the bottom where it emitted a loud metallic thud as it finally came to a halt. The car, like the driver, was unequivocally dead.

CHAPTER THIRTEEN

Within two years Helen had experienced both the joy and misfortune of being a bride and then a widow. The news of Denis's death had proved difficult for her to comprehend and accept, particularly the number of unanswered questions relating to the purpose of his journey to Haxton and the contributing factors to his neglectful driving. It was true that he could be wild and racy behind the wheel, but it had always been a decadent show of manhood that he had been able to control; his prowess relied upon his mastery at the wheel. Men had always viewed such masculine capability as a potent aphrodisiac to the female sex. Such men were survivors and Helen had somehow always assumed that Denis was indestructible.

Richard and Diana had cut short their honeymoon. Their evident happiness almost served to promote hurt and pain in Helen. She was ashamed of such feelings as she recognised that she had succumbed to a generous bout of jealousy and an even larger self-indulgent dose of pity. The funeral, she hoped, would bury her husband and these despicable thoughts. It would be the ending and the beginning, from the old life into the new. This of course was not the first time in her life that she had transcended into new territory, nor, she felt, would it be the last.

Throughout the proceedings, Helen had been oblivious to his presence. There had been a large number of people present, some she knew but many she had never met before. She had concentrated upon the young women's faces, wondering if they had been charmed by Denis's ways as she had been. She wondered if his life would have been different if he had married one of them. She had been so preoccupied by such thoughts that she had failed to notice Harry who had scrutinised her every move throughout the funeral. He had withdrawn and blended into the background and, like the predator he was, would only strike when the time was right.

As anticipated the majority of people continued to pay their respects and accompanied the family back to Horton House. A table of light refreshments had been set out and the family members afforded propriety and hospitality to their guests by inviting them to partake of food and drink. Understandably Helen found the procedure of offering small talk to strangers both tiresome and draining but took comfort in watching Diana undertake the challenge with a renewable gusto. She seemed to relish every sentence and unknowingly provided Helen with sustainable strength via each performance.

The voice was recognisable before she saw his face.

'Helen, what a tragedy you are facing.' Harry's eyes were full of derision.

'Thank you for your concern Harry.' Helen now began to sense intense unease and began to move away but she felt his warm breath upon her face.

'Not so quickly, otherwise I'll have to find someone else to talk to and I doubt you would like that.' Helen froze, dreading his next move. He intimated for her to follow him as he proceeded to the library, closing the door behind them.

'The last time I saw Denis he was in a bit of a state. Don't suppose you knew that because I was probably the last person to see him alive. Oh don't look so shocked, I didn't kill him. You managed to do that all by yourself.'

Helen sat down, speechless and shocked. Harry crept up slowly behind her and quietly whispered into her ear.

'He knew, Helen. He knew!' Triumphantly he moved away and waited for her reaction.

'Why did you tell him?'

'I didn't. When I last saw him he was driving madly having just received the results from his doctor. He knew that he had never, and could never, father a child. Lucky for you that he died when he did. I can't see his father welcoming you with open arms, if he knew all the facts.'

'What do you want Harry?' The usual question always seemed to follow.

'Mutual respect. You ensure that I'm given what I deserve in respect of the business and I'll respect your indiscretion and remain quiet. I can't say fairer than that. It's not much to ask when it's family, would you say?'

The nightmare had started again. Helen knew exactly what was expected of her but she also knew that her father-in-law would not tolerate scoundrels. He would not be swayed by sweet-talk. Hard-nosed business, as usual, would be the order of the day.

****

The loneliest times were normally at night when Helen could not sleep. Every audible sound could be heard, from the whistles of the wind to the familiar creaks within the house; every sound that was, except the one that she longed to hear: the gentle breathing of her husband lying next to her. She missed him and continually tortured herself by trying to recreate his final thoughts and moments of life. The thought of discovering that his wife had duped him or been unfaithful sickened her. The thought of discussing such revelations with Harry was a total nightmare scenario. Every night she revisited these thoughts until she made a decision. She labelled herself as a fraudster and decided that the best course would be to leave Horton House and Beckston forever.

Events were to take an unexpected turn in Helen's life. She in particular had been oblivious to her own dispirited nature. At times she appeared to the rest of the family, including Diana, to be withdrawn and morose, so unlike her usual self. Initially this was attributed to her grief of bereavement. Agitation, headaches, difficulty in sleeping and a lack of interest in food all contributed to Helen's physical exhaustion. She complained of a sore throat and her complexion became pale and toxic in appearance. The family were naturally concerned and insisted upon a doctor's opinion. Helen's resistance to this finally yielded when she collapsed and had to be put to bed. The diagnosis was twofold: physical exhaustion and diphtheria, the first paving the way for the second.

Helen was admitted to hospital and carefully nursed to ensure that her heart had not been affected, as diphtheria was known to cause cardiac damage. Initially Helen's legs had been partially paralysed and therefore for four weeks she had been nursed flat in bed. Slowly she began to show signs of improvement and welcomed the regular family visits. Both Edward and Richard regularly visited and were clearly concerned about her health, but the best tonic came in the form of Diana. Her sparkling humour and effervescent personality provided the ultimate dose of medicine. As Helen's strength grew so did her urge to return home. Diana voluntarily offered to look after the patient and the doctor therefore willingly discharged Helen on the understanding that she did not overexert herself. Diana was as good as her word. Her nursing qualities far exceeded everyone's expectations, including those of Edward who now began to soften his opinion of his sister-in-law.

Diana maintained a very close vigil upon her friend. She sacrificed her own slumber to attend to her and constantly waited upon her with unswerving devotion. This homely nature seemed to contradict her normal gregarious personality, normally always in need of crowded recognition. Helen observed her with increasing curiosity and wondered why there had been this transformation.

'Since your wedding you haven't been involved in any performances. Don't you miss them? Are you just waiting for the right one to come along?' enquired Helen.

'No I don't miss them Helen. The simple truth of the matter is that I've been there, done that and something that I thought I couldn't live without is now no longer important. If you're wondering what I'm talking about, it's the fact that for once I feel really happy. I feel wanted and I love being married. I wasn't going to mention this yet, but I can't keep it a secret any longer: I'm pregnant. I... I hope you don't mind...'

'Of course I don't mind. Diana it's wonderful news. I bet Richard is over the moon. You've transformed his life completely. Oh, what about Edward, does he know?' Diana shook her head.

'No we haven't told him yet. We wanted you to know first.'

'You must tell him. He has so longed for an heir. This will be so important to him. Diana, I really don't think it could have come at a better time. You know I do believe our luck is changing.'

The metamorphosis from flamboyant showgirl to wholesome wife had begun slowly, but soon the changes became evident to all. Richard doted upon his young wife whilst Edward began to slowly reappraise his initial judgement of her qualities. To Helen she was the perfect friend and confidante. However, as family life in the Tetlow household exuded a settled contentment, their province of business began to reveal cracks of alarming magnitude. The firm had managed to survive the effects of the economic depression during the early years of the thirties. Textiles, as was so often the case, had been the first to suffer with a decline in sales and the inevitable associated loss of earnings. It now became apparent how good a sales manager Denis had been. It also highlighted Harry's persuasive business acumen. For this reason alone Edward condescendingly agreed to retain Harry in the firm, much to Helen's relief.

Competition from abroad began to flood the market and British manufacturers were waking to the reality of enforced change or liquidation. Mass-produced fashion now ensured that Parisian styles could be copied, often in cheaper synthetic fabrics such as rayon, and launched in the shops. The glamour of Hollywood and the powerful influence exerted by magazines, using photographic cover images, caught both the eye and the imagination of women throughout the land. Men were also targeted through the consumer revolution; using the latest tailoring technology it was possible for most to afford made-to-measure suits.

'Diversify or Die,' became the salient motto. As a well respected gents clothing manufacturer Tetlow Brothers rested upon an image of staid foundation; ideal for the older gentleman but an outdated label for the young. The old adage of having to speculate to accumulate and possibly secure bank loans, seemed to be less than attractive to the minds of two men whose forefathers had built up a sound business based upon Victorian values. The challenge of persuasion became irresistible in Helen's mind. With renewed health she began to take an active role in the assessment of the firm's financial figures. The analysis of her findings encouraged her to reassess the future of the firm. Working together with Diana she realised that there had to be a colossal investment in the training of the workforce and machinery if they were to deliver the necessary goods and satisfy the demands of the customer. It was time to appeal to the fashion conscious female as well as the male; a thought which struck horror in the confines of a previously male dominated business. With Diana at her side, she knew that any objections could be over-ruled.

Although the two women were bursting with ideas, neither had been trained in design and couture. In order for the business venture to succeed they needed professional assistance, but at a minimal cost. Diana, as always, had the answer. Her theatrical costumes had in the main been designed by a talented young woman, Sarah Nussey, whose talents clearly exceeded the short span of sensationalism required by the stage.

As expected, Sarah arrived at Horton House carrying a number of sketchbooks. Turning the pages Helen and Diana instantly recognised the young woman's talents. Her design ideas clearly conveyed her aptitude for draping and manipulating fabrics in dramatic style. The collection of clothing designs revealed an artistic ownership of unique inspiration which had the potential of selling escapist fantasy. Coupled with that quality was her ability to accommodate commercial trends and avoid way-out sensationalism. This was definitely the key to success in the fashion industry.

Initially Sarah was given a small, unused bedroom at Horton House as her working design room. The Tetlow men were still sceptical as to the feasibility of the project and therefore both Helen and Diana decided that it would prove more advantageous if the designs were produced unobtrusively away from the business; that way Sarah would be afforded the time and space to be successful. This venture depended upon total success. Whilst Sarah gathered ideas from current fashion magazines, Helen and Diana contacted and visited Northern mills that were experimenting with crepe; loop, knop and various other fancy yarns to produce novelty fashion effects. There had been a complete revolution in the manufacturing trade with the introduction of washable, easy-care luxury fabrics and, together with the development of man-made fabrics and improved methods of manufacturing, it became difficult deciding which area of fashion to concentrate upon. Even Ladies' tweeds demanded colourful hues including flame poppy, hunter's green and kingfisher blue. It was clear that the fashion conscious woman of the mid-thirties required a wardrobe of specialist outfits for every occasion and in each one she demanded elegance and sophistication. She expected to convey femininity, modernity and independence.

The decision was finally made. As a firm of established tailored outfitters, albeit to men, the new collection would concentrate upon fitted daytime wear, such as coats, ladies dresses, and suits. If success followed then the collection would be widened to include eveningwear, both formal and informal, sporting and spectator sportswear, blouses, nightdresses, underwear and accessories. The list of possibility was endless.

Sarah very quickly threw herself into the venture with total commitment, working long into the nights. She clearly lived to work and spoke of nothing more than of dissemination of fashion plates, creative designing and the production of the pattern blocks. At this point she then began to transform her ideas into reality as she proved how professional and talented a dressmaker and tailor she really was. Intricate shapes of fabric were manipulated with seams and darts, shaped with padding and decorated with fastenings and trimmings, until the final masterpiece revealed couture that would not have been out of place in Hollywood. The figure-hugging silhouette, which accentuated the waist and shoulders whilst narrowing the hips, could not fail to appeal to the fashion conscious woman. The designs were a fusion of glamour for women and sex appeal for men. It was therefore ironical that this mistress of creative vision, who could capture the essence of arousal within a garment, was unreservedly modest and retiring. By her own admission she herself could never wear such apparel, preferring to blend unassumingly into the billowing, bohemian dresses which were shapeless around her. The characters of Sarah and Diana could not have been further removed, but perhaps it was for that very reason that they respected one another and worked so well together.

Diana had always been flamboyant but even she now recognised that sleek fitting styles were inappropriate for her blossoming figure. She was six months pregnant and totally averse to her husband's suggestion of working less and resting more. She knew that their first collection had to be marketed with sufficient impact. Visual advertisements in magazines would be expensive and could not capture the fine details of cut, texture and surface decoration. Rigid figures could not convey the sensual sway of a drape cut on the bias or the soft structure of a crisp tailored suit. Only one thing could do that; the rounded contours of female bodies.

It only became apparent once the arrangements were in place how skilled a negotiator Diana was.

'You've done what?' Helen asked in disbelief.

'I've secured a late night opening at Brown Muffs in the ladies fashion department so that we can host our own fashion show. This is our chance to promote what I hope will be the first of many collections.'

'What about the models?' Helen was initially concerned that Diana had overlooked the necessary detail.

'No problem! I've enlisted my friends from the theatre. The girls were only too happy to have the excuse to parade about in desirable fashion. With their figures we're onto a winner; every woman around will automatically think that they will look just like them. I've also drawn up a list of desirable clients, including the wife of the bank manager. If we're going to be repaying our loan to him and his bank I thought we might as well get his wife to pay a little back.' Diana was totally incorrigible.

The weeks that followed were immersed in total dedication. Sarah seemed to work night and day, adapting and perfecting, whilst Helen and Diana co-ordinated the processes from designing to manufacturing to the ultimate marketing ploy: the hosting of the fashion evening. Some of the machinists at Tetlow were enlisted with the lure of overtime to produce these one-off products. Helen and Diana provided extra pairs of hands as they shadowed the workers and assisted with any menial tasks, from sewing on buttons to final pressing. Helen organised the event's publicity with advertisements, which she herself designed, she invited a number of Beckston's elite with their wives and managed to persuade the local press to be present. Diana acted as the choreographer, encouraging her models to move gracefully to music whilst exhibiting their garments with both decadence and decorum. She was a past master of modest exposure and no one knew better how to alluringly tease under the veil of refined sophistication. The evening had to appeal to both sexes.

The ladies department at Brown Muffs was housed on the first floor and had centrally positioned a most imposing oak staircase which ascended before subdividing into two further stairs leading off at right angles. The effect was theatrically majestic and perfect from which to introduce the new collection. It soon became apparent how effective the advertising campaign had been as large numbers of people began to assemble. The staff from Horton House obligingly volunteered to mingle amongst the gathering, supplying ample refreshments of unreserved drinks and canapés, in order to ensure that the evening began successfully. All the arrangements seemed to be progressing well until it was discovered that one of the girls had sprained an ankle in a fall the previous day which had repercussions for the finale.

'We need another model in order to show the full final collection,' snapped Diana.

'Surely the girls could double up and change?' Helen enquired tentatively. Diana was in no mood to accept unworkable solutions at this late stage. She could hear the assembled party chattering with excitement, devouring the free refreshments as they spoke.

'There wouldn't be time for that.' Suddenly Diana stepped back and encircled her friend. 'There's only one thing for it, you'll have to make up the numbers.'

'Me! You must be joking. I'm not a model and certainly not a dancer. I really wouldn't be happy in the limelight.'

'Well it'll be down to me then,' Diana snapped. 'Just don't be surprised when we don't get any orders as the audience see me swaying down the stairs carrying everything in front of me. Actually, when you see some of the elderly matriarchs out there, they probably have bigger stomachs than I do!' Diana always knew how to puncture the intensity of adversity with humour, making light of difficult situations. She also had no intention of participating as a model herself and knew that Helen would not refuse her.

Diana excelled in her role as compere, introducing each aspect of the show with the thrill of anticipation. The assembled audience were enthrallingly beguiled as the girls flowed down the staircase in front of them, mingling within the audience just sufficiently long enough for the interested parties to be able to closely scrutinise the quality of the couture, before ascending in synchronised form and disappearing from view. There were gasps of admiration punctuated by intense applause as each microcosm of delight came into view, entertained and disappeared. Padded shoulders, large collars, wide lapels, V-shaped necklines and cuffed sleeves, all made their debut in the collection of ladies coats, dresses and suits. Behind the scenes Helen and Sarah worked frantically assisting the girls in dressing and undressing. Sarah was a perfectionist and refused to allow any mistake to show. Last minute adjustments were made with her nimble seamstress fingers and fine needle and thread.

As the finale approached Helen began to feel nauseous. She was afraid of letting everyone down by her inexperience. Sarah psychologically cajoled her with confidence as she helped her to prepare and finally the time had arrived. All the girls, including Helen, were wearing woollen-tweed coats. They made their entrance as Diana introduced each one with fine adjectives and perfect fashion prose. Each girl lined both sides of the staircase in a stationary manner, awaiting the arrival of the final model. Helen appeared at the head of the stairs, momentarily stopped, unbuttoned her coat and allowed it to fall behind her as she stepped forward revealing a black lace and chiffon evening dress. The ruched bodice partially eclipsing the bust line, emphasised the rounded contours of her feminine form and as she moved the black pleated silk chiffon trails falling from her shoulders to the ground, swayed against her back whilst the full length panelled skirt flared from the knees as the circular-cut inset godets fanned outwards. The eyes of every woman and man remained avidly on her, including those of the local press who quickly wished to capitalise upon the moment and capture the vision. The repeated flashes of the camera signalled to all that the last minute decision to include eveningwear had been a recognisable triumph.

The enthusiastic applause emulating from the audience continued for some time. All the models beamed with delight as appreciative recognition echoed throughout the store. Helen positively glowed with excitement, totally unaware of the many envious looks of admiration she was receiving from the ladies and the equally licentious ones from the men. Even Diana acknowledged to herself how radiant Helen's beauty was. It had always been there but the dress and slight make-up had merely emphasised it. As the applause finally abated it was with total surprise that Helen stepped forward and expressed her gratitude to the audience.

'May I take this opportunity, ladies and gentlemen, to thank you for attending our special inaugural evening which has witnessed the launch of Tetlow Brothers Ladies collection. We do hope that you have enjoyed our latest selection and indeed will want to support us further by purchasing from us. We have for many years been recognised as one of the finest gentlemen's outfitters and that of course will continue, very much to both my father-in-law and brother-in-law's satisfaction. This evening would not have taken shape without the inexhaustible efforts of my sister-in-law, Diana. However a new era beckons and both Diana and myself welcome the challenge of fulfilling the dreams and desires of every fashion conscious woman. Wishing to do that and being able to put it into practice is of course not an easy feat. This evening would not and could not have been possible without the indisputable talents of Miss Sarah Nussey.'

Helen and Diana beckoned to Sarah to join them and receive the applause but she seemingly preferred to remain on the sidelines. The two women refused to allow that to happen and collectively manoeuvred her onto the middle of the staircase. Blushing and bewildered she reluctantly received her share of the adulation.

Only one member of the audience continued to scrutinise her. Throughout the remainder of the proceedings he looked at no one else, including Helen or the numerous beautiful models in the store. Sarah was plain and unremarkable in appearance. She possessed great talents but covered herself in shapeless, unnoticeable apparel. Simple and unadorned, she was his perfect choice.

CHAPTER FOURTEEN

The summer of 1935 witnessed enormous changes in the Tetlow family, both in business and at home. Risk and enterprise had become successful bedfellows following the catalyst of the fashion show. Publicity in the press had had a marked effect upon Beckston's community, but it had not been long before the firm had become overwhelmed with orders from the continent. The employment of more workers and machinery had even necessitated the move to larger and better premises as the firm continued to prosper. Sarah had been given her own design room, where she continued to conceive the desires of the fashion conscious woman, avidly bringing them to fruition in a wealth of stylish materials. Helen had found herself imbued with a new form of confidence which she exploited to the full as the marketing representative for ladies' fashion. It was her job to launch Sarah's ideas and maximise potential client interest.

Life had definitely changed for the better. It had, however, changed unequivocally for Diana and Richard who had now become the proud parents of a son and, as Edward had pointed out, 'a long awaited heir to the Tetlow firm'. Everyone seemed to be happy, content and oblivious to the thoughts of adversity. Their preoccupied and diverted attention had overlooked the possibility of a cuckoo, or rather a vulture, in the nest.

The orders continued to flood in whilst the workforce continued to sustain the output. Sarah persisted in her diligence and whilst the rest of the Tetlow family were enveloped in thoughts of infancy the designer continued to produce further avant-garde creations. Her ideas seemed to know no bounds and as the public clearly craved her styles she now began to channel her energies into other fields: men's fashion. Weeks of unstinting hard work abruptly ceased as Sarah suddenly announced that she needed some time away. The request, although somewhat strange in timing, could not be denied and was accordingly assigned as being a necessary reward for dedicated work. Surely, it was argued, the launch of the men's collection could wait. Everyone understood that the creative genius was exhausted and needed to replenish her energies. The firm would surely manage without her for two weeks.

****

The telephone call could not have coincided with a busier time for Helen. In Sarah's absence it had become quite noticeable how much the designer was needed. Coupled with this Diana was also unavailable as she begrudgingly adhered to the wishes of her doctor and husband and rested at home with her new son. There was little time for Helen to socialise but she instantly recognised something in the tone and nature of his voice and understood instantly that he needed her. It was William Fawcett on the line for her and yet when she listened to his voice it sounded slow, slurred and so unlike her grandfather. All that he would say was that he wished to see her. There was no reference to the fact that he had not contacted her for more than a year, a year in which she had lost her husband, suffered illness and helped restore a business which may otherwise have floundered. That something in his voice made her forgive him for any transgressions.

As before he sent his car and chauffeur to collect her and bring her to him. Mount Hall had maintained its imposing air of superiority, but this time Helen felt more at ease as the butler welcomed her and led her through a library lined with faded antiquarian books. At the far end he opened the French windows and signalled to her to join her grandfather who was seated on the terrace overlooking the wide expanse of grounds. He was seated with his back to her and thereby accorded her the advantage of greeting him first. As she spoke he turned slowly and afforded her his arms.

'Helen, thank you for coming. I have so wanted to see you again but I didn't want you to see me. You must forgive me for being slow to speak and act but I suffered a stroke a little over a year ago. Please don't look so worried. I'm alive and fortunately have regained my speech and movement. I may not be quite as agile as I once was, but I can still enjoy life.' He reached for her hand clumsily and Helen immediately noticed an element of stiffness, no doubt a legacy left from the initial paralysis.

To avoid undue embarrassment Helen tried to introduce conversation and chatter to him, to allow him to rest and, although he was extremely interested to hear of the recent changes in the Tetlow business, he refused in his stubborn manner to be a spectator. He seemed undeterred by his slurred speech impediment or by the fact that he now relied heavily upon the use of a walking stick and was adamant upon showing Helen some of the grounds. As he moved Helen witnessed an occasional grimace and realised that the paralysis had affected the whole right side of his body. The appearance of a large tea tray was a welcome relief, no doubt to them both, and signalled their return to the comforts of the terrace.

'I was extremely sad to hear of your loss. It's so cruel to lose someone so young.' The sentiments were aired with understanding and, as Helen thought, sprang from experience.

'Thank you. It was a terrible shock. As you may have heard it was an accident.'

'Yes, those are always the worst to bear. The chance factor always makes you question whether it could have been avoided.' His eyes bore into her with a depth of penetrating scrutiny.

'Well my entire life has changed now, thanks to Diana, Richard's wife, who has been a very good friend to me since schooldays. It's also thanks to Diana that the Tetlow business is doing well and I now have a purpose in life again as the marketing rep for ladies' fashion.' Helen spoke with true pride about her new life.

'Yes, I must say that I'm pleased for you and the Tetlow family. I've known Richard for many years and from my sources in the know I hear that he's never looked so well as he does at the moment. All I can say is good for him. That's what a young wife and baby can do for you.' As William Fawcett mouthed the final sentence Helen immediately felt a sense of empathy for him, for the loss of his wife, her grandmother, in childbirth. She gripped his arm affectionately and he returned this affection with a knowing smile and a nod of the head.

'You never had experience of that, did you?' As she prompted the question her face wore an expression of total understanding.

'For someone so young you have an immense sense of feeling, my girl. Perhaps that's not so surprising, when you consider what you've been through, even in your short life. Helen, as an old man who has witnessed most of life's dealings, I want to give you some advice. Live life to the full. Grasp opportunities when they come your way, and they will believe you me! I understand that you're enjoying your work and sharing your life with others, but you must have a life of your own. When I look at you I still see Helena. You're a beautiful girl Helen and deserve to be loved.'

'I have been! I have been married to a man who loved me.'

'Yes, I'm not disputing that Denis Tetlow loved you. He did have somewhat of a reputation with the ladies and would not have married you if he hadn't been in love. However Helen, did you love him? Can you actually say that you were in love with him? I have been in love and I'm sorry Helen I don't see that look in your eye when you speak about Denis. It may sound harsh in view of what happened, but I also have a reputation for speaking plainly.' He had definitely exposed a raw nerve as Helen battled to fight back the tears.

'I have been in love and I do know what it feels like. You don't solely have the rights on those feelings you know. But I also know what it is to feel hurt as a result of intense love and all I can say is that it is easier to love someone with less fervour who will not shatter your world.'

'Helen, it may be easier but it is worthless love in comparison.'

For many days following her meeting with her grandfather Helen found it difficult to refrain from thinking about Thomas. She tried to imagine where he was and what he was doing. She still found it difficult to accept how so much pain could develop from so much love.

****

The day had been glorious and the family had chosen to spend their Sunday in the grounds of Horton House, being frantically entertained by the antics of Jack Tetlow, a highly spirited infant who crawled with alarming speed towards anything that represented danger. Edward Tetlow and his brother Richard frequently remarked how the little boy reminded them of Denis, who from childhood onwards had refused to be daunted by the fear of risk. It was only in Helen's presence that each brother threw a cursory glance to the other to signal that such reminders were inappropriate.

Their visitors were totally unexpected. The fact that they arrived together was alarming enough, especially to Helen. No one was prepared for their news. Sarah proudly raised her left hand and tried to dazzle the spectators with the small solitaire and the wedding ring below it.

'We didn't tell anybody because it happened so quickly. It's just been a whirlwind romance,' Sarah announced.

Helen stared, first at her and then at him. She questioned how anyone with so much talent as Sarah possessed could be duped by such a man. Callous and rapacious, Harry only ever did anything for self-gain. He could never understand the meaning of romance. She truly felt sorry for Sarah.

Edward and Richard played the convivial hosts congratulating and toasting the couple with champagne. Diana, understanding of Helen's feelings, was more reserved in her own expression of felicitations than the men. Helen mumbled a quiet word of 'congratulations' and moved away. She was unaware that he had followed her to the edge of the garden.

'Well Helen I know you're so pleased for me.'

'Why Harry? Why have you married her? You don't love her,' Helen declared.

'Needs must Helen, needs must! You more than anyone know all about that. Remember your own wedding day and why you married Denis?'

'You're despicable! She'll soon see through the veneer and realise what a grasping, extortionate predator you are.'

'My, you have learnt some big words Helen. Must be all that marketing you've been doing. Anyway I can't stand here all day talking to you, as much as I would like to, I am now married and must return to my wife. We don't want her becoming jealous of you, do we?' Harry retreated definitely pleased with himself and left Helen to contemplate his next tactical manoeuvre.

Within a matter of weeks the reason became all too clear; Sarah declared that she had been offered a position elsewhere. It would only be in her best interests to remain at Tetlows if she was offered some future security. She wanted to be more than just a paid employee, she wanted a partnership and thereby some ownership of the firm's profits. Harry's demands had begun to take shape. However, what Harry had not anticipated was the tenacity with which Edward Tetlow was determined to hold onto the business.

'I'm sorry Helen if you think I'm speaking out of turn, but I'll not sit back and see a respectable business, which was founded through hard graft by my father, be siphoned off by a charlatan like him. He is behind all of this. I don't like the man, I never have, and I would never trust him. He hoodwinked Denis and clearly he has the same effect upon his wife. He may be your cousin, but as soon as I can find a way to get rid of him, I surely will.' It was clear that Edward had long wanted to express his feelings about Harry but for Helen's sake had kept them to himself.

'I certainly couldn't agree with you more. We may be related but we are definitely not close. However Sarah is our greatest asset and we run the risk of losing customers, or even allowing our competitors to take her from us and use her against us. If that happens the business will suffer,' exclaimed Helen.

'She may be a good designer but she's not the only one around,' snapped Edward.

'That is true, but her designs have become something of unique status. The profits will definitely suffer without her.'

Edward was a businessman and a very shrewd one. For a moment he scrutinised his daughter-in-law and accepted the facts.

'Very well. We'll put it to the others for agreement. I suggest we offer her an increased salary and fifteen per cent of all net profits for the time that she remains employed with us. That is a remarkably fair, indeed more than fair, offer,' remarked Edward.

Helen agreed that the deal was a generous one and did not anticipate any objections. She was, however, ignorant of the fact, as Edward was, that their conversation in Edward's office had been fully overheard by an eavesdropper. The old adage that eavesdroppers never hear any good of themselves did not unduly concern Harry.

The deal was accepted and the business continued to flourish. Helen regularly visited her grandfather but kept the visits clandestine with the exception of Diana. She did not want Harry to hear of her meetings in case he decided to use that information to his own advantage. The less he knew the better.

As another collection was about to be launched Helen found herself spending more and more time at work. In order to meet deadlines this necessitated working late at the office. One evening she was aware that she was the only person left in the building but she suddenly became conscious of a presence.

'My we are jumpy Helen. What's the matter? You seem surprised to see me,' Harry enquired.

'I am rather. It is late. What do you want?' Helen asked, irritated by his intrusion.

'Why do you think I want something?' Harry asked in his own bemused way.

'Because you always do!' Helen snapped.

'Well we're not too friendly tonight are we? I had hoped that you'd be a little more approachable, seeing that I have a little proposition to put to you.' The word 'proposition' immediately commanded Helen's attention.

'Go on, I'm listening.'

'Our married quarters are what you might call, a little cramped. Oh, don't look so worried I've not got her in the family way. You'd know all about that from your past experience. No, she's far too useful to me, working towards the profits as she does. What we thought would be nice, rather than living in a flat, would be a house of our own. That's where you come in! As you haven't yet given us your wedding present I thought you might like to make a little down payment.'

'You're asking me for money? How much Harry?'

'A couple of grand would be very helpful.'

'Two thousand pounds! I don't have that sort of money. Denis left me nothing having gambled everything away with you. Where am I going to find that sort of money?' As Helen looked up from her desk Harry was closing the door behind him.

'You'll think of something Helen, you always do!' His parting words did not imbue her with confidence.

****

Diana had noticed a distinct alteration in Helen's demeanour. The workload was understandably demanding at this crucial time prior to the launch of a new collection, but she knew that there was something else troubling her friend. She waited for an appropriate time when the two women could speak freely without the risk of interruption.

'Helen, is everything all right at work? I know that I haven't been there with you, but it won't be long before I can persuade Richard to let me return. You know that you can always ask me to help you, don't you?' Diana suggested.

'Yes, of course I do.' A long pause followed.

'Helen, we've known one another too long to pretend. What's the matter?'

'It's the same thing, over and over again. He won't leave me alone. He's always there and I don't think I'm ever going to be free of him.' The emotion began to show in Helen's eyes.

'Who are you talking about?'

'Harry! Bloody Harry!' Diana was genuinely startled by Helen's choice of expletive. She had never heard her swear before.

'He wants two thousand pounds, which I certainly haven't got. He's calling it a belated wedding present, would you believe? But as you and I both know, it's just another way to describe blackmail.'

'Two thousand pounds! What does he want, Buckingham Palace?' demanded Diana.

'He might as well as. I'll never be able to raise that amount. Where can I find that sort of money?'

Diana remained unusually silent for a short time.

'What will happen if you don't pay?'

'That doesn't bear thinking about. The word 'disgraced' springs to mind. He intends to capitalise upon my past.'

'Normally I wouldn't tolerate blackmail, but in this case I think there may be a way to hopefully settle this matter once and for all,' declared Diana. She left the room quickly; in her absence Helen remained transfixed in bewilderment. Moments later she returned and was unlocking a small, undistinguished looking wooden box whose exterior belied its contents. Inside fabulous jewels sparkled with promise, some of which Helen had seen before.

'Aren't these the pieces that Mr... '

'Yes, that Mr Godwin gave me,' interrupted Diana. 'I'm never going to wear these again. This was my old life, now I have a new life and one which I'm very happy with.' She handed the box to Helen. 'Let's pick out a few choice pieces. If you make him a genuinely irresistible offer perhaps you can persuade him to leave you and even Beckston for good.'

'How I wish that could be possible,' murmured Helen.

'Of course it is! There are enough diamonds, emeralds and sapphires here to convince him of that fact. There is certainly more than two thousand pounds worth here! All these pieces were commissioned based on the Art Deco style. There are plenty of buyers who would snap these up today. Just tell him that Denis gave them to you and hopefully he'll get the message that there will be no more forthcoming. The deal is that he can have these only if he assures you that he will never bother you again.'

Diana in her matter of fact way had made it sound so simple. The only difficult part was accepting that Harry would agree to the deal and maintain his word.

****

For the first time in her dealings with Harry it was Helen who determined the exact time and meeting place. Mixed emotions coursed through her body as she awaited his arrival. She had chosen her office, late at night, to ensure privacy and to give her a feeling of confidence, being as it were, on home ground. He entered, listened, agreed, accepted and left Helen with a feeling of numbness. The expected state of euphoria failed to transpire as the entire transaction had been too easy. Nothing was ever that easy with Harry. She had made it blatantly obvious that she had nothing else of consequence to give him. He took the jewels only on the agreed understanding that he would walk out of her life forever. There had been no argument or negotiation necessary; he just accepted her terms and left.

It was only the next day when Sarah announced that he had walked out on her, their marriage and Beckston that Helen began to feel hopeful.

****

Helen found it inconceivable that Sarah had become so distraught in his absence. To Helen it was jubilation, admittedly internal jubilation, as any expression of relief in his departure served merely to reinforce the abandonment of his wife. He had been the one and only 'love of her life' and as the weeks passed time failed to heal Sarah's distress. She refused to hear anything detrimental said of him; neither Helen nor Diana could persuade her otherwise. At first she appeared to find solace in her work but gradually an inertia of ideas descended into desperation and ultimately depression. She had difficulty sleeping and no longer seemed to care whether she ate or drank. She no longer seemed to care about her appearance. In fact she no longer seemed to care about anything. An invitation to stay at Horton House was declined, as was the opportunity to take a holiday.

It became increasingly difficult to approach her or work with her. Something had to change and it finally did. Three months after Harry's departure Sarah suddenly failed to appear at work. She failed to contact anyone and she also failed to answer her door. The decision to involve the police was the ultimatum which could not be ignored. It proved necessary; they were the ones who discovered her lifeless body.

CHAPTER FIFTEEN

Helen and Diana's insistence upon calling the police so promptly had unmistakably saved her life. A hideous cocktail of tablets and alcohol had fortunately failed to induce the intended suicide. It was so pitiful, the fact that someone with so much talent could have been brought so low as to contemplate such action. The end would never have justified the means, certainly in Helen's eyes. She resolutely reiterated, 'no one, especially Harry, is worth taking your life for'. Diana repeatedly nodded in stunned silence.

The two women were adamant that upon her release from hospital, Sarah would join them at Horton House. Diana once again took it upon herself to organise the care of the patient and, with Helen's assistance, Sarah was nursed and attended to with untiring devotion. Gradually her stamina and interests began to return once she requested paper and drawing implements. As she sketched it became very clear to everyone that she had been reunited with something worth living for. The inherent drive for perfection shone through with a modicum of humour.

'I cannot believe what some women are prepared to wear!' Sarah announced.

'What do you mean?' The question fell from the lips of both Helen and Diana simultaneously.

'Being in hospital gave me a chance to do a little research. Nightwear and lingerie have been neglected for far too long. We need to launch a collection soon. In fact I would say the sooner the better. If I design it, will you two do the necessary?'

It would have been futile to suggest that she should rest. The perfect tonic for Sarah's recuperation was work, plenty of work. Filling her time this way would ensure that she did not stray into unsavoury thoughts. She had already subtlety removed her wedding ring and had not once mentioned his name. It almost felt as though Harry had died. Helen reluctantly admitted to herself that unfortunately it was nothing more than wishful thinking. Dreams, of course, sometimes had a way of coming true whilst nightmares always seemed to reoccur. That was the problem.

****

Fashion continued to brighten the lives of the population and for those that could afford it the new collections were avidly snapped up in orders. The emphasis began to be placed upon mass production where the most popular lines were manufactured in large quantities, often in cheaper synthetic fabrics, before gracing the rails of stores such as Brown Muffs. Tetlow Brothers continued to diversify, producing both haute couture for special commissions and fulfilling volume orders for London retail stores. It literally felt as though the Tetlow family and those closely connected had simply struck gold. Fortune may indeed favour the brave, but for those not on the receiving end, envy can be a dangerous motive.

Large orders necessitated long working hours. The prospect of a holiday was always a discreet incitement to work harder but the irony was that hard work induced success which in turn produced further orders and more work. Helen, Diana and Sarah were reluctant to take leave of their success, albeit in a temporary way. Richard, although not on holiday, was currently away on business which required Edward to have to step into his brother's shoes and receive an important client, Mr Trenchard, from Trenchard and Sons, a large retail company. Edward was always far happier working amongst his employees and totally disliked the niceties of business. A new client who specified dealing with a man, rather than having to respond to feminine control, may be an insufferable bigot but was not one to be shunned. Such an important client was at liberty to determine the date and time of a business meeting. The choice was Friday morning and the terms of 'take it or leave it', clearly indicated that there was no room for negotiation. Therefore the weekly routine of collecting the wages from the bank would have to be changed. Procedures were put in place and reluctantly Edward visited the bank a day early. The firm's wages would surely be secure overnight in the large office safe.

Throughout that Thursday the workload had been unrelentingly unmerciful and Helen accepted that her working day would continue into the late hours of the evening. She knew that she would not be alone as Diana and Sarah were also facing the pressure of meeting the time schedule. They worked together as a collective team on any project and that was their success.

Helen left her office only once to visit the ladies and make herself a drink and when she returned, she found her chair occupied. The nightmare had returned to haunt her. He sat there and epitomised every inch the harbinger of doom that he was. Helen was totally speechless.

'Now I know what it is like to sit in the seat of power. I've never before tasted it.'

'What are you doing here Harry? You promised me you would go and leave me alone.' Helen was clearly distressed and showed her anxiety by spilling the contents of her cup.

'Careful. I think you had better sit down whilst I run you though one or two issues. Firstly, I just wanted to taste a little of what you always seem to end up with. You were born with a silver spoon in your mouth and whatever happens you always end up with the Midas touch. As for me, I'm always on the scrap heap, whatever I do. Secondly, you should know me by now Helen, I may have given you my word but of course I never stand by it. Thirdly, it appears that your word, or rather your gems, are worthless.' Helen remained transfixed whilst Harry calmly positioned a large diamond pendant, one which she recognised that had been Diana's, onto the desk before revealing a hammer from his jacket pocket. Swiftly he brought the hammer down, smashing the jewel into fine pieces. Picking up a minute shard he held it close to her cheek and felt her involuntary trembling. He felt empowered by her anxiety.

'Scared are we? Or are you just shocked that Denis's feelings for you didn't amount to very much. The diamond is a precious stone of pure carbon. Did you know that carbon is the hardest natural substance on earth? No? Well I didn't, but I've had to have some investigations done on your jewels and it turns out that they're worthless. Just like you! A true diamond would not shatter under a hammer. I did consider that you might have tried to fob me off but then decided that even you were not that stupid. You must have known that I'd find out. So for once in your life you were the one to be deceived. You know I kind of like it. Revenge from the grave you might say.' He leaned back into the chair, folded his arms and smiled so smugly that Helen began to feel nauseous in anticipation of his next move.

'What do you want me to say or do, Harry? I don't have anything else of value to give to you.'

'Now that's where you're wrong, my dear little cousin. You have all the week's wages just sitting in the safe.' The bewildered look upon her face momentarily stopped him from continuing.

'How, could you possibly know that?'

'Because I do! I've told you before, don't ever underestimate me Helen. Whatever it takes, I'll do it and survive. I'll take anyone down who tries to sell me short; that includes you, definitely you!' A look of hatred flashed across his face.

'I don't know the combination for the safe. Only certain people know that.'

'Like Edward for one?'

'Well yes.'

'That's all right then. He's still working in the cutting room. Obviously working late so that he can spend his time tomorrow entertaining Mr Trenchard, who of course won't be coming.' Harry suddenly began to guffaw with unrelenting laughter.

'It was you who set all this up?' Helen enquired incredulously.

'Yes, my naive Helen, it was me.'

The unrecognisable strains of a man's mocking laughter were sufficient to disturb both Diana and Sarah who were curious to know who was on the premises. Their unexpected interruption provided relief for Helen until Harry's persuasive invitation made them enter and sit down. There were no arguments as he held the small gun at Helen's head. Dispassionately his eyes fell upon his wife.

'Go and tell Edward I want to see him, now.' Sarah quickly rose to her feet and left the office. Almost immediately the gruff tones of Edward could be heard down the corridor.

'You bloody fool, put that down.'

'Don't provoke him, Edward!' pleaded Diana.

'Tell your father-in-law what he needs to do,' Harry said jolting the pistol into Helen's temple.

'He wants you to open the safe.'

'Not on my bloody life,' snapped Edward.

'That can be arranged but you must get in the queue. Helen's first.'

'You wouldn't. You don't have the guts!' Edward said disparagingly.

The unmistakeable sound of the firing lever being raised was enough. Shrieks of anguish rang out long after the gun had been fired. Edward collapsed to the floor, grasping his left arm which was quickly becoming saturated with blood.

'The next one's for real,' Harry replied calmly. No one disputed that fact.

There was no choice in the matter. Everyone obediently walked to Richard's office as Harry maintained his grip upon Helen, pressing the pistol indefatigably into her head. Diana's improvisational skills turned her stockings into a makeshift tourniquet which seemed to stem the flow of blood from Edward's arm. Harry intimated the next move. Showing no remorse he pointed at the safe, quickly glancing towards Edward who was visibly in pain and beginning to show signs of shock.

'Open it!'

'Can't you see he's injured and needs treatment?' sobbed Helen.

'He'll get it, when I get what's due to me,' Harry snapped. 'Now open it!'

Diana and Sarah supported Edward on either side and led him towards the large safe. His pallor was extremely pale, his respiration rapid and shallow and, although seemingly drowsy and weary in appearance, he was still conscious. The women guided his hands to the lock where he began to move the combination dial slowly and jerkily.

'Come on, hurry up!' Harry snapped.

'For Gods sake, the man's been shot. How can you be so unfeeling?' demanded Sarah. 'You're not the man I married. You can't be. That time we spent together, did it mean nothing to you?'

'Absolutely nothing,' came the cold reply. His eyes were fixed upon the safe; he failed to blink as the door was finally opened.

With the money placed in front of him a wry smile pervaded his face. His hands grabbed at the notes before they were swiftly concealed into every available pocket about him.

'Well, thank you everyone. I won't be so rude as to leave without giving you something back. Helen has probably never mentioned it but the grandchild that she almost gave you Edward, wasn't Denis's. Your son who had such a reputation with the ladies couldn't manage that. It didn't matter however as Helen was pregnant with her cousins when she married your son. The best laugh is that Denis felt he had to marry her because he thought it was his!'

'You lying bastard, Harry! You're nothing more than a low life and I'll make sure you pay for this. Helen and Diana have been the best things to come into my family. How dare you... ' The sentence was punctuated by the simultaneous sounds of the shot and the screams. Edward had been shot through the heart.

Callous by nature Harry had now proved himself to be a cold-blooded murderer. As he made his way to the door his captive's eyes were rigidly fixed upon the pistol. The recognisable sound of the firing lever being raised again signalled a dire warning. The consequence for killing again would be no more severe than for killing only once. As the pistol became aimed towards Helen Diana sprang with swift alacrity and threw herself towards the killer who momentarily staggered in his stance being totally unprepared for her defensive action. The force of her body completely overwhelmed him and the short scuffle was brought to an abrupt end with the noise of the gunshot. Harry left his victim to writhe in pain having shot her at close range in the right leg. He left alone. No one followed or saw his next move.

The corridor quickly became saturated with the contents from the carefully concealed petrol can. Premeditation was the only word to describe the scene that followed. Flames licked through the structure of the building with voracity causing windows to shatter or explode whilst the intense heat entangled the internal framework into a mangled heap of destruction before being engulfed in thick choking smoke. The office buildings and the majority of the works had been totally ravaged in the fire by the early hours of the next morning. All that remained were blackened piles of smouldering rubble.

CHAPTER SIXTEEN

'I sentence you to be taken from this court to a place of execution where you will be hanged by the neck until you are dead. May the Lord have mercy upon your soul.' The judge's words were final and irrevocable.

Harry remained stationary in the dock; his face wore an impassive look. The police guards flanking him, each grabbed one of his arms to lead him away down the staircase. Before turning, he threw an insidiously penetrating stare towards Helen who likewise returned his gaze with dispassion.

Throughout the proceedings of the trial his demeanour had been one of calm impunity. The evidence presented had been overwhelmingly in favour of his guilt. Although he showed no remorse for his actions he sought neither to defend himself nor did he choose to further his cause with sensational revelations about Helen. Instead he appeared to accept the prosecution's proceedings without retaliating via his own defence. The result was a foregone conclusion of everyone's expectations. The only worry was why he had been so accepting of his fate. Had his actions finally made him realise the evil he had committed? Probably no one would ever know the answer.

There had been no compassion that night when he had doused the exit route for the three women with petrol before torching it and escaping, knowing that the inferno would destroy buildings and human life without selection. He had murdered Edward in front of them, attempted to shoot Helen, instead he had wounded Diana and his finale had been the ultimate cleanser of guilt, the spread of fire. The most disturbing fact of all was that seeing all three women alive in the court could not even spark a modicum of surprise across his countenance.

All three were, without question, survivors. Sensing the rapid approach of the fire their initial response had been one of despair and hopelessness. Diana was in great pain, having been shot in the femur she was quickly losing blood and consciousness. Sarah attended to her, again applying a makeshift tourniquet, whilst Helen deliberated possible options. The window was too elevated from the ground, even for the able-bodied, whilst the corridor was non-negotiable as smoke began to seep under the door. In panic she began to hyperventilate, avidly scanning the room for any way out. Suddenly her eyes became fixed upon a large cupboard which she proceeded to randomly empty. The furniture was large, heavy and totally unmovable with its contents but, once emptied, Sarah and Helen applied desperate force to move it. Slowly it yielded to their combined efforts to reveal a window hatch which Helen had recalled seeing in the office next door. It had been a connecting hatch between the offices which was no longer in use. This office not only led into the corridor but also had a door into the cutting room. If they could only reach the works they would then have access to the outside.

As the smoke began to billow with more urgency under the door and the flames crackled along the corridor panelling, Helen felt impelled to work faster. She smashed the painted window out using chair legs and then attempted to clear any excess glass from the frame. Helen had to be the one in charge. Removing her dress she covered any undetected shards of glass with the fabric before insisting that Sarah wriggle through it. Lifting up the almost unconscious Diana Helen laid her onto her back and began to pass her through the hatch headfirst to Sarah. A deep groan signalled to both the intensity of pain that Diana was experiencing as her legs were raised and transferred through the hatch. Helen finally followed and the women were at last safe as they managed to find an outside door which could be opened. To the outside world they presented a most motley and dishevelled, grimy sight: Helen half-naked, Sarah sobbing and Diana heavily bloodstained and unconscious. They could not have been more joyful; they were all alive.

The trial had attracted a great deal of interest. The final day had been no exception as the public gallery became crammed with individuals eager to know whether there would be an execution. Human nature has always been intrigued by morbid curiosity; public executions have testified to this through the centuries. However the one person Helen had not expected to see appeared in full view. William Fawcett did not seem the type of man to be swayed by public curiosity. His presence no doubt, Helen felt, was down to the fact that Harry was her cousin. He was obviously there as a gesture of support to Helen. It was strange, however, that he made no attempt to catch her gaze or contact her before or after the proceedings. The strangest thing, however, was that he left the court whilst the judge was delivering the death sentence.

At last it had come to an end, not just the trial but also the relentless torment continually perpetrated by Harry. Sarah had again been faced with emotional turmoil but it appeared that her earlier treatment by her husband had almost promoted some immunity against his final attack. Surprisingly this time she seemed to handle the experience with pragmatism. Helen found it difficult to believe that his blackmailing days were over and for many months endured disturbing nightmares. All three women at the trial had given evidence and, although the jury sympathised with Helen and Sarah's accounts, it was Diana with whom they empathised. Unable to walk and confined to a wheelchair her physical state touched their hearts immediately. It would be many months before the doctors would ascertain if she would ever walk again. It seemed to be the cruellest cut of all, a talented dancer imprisoned in a chair. One man murdered and a young mother's future destroyed provided sufficient cause for just retribution.

****

The prison wardens at Umstanton never complained about their charge. He was quiet, polite and mild-mannered. It seemed strange that such an individual received no visitors, never referred to his family or friends and coped far better than other inmates who pleaded their trust in clemency. This prisoner was not reliant upon the substitution of a life sentence for the death penalty. He came in with no false hopes and would leave with none.

As the two prison wardens entered the condemned cell they realised not only was it their last night shift for the week but the last shift with Harry Ledgard. They relieved the other wardens, exchanging nothing more than a brief nod of the head. The atmosphere in the small room now seemed too oppressive and charged with emotion to warrant verbal communication. Harry was lying still on his bed, his arms crossed beneath his head staring at the ceiling.

'Anything, we can get you Harry?' The question was always the same.

'I'd like a pen and some writing paper please.' The request was unusual as this was the first time that he had ever asked for anything. As they waited for the items to be brought each man couldn't help but wonder whom the recipient of the letter would be.

Silence once again prevailed with only the occasional sound from the pen pressing into the paper. It would be a long night. The two warders removed their hats and unbuttoned their tunics in an attempt to make themselves more comfortable. Neither man could see what was being written. Once completed Harry retained the letter and then agreed to play cards calmly, in a convivial manner. In the early hours of the morning he fell asleep and was awakened as new wardens entered the cell.

Dressed in an open necked prison shirt Harry refused the tot of whisky offered to him. He passed the letter to the prison chaplain who affirmed with an understanding nod of his head that it would be posted after the event. Harry had to accept that it would be checked and read by the authorities but consoled himself with the thought of the impact it would have upon the intended recipient. That thought and only that thought remained in his head. The time was now 7.55 am and the approaching footsteps heralded the arrival of the hangman. The governor, lord lieutenant of the county and other official witnesses were already waiting at the scene. His arms bound behind him by a leather belt, Harry heard the first strike of the eight o'clock chimes. Suddenly he was frogmarched from the condemned cell, through the open door and into the final room where he was stopped abruptly with ultimate precision on the trapdoors. Whilst a leather strap was being placed around his ankles his world turned dark as the black hood and noose were slipped over his head. He felt the rope being turned to ensure that the knot was at the side of his neck and then the wardens released their grip of his arms. The room was silent, everyone waiting for it to happen. As his body momentarily tensed he thought about the letter. By the eighth chime of the clock he was dead.

A couple of hours later his body was taken down, the hood still covering his head. Later that evening he was buried within the walls of the prison in an unmarked grave. He was just twenty-six years old.

****

There was no explanation for it but as Helen picked up the envelope a shiver ran down her back. It was clearly addressed to her but she did not recognise the writer's hand. As she began to read the letter's contents she understood the reason for her feeling of foreboding.

Dear Helen,

When you read this letter I will be dead. That of course is what you want. You always wanted me out of your life, as I wanted you out of mine. I will have taken my last breath before that rope tightens without mercy around my neck, before snapping it to end everything.

Don't get me wrong I am not feeling sorry for myself because I do deserve it. I think I must have been born evil. I've always hated you from the minute you came to live with us. You were the little girl that mother had always dreamed of. She simply switched her love for me to you. Even Thomas doted on you. Father didn't but he was more interested in the pub than me. So you see Helen, you came to us having been born to your fine mother and stole mine. I decided very early on that I would simply take what was owing to me – anything that was yours – family, friends, money and even your affection.

Wonder what I mean by affection? This is the best bit, which I've saved until last. You were carrying my child, not Thomas's. I hit him from the back and he was laid out unconscious. He thought he'd passed out with too much drink. He even thought afterwards that you were mad with him because he was drunk. I was the one that climbed into bed with you. I was the one that got you pregnant. It was a masterstroke as I was then able to profit from your guilt by reminding you of your little mistake. Thomas was the one man in the world that you loved and I managed to turn you against him.

I go to my grave knowing that you have not got everything in life that you wanted.

Your cousin and lover, Harry.

Helen suddenly felt overwhelmingly nauseous.

CHAPTER SEVENTEEN

The sensationalism created by the trial and execution finally began to wane in Beckston as public interest focussed upon royal events. Patriotism became endemic as the previous year had witnessed the Silver Jubilee joyously proclaimed throughout the realm by fireworks, street parties and the melodious peal of church bells. However the high hopes of a nation for a continued long and stable reign were dashed in January 1936 when George V died. In a historic gesture Queen Mary, upon her husband's death, took the hand of her eldest son and, stooping, kissed it. The king would live on; the realm renewed its urge to celebrate as preparations were put in force for the 12th of May 1937, Edward the Eighth's coronation date.

Amidst a background of constitutional change the early months of 1936 also witnessed changes in the Tetlow household. Edward Tetlow was buried with the full recognition that he deserved. A pair of elegant black horses, heads held high and topped with black plumes, walked with dignity behind the funeral director as they pulled the carriage of the glass hearse through Beckston. The mere sight of the horse drawn hearse was enough to demand total respect from every onlooker. Helen and Diana both shed tears as they recalled his final touching words which each woman knew had been truly meant. Richard refused to allow anyone else to push his wife's wheelchair at the funeral, it appeared that he wanted to be as close to Diana as he could, she had undergone both the shooting and a painful operation to remove the bullet. His constant attention to her and the numerous occasions that he held her hand or touched her shoulder with tenderness, indicated to all his gratitude for her life.

The funeral had been well attended and it was only later, as the family began to leave the graveside, that Helen became aware of his presence. It was still a relief not to be accosted and startled by Harry. That was a spectacle she knew she would never have to face again. This time the unexpected was a pleasant surprise, William Fawcett, her grandfather, had come to pay his respects, no doubt as a fellow businessman. He offered his condolences first to Richard and Diana and then proceeded to accompany Helen to the waiting cars.

'Your presence here today is greatly appreciated. Thank you.' Helen spoke with gratitude as she gripped her grandfather's hand. He still relied upon the use of a walking stick but his speech and movement were noticeably improved.

'It was the least I could do, believe you me Helen. The very least!'

'You will come back to the house for some refreshments?'

'I don't know. I don't want to impose.'

'You wouldn't be. You're family,' insisted Helen. William almost seemed embarrassed by this remark and as they turned towards the car Helen heard him faintly whisper, 'I don't deserve you.'

The evening witnessed the departure of the final guests, with the exception of William Fawcett. It had been a long day for the Tetlow family, including Sarah, and everyone understood that the final act of burial had laid to rest both Edward as well as his murderer. An uncertain future lay ahead and no one quite knew how the phoenix would rise from these ashes, but rise it must.

The suggestion was totally unexpected and a sea of faces stared back at William Fawcett.

'That is a very generous offer William. It's certainly good at a time like this to know that we have friends to fall back on, but we need to work this out ourselves.' Richard had been visibly moved by the kind offer.

'What is there to work out? I own some very large mill premises, a great deal of which is nowadays never used. You would be doing me a favour by setting up your new business in them.'

'As kind as your offer is we could not accept rent-free premises. In the past we have always owned our buildings and that is really what I am hoping to do again,' Richard said apologetically.

'Come and take a look and tell me how much space you need and the buildings will be put into your name, Richard. You will own them.'

'You want to give away part of your business William? Why do you want to give it to me?' Richard was totally perplexed.

'Because everyone in this room has done far more for Helen than I have ever done. As her grandfather I owe you some gratitude and it's my way of trying to correct some of the wrongs that I've done in my life.'

The public acknowledgement meant a great deal to Helen. Finally she knew that all the secrets were out in the open and Pandora's Box was completely empty.

****

He was as good as his word. Within weeks Tetlows was firmly established in the west part of Fawcett's mill, the legalities having been signed, sealed and delivered. Richard's misgivings of usurping Helen's legacy were laid to rest when William quietly reassured him that the gift was but a very small part of her considerable fortune. He was adamant that he wanted to donate his thanks in this way and to refuse his offer would be seen as churlish upon Richard's part. The new machinery, followed by the old employees, began to filter into the new premises. A state of the art design studio was produced for Sarah. A joint welfare committee was established for the employees of Tetlows and Fawcetts, whereby the companies ran trips to the Yorkshire Dales and the East and West coasts, as well as establishing cricket matches, tennis and football tournaments. His employees described the radical change in

William Fawcett as the *Christmas Carol* effect; Scrooge had certainly reformed.

Helen had had little time to reflect upon the contents of that letter. Sometimes she knew that she had mentally tried to erase it from her memory by totally immersing herself in her work. It was certainly true that there had been a great deal of work to do, all within a short period, but on the odd occasions when her thoughts had drifted to the events of that fateful night she cursed herself for ever doubting Thomas's actions. Often she would try and imagine where he was now and whether he had married and become settled with a family. Such thoughts stung her with remorse and regret and culminated in hot tears trickling down her cheeks. Everything connected with Harry was still too raw to mention and the mere sight of Diana confined to a wheelchair was enough for Helen to not confide in her friend. William Fawcett had done a great deal more for the Tetlow family than he probably realised and his benevolence had only just begun. His unexpected visit one evening to Horton House was so unlike his usual pre-planned affairs and the excitement upon his face, quite out of character.

'I've decided to do something that I've always wanted to do,' William blurted out.

'Well good for you! Whatever it is, we can see that it's put you into a bit of a frenzy,' Richard remarked.

'Oh it certainly has. I have always wanted to travel on an ocean liner but I've never had the time or the companions to do it with. I felt that if I waited much longer it would be too late. So I'm going to sail aboard the Queen Mary on her maiden voyage and you're all going to come with me! It will be my treat and I refuse to take no for an answer!'

The old adage, 'Generosity knows no bounds' could aptly be applied to William who appeared to be at his happiest when giving. No one had been overlooked. Richard, Diana, their infant Jack and his nanny, Helen and Sarah were all William's travelling companions. The prospect of a voyage aboard one of the largest and most luxurious ocean liners ever built did not fail to be an invigorating tonic for life's past experiences.

The Queen Mary had been launched in September 1934 but it was not until the 27th May 1936 that she departed Southampton on her maiden voyage, arriving firstly in Cherbourg before crossing the Atlantic to arrive in New York; crossing time from Bishop Rock to Ambrose Light Vessel, 5 days, 5 hours and 13 minutes. Such knowledge would indeed be a topic of conversation in many gentlemen's clubs in the land.

A voyage as a first-class passenger provided a unique experience of travelling luxury at times extremely insular as each of the three classes were separated to keep them apart. First-class or cabin-class, passengers had exclusive use of the upper decks of the ship where their staterooms, lounge and dining room were situated. Second-class accommodation was in the stern whilst third-class accommodation was down in the hull. Helen had not anticipated how luxurious a ship could be and found every experience and vista offered to her as a first-class passenger quite overwhelming. The splendour of Art Deco was at its most magnificent throughout the lobbies, corridors, staterooms, ballrooms, restaurants and bars. Just when Helen thought that she had viewed every stunning location she found another to take her breath away. She marvelled that a ship could hold a swimming pool with heated water as well as boasting deep and shallow ends. The amazing Atlantic map in the cabin-class restaurant allowed passengers to take note of their journey as they watched a crystal model of the Queen Mary, lit with a bulb, make its way across the map. Such sights were mesmerising but the most awe-inspiring was the cabin-class dining room. Situated centrally in the ship it was three decks high in the middle, 48 metres long and the full width of the ship. Panelling in hues of browns, bronzes and gold covered the walls whilst being complemented by seating upholstery in rose pink. The menu revealed a mouth-watering selection of at least a dozen courses; the enormity was put into perspective when one realised that at one sitting, 815 passengers could be amply wined and dined.

Opulence was not just restricted to the liner; its first-class passengers paraded along the decks in their finery and utilised every social occasion as a reason to change and display their outfits. Whether time was to be indulged reading a book from the liner's library, selecting from the luncheon menu, indulging in the deck games or the gymnasium or simply taking the air on deck, each activity demanded suitable attire. Helen, Diana, and Sarah eagerly scrutinised the fashions paraded in front of them. The best, of course, was reserved for the evening when the ladies, in particular, displayed wealth in sumptuous cocktail dresses and undisputed genuinely expensive jewels. Neither Helen, Diana nor Sarah could hope to compete with the abundance of riches surrounding them but each woman rose to the challenge with the items in her possession.

The first evening on board Diana invited Helen to her stateroom to assist her with her choice of jewellery. Richard had politely left for an early cocktail in order to give his wife time to indulge herself in her preparations for dinner. The jewellery that Diana was considering were pieces that Richard had bought for her; tasteful and simple in design, they lacked the impact of her previous jewels which Mr Godwin had bestowed upon her.

'It's alright Helen, you don't need to give them such a disparaging look,' remarked Diana.

'I wasn't. I was thinking how beautiful they are.' Helen seemed to have been momentarily caught off guard and tried to reassure both her friend and herself of her envy of them.

'These are all real. I saw what Harry did to the others that night. They were all fake, rather like my relationship with Geoffrey Godwin.'

'Your relationship with Geoffrey Godwin?' Helen repeated his name in a bemused manner.
'Yes, Helen, Geoffrey Godwin. You shouldn't believe everything that you hear. I'm afraid I did lead you on somewhat.'

'You mean that you and him were not... '

'Yes Helen, I was very much a virgin when I married Richard.' A look of relief began to penetrate across Helen's face even though her friend had an aptitude for embarrassing statements.

'What about the trips to London and abroad?' Helen enquired.

'I fabricated everything.'

'Why did you do that?'

'For the glamour. Goodness knows, my mother brought me up to expect the best out of life and I wanted you to think that I was leading a truly sophisticated existence. Your life always seemed to revolve around excitement and secrets and I suppose I just wanted some of the same.'

'You know Diana, I was totally convinced that you were a woman of the world.'

'So my acting ability has not gone to waste?'

'Certainly not.'

'Well Helen, let's go and join the others. I feel like knocking the men dead tonight with our sex appeal.'

Helen quietly smiled to herself. The revelation had rejuvenated Diana with an energy that had been sadly absent for too long.

There were many beautiful women in the cabin-class restaurant. Some were true aristocratic beauties with a fine lineage which explained why the chiselled bone structure of their faces would inevitably attract the attention of exceedingly wealthy American men, whose sole ambition was to mix their new wealth with the old titles of England. Diana still retained her audacious spirit as she allowed the front split in her skirt to fall open and reveal her shapely legs. As Richard tried to manoeuvre her wheelchair along corridors and through doors men seemed only too happy to be of any assistance that they could. Her smile provided sufficient gratitude and indicated to Richard that his wife's confidence was returning.

Sarah, as always, preferred to attract the least attention from male admirers and she provided no encouragement in that quarter.

William, however, was fully aware that Helen neither encouraged nor rebuffed any advances. She was an exceedingly beautiful woman and her face, like others in the room, was dependent upon her ancestry. Every time he looked at her, he saw Helena, which made his heart stir a little. One day she would marry for love as he had done, but hopefully the match would be bound by mutual feelings.

On the third evening of their voyage William and Helen found themselves alone together as the others had succumbed to an early night. As they relaxed in a quiet corner of the observation lounge, satisfied and seemingly happy with a glass apiece in front of them, Helen was totally unprepared for her grandfather's outburst.

'The Tetlows are good people, Helen. Never, ever doubt that,' declared William.

'I do know how good they've been to me. However you have been extremely good to them. Diana and Richard were telling me that you've arranged an appointment for Diana to be seen by a specialist in New York and that you've insisted on paying for the consultations and treatment.'

'It's the very least that I can do!'

'The very least! You've done more than enough,' Helen insisted.

'But I haven't! I owe them, you and Sarah a great deal.' William suddenly leaned forward. 'There is something that I need to tell you. I've pondered long and hard over the implications of this but have decided in the end to tell you the truth.'

'What is it?' Helen found the severity of the conversation had obliterated everything around her. She stared hard at the elderly gentleman and waited for him to begin.

'I feel responsible for everything bad that has happened to you and your friends. After I lost Helena I seemed to lose the will to live. Nothing else mattered. I married Helena knowing that she was carrying another man's child. That didn't bother me because I was totally in love with her and hoped in time that she would reciprocate my feelings. Although Arabella was not strictly my child I did love her as though she was. The trouble began when she went against my wishes and decided she was going to marry into the working classes. I know now that that sounds so arrogant but I had only wanted the best for her. She refused to listen and therefore I washed my hands of her.' Tears began to appear and dribble down the faces of each party.

'You have nothing to reproach yourself for. You did all that you could have,' pleaded Helen.

'But that's where you're wrong. It's what I did later that I shouldn't have done.'

'What do you mean?' Helen tentatively enquired.

'After losing Helena I never sought female company again. I simply immersed myself in the business. That was, until many years later, when a kind housemaid at Mount Hall showed compassion and interest at such a level that I began to have feelings for her. I know it was wrong but I took advantage of her. She suddenly left and I simply forgot about her, business being more important as always! Then a few years ago, out of the blue, I received a letter from her. She hadn't been feeling very well and felt she ought to let me know that although she'd married, she'd given birth to my son. By then the boy was a man. I later heard that she had had good reason for writing as she died soon afterwards.'

'How can you be sure that this man is your son?' enquired Helen.

'I wouldn't have doubted anything that this lady told me. She was as they say as straight as a dye.'

'But nothing that you have told me has any bearing on the Tetlows.'

'That is where you are wrong Helen. It has everything to do with them, you and Sarah. The son I sired was bad through and through. Harry Ledgard was my son.'

Silence prevailed as each one contemplated the effect of these revelations. Helen found it difficult to comprehend that Annie could have been unfaithful, particularly with the obstinate father of Arabella, the man who would not accept her marriage to Robert Siddall, Annie's brother. Then she pondered over the disclosure that William Fawcett was not Arabella's father and indeed not her own true grandfather. At this moment in time she preferred not to pursue the line of enquiry as to the true lineage. Her mind whirled undoubtedly with the fact that this great stalwart of a businessman in front of her was Harry's father. Suddenly the look of shock across her face began to disappear and was replaced by an uncharacteristic smirk.

'Harry never knew that you were his father, did he?'

'Certainly not,' came the emphatic reply.

The confirmation turned the smirk into laughter which disturbed William.

'What is there that can possibly make you laugh from all of this?' William enquired.

'Don't you see, Harry spent his life hating me because he was jealous of my background. The irony of it all is that, unbeknown to him, his father was a rich and successful businessman. He stood to inherit far more than me but just did not know.'

William remained silent and sceptically doubtful of Helen's remark.

Silent and pensive, each party rose from their seats and left the observation lounge without conversing. They eventually parted with little more than a brief glance in the other's direction before retiring to their respective staterooms alone and undisturbed. Sleep did not come naturally to either one that night.

**.

'Penny for them? As the English say?'

The question momentarily startled Helen who had purposefully made her way alone to the Promenade deck before breakfast. She had been deep in thought until the unfamiliar accent interrupted her.

'Them?' repeated Helen.

'Your thoughts. I've been watching you for some time and you may appear to be looking out at the ocean, but you're clearly not seeing it. Is there a pun in there somewhere? Let me introduce myself, I'm Henry Bletchley Barrington, family originally from Baltimore but now living in Boston. Yes, it does seem as though the family has been rather too greedy where the letter 'B' is concerned. I'm just thankful that my folks didn't call me Bertie.' The well-dressed gentleman offered his hand and beamed with delight as Helen shook it.

'And your name?' Helen blushed slightly, aware of her impoliteness, to introduce herself.

'Forgive me. I'm Helen Tetlow from England.'

'I could surely have put money on it. A true British beauty!' The remark served only to deepen Helen's embarrassment; the man was without reticence and overtly familiar, traits which did not figure prominently in England. Nevertheless there was a refreshing honesty in his style which the compliment helped to deliver.

During the following two days at sea Helen found herself often in his company. The only child of a wealthy American industrialist, Henry Bletchley Barrington had capitalised upon his fortune of being born into a financially successful family and was now himself an independently wealthy Boston banker. The perpetual alliteration of the 'B' consonant had made Helen smile when this bachelor spoke of his life. Striking features and an assured but relaxed manner helped to make him congenial company. Many female heads turned as he strode along the decks, beaming with delight as Helen came into view. The smooth and polished exterior, however, did not totally conceal the workings beneath the surface. Helen caught a glimpse on a couple of occasions of a dominant and rather arrogant individual who refused to be contradicted. Surrounded by a party of men it was clear that he was used to getting his own way as he argued or rather 'discussed', in his words, national and political issues. He held total belief in himself and expected others to do the same. He later confessed that he held hopes of running for the senate and Helen instinctively knew that his powers of persuasion would be the success of electioneering. As New York began to loom upon the horizon Helen instinctively put their meeting and friendship into the transient hold of life; a chance encounter of the appropriate proverbial 'ships that pass in the night'. Hopeful travellers would exchange many farewells, whether first, second or third class, they had all encountered friendship throughout the five days at sea.

Britain's pride was indisputable as the indomitable liner sailed majestically past the Statue of Liberty into the largest port in the world, New York. This was the gateway into the New World. It seemed fitting that a city of 7 000 000 people should be allowed to host her entrance and pay homage to this almighty spectacle: two heavy weights lying side by side, each gigantic in their own respective way. New York City, constricted by its island site, had continued to expand in the only direction accorded to it: vertically. The horizon was said to be constantly changing as skyscraper followed skyscraper, each towering over its predecessor with more reinforced concrete and steel and iron girders. The Woolworth building had been the highest on earth but the Empire State building, a feat of engineering at 102 storeys and 1,248 feet high, had subsequently succeeded that. When it was announced that this wonder was 200 feet higher than the Chrysler Building, itself three times the height of St. Paul's, gasps of disbelief emulated from the passengers. Some even swooned with vertigo at the mere thought of such heights.

Helen and her family viewed the city in awe. Beckston and its troubles seemed far away and even the latest revelation was not going to spoil this wonderful experience. Before disembarking Helen glanced at William, then at Diana, before surveying the unique outline of New York. She had overheard a conversation by a fellow passenger who described the city as a 'portent', indeed a prodigy of its time. Another had described it as the gateway into a New World. To Helen, for the sake of her family, she hoped this 'portent' would be the sign of something good to come and the start of a new and untroubled life. Perhaps luck would at last be in the air.

CHAPTER EIGHTEEN

Stepping into the great city began with a plethora of sensations, all exaggeratedly tantalising to the senses. Noises, smells, and sights both delighted and confused and initiated visitors into the American way of life. Coffee and bagels, soda and vermouth, downtown cabs careering with speed, were but a few of the peculiarities of this country. New York itself throbbed with cosmopolitan energy. Jews, Italians, Russians, Germans, Irish and British settlers had all entwined a customary legacy into the heart of this city from their own particular homelands. The result was an unplanned mishmash of culinary, religious and cultural differences which gelled with complementary satisfaction. Locals, visitors and immigrants mixed accordingly with ease, on occasions albeit reservedly distrustful, but given time reliably relaxed.

The luxurious lifestyle was to continue at the Waldorf-Astoria Hotel, situated on the acclaimed Park Avenue, Manhattan. They had a reservation for a week, time in which to explore the city and allow Diana to visit the consultant.

The Art Deco landmark stood defiantly proud on its base of granite facing before soaring with monumental splendour to an upper façade clad in brick and limestone. Solid and dependable, the exterior housed a prestigious destination for its visitors. Fame preceded it as its name had been firstly synonymous with a salad, and then Cole Porter's 1934 song which contained the lyric, 'You're the Top, you're a Waldorf salad'. Notwithstanding its famous connections, the quality of its interior was sufficient to earn it the reputation of being one of the world's best hotels. Numerous corridors and lobbies ran like arteries from the heart of the building, all decorated with splendid murals and notable pieces of artwork. The central lobby itself housed a three metre high clock decorated with portraits of American Presidents and even

Queen Victoria. Its quarterly chimes, echoing those from the London's Westminster Cathedral's clock tower, never failed to make transatlantic travellers feel at home. The hotel epitomised wealth and thereby success. Despite the cost William Fawcett would clearly accept nothing less than the best for Helen and her family. Helen began to realise that this was the only way that he could atone for past mistakes. She therefore decided to put all thoughts of the past behind her. Life was for living and there was plenty of that to do in New York.

****

She had agreed to meet everyone in the central lobby in order to take in the sights and enjoy an indulgent shopping spree. The clock had caught her attention, as it always did with guests; that is, until his voice broke her reverie.

'Penny again for them?' The once unfamiliar accent was instantly recognisable.

'Hello, what are you doing here? I understood that you were returning home to Boston. Are you staying here?' Helen felt herself becoming quite flustered in her questioning.

'My intention was to return back home but I found myself with some unfinished business.'

'You mean with the banks here. Of course New York is famous for Wall Street.' Helen suddenly found herself rambling, not knowing quite what to say next.

'Money doesn't even enter into it. You can't measure love in cents and dollars or even pennies and pounds! Remember I'm a banker and I should know. I'm staying in New York because there's a certain British interest that has caught my eye which I'm going to pursue and marry!'

The man was nothing less than forthright. Helen blushed profusely and was totally speechless. There was nothing that she could say. The only worry was that he had made up his mind without giving any thought to her decision. He certainly had the makings of a prominent politician.

The consultant's prognosis was extremely favourable. All welcomed his recommendation of the use of physiotherapy rather than operative work. He suggested the name of a colleague he knew of, working in Britain, who would be able to apply physical methods such as massage, manipulation and infra-red treatment to Diana's injuries. Furthermore he saw no reason why she would not walk again. His words imbued hope and confidence in everyone. The rest of the week could now be spent in indulgent activities: sightseeing, shopping and dining. For Helen, of course, the week was to prove somewhat of a turning point in her life.

She knew that he was wealthy but she didn't know how relatively wealthy he was. Her measurement of wealth had initially been influenced by the comparison of Milldyke against Highbury in Beckston. This, however, was America: big and bold in comparison to England and everything in it seemed to be scaled accordingly. Henry's suggestion of an excursion for the two of them transpired to be a flight from New York to Boston. If that wasn't enough to impress a girl he made sure by flying the plane himself. Having his pilot's licence was, in his words, 'no big deal' and merely served to reinforce how privileged he was. It was true; he could not refute his fortunate background, but equally so he appeared to be ignorant of his good fortune.

This was the first time that Helen had flown. She marvelled with both delight and some initial trepidation as Henry gained sufficient speed to propel them into the air, leaving the ground far below them. She acclimatised herself quickly to the noise, motion and ever-diminishing views of the New York skyline, strongly denying herself thoughts of all the potential dangers. Henry, as always, was in control.

Bathed in sunshine Boston seemed pleasant enough. It possessed a charm lacking in New York but reminiscent of England. The place abounded in history. Old world charm had been deposited upon its shores by the arrival of the Mayflower in 1620 and its human cargo of English Pilgrims. They were Puritans who had fled England to escape religious persecution. Their hope of living in peace abated in 1692 as religious hysteria led, firstly, to the renewal of persecution followed by executions for alleged witchcraft. They had, however, left a legacy of English style and familiar sounding names throughout New England which could not fail to fascinate and delight. Helen, like most visitors, quickly became entranced by the charms.

'Do you like?'

'Yes, very much.' Helen's emphatic reply merely served to confirm Henry's hopes.

'Wait until you see the house.'

Pastel hues of every colour existed on the timber clad homes. Helen had heard that New England was the place to visit for its array of autumnal colour but she had not expected such visual sensations to abound on its buildings. Beckston, by comparison, with its dark stone would now appear even more dismal.

Henry's house was constructed of white stone. Built in 1905 in the Georgian Revival style it was modelled as a small-scale mansion and appeared to be totally extravagant for a bachelor, a housekeeper and a handful of servants. Helen avoided the obvious remark in case it was judged as a matrimonial indictment. Elegance from an earlier age pervaded throughout the house. The hallway was dominated by an impressive winding staircase that led the visitor's eye upwards before transfixing it upon a huge dazzling crystal chandelier, hanging magnificently in the atrial cavity. The smell of polish wafted in the air, no doubt as a result of the numerous pieces of very fine antique furniture positioned in every room.

The housekeeper warmly greeted the couple and informed them that their rooms were ready, as instructed, and that dinner would be served accordingly, later in the evening.

'What did your housekeeper mean? The rooms are ready; why do we need rooms?' Helen enquired.

'I rang through earlier and made arrangements.' In his matter of fact way Henry considered that everything was under control.

'You did what? My family are expecting me back tonight at the hotel.'

'No they're not. At the same time I took the liberty to also inform them that we would not be returning tonight.'

'You certainly did take the liberty. It would have been nice to have been asked first!'

'Well it's done and settled. Come and see the rest of the house before we go and explore Boston.' Henry continued totally unaware of Helen's feelings.

As they viewed the sights of Boston and its surrounding area Henry talked and Helen listened. He spoke of his childhood, his privileged background, his banking profession and of his overriding ambition to run for office.

'You see Helen, I have such an abiding love for my country that its my duty as an American citizen to work for the good of others and never allow history to repeat itself. Do you know that when the Depression hit us in 1928 the consequences were unbelievable? Millions lost their jobs. Businesses, works and factories closed; crops and manufactured goods could not be sold or had to be practically given away; banks failed and thousands of people were very near to starvation. Since 1933 President Roosevelt has led a mighty effort to set things right and has done all in his power to get the financial and industrial systems up and running again.' At this point Henry paused for a moment, glanced at his companion and added, 'You being a woman and an English one at that, I doubt that you can appreciate how I'm governed by such a true vocation in life. However I'm determined to succeed and be up there with the President himself. It's time you told me a little bit about your life.' Helen didn't quite know what to say. She was certain that tales of Beckston could not compete with dreams of Washington and all too soon found herself hearing about Congress, or for her understanding, Parliament and its two houses, the Senate and the House of Representatives. By the time they reached Henry's house again Helen felt as though she could have stood for the Senate herself. She welcomed time alone to freshen up for dinner.

With the bedroom door closed and locked she leaned against it and breathed a sigh of relief. The man was insufferable, chauvinistic, boring and selfish. Riches alone were insufficient inducement for marriage.

Her room had a warm and welcoming feel about it. The four-poster bed provided a homely indulgence with its boldly coloured patchwork quilt and large lacy bolsters, which doubtless would instantly induce an acute soporific feeling to the recumbent visitor. She lay down, intending to rest, but quickly found herself falling into a deep sleep.

The wind was causing the thundering waves to crash with tremendous force against the granite rocks below. This seemed to be such an inhospitable place, both on land and out at sea. The ferocity of the weather would make survival only possible if there was somewhere to shelter. In desperation she avidly scanned the wild and windswept landscape but could see nothing except a miniscule shimmering light on the far distant inland. Battling against the weather she tried hard to make her way towards it, knowing instinctively that if she could just reach the source of the light, she would be safe. At first it seemed that the more she tried the less successful she was. The light continued to twinkle like a beacon until she suddenly felt herself lifted from the ground and carried by the wind to the door of a small isolated cottage. Peering through the windows she realised that the light was coming from within; there was a warming fire in the hearth which she could not resist but she could not see anybody there. She didn't think anyone would mind her entering the cottage and warming herself by the fire. It appeared that there was only one room and it was sparsely furnished but it had the most welcoming presence that she had ever encountered. She lay down on the small bed, pulling the covers around her feeling warm and safe. The sensation was only interrupted when she heard knocking at the door. She was reluctant to leave the bed but the unmistakeable sound of his voice calling her name made her eagerly run to open it. Her feelings now were governed by a tremendous surge of happiness as well as indisputable passion. It had been many years since she had last experienced such feelings. The door, however, refused to open. Anxiously she turned and pulled the handle but still the door would not open. He began to call out her name with repeated intensity until the climax was reached. Suddenly it was at an end and she opened her eyes focussing upon the drapes of the four-poster bed. The knocking at the door continued until she unlocked and opened it. The maid apologised for disturbing her but, on Mr Bletchley Barrington's advice, had come to prepare her bath and deliver a large box. Helen opened the box and lifted out an evening gown, lingerie and matching nightdress and negligee. Everything was of the finest quality; the store had delivered to his exact specifications. Helen laid everything on the bed and then lay down at the side of them. Closing her eyes she tried unsuccessfully to return to that cottage but the moment had gone and its retrieval now eluded her.

Helen found it difficult to concentrate upon the topic of conversation. The intimate candlelit dinner setting for two amidst the splendour of crisp table linen, sparkling crystal and shining silver offset by antique furniture, was devoid of any romance in Helen's mind. As before Henry talked but this time Helen failed to listen. Only the appearance of the small, leather box placed in front of her curtailed her daydreaming and brought her rapidly to her senses.

'I would like you to do me the honour of being the next Mrs Bletchley Barrington. I doubt you'll get a better offer than that!' His smug impudence was more than she could bear.

'I wouldn't say that. Not all English men are wealthy but at least the majority are gentlemen and know how to treat a lady, which is more than I've found in America!'
Helen's remark was enough to unleash the host of demons in his anger.

'How dare you insult my family name and my fellow countrymen?' Vehemently he rose to his feet, causing his chair to fall backwards to the floor and strode towards her. He struck her across the face as Tom had done many years before and then pushed her to the floor. The sudden noise alerted a servant to peer around the door. Their enquiring manner served only to infuriate him more and he hastened their retreat with an aerial bombardment of plates and cutlery.

'It's my turn now to insult and defile you. You'll soon be able to decide whether American or English men give the most pleasure between a woman's legs.'

Frantically she tried to fight him off but his indomitable strength became overpowering. Tearing at her dress he began to shred any vestige of decency left, wilfully exposing her body to his vindictive desires.

'No Harry. Stop!' Helen found herself suddenly back in England on that previous fateful night. The more she tried to resist the more it seemed to inflame him until she realised that he was on the verge of entering her.

'No not again! For God's sake, let it be Thomas.' With all her strength spent in this final cry she found herself resigned to the inevitable and surrendered. At that very moment she felt him roll away from her. Slowly he rose to his feet and as she opened her eyes she found him staring down at her. Minutes seemed to elapse before he spoke.

'Jesus, when a woman calls out another mans name during love making that's off-putting. You called out two different names. Do you know what that makes you?' Helen found herself unable to speak.

'No! Well I'll tell you. An English whore.' She felt a sudden kick of his foot against her side. As he left the room he violently slammed the door, leaving her to gather both her thoughts and her clothing. She quickly retreated to the safety of her room, taking care to lock the door behind her before contemplating what to do next. An unexpected quiet tap at the door once again aroused her fears.

'Madam, are you alright? It's Lizzy, your maid.' The voice like the tap against the door was purposefully hushed. Opening the door she recognised the maid as the girl who had previously delivered the box and prepared her bath. This time her face wore an expression of concern.

'What has he done to you?'

'Nothing.'

'I wouldn't call that large bruise on your face 'nothing'.'

Helen allowed her into the room, taking care once more to lock the door behind her.

Staring into the dressing table mirror she saw her own face staring back with a distinct red swelling over her left cheekbone. Lizzy attended to her by applying a cold compress to her face and later to her right side, near her ribcage, which was beginning to swell and throb. The girl also allayed any doubts about leaving the house that night.

'You must stay here tonight and rest. Don't worry, you will be safe. If you want me to I will stay with you. Mr Bletchley Barrington has a violent temper which can be brought on by little things. For a time he's like someone else possessed and then he's fine again. It's said that his mother suffers from the same thing. It seems as though it runs through the family. In the morning he'll be back to normal.'

Helen found sleep elusive that night. Her cheekbone and ribcage throbbed continuously and as each injury was situated on the opposite side of her body, there was little chance of finding a comfortable position. Coupled with her physical pain her mind whirled with suppositions. After all, Henry was practically a stranger to her and an unpredictable one at that. He had in effect kidnapped her through deception, abused her and held her against her will. The question was, would he readily release her?

Lizzy's words were truly prophetic the next morning, laying claim to the fact that Henry's behaviour was obviously customary throughout the household. As he kissed Helen he appeared oblivious to her flinching but was extremely concerned about the bruise upon her face and the nature of its cause. Cradling her in his arms he accepted her version of falling against the side of the bath adding that it was time for someone to protect her. Helen had avoided telling him the truth in case it once again inflamed his temper.

'You know Helen, I'm the man for you. I will always love you and look after you and not allow any harm to come to you. Please make me happy and accept my proposal of marriage? I've wanted to ask you from the very moment we first met. Somehow I just didn't have the courage to ask, until now.'

Helen stared incredulously through the window out towards the finely manicured lawns which stretched the eye further to the equally manicured hedges surrounding them, all laid out in grid formations.

'You're speechless Helen. I shall take that as a good sign. I don't want to rush you into anything. Therefore I'm going to fly you back to New York to give you time to consider. I'm also a firm believer that absence makes the heart grow fonder and a short separation can do nothing but good.' Helen truly agreed with the last sentiment. Indeed she would have agreed with any sentiment in order to reach New York safely.

CHAPTER NINETEEN

England, in comparison, appeared small, modest and predictable against its transatlantic neighbour. The simplicity and pleasantries of English life held the promise of both romanticism and sensitiveness, so apparently lacking in the brash exterior of the larger than life American culture. Such thoughts were unkind and could not be sweepingly applied to all aspects and all citizens of the States. It was just that Helen had had a bad experience and now longed for the safety of home. Absence had indeed made the heart grow fonder as Helen found that to leave a place for any length of time made appreciation for it all the stronger. She appreciated returning home with her family and friends and she appreciated distancing herself from the unwanted attention of Henry Bletchley Barrington. It was only upon her return home that the thought struck her how similar the two names were and how synonymous they were in character. Harry and Henry. In fact Harry was the accepted diminutive form of Henry.

Helen had chosen to confide in no one regarding her experiences in Boston. She attributed the bruising upon her face to the fabricated fall against the bath, hoping that the whole scenario of that time would fade into oblivion. Conversely however, by choosing not to discuss the enforced elopement, everyone was convinced that matrimony to the wealthy banker was a certainty. They interpreted her silence as a measure of true love. William seemed to beam with pride whilst Diana and Sarah held quiet conversations, no doubt predicting the bridal fashions for the following year. No one, including Diana, asked her directly; they all just wished for the fairy tale ending.

As the ostrich proverbially buries its head in the sand, Helen refused to accept what was probable. She had agreed to contact him, regarding her answer, to avoid disclosing her own address or telephone number. As the days and weeks passed by everyone looked anxious and failed to understand Helen's relief at the distinct absence of contact. When it almost seemed likely that she would never hear from him again, that is when it began. Extravagantly presented floral bouquets and boxes of handmade chocolates arrived with regularity and, upon unwrapping, yielded written messages of love as well as the occasional piece of jewellery. Art Deco designs portrayed in brooches, necklaces, bracelets and earrings tumbled from their wrappings or twinkled tantalisingly next to hard nut clusters and fondant fancies. It was clear that he was skilled in the art of seduction and, with an exceedingly wealthy bank balance of his own, Diana could not understand her friend's reticence.

'He's crazy about you. If I weren't married, I'd snatch his hand off. Helen, you'd be a fool to let this one get away.'

'Even if I had to put up with the occasional black eye or cracked rib?' The question abruptly broke any further admonishment of envy.

'Oh, Helen why didn't you tell me? I've been so wrapped up in myself and so preoccupied with matchmaking, that common sense seems to have abandoned me. Even Richard and William made me promise not to interfere and question you, for fear of upsetting the deal... I mean the romance.'

'The deal? Am I now being traded as goods on the open market? How much have I been sold for?'

'Nothing.'

'Perhaps that's all I'm worth Diana!'

'It's not what you think. Oh how I wish I could cut my tongue out! I used to be the level-headed one, the one who always came up with the plans but lately all I can think about is getting out of this wheelchair. Reason seems to have flown out of the window!'

As their eyes met each felt compelled to smile, grin and emit a spontaneous giggle.

'You know Diana, I think you're right. The tables have turned somewhat and I suppose I'm going to have to be the one to be the impresario. That is, I would if I knew all the facts. Now like the old Diana you need to bare everything to this interested audience. I need you to tell me all that you know.'

The revelations provided a relief to Diana who had disliked the thought of not confiding in Helen, but to her friend they were a source of concern.

Richard Tetlow had been persuasively encouraged to turn his business into a much larger concern and thereby utilise the potential at his disposal. A cautious person by nature and never one to take a risk, certainly not a financial one, Richard had obviously been highly inspired by the words of Henry Bletchley Barrington. Expansion in order to capitalise would demand new machines, an increase in workforce and an increased stock of new fabrics, all of which necessitated a healthy injection of disposable cash. As a banker and the son of an industrialist Henry knew all too well the stories of firms with long and honourable pedigrees who defied progress and refused to invest for their future. They were the ones who closed their doors for the final time. Coupled with this was the emphasis on making garments for the ever-fickle fashion conscious. Even *The Times* had noted in 1913 that women had become 'quick-change artists'. As Henry pointed out, in the future only the strongest would survive and the bigger and stronger the firm was, the more chance there was for its survival and its ability to satisfy consumer demands. It had happened in America and it would surely follow suit in England. To be forewarned was to be forearmed and for once Richard had listened and decided to act upon the advice of a stranger.

The offer had at the outset seemed a benignant one, on the part of Henry. There were few bankers who would arrange a sizeable loan and expect neither interest nor specified security in return. Richard needed the additional funds for his entrepreneurial future as well as meeting the regular, but necessary, physiotherapist's fees for Diana. William Fawcett's generosity had known no bounds and Richard could not and would not ask the man for more. It appeared that there had been an unspoken agreement between the two men suggesting that Henry would, after all, profit from this deal. The assumption was that favours for family were different to favours for friends or acquaintances.

Helen felt completely cornered in this ménage à trois business deal. She was angry that she had been put into this position, through no fault of her own, and yet the very people who she loved the most stood to be ruined by her decision. Confiding in Diana she then made her friend promise that Richard would hear nothing of their conversation; the poor man had had enough problems lately.

****

William studied the young face in front of him, staring back at him with conviction.

'50 000 pounds is a large sum of money Helen and I'm not certain that I could raise that amount. I may look wealthy but the majority of my assets are in stone.'

'I see. Well, thank you. I'll not detain you any longer Mr Fawcett.'

'Mr Fawcett! How can you be so distant Helen?'

'It was to have been a business proposition. I am certainly not asking for charity. However it was totally wrong for me to come here, I see that now. We're not even related and I cannot expect anything from you.' The old man suddenly realised the scale of effect that adversity had had on this young soul.

'Please sit down Helen. We have some unfinished business.'

'I don't think that there is anything else to say.'

'That is where you are wrong. I know that you're angry with me and rightly so. What troubles me the most Helen is since that night when I confided in you there has been no reference made to the revelations on your part. I've waited for some form of response, anger or pity I could tolerate, but the indifference has been the bitterest pill to swallow.'

'There is nothing for me to say. What is done is done. My life has always had so many twists and turns to it that I've come to accept the unexpected. To be told that my grandfather is not my grandfather and to learn that Annie had given birth to your son, instead of her own husband's, however despicable he was, is all part of life's rich tapestry some would say. Fate I can accept but the thought of being the architect of my own destiny is what disturbs me.'

William studied the young face once more and realised how indebted he was to her. His intuition, however, made him realise that there was something deeper troubling her.

'Helen, please don't hide behind a façade. What is it that you're not telling me?'

'The truth! The whole truth.'

Surprisingly he was a good listener, a quality that inspired Helen to unburden herself of all the anxieties which had tormented her through the years. She described that fateful night when Harry had raped her and how she had used the ensuing pregnancy to deceive and dupe Denis Tetlow into marriage. Her actions still disgusted her morality and sense of justice. As a result of marrying into the Tetlow family her life had dramatically altered and the lives of those around her had also irretrievably changed. Her association with Harry had resulted in Edward Tetlow's death, Diana's paralysis and Sarah's attempted suicide. To reject Henry Bletchley Barrington's marriage proposal appeared little short of churlish, particularly as Helen knew that a refusal would no doubt instigate the demand of the complete loan payment, and Tetlows, as a result, would be ruined. Marriage into such affluence, of course, would come at a price and Helen, although feeling decidedly cowardly, could not face life with a violent schizophrenic.

The full disclosure was little short of a confession and similarly provided spiritual cleansing for Helen's soul. William as the absolutist quickly tried to assure Helen that the blame could no longer be attributed at her door. Tears ran down the elderly stalwart's face as he embraced her and held her close to his breast.

'Helen, you must not marry that man. Do you remember that I once talked to you about love? Well it's time that you felt intense love in your life. Never ever contemplate marrying for money as you will have a poor life. I will find the money for you, rest assured of that.'

'But from where? It is a very large sum.'

'Where there is a will Helen, they do say there is a way. Leave the monetary side to me. I will not let you down.' Once more the old man held her tightly to his breast and felt the tears run down his cheeks. At that moment he experienced such an intensity of love for the young woman in his arms and as he gazed into her face he momentarily saw Helena smiling back at him. He blinked and Helen's features reappeared.

'You'd better leave now Helen. Remember not to say anything to the Tetlow family or indeed to anyone else. I will be in contact with you soon.'

She had stirred such feelings in him which he had thought were long ago extinguished. Helena had always had that power over him, power which could persuade a man to do anything for a woman. Later that evening he reflected upon the events of the afternoon and knew instinctively what his next move must be. He was certain that it was Helena who had visited him for those brief moments and that was a strong enough omen for him to know that his earthly life was almost at an end. He had, over the years, heard countless stories from elderly weavers who talked of deceased loved ones visiting the deathbeds of their relatives, whilst assuming the identity of the living. William was not confined to his deathbed yet, but he was aware that the stroke had weakened him and no doubt was a catalyst in the life cycle. Life was for living and for the young and he knew what he had to do. He picked up the phone and made the call.

The recipient of his call remained customarily cold.

'Well?'

'I need a favour.'

'A favour?'

'Yes, I would not ask if it was not necessary.' William began to relate the full nature of the conversation he had had with Helen.

A pause occurred whilst the listener decided upon the ensuing course of action.

'Very well Fawcett. You can have the money but in return you relinquish your mill.' The voice remained cold and devoid of emotion.

'My mill? That was built up by my father and his father before him. What use would it be to you?'

'It all depends on how much you value the girl. I'm just testing whether you'd still do anything for love. You certainly once did.'

'I would still do anything for her, as you well know.'

'And her granddaughter?'

'Likewise.'

'Then I think we have a deal. Contact your solicitor and have the necessary paper work conveyed to me. You know the address.'

Suddenly the line went dead and William fully accepted the consequence of past actions which had been set in motion almost half a century earlier.

CHAPTER TWENTY

A rnie Barraclough possessed sufficient charm, talent and flair to be self-employed. He was widely recognised as a highly professional photographer who had worked for many years at the Beckston Gazette. His shots had included local interest as well as royal visits. However, for Arnie, only one photograph remained of special interest to him: the one of Helen wearing that tantalizingly, seductive black lace and chiffon dress at the fashion show. Arnie, along with a handful of other local pressmen, had captured the moment for posterity but only Arnie recognised the potential at his fingertips. He instantly recognised the impact that a beautiful face and figure would have upon the public and, accordingly, upon his own career. It was at this point that he had decided that one day he would put into practice his long cherished dream. He made an appointment to see her and realised that the time had finally dawned as he was shown into her office.

'How can I help you Mr Barraclough?' Helen's voice was clear and businesslike. As she shook his hand she felt that his face was vaguely familiar.

'Please, its Arnold or Arnie. I have a proposition, a business proposition, which I'd like to put to you.' Helen was both intrigued and rather amused. She smiled with relief for this at least was not a marriage proposal.

'What I have to say I feel could be of mutual benefit. For many years I've worked as a photographer for the Beckston Gazette. I love my work but I've long held a dream of branching into freelance photography. To do that I would need to establish myself with unique and high quality work. I need a subject and location to do this, both of which have to be stunning. My work also needs to appeal to a certain niche or market for it to be recognised and gain patronage. What better area than the fashion industry? What better model than you, wearing and therefore advertising your own collections from the firm?'

The idea was certainly avant-garde and also appealed to Diana and Sarah. The more it was thrashed out, the more appealing it became. Sarah's new collection, which she had been working on since her return from America, had a nautical feel about it. This in part was due to two reasons: the experience of having sailed aboard the Queen Mary and in celebration of the forthcoming king's coronation. A collection inspired by the sea would provide a patriotic feel and could be produced and unveiled for the coronation in 1937. The forthcoming year would promise to be historically memorable with the inauguration of a new monarch and with that in mind Helen suggested the release of a fashion calendar. Against a competitive market, twelve different shots and a cover picture would introduce and advertise a new collection across a wide audience.

Everyone was happy. William Fawcett had been true to his word and had managed to produce the 50 000 pounds. Helen now knew that they would no longer be reliant upon the Boston banker and felt the printing costs would eventually transpire into financial gains by increased orders. Arnie had saved up sufficient holiday leave to be away from the Beckston Gazette and had already pin pointed the exact location for the stunning backdrops: the Cornish Riviera. The choice of location was based primarily upon reputation. Arnie had never visited the region but had witnessed sufficient accounts and gazed with admiration at colleagues' photographs to know that this county had ample supplies of rocky coves, granite cliffs and moor land to create atmosphere. If further dramatic artistry were needed to compound the setting the great Atlantic rollers would offer an insurmountable surge of indisputable power in nature's wild showcase. Everyone agreed that Cornwall would provide the perfect setting for a nautical collection.

The ensuing months witnessed the necessary designing, making and final preparations. September was designated as the month for the fashion shoot, a quieter time when the weather was still as reliable as English weather can ever be. It was agreed that the shots would be taken over a period of a fortnight and Arnie's flattery persuaded Diana that she should also act as a model. His compliments to Sarah, however, could not induce the same effect. Nevertheless a bond of friendship began to form between the designer and the photographer. They both had plenty in common, naturally artistic and both seemed to conform to a slightly bohemian outlook. Arnie, like Sarah, was a perfectionist in his work but his outward appearance was little short of dishevelled. It seemed that work took over to the detriment of personal grooming. His suit had been well-worn to such an extent that it sagged with age whilst a neglected haircut, moustache and beard presented a Neolithic look. None of this was important as everyone knew that it was the person inside that mattered, no one more so than Helen.

As September drew near it was agreed that Arnie would drive down to Cornwall ahead of everyone and seek out the best locations. His pride and joy was his Model Y Ford. Although rather slow, and with the tendency of its suspension to wander from side to side on the road, the car provided Arnie with freedom. Helen and Diana felt it would be safer to fly down to the West Country, particularly in view of the necessary luggage. However it was not entirely a surprise when Sarah announced that Arnie had asked her to accompany him on the journey down through the country in order to check out locations.

A wink and a nod from Diana would have been sufficient but the old Diana could not resist teasing.

'What will you exactly be checking out Sarah – single or double beds? I'm sure that a fellow with his artistic traits will have plenty of lead in his pencil!' Even by Diana's standards the remarks appeared risqué. The momentary gasps and exclamations of 'Diana!' merely precipitated girlish giggles in all three women. The comments had served a purpose, they were not there to shock but to signify that Diana's confidence and spirits had returned. Everyone knew that the forthcoming trip was one to look forward to.

However, before the journey could begin for Helen, she decided upon finally suppressing any misguided hopes of a transatlantic marriage. She returned every piece of jewellery and penned the letter that would leave Henry in no doubt of her refusal to marry him. The matter was now resolved, especially as Richard had also contacted him with regard to no longer requiring a loan. Any connection with Henry Bletchley Barrington was totally severed. Relief and hope had begun to finally filter through.

****

The look upon Sarah's face was of little surprise to either Helen or Diana when they were collected from the Cornish airfield. It was clear that a week in Arnie's company had produced a bloom in her face that could only have developed from genuine affection. He had always seemed an affable character but the mutual affection was also recognisable in his face and behaviour. Fleeting eye contact and contented smiles expressed the start of something more than a working relationship. Helen and Diana accepted that they would be gooseberries but once the shoot was over they could give the amorous couple privacy of their own company.

The hotel at Mullion Cove was like many Cornish hotels, substantially built, no doubt to withstand the extremes of weather witnessed in this region. Positioned on the cliff edge it commanded a visual vantage point of the jagged rocks and unforgiving sea below whilst inside the comfort of the guests was paramount. Fresh flowers and up-to-date periodicals adorned the lounges whilst the dining room was famed for serving local produce and hosting a first class wine cellar.

Arnie and Sarah had already spent many hours travelling around the coastal villages that so often seemed to precariously cling to the rocky inlets, scalloped by the sea. They excitedly showed Helen and Diana numerous harbours, villages and coves, dotted around England's westernmost tip, before traversing inland; this, in contrast, proved disappointing as the land had been encroached upon by manmade structures, the relics of tin mines. The true charm of Cornwall definitely rested around the coast. It was the unpredictability of the sea that had provided and embellished the legacy of legends.

Reality and superstition readily blended into belief in such surreal surroundings. The strange sounding place names seemed to confer genuineness whilst the stories of lost lands, such as Lyonesse, seemed not so much to be just an Arthurian legend but a statement of fact. If evidence was required. as the locals pointed out, then evidence was there. The large granite block, Table Maen at Sennen, was proof of King Arthur's existence; this was where he had feasted with seven Cornish kings to celebrate victory over the Danes.

There were sufficient boulders around Cornwall to believe that Arthur had existed. Any boulders connected with this king were often believed to possess supernatural powers. The weather had fashioned many over the centuries so that they now assumed unusual outlines, resembling human beings, animals and familiar shapes. Those with holes were esteemed to possess special powers whereby a child could be made strong again by passing it through the hole against the direction of the sun. It would only be effective if the ritual was repeated nine times. Such potency against misfortune was needed, especially in a land where the devil was known to travel at alarming speeds, often reputedly leaping over obstacles, such as ravines. It was little wonder that the population had erected round cottages and topped them with crosses. These peculiar whitewashed structures had been built to prevent the devil from hiding in dark corners.

Satan, however, was not the only one who had been feared in this land. Cornish smugglers had plundered ships for 200 years, as ill-gotten gain provided a lucrative trade. Cunningly concealed coves leading into caves, which in the main were both secluded and primarily inaccessible, had long been known as smugglers' store-places. Honeycombs of passages ensured that contraband could be concealed from the authorities. So lucrative was the business that often magistrates themselves had been in league with the smugglers. Who could blame them when as much as sixty gallons of French Brandy could be brought ashore in a year, in just one Cornish location? Houses, inns and even churches had all surreptitiously participated in the provision of an honest cover for a dishonest trade.

Tales and legends from the past added magic to this land. No one questioned the authenticity of them, it was enough just to be there, to allow the charms to metaphorically wash over you. Surprising results had already occurred. Arnie and Sarah seemed very much in love and Diana was at last beginning to manage to walk with only the assistance of sticks. Obviously the expense of a physiotherapist was at last beginning to prove advantageous, but her recovery appeared to excel in the Cornish climate. Sharing a room with Diana, Helen was the first person to understand why.

'Richard doesn't even know yet! Oh Helen I do wish he were here. It's not right for me to tell him over the telephone that he's going to be a father again.' Helen nodded in agreement. Such news needed to be shared with an intimate one in an intimate way.

Diana continued, 'We had always thought that it would be good for Jack to have a brother or sister but with the accident somehow we had begun to doubt whether that would ever be possible.' The word 'accident' blanketed that horrendous turn of events with a euphemistic memory.

'Diana, I am so pleased for you both. God knows that you've had your troubles and now it's time for some happiness.' Diana reached out and grasped Helen's hand. For once her persona seemed grave and intent.

'Do you know what would make me really happy Helen? To see you in a similar position. There is only one man that could make that happen. Why don't you find Thomas?'

'Thomas?'

'Yes, Thomas. I know that you've always loved him. I think that I've always known that. You need to find him.'

'How and where? He left Beckston many years ago because of me. He doesn't know the truth, thanks to Harry. He probably hates me.

And I expect by now that he's married and has a family of his own. Besides which I would not have the first idea of where to look and even if I did find him, I would not have the first idea of what to say to him.'

'How would you feel if he's still single and in love with you? Under those circumstances wouldn't it be a crime not to look for him?'

'The chances of that are very remote.'

'Helen, you only have one life. This is not a rehearsal and…' Helen suddenly began to laugh.

'Diana, I never had you down as a philosopher.'

'Whatever it takes Helen, I'll do whatever it takes to make you see reason, even if that means hiring a private investigator.'

That night Helen had a very strange dream. She found herself inside a small cottage. Indeed there was a familiarity about it as she sensed that she had been there before. The room appeared small and dark and as she peered around the dim interior she suddenly became aware of a presence in the room. The darkness prevented her from discerning her mystery companion except that the build and outline led her to believe that it was a man. The only glow in the room came from the dying embers of the fire. As she walked towards the fireplace and the figure huddled in a large chair at its side, incessant knocking at the door commanded her attention. Now curiosity began to pull her in contrasting directions. The decision was made for her as she instantly recognised the sound of Thomas's voice calling out her name from the other side of the door. Once again, as in the previous dream, she experienced feelings governed by happiness and inexpressible waves of passion. Once again, as in the previous dream, the door refused to open. He repeatedly called out her name with an ever-increasing intensity which made her frantically claw at the door. In desperation she cried out to her mystery companion to help her but her pleas had no effect. Finally she tried to run across to the stranger and implore him to help her, but she found it impossible to reach him. As she moved it appeared that the fireplace and its surroundings also moved, making them unattainable. She tried to propel herself with force and outstretched her arms and hands as far as she could but still remained inert and unable to advance across the room. Weakened and weary she found herself withdrawing from this unattainable pursuit at which time the figure slowly began to rise to its feet. The movement in such a still and seemingly inanimate body produced a premonition of fear in Helen. She stared in disbelief at the faceless shape in front of her, realising that it was little more than a blackened shadow. There was no one else in the room or indeed adequate light to cast such a presence. Hearing Thomas's voice calling out to her she cried out for help.

The face looking tenderly at her was warm, welcoming and very familiar.

'Helen, everything's all right. You've obviously had a bad dream.' Diana embraced her, drawing her close to her for reassurance. Like a small child Helen clung to the warm and tangible body surrounding her, thankful that the disturbing scenario had been but an unpleasant dream.

Describing the dream to Diana made it appear less sinister but solitary thoughts presented a different interpretation. Helen had now experienced this nightmare twice. Each time there had been the cottage and the prevention of admitting Thomas into the cottage. She was certain that her subconscious state was trying to impart a message. The idea was not as crazy as it might appear; the Austrian psychologist Sigmund Freud had even presented theories regarding the unconscious mind and sexual repression and was indeed famous for his methods of psychoanalysis. Dreams were one way in which the mind was unconfined and unshackled by convention or by reason. The overriding questions were: why was she prevented from being with Thomas? Events in her life had prevented them being together. What was the significance of the shadowy figure? There had been a malevolent feeling imparted by its presence. Unable to distinguish its true identity Helen began to question whether her mind was alerting her to the possibility of yet further evil in her life. Her thoughts returned to her schooldays and a famous novel that she had once read by Charles Dickens. She recalled the character of Ebenezer Scrooge in *A Christmas Carol*, remembering his fear of being visited by the three spirits. Of those the one he feared the most was unquestionably the Ghost of Christmas Yet to Come. Helen likened her fear to these three spirits. Harry was now the Ghost of Christmas Past, dead and unable to affect her, Henry Bletchley Barrington was hopefully now out of her life but for the time being could be assigned to the title of the Ghost of Christmas Present. The Ghost of Christmas Yet to Come was an unknown quantity and in the novel had been silent and shrouded. Like Scrooge, Helen feared the last of the trio the most. She understood that a force even greater than fate had governed her life. At that moment she realised that the Ghost of Christmas Yet to Come resided very much in the past. Unlike Scrooge, however, she did not feel that her actions were solely responsible for its raison d'être.

CHAPTER TWENTY-ONE

It had long been accepted that Parisian design influenced and directed the fashion talent of its competitors; the latter undeniably understated in both Britain and America. Paris had a self-imposed prestige which had managed to eclipse the brilliance of rising stars outside the French capital. Sarah Nussey's name may not have been internationally synonymous with the couturier Elsa Schiaparelli or the designs of Chanel, Vionnet and Paquin, but the success of the 1937 Tetlow collection was paramount to the survival of the firm. Sarah was now enjoying some well-earned romance but she had had to use an enormous supply of midnight oil to attain it.

The plentiful supply of backdrops and improvised props for the shoot made the final choice of location extremely difficult. An abundance of rocks, coves and cliff tops vied with the picturesque ports, home to both fishermen and artists. Small boats bobbed in rhythm against the faint breezes at the waterfronts whilst palm trees, camellias, rhododendrons and hydrangeas all flourished in a climate which could alter dramatically overnight. The charm of Cornwall definitely lay in its transient beauty.

Against a panorama of visual delight Arnie positioned his models to maximum effect. Helen and Diana eagerly complied with his requests of arrangement: seated, standing, leaning or relaxing, they worked hard and always with a smile. Diana was now able to stand for a short time without relying upon support from sticks and was keen to be photographed in this way. Beautiful models and beautiful scenery guaranteed the venture would be a success, but if there had been any doubt Sarah's collection dispelled any misgivings. She had worked tirelessly to produce a range of couture that would happily have graced any Parisian catwalk. A white linen trouser suit, edged with a blue silk binding and further complemented with a matching blue blouse and waist sash would no doubt appeal to the modern free-spirited woman. Wide trousers, enhanced by wide turn-ups, instantly provided that nautical feel that Sarah had been so inspired by. The elongated suit emphasised Helen's gracefully slim figure which she further maximised to effect by placing a straw beret jauntily at an angle on her head. Diana meanwhile utilised her natural assets when she appeared in a figure hugging evening dress that allowed her to move only by means of a very long side slit. She knew precisely how to position herself towards the camera, supporting herself against a large boulder, dramatically perched on the cliff top, presenting both a coy yet salacious look at the same time. Displaying a long and shapely leg she defiantly subjected any future gazer to look firstly at the body and then at the garment. No one objected as they had waited long enough to witness the return of their old friend. Helen was also well aware that the figure hugging dresses would shortly be out of bounds for her friend.

Day and eveningwear, coats and leisurewear were modelled and photographed against a varied selection of locations. Frequently both models would appear in one shot so as to maximise the number of garments photographed for the calendar. Shot after shot was taken so that the best ones could be selected for printing. Finally they had achieved what they had set out to do as well as a little more.

The final afternoon Helen and Diana enjoyed a well-earned rest before packing and changing for their last dinner at the hotel. Arnie and Sarah had been noticeably absent throughout the day but understandably they needed time alone. When they did appear both seemed flustered, rather nervous, but exceedingly happy. Arnie had used the dramatic scenery at Land's End to good effect. No woman could forget her proposal of marriage as her suitor, in the time honoured tradition, fell onto one knee, offering himself and all his worldly goods with only the Atlantic Ocean 250 feet below them. Sarah had needed no convincing; Arnie was definitely in love with her. Harry and Arnie were totally dissimilar in every way and both Helen and Diana were extremely pleased by the news. An impending marriage would require planning and all three women avidly discussed fashions for 1937 until they realised that it was incorrect for the intended groom to be party to such discussions. The trio giggled whilst Arnie looked uncomfortably around him. He realised that he was not just marrying Sarah but her way of life as well. He understood the importance of such friendship and accepted that it was more than just business. His experience of friendship in the past had made him extremely wary and for this reason alone he recognised the importance of true and loyal friends.

'Sarah and I haven't yet discussed wedding plans. Personally I'd like it to be as soon as possible and as informal as possible,' Arnie assured the assembled party. Sarah threw a warm smile back to him and nodded in agreement.

'I agree. I've never been one for pomp and circumstance, always preferring to be in the background. I certainly don't welcome the limelight. As you all know I've tasted marriage once and don't see the point of getting carried away with a big do. A small, select gathering at a register office would mean more to us than a large church wedding. We'd like our true friends to witness the love between us on our special day.' Sarah's words were heartfelt and truly poignant. Helen and Diana were acutely aware of the perfect match standing in front of them. A civil ceremony would work just as well in binding these two soul mates together. Nothing else was required.

'Besides which, we don't wish to be responsible for taking the limelight off the royal couple,' Arnie announced in an uncharacteristic joking manner.

'The royal couple?' came the reply in unison.

'Yes, Edward and Wallis Simpson, the divorcee from Baltimore. Not only that, but shortly to be twice divorced! Quite a coup d'état for the old establishment to have to face.'

Helen began to witness Arnie in a new light. He seemed to relish imparting news which no one else knew. Through his connections with the newspaper business he had built up a small network of colleagues, likewise working for the press, such as photographers and journalists. Some of these had connections themselves with the American press who were avidly enjoying reporting details about the royal love affair. King Edward VIII had chartered a yacht, the Nahlin, during August thereby breaking with the expected tradition of grouse shooting. He had cruised around the Adriatic coast with some close friends, in particular a Mrs Wallis Warfield Simpson, a married American woman, and as the American press knew only too well, unlike the restrained and loyal British press, the couple were in love. It was being predicted that once Mrs Simpson obtained a divorce and became free she would marry Edward and become Queen Consort and Empress of India. The next few months would certainly see the Constitution of the British Empire and of the British Monarchy tested to its limit. During dinner that night, as everyone eagerly discussed the news of the two impending marriages, Helen reflected upon her own thoughts. Wallis Simpson was not the only person to come from Baltimore.

Helen and Diana left both the Cornish charms and the courting couple behind the following morning as they returned to Beckston. Each couple returned respectively as they had arrived, by either aeroplane or car. For Arnie and Sarah the meanderings of the long journey would only serve as a preliminary honeymoon whilst, at least for Diana, the shortest time for travel arrangements was of paramount importance. Richard met them and throwing his arms tightly around Diana, suddenly beamed with delight. Allowing the couple some space Helen had stood some distance away and understood from his reaction that he now knew of Diana's news. Conversely, his reaction to Helen was quite different. His facial expression was charged with distress as he protectively embraced her.

'What's wrong, Richard?' Helen asked, bracing herself for the unknown.

'I'm sorry Helen. I was not going to tell you this until we reached home. I'm afraid that your grandfather has suffered another stroke. He's very weak and is asking to see you.' Helen made no reply. Her silence conveyed her emotion. The word 'grandfather' may not have been a true description but this thought never even entered Helen's mind now. He was her only link with the past and she had to see him.

Absurd thoughts often prevail at stressful times; whether it is the mind's way of dealing with the inevitable remains open to debate. As Helen entered William's bedroom, a room she had never seen before, she experienced agitation, grief and folly. William Fawcett was heavily propped up with an abundance of pillows in a full-tester bed with heavy drapes. Momentarily she recollected Diana's mother describing this room, using second-hand accounts. She even recalled the joke that the bed was so large that he could fit all of his workers into it. That had been at a time when she had never met this man, a time when Diana and herself had improvised to see Mount Hall. She blinked and the reality crushingly hit her. He was weak and needed her now more than ever.

A mumbled word fell from his lips as Helen approached the bed. She realised that he was trying unsuccessfully to say her name. As before, the paralysis had affected the right side of his body thereby necessitating a total reliance upon the left side. The gesture of a smile turned shockingly into a fixed grimace as the right side of his face refused to cooperate. Helen looked into his eyes and witnessed his thoughts: fear and frustration were clearly evident.

'It's all right. I'm here now. You don't need to try and convey anything to me. Just rest and get strong again.' Helen spoke clearly and calmly. His left hand began to grip her arm tensely.

'I promise I won't leave you. If it's fine by you I'm going to come and stay with you until you're well again. Tetlows can manage without me. That's what Richard said to me anyway.' The tense grip relaxed and relief began to filter across his face. She remained at his bedside until slumber intervened and he fell asleep.

The doctor's words served only to confuse and disturb. A long-term prognosis of a stroke or apoplexy, dependent upon the haemorrhage or embolism in the brain, was difficult to ascertain, particularly with a patient of such advancing years. Helen persisted with her questions to try and elicit some form of hope, however small that may be, but medical rhetoric truly did not exist to cushion the anxieties of loved ones. Only time would tell.

As the weeks passed William began to show definite signs of recovery. Helen provided fulltime care. She fed and bathed him, read to him and repeatedly encouraged him to tackle the most mundane of tasks. Any technique would be employed if it could be effective; she persuaded, cajoled, harried and even bullied him into recovering. She worked tirelessly with him, gesticulating and accentuating the pronunciation of repeated vowels and consonants, until they formed recognisable words. She pushed him around his grounds in a wheelchair before encouraging him to walk again, albeit a shambling gait, with just the assistance of her and a walking stick. More than anything she gave him back both dignity and self belief. The doctor described the transformation uncharacteristically as a miracle.

William Fawcett would never be the man he once was, but at least he was living and experiencing a modicum of the quality of life. Although Helen was very grateful for this she also regrettably admitted to herself that, in order for this to continue, she would have to remain living at Mount Hall. She missed her family and friends at Horton House but conceded that his needs were greater than hers. Helen was reluctant to leave her grandfather, even for short periods of time, and regularly turned down invitations. Finally Diana and Richard issued a dinner invitation that it would have been churlish to refuse; Arnie and Sarah had agreed upon the date of their forthcoming wedding and the evening would be spent discussing their plans.

'We've both decided that we'd like to be married before Christmas and before the year is out. The registry office is booked for December 3rd and we just want Richard, Diana and yourself there to be our witnesses.' There was no ulterior motive for bringing the date forward other than two people who loved one another wanting to be together. Sarah as always was honest and businesslike in her approach to matrimony.

Celestial influences did indeed govern the affairs of the heart in December 1936. The day on which Sarah and Arnie exchanged their vows in a civil ceremony also saw the London newspapers revealing the constitutional crisis; a King of England was shortly going to resign the crown in favour of love. Poor Queen Mary, an elderly matriarch, she had survived widowhood in the previous year, witnessed the smoking ruins of the Crystal Palace which had burnt down within the last week and now faced the uncertainty of the royal lineage. These were indeed uncertain times but a wedding was always a time for a celebration, at least when it did not jeopardise constitutional law.

The small party returned to Horton House for the reception. Arnie's father and Sarah's parents had attended the wedding and likewise joined the party for the wedding breakfast. There was nothing unusual or remarkable except for Arnie's appearance, which had been truly transformed, a point not totally rare upon a man's wedding day. However, for the first time he looked groomed. His hair had been drastically cut and he was completely clean-shaven. Helen now knew why he had appeared familiar to her as she recalled the small boy who had always complied with his friend's wishes. Arnold had been the downtrodden friend of Harry.

The realisation caused Helen to quietly reminisce. She retreated to Richard's study in order to find solace and probably would have remained there longer if she had not been disturbed.

'There you are Helen. We were just wondering if the effects of the champagne had become too much for you.' As Helen gazed at the newly transformed Arnie she too began to wonder if the drink was beginning to take a hold.

'No, I'm fine. Thank you. You really should go back to Sarah and your guests.'

'You're one of our guests too and one who we really want to share our celebration with.' Arnie was totally unprepared for Helen's next remark.

'Arnie, or should I call you Arnold? I just wish you had been straight with me. Why the pretence?' Arnie began to look decidedly uncomfortable and cast his eyes away from Helen's stare. Silence prevailed for a short time.

'I should have known, the beard and the hair unwittingly were my camouflage. I didn't grow them on purpose; it's just the way I am. When I first saw you at that fashion show I recognised you instantly. You were always a beauty Helen. That was another reason for Harry to hate you. To him you had everything. When I approached you with my business proposition I didn't think a connection to Harry would help my chances. You didn't appear to recognise me therefore I decided not to refer to the past.'

'And Sarah? Does she know that she has just married the best friend of her late husband?'

'No, she does not and I would like it to remain that way. I don't want to cause Sarah any further heartache over him. Oh, and just to put the record straight, he and I were not best friends. He may have bossed me about when we were children but as I grew up I decided enough was enough. Only Thomas had enough sense to get as far away as possible from him.'

The unexpected reference to Thomas completely stunned her.

'Thomas? What do you mean, 'as far away as possible'?'

'As you know, Cornwall is just about as far as you can go. Old Tom Ledgard showed me the postcard he'd sent. Even said I could keep it as it was of no interest to him. To be honest with you, it was that postcard that made me crave to visit Cornwall. Never before had I seen such rugged beauty. Somehow inside I just knew that it would be the perfect place for a photo shoot. I wasn't wrong was I?'

'No, certainly not! Arnie, do you still have the postcard?'

'That was my inspiration! I wouldn't throw that away. Would you like to see it?' Helen smiled and nodded eagerly.

Arnie and Sarah had decided to delay their honeymoon until the spring. Their reasons were manifold: the launch of the calendar, the final preparations for the 1937 fashion collection and their choice of honeymoon location, which came as no surprise as being a quiet hotel in Cornwall. The latter determined that an Easter honeymoon would be preferable to a Christmas one on the wild windswept Cornish cliffs. Besides which, Christmas was a time to spend with family and friends. Helen therefore waited anxiously, hopeful that Arnie would find that postcard. In her own mind she felt that it would be her best seasonal present.

A week had passed and Helen, still caring for William had heard nothing from the newly married couple. She began to chastise herself for she knew that they were both heavily involved with work whilst the days for her were long and at times insignificant. The long wait felt like the lull before the storm and Helen's thoughts constantly returned to memories of Thomas. She longed for change but like the rest of the nation was unprepared for it when it came.

The invitation to the small dinner party had been given to Arnie, Sarah, Richard and Diana a week previously. William, like Helen, wished to toast the happy couple and extend their hospitality, little knowing that the occasion would be governed by unprecedented news. December 11th 1936 would become one of those occasions in the future when you would always remember your exact location and what you were doing. Years would pass but it would still be possible to pinpoint the situation. They all knew that as they listened to his words:

'I have found it impossible to carry the heavy burden of responsibility and to discharge my duties as King as I would wish to do without the help and support of the woman I love.'

King Edward VIII's radiobroadcast to the nation brought his 325-day reign publicly to an end; he had signed the Instrument of

Abdication on the previous day. Reverting to the status of a Prince he boarded the Fury, a Royal Navy destroyer, in Portsmouth and prepared for a life of exile in France with the woman he loved. His resolve to marry her had remained steadfast. The prime minister, Stanley Baldwin, had finally told him to choose between the throne and Mrs Simpson. To some he would be seen as a traitor whilst to others just a romantic.

Everyone remained silent in the room, no doubt trying to comprehend the severity of the situation. William suddenly fumbled for his stick and rose to his feet. His hand and speech were clumsy but his gesture was clear.

'God save the King! To King George.' Everyone rose to their feet and toasted the future monarch.

'To Arnie and Sarah!' William once more led the toast and everyone chinked their glasses before drinking to the couple's happiness.

The events of that fateful day admittedly had put everything else into perspective. A tone of quiet harmony pervaded for the remaining part of the evening. As the guests expressed their gratitude and said their farewells Helen accompanied them into the entrance hall where a maid graciously assisted them with their coats. They were already getting into the car when Arnie turned swiftly and hastily returned to the front entrance where Helen was standing. He reached into his pocket and motioned to her to take the item from him.

'I almost forgot to give you this. Keep it as a souvenir.'

Before Helen could say anything Arnie had run back to the car, leaving her to wave goodbye. The postcard was a black and white picture of Land's End with jagged rocks battling their way through the waves and surf. The scene was harsh and unrelenting but familiar to Helen who instantly recognised the wild Cornish beauty set against the Atlantic coast. On the reverse side she fingered the writing, following the flow of the writer's pen. The message to his father was insignificant;

a couple of lines informing him that he was safe and happy but the final words were the ones which Helen continued to repeat:

'Give my love to Helen.'

Unable to sleep that night Helen knew that she needed to revisit her past, however painful that might be.

****

Standing at the base of the two steps she summoned up the courage to reach out and knock on the shabby brown door. The houses and the passageway appeared to conspire to surround her with a feeling of claustrophobia. She felt trapped in this depressing environment and was contemplating leaving unseen until she heard voices and realised the door was beginning to open. A face stared back at her.

'What do you want? If you've come for money, we aint got any, so don't bother asking.'

'Please, I don't want money from you. I just need to talk... '

'Talk? What could the likes of you want to talk to us about?'

Helen looked at the old wizened face and decided that the woman's lack of aptitude for hospitality lay in her fear for survival. She had forgotten the weekly rounds of the rent man or the tallyman and the ingenuous accounts needed to stave off their demands.

'Does Tom Ledgard live here please?' Helen tried to move the situation on.

'Who's asking?' The grey haired crone was beginning to present a parody of a parrot.

'I'm Helen, Annie's niece,' she said calmly.

'Never heard of you.' The viperous doorkeeper was beginning to close the door until Helen thrust her foot over the threshold.

'I used to live here with Tom and his family. Please, I just need to talk to him.'

The eyes momentarily squinted in an attempt to examine her closely and no doubt assess the potential pecuniary advantage of allowing her access.

'Wait here. I'll see if he's at home to visitors.' The door was closed abruptly. Helen had little choice but to wait. The invitation to enter slightly chilled Helen with an apprehensive spasm of fear. A combination of treading into the past mixed with an uncertainty of his reception of her momentarily terrified Helen.

The room had changed little except for the additional years of neglected housekeeping. Annie's high standards had always ensured cleanliness and a modicum of comfort. Even the ample charms of Mary Brooke, the warm hearted woman Tom had installed into his home following Annie's death, were sadly missing. As Helen's gaze fell upon the old man slumped in a chair she understood why his companion was a harridan of discomfort.

'Say what you've got to say and get out.' The viper clearly had no compulsion other than to offend.

'If you don't mind I'd like to speak with Tom alone.' Helen was determined to stand her ground.

'Fancy him for yourself, do you?'

'That does not even warrant a reply,' snapped Helen.

'My, we are hoity-toity madam. Bet you've had a bit of rough in your time.' The poison spewed from the stranger was beginning to distress Helen. Her resolve to be neither drawn nor intimidated was beginning to weaken. She turned and began to walk to the door.

'Enough! Helen, come here and you, woman, make yourself scarce.' It appeared that little had changed; Tom still dominated with the final word.

Alone with him she was still fearful, notably of his temper, but time and infirmity had obviously weakened the aptitude for physical retaliation. Following his outburst he coughed which seemed to cause clear distress to his inhalation before once more returning to his shallow breathing.

'Don't look so worried girl. I'm not ready to peg out just yet. Years of working in a bloody spinning mill haven't made me a picture of health, but my time isn't up yet. What do you want?' Tom was still direct and very much to the point and because of this Helen decided that she too must adopt the same stance. This man would not tolerate sentimentality.

'I want to find out where Thomas is.' The words fell from her lips with ease.

'Why?' The question was unswervingly to the point.

'Because... because ...' Helen was now beginning to falter at the crucial moment.

'Let's face it Helen, you've had one of my sons, so you might as well have the other bugger. Was that what you were trying to say? Harry always maintained that you gave him a job in the family firm so as to seduce him. He had to show his gratitude in a certain way.' Helen remained silent; she decided there would be little point trying to confer the truth. Any transient feelings of compassion for him had quickly faded. He was still the man she remembered.

'I'm sorry, I shouldn't have troubled you.' She rose and once again began to walk towards the door.

'In truth I haven't set eyes on him since he left Beckston. He sent a postcard from somewhere down south. It meant nothing to me. I don't expect I'll ever clap eyes on him again. I once had two sons but now they're both dead, or so it seems.'

For the first time Helen felt some sympathy for the old man. He sat there, looking rejected and forgotten, and she knew that there was some truth in his words. It was almost Christmas and yet she sensed that there would be little festive cheer in this house. She did all that she thought she could do she left the contents of her purse on the table.

'You can take that back where it came from,' Tom demanded. 'I'm not a bloody charity case.'

'No one said you were. I just wanted to help you.'

'Why, because you think you're lady bloody bountiful? Couldn't wait to leave and marry into the upper crust. Didn't give any of us a second thought then. Why bother now?'

Helen summoned up the strength to tell him the truth, despite the fact that she knew it would be of little consequence to him.

'I've always loved Thomas but I've never had the opportunity to tell him that. It's probably too late now but I've wasted too much time already. I would just like the opportunity to see him. Is that so much to ask?'

'It all depends on whether he wants to see you again. The daft bugger always had a fondness for you. He certainly didn't get that namby-pamby way from me. Come to think of it, Harry was always more like me.' Helen cast her eyes downwards and recalled the irony of Harry's letter: 'It is a wise child that knows its own father.' Conversely, she also admitted inwardly that it is a wise father that knows his own child. How true that statement was.

'Is Thomas more like his mother? I heard that she had a beautiful voice and enjoyed singing,' enquired Helen.

'He hasn't got a bad voice but it's not of her ilk. No, I tell a lie, he did take after me.' Tom reached down by the side of his chair and picked up some pieces of paper. 'Here take a look at these. Bet you didn't know that someone like me could do something like this?'

The papers held pen and ink images of the locality, the formidable gates and stark lines of Padgett's mill, the cobbled streets of terracing and the careworn faces of the local inhabitants and workforce had all been captured for posterity. Helen shook her head in disbelief at the evident talent of the uncaring man in front of her.

'No, you're like all the rest. Only see what you want to see,' Tom snapped. 'I've had a bloody hard life which has made me how I am. It doesn't mean that I can't be good at something. I never had the time before to draw. Always too busy working, trying to put enough food on the table. Now that I don't have to traipse each day to the mill I can still look at it and those I worked with, not just in my head but on paper.' Tom suddenly snatched the papers back and returned them to the floor.

'Could I buy them from you?' Helen enquired.

'They're not for sale and never will be to you. I don't want my stuff on your fine walls.'

Helen felt the turn of the conversation was her cue to leave. As she rose once more to her feet, Tom felt compelled to have the last word.

'If you think these are good I'll tell you now they're nothing in comparison to what Thomas can do. Didn't know that, did you? He really is an artist. It seems the gift can be passed down from generation to generation.'

As Helen walked down Paradise Street she felt a wry smile drift across her face. Tom had unwittingly complimented his son, a rarity in his vocabulary. He had also given her something to think about.

CHAPTER TWENTY-TWO

Mount Hall seemed safe and welcoming. Helen had forgotten how wide the social divide could be. Beckston was not unlike anywhere else in the country in that it housed a complete spectrum of society, but its inhabitants seldom mixed within its hierarchical strata. Helen refused to feel guilty. She had offered help but Tom's stubbornness had prevented even pecuniary assistance. He would never change his abhorrent dislike of her and she could never truly admit to enjoying his company. Fortunately there was a great deal to do and an industrious mind would always be the best antidote for a dose of depression.

William's evident recovery perfectly coincided with the necessity for Helen to return to work. Edward VIII's abdication had caused an enormous amount of distress, not least to the numerous manufacturers of pottery mugs and other souvenir memorabilia, who had eagerly seized the enterprising spirit of the forthcoming coronation to apply the well-known likeness of the king to anything saleable. There would still be a coronation but some changes would have to be made. Thankfully the fashion calendar could still go ahead with only minimal alteration. As Helen returned to work Diana took her leave, much to her husband's satisfaction, so that she could rest, have time with Jack, who was proving to be quite a gregarious little boy, and prepare for Christmas. This year Horton House would play host to all with its own brand of seasonal festivities.

The blossoming family, the newly weds and a well-recovered patient and his diligent carer, were all looking forward to the indulgences of Christmas and the hopes and expectations which a new year would bring. Their thoughts were far from Europe and the threatened war which was beginning to plague the memories of those who had not forgotten the effects of warfare two decades ago. The Spanish Civil War had already broken out between the governing republicans and Francisco Franco's nationalist party, the Falange. As serious as this was it no longer solely dominated the news; Benito Mussolini, who was rising to power in Italy and Adolph Hitler, who was intent upon seizing absolute power in Germany, vied for maximum coverage in the press, or so it appeared. Horton House, like many homes in Britain, had little to worry about that Christmas; the events taking place on the continent would not affect this side of the Channel. There was so much to look forward to that nothing could spoil the festive celebrations.

****

It was Christmas Eve, that very special time of year when youngsters all too readily agree to go to bed. The little ones, intent upon keeping at least one eye open for Father Christmas, find that slumber intervenes and their waking memories consist of the weight of a stocking or pillowcase filled with presents laid across their bed the next morning. Ideally that would be the wish for every little soul but as Helen knew in reality there were few homes where children woke to an abundance of gifts. The Tetlow firm had tried to address the imbalance by giving their employees presents and those with families fabric sacks filled with an imaginative array of gifts. Helen had orchestrated this philanthropic idea many months previously. It was ideas like this that fuelled the employees' unswerving loyalty to Tetlows and hailed them as model employers.

The firm had closed early that day and as Helen returned to Mount Hall to prepare to leave for Horton House with William later that evening a loud knock at the front door startled her. All of the staff had been given time off during the Christmas period to be with their families. Even the chauffeur had just left as a car was being sent from Horton House later that evening. Without reason Helen momentarily hesitated until the resounding sound beckoned once more. Premonitory feelings surged through her body for no reason. That was of course until she opened the door. The familiar face was one that she had hoped she would never see again.

'Hi Helen. Bet you're a little surprised to see me. I kind of thought it would be a romantic gesture to appear on Christmas Eve.' The American accent was the prime catalyst in recalling well-buried memories.

Helen remained transfixed; unable to speak she simply stared at the manifestation in front of her. Henry Bletchley Barrington always appeared to be enveloped by an air of superiority, the result, no doubt of a privileged upbringing. He smirked with conceited delight as his eyes ran over Helen's motionless outline.

'It's a little cold out here, Helen. Can I press you to invite me in?' His eyes teased with a mixture of coy reticence whilst harbouring an undercurrent of fixed determination. The man was certainly used to getting his own way, a premise that Helen was acutely aware of.

She led him into the drawing room, taking care to close the door behind them so as not to disturb William who was resting upstairs. Henry sweepingly surveyed the room before being captivated by the large oil painting hanging resplendently above the fireplace.

'Now that is what I call a masterpiece. The artist could not have failed when being presented with such a beautiful subject. He just painted what he saw when he looked at you Helen.'

'No, the portrait is of my grandmother,' Helen quickly corrected him.

'Well the likeness has been well carried. It will be good to think that our grandchildren will carry these looks.' The assumption was exceedingly alarming to Helen's mind.

'Our grandchildren? Henry I thought that I'd made it clear to you that I do not wish to marry you. You must have received my letter and the return of the jewellery.'

'What a woman says and what she wants are, from my experience, two different things.'

'Well, I can assure you that that is not the case with me,' Helen snapped. Recollections of that night began to enter her mind. She needed to handle him carefully in order to avoid the spark of a confrontation.

'Please, I don't want to be rude or ungrateful Henry. Someone in your position demands a wife of a certain standing, who can support you and have exemplary standards. A woman of class.' Helen was keen to offer compliments in a bid to placate him. The smile that played across his face confirmed her skilful approach to a delicate situation. Her words had been carefully chosen to appeal to his egotism.

'I'm in no doubt, Helen, that a man in my position requires a very special lady at his side. I'm on the brink of running for office.'

'Congratulations. That's exactly why you must select your wife carefully. In fact I'm sure that an American lady at your side would appeal to the patriotic voter.' The sentiment was one which Helen knew would appeal to his fervent love for his country.

'That is very true. However I view it from the point of bridging the Anglo-American divide. After all, both nations have been captivated by the recent news. If Wallis Simpson can get her prince then anything is possible. By the way, did you know that Wallis originally hails from Baltimore? Can you imagine how I could use that in my campaign? I kind of like the romantic overtones there. Me from Baltimore and you from England. It's surely meant to be Helen.'

Subtlety did not work with this hard-nosed politician. The direct approach, which Helen had hoped to avoid, was necessary.

'Henry, there will never be the remotest possibility, either now or in the future, when I will become your wife. I simply don't love you.'
'But that is not to say that you won't in the future though? I can give you anything that you could possibly want.'

'I know that, but it's not enough.'

'Jesus Christ, not enough? Then what do you want?' He looked at her momentarily before asking the question. 'There isn't anybody else, is there?'

'As a matter of fact, there is.' The words had tumbled out so easily because they were true. They also ignited an emotional touch paper which instantly turned Henry's calmness into cataclysmic rage.

The tirade of abuse was relentless. It began verbally by defamation of character but quickly escalated into a tyranny of physical assault as Henry hurled any item within his reach in a manic, uncoordinated attack. As Helen tried unreservedly to reach the door he lunged towards her, propelling his body in frenzy until his arms grasped around her, pulling her to the floor. Lying on top of her Helen became fearful of the previous encounter and began to fight him, pushing and kicking in a bid to disarm him. His behaviour, at best, was reprehensible and, at worst, would prove devastatingly consequential. Helen's limbs began to thrash around in desperation, eager to unlock and alleviate the painful and constraining hold his body was subjecting hers to. The antique contents of an equally aged and rather delicate looking cabinet, lacquered in the chinoiserie style, began at first to tinkle with the rolling motions of the bodies, then tremble and finally rattle as the onslaught of the prolonged physical assault heightened. Two vases crashed and accordingly broke as they fell, one from a jardinière and the other from an occasional table, before the mahogany table itself also toppled from the constant wrestling of the two bodies.

The stranglehold imposed by Henry was intensified by an inordinate power of strength, no doubt a result of angry delusion and derangement, which worked together in his mind to provide a superhuman force. Each time she fought him he returned the blow with a vigorous punch which equally incapacitated and weakened her resolve to retaliate. Her face and her body were sore and she tasted blood in her mouth. She could no longer summon up the strength to either fight him or defend herself but, as unconsciousness began to take hold, she inwardly knew what would come next. She sensed he was unbuttoning himself and felt her dress being raised. He ignored her pitiful pleas, denouncing her protestations with derision.

Helen was only aware of his presence when she heard his voice.

'Leave her alone.'

'What can you do to stop me, old man?' came the taunting reply from Henry.

William remained at the door his face white with agitation. He seemed to be leaning against the door case, in need of support. Slowly he raised his concealed arm revealing a pistol in his hand. His trembling fingers gripped the handle tightly but not steadily, as the barrel seemed to constantly quake.

'Are you going to take me out with that?' Henry rose to his feet and began to laugh hysterically. 'I like it. An old man with an old shooter. Back home you could go to the chair using that, but old man, I don't think you've got it in you to do it.'

The hysterical laughter suddenly stopped, punctuated by the single shot, and the arrogant tyrant dropped dead to the floor. Henry Bletchley Barrington would never get to run for office now.

****

'What have I done Helen?' William stumbled to a chair and every inch resembled the apt description given him, of 'old man'.

'You did what any decent man would have done.' Helen mustered up sufficient strength to pull herself up and made her way towards him. Bending over him she cradled William in a supportive embrace. They held one another closely both fighting back the tears with staunch resolve.

'I shouldn't have killed him.'

'What was the alternative?'

'I don't know.' William began to shake his head. 'Not this.'

'You may say that, but his temper was uncontrollable. He was sick and needed help but without you here today he could have murdered me. You did what you had to do in defence of me.' William nodded accordingly as he gazed at the bruised and swollen face in front of him. Tears ran down the old man's face as he attempted to gently caress the unaffected areas of her face.

'I know that Helen. I truly would do anything for you. However it doesn't make it any easier to bear. I've just killed a man.' They each looked into one another's eyes and slowly began to realise the implications ahead of them. Helen rose to her feet and, with a look of purpose in her face, walked towards the door.

'Where are you going?'

'The police need to be informed,' Helen said. 'The quicker this is sorted, the better for both of us. If I ring them now they'll understand why you had to defend me. Leave it and they'll be suspicious. Don't you worry, they'll understand.'
'Helen, please sit down.'

'I've told you, there is nothing to fear,' Helen stated assertively.

'Perhaps not this time but I need to atone for my past mistakes. The time has come to do just that.'

Helen sat down facing him without uttering a word. Instinctively she recognised the signs that further revelations were about to be disclosed. Minutes passed before William spoke and as he did he pointed with indignation at the lifeless corpse.

'He had to die for you to live. No one can question that.' Silence once again prevailed. 'But if a man wants something so badly that he takes another man's life to get it, surely that is wrong. I did that Helen. I killed a man and took something that was never truly mine. I thought it could be in time but how wrong I was.' William stopped in his preamble to stare at the young woman opposite him. 'You don't know what I'm talking about, do you?' Helen shook her head in response.

'Do you remember me telling you that when I married your grandmother she was carrying another man's child? Helena had been a free spirited young woman who was not going to abide by the strict wishes of her family. Her brother, Lord Petheridge of Stansdale, had high hopes for his beautiful sister marrying into further aristocracy and bringing yet more wealth into the family coffers. However Helena fell in love with one of the workers on her brother's estate, a lowly horse groom and a married one at that. Petheridge certainly wouldn't tolerate her eloping and marrying 'a low-life', as he referred to him, nor could he expect a marriage into the nobility as she carried another man's child. To him I was the acceptable solution. I had always loved Helena but could never hope to compete for her hand. Petheridge made me a proposition which I could not refuse. 'Kill the 'low-life' and take the prize.' Mistakenly I thought it would be as simple as that. But it was not simple, not simple at all. Nor was it right.'

William fell silent for a moment, giving Helen the opportunity to judge and question, but she preferred instead to remain reticent. The woeful look upon her face was sufficient sentiment, although William could not decide whether it spoke of merely distress or of disgust at his action. Nevertheless he continued.

'I gave no thought or feeling to that man or his family, waiting until there was just him and me alone together.' William stopped again, unsure of how to proceed.

'And?' came the pre-empted question which William was striving to avoid.

'We were both of an equal size, making the job difficult, but I managed to overpower him before strangling him. Petheridge had insisted that the job had to be done cleanly. No firearms or knives. That way there would be no evidence.'

'Only a body,' Helen said mockingly.

'There was not even that. I torched the barn where I'd killed him and slipped away unseen as well as unknown to anybody on the estate. The police found nothing more than the charred remains of a man's body and the inquest returned the verdict of death by misadventure. A naked flame and bales of hay are combustible bedfellows.'

'What about his family?' Helen enquired poignantly.

'That thought has returned more and more to haunt me. He was married with a son. Not a happy marriage by all accounts, but still, I left a woman without a husband and a son without his father. I don't know Helen. I'll never know what happened to them. He would have left them, no doubt, for Helena but that doesn't make what I did right.'

'Did my grandmother ever know about this?'

'Never,' came the emphatic reply. 'As it was she never ever loved me. Merely tolerated me. She followed her brother's wishes in marrying me to be respectable. I think with the birth over she gave up the will to live. I loved her and always will. Nothing can change that.'

It was not in Helen's power to be outwardly judgemental. Inside she was, if the truth was admitted, shocked by this recent revelation of the skeleton in the family cupboard. Cold-blooded murder had taken place for purely selfish reasons. She had to think quickly and at the same time be pragmatic. The incident, however repugnant, had occurred over half a century ago. William, now an elderly man and an infirm one at that, had no doubt imposed his own mental punishment by living with such knowledge since that time. Helen could see no advantage in informing the authorities about a case that had been assigned to oblivion for the sake of posterity. She had of course overlooked one detail.

'Helen, promise me one thing. Marry for the right reason. Marry someone you love and who loves you. Don't be swayed by anything else, especially money.'

Helen quietly rising to her feet kissed William on the forehead before assuring him that his disclosure needed to be buried once more. She reminded him that only the earlier incident of the afternoon needed reporting and left the room to ring the authorities. Having dispensed with these formalities she made her way back to the drawing room, mindful of the officer's insistent advice at the other end of the telephone: 'do not touch anything.' She was certain that this advice would be complied with as there was only the two of them in the house. No one else knew anything about what had happened. That was when it struck her. The one detail she had failed to overlook; Petheridge, her grandmother's brother, the accomplice who orchestrated the murder; what of him?

As Helen reached to open the drawing room door the unmistakeable happened. The single shot, fired at such close range, could not fail. Suicide would have given complete closure if Helen had not been chosen as his confidante.

CHAPTER TWENTY-THREE

The old adage, 'Neither time nor tide waits for mankind,' was a saying which Annie frequently used. Helen could now fully appreciate its true meaning as the course of events began to unfold. The actions of that afternoon had set into motion an unstoppable sequence of circumstances which only time would realise the destiny of. A succession of police officers, steely detectives, finger printing experts and questions, continual questions, inevitably followed. Helen also knew that an inquest and the probability of a trial would develop later. Public interest would definitely take a hold when everyone realised the identity of the dead body; an exceedingly wealthy American who was practically a senator, 'up there' with the President himself. If further sensationalism was needed the press would indeed be able to fan the flames of this fire with revelations about the alleged murderer, William Fawcett, a well-known and respected local businessman, who had shot the American before committing suicide. Helen could not stem this imposition of privacy but she was secure and grateful in the knowledge that no one would find out about William's earlier confession. It had been a dying man's confession and as such would be allowed to go to his grave with him.

The relentless questions continued. Every aspect of Helen's life was thoroughly probed with meticulous inspection. Her relationship with Henry Bletchley Barrington was cross-examined repeatedly, often, it appeared, with some distrust, as the prospect of marrying such a prominent and wealthy man did not sit easily with rejection. The detectives observed scathingly that it would be every girl's dream to receive such an offer of proposal that it would never be rejected. They seemed sceptical in the belief that a prominent politician could double as a violent schizophrenic and walked away shaking their heads, unconvinced.

'What if there was someone who could verify the truth?' Helen queried.

'That would help,' came the far from hopeful reply.

'There is somebody. A maid at his house. She knows what he was capable of. She was the one who tended to my injuries. Her name is Lizzy. She'll tell you that it runs in his family. Apparently his mother suffers from the same thing. Please speak to her and you'll see that he was shot in self-defence.'

Helen realised that she was beginning to ramble but she was desperate to make them understand why he had been killed. Even the injuries on her body had not been sufficient to convince them. She was desperate to make them realise that her grandfather, as she convincingly maintained the title, had against all opposition of infirmity defended her in order to save her life. He was not a murderer but a hero to be admired for his courage. The trouble was convincing the police, particularly as he had thereafter committed suicide.

The questions continued with relentless pursuit even throughout the sensitive period of William's funeral. Following post-mortems on both bodies Henry's was returned to his homeland by request of his family. Helen was only too pleased to return immediately to Horton House where she enjoyed the loyal support of her family and friends. The scars from the physical torment which she had endured from Henry were beginning to heal, but mentally she often found herself troubled by disturbing dreams of that afternoon which all too regularly interrupted her sleep. Even Diana's consoling words of 'the memory of that day will fade with time,' did not totally convince Helen. None of this would, or could, subside until the legal proceedings were finalised. A trial or inquest would only do that and as either of those would take an inordinate amount of time to arrange, Helen accepted the inevitable task of waiting.

Quite unexpectedly two American detectives, in the presence of two of the former steely detectives who had previously questioned her, visited Horton House. She was asked the same questions again but this time there was far more interest taken in the possibility of a witness to Henry's behaviour. Helen eagerly described Lizzy, the maid who could testify to his unpredictable outbursts and the pain that he was capable of inflicting. The British detectives had previously seemed so disinterested unlike their American counterparts who positively lapped up any forthcoming information. Helen had been only too willing to assist with their enquiries.

A month later an inquest was held which concluded that William Fawcett had taken the law into his own hands; believing that an intruder had entered his house he had mistakenly shot the man in what he assumed was self-defence. It was recorded that William was a man of advancing years and one who had recently been subjected to excessive frailty and feebleness through infirmity. The inference here was that he had misjudged the situation and as a result of his error had decided to take his own life. It was a forgone conclusion that it had been an accidental shooting followed by a self-imposed suicide. The case was closed and there would be no requirement for a trial.

Although Helen was relieved by not having to suffer any further intrusion into her life she was perturbed that William had shouldered the full blame posthumously. She enquired why Lizzy had not been found in order to present a more enlightened and truthful account of Henry's actions.

'Surely those American detectives questioned Lizzy?' Helen enquired. The two British detectives stared back at her with deadpan expressions.

'The matter's best left alone.'

'How can you say that? The inquest did not present a full account. What occurred that afternoon would never have taken place had it not been for Henry's obsessive behaviour. Why was that not made public?'

'One word. Politics. This was proving to be a hot potato that no one wished to handle. Our American friends made that very clear.'

'But they seemed so interested in what I told them. I felt certain that they would find Lizzy.'

'Well, yes, they did. We knew then that it was best not to take it any further.'

'What do you mean?'

'The girl suddenly went missing and was found dead some days later, apparently as a result of an accident. Allegations that a leading politician is a madman would be seen as nothing less than scandalous. The powers that be stopped us going any further. Just be thankful for that. You had a very narrow escape.'

'Is that what you call it? What about poor Lizzy? She didn't have a narrow escape. It was me who led them to her.' Helen was clearly agitated and upset by the revelations.

'No, you didn't. If it's any consolation she was in the process of doing that herself. She was about to sell her story to the press but it didn't quite happen. The rich and powerful have ways of preventing that sort of thing. You just confirmed what they already knew. With or without you, the ending would have been the same.' The two detectives leaned back in their respective chairs, folded their arms and gazed at Helen.

'Is that it?' enquired Helen.

'Yes, it's all over and done with. Our advice is to keep what you know to yourself. Go home and forget about it.' Both detectives appeared quite nonchalant in the handling of the affair.

Helen knew that as long as she lived she would never forget it.

****

The little Model Y Ford trundled happily along the winding Cornish lanes. It was not the most stylish or the most reliable of vehicles but what it lacked in engineering and aesthetical appeal, it made up for in characteristic charm. It had served them well during their early days together and now fittingly was the perfect mode of transport for their honeymoon. Arnie and Sarah revelled in one another's company. They complemented each other being perfect soul mates.

They returned to the Mullion Cove Hotel where they had previously stayed during the photography shoot for the calendar. Numerous people had remarked on the artistic professionalism of the pictures which had further triggered the need in Arnie to investigate whether his work was good enough for freelance photography. Colleagues had suggested the name of a man who would be able to advise him. Puck Evans, a former Welsh man, was revered as a leading authority in the world of photography. He now lived and worked in Cornwall and it was by no coincidence that he frequently mingled with the colony of artists, now established around the small fishing ports of Newlyn and St Ives. Painting and photography were not dissimilar in that they each relied upon artistic stimulation which would appeal to the onlooker's eye. The skill of course was in the application.

Mr Evans was affectionately referred to as 'that Welsh Wizard', on account of his mastery and skill in photography. It seemed rather apt that he was associated with the term which had previously been applied to another fellow Welshman, David Lloyd George. Small in stature, around fifty years of age, he possessed the most hypnotic, sparkling, emerald green eyes, which Arnie and Sarah had ever seen. His studio was housed in the front room of his cottage where the walls were lined with numerous framed photographic memories. There was an instant rapport between the two men as they eagerly discussed the evident merits of the Leica and how the interchangeable lenses had enabled photography to be spontaneous. This was then avidly followed by the technical refinements of using Zeiss lenses and the unbelievable excitement of using cameras with shutter speeds of 1/500th of a second. Arnie had for the first time during his honeymoon forgotten about his new wife but Sarah allowed him the indulgence of talking passionately about his other love with a fellow enthusiast. It was not every day that like minds met with such intensity. Sarah smiled, secure in the knowledge that her husband was totally passionate about a camera but would never deceive her with another woman. She indulged him and allowed him all the time that he needed to satisfy these passions.

'Well then boy, let the dog see the rabbit.' Arnie seemed dumbfounded by Evans's request.

'The dog see the rabbit?' repeated Arnie.

'What I mean is, show me your photographs boy.'

'Of course. Here they are.' Arnie proudly passed the calendar to Evans. Silence prevailed as the master studiously examined each picture. Arnie appeared uncomfortable, almost like an interviewee awaiting the ultimate decision. Minutes seemed to have passed, indeed to Arnie hours had elapsed, before Mr Evans voiced any form of opinion.

'I'll grant you boy, you've got a talent.' The master's word was sacrosanct in the photographer's world.

'Enough to go freelance?' Arnie enquired tentatively.

'I'd say so,' came the affirmative reply. The opinion was one that they had hoped for but the finality of hearing it made both Arnie and Sarah eagerly embrace each other with great affection. Momentarily they had forgotten that they were in company.

'I'm sorry for our behaviour. We're just so delighted to hear your opinion. And as well as that, we're on our honeymoon,' Arnie announced proudly.

'Well my boy, you don't need to apologise to me. It's congratulations all round. It makes for a fine start to your married life.' The emerald green eyes twinkled as the Welsh Wizard winked and smiled at the happy couple.

'There's just one thing I'd like to ask you,' came the melodious Welsh accent resounding through the hollow vowels.

'Yes, yes, anything!' Arnie was eager to please.

'Who is the model?'

'Yes, I thought you might notice Diana, or rather her long legs. I should have known the pictures would be successful with her frame to adorn them.'

'No boy, you misunderstand me. Granted the one with the legs is lovely, but I'm talking about the other girl. She's beautiful and certainly deserves to have been painted and now photographed. I've seen her face before in a painting. It was definitely the same girl, of that I'm certain. The trouble is the memory is not what it used to be and I can't quite recall where it was that I saw her. Don't worry, it'll come back to me and when it does I'll let you know. You're on honeymoon you say, so doubtless won't be hurrying off just yet. Give me the name of your hotel and I'll be in touch.'

Both Arnie and Sarah enjoyed the prospect of a good mystery. The superstitious charm of Cornwall combined with the wizardry of a Welshman would definitely make for a good tale on their return to Beckston. They were acutely aware that at the centre of this tale was Helen, their close friend, who had suffered enough of late and who could definitely benefit from a light-hearted anecdote. However, if they were lucky enough to view this painting, they imagined that the model would bear little or no resemblance at all to Helen. They both decided that they would spare Mr Evans the indignity of attributing his mistake to either a failing mind or deficient eyesight, merely the old adage of 'Beauty being in the eye of the beholder', whether it was a case of mistaken identity or not.

****

The attractions of Cornwall were indisputably unprecedented. Each of the senses could be stimulated, aroused and excited by the myriad of seafaring and nautically associated sensations. The pungent smells of both sea and freshly caught fish mixing with the rising acrid smoke from sailors' pipes of tobacco were constant reminders that the community both lived by, and from, the sea. However it was no coincidence that a very different type of community had been drawn to Cornwall's shores by these sensations and they too, albeit indirectly, lived likewise by and from the sea. These groups of people had been influenced by the tenacity of the population living there, their resolve to survive as well as the remarkable landscape and, most crucially, the poignant intensity of the light. Not surprisingly Cornwall appealed to the artistic traits of painters – traditional, modernist and contemporary – as well as to the literary talents of artists and the surrealistic interpretations of sculptors. The small fishing ports of Newlyn and St Ives attracted such talent from the artists' colonies of France, the Barbizon and Pont-Aven as well as the painting schools of Paris and London. Already well versed in their particular areas, these artists established their studios in the atmospheric cottages and lofts lining the ports and looking around them drew their inspiration from the working lives of the fishermen and their families. These were the types of communities that Puck Evans mingled at ease with and they in turn gave back a distinct mutual respect.

Puck Evans very quickly recalled where he had seen the painting. Arnie and Sarah welcomed the opportunity to provide the transport in return for their navigator's skills, a necessity along the unfamiliar lanes. Their journey ended just north of Mousehole where a little harbour protected by curved stone quays and a narrow entrance provided welcome refuge for sailors and fishermen. As they walked to the small stone-built cottage the rays of the sun beamed down and glistened upon the gentle waters in Mount Bay. The tranquil scene was an exception in this land of ferocious gales and shipwrecks but a very welcome contrast. There was no reply as Puck Evans knocked at the door but quite unashamedly he opened the door and entered. Sarah, realising that this was someone's home, drew back in astonishment until summoned.

'Come in girl. Don't be afraid. He won't mind. We don't lock the doors around here. There is never any need. No doubt he'll be down at the quay working on his nets. You see he's a fisherman by day and a painter by night. Come and look, he has talent. No doubting that.'

The interior of the cottage was quite sparsely furnished in contrast to the decorative proliferation. Every wall was lined with both simple pencil sketches and watercolour paintings depicting local scenes. Pale grey slate roofed cottages curved around harbours as narrow twisting streets darted into oblivion. Moor lands, cliffs, churches, and banks of wild flowers, and of course the sea, always the sea, stared back with a visual realism showing that this artist held a true affinity with his surroundings. Both inspired and entranced by the mastery of such exhibits their reason for coming had been almost overlooked until they saw the painting.

As Arnie and Sarah gazed at the painting they immediately realised their mistake. Long, thick dark eyelashes framed the beguiling blue eyes. The artist had captured the essence of her innocent smile, implanting dimples in her soft rounded cheeks whilst the full sensuous mouth added a decidedly provocative demeanour to the beautiful face.

'Well, am I right or am I not? Is she not the girl that you used in your photographs?' enquired Evans.

'Yes she is,' came the emphatic reply from both Arnie and Sarah.

'She's definitely a beauty. The trouble is he refuses to part with her. Everything else is for sale but not this beauty. By the way, what is her name?'

'Helen.' The sound of her name made all three of them turn to face the open door. The sunlight streamed in through the open aperture momentarily blinding the onlookers until they acclimatised themselves to the brilliance of the light. The black silhouette of a man remained in the doorway.

'Her name is Helen,' came the definitive reply. As her name fell from his lips he began to enter the cottage, enabling the party to finally see the face of the artist. Sarah was the only person who did not recognise or know him.

CHAPTER TWENTY-FOUR

Easter had proved to be an exceptionally busy time. The absence of both Sarah and Diana in the office had placed additional but welcome responsibility and workload upon Helen's shoulders. She was the one who had been adamant that Arnie and Sarah continued with their honeymoon and that Diana enjoyed a proper period of rest prior to her confinement. Against their protestations she personally ensured that a fully occupied mind would have little time to dwell upon the events in her past. She needed to be fully industrious and her hopes were definitely realised. The machinists in the factory were working tirelessly to fulfil the orders for Sarah's new collection; the patriotic look so perfectly conceived by the designer, displayed by the models and captured by the photographer, had ensured that the calendars delivered to Tetlow's customers attracted sufficient business. The imminent coronation of King George VI and Queen Elizabeth on 12 May 1937 provided the perfect reason for the nation to celebrate and the fashion stores duly seized the opportunity and quickly overwhelmed Tetlows with orders.

Helen and Richard worked long hours to ensure that the business ran smoothly. Although no longer a young man, Richard had, in recent years, recouped a little of his youth which Helen attributed to the beneficial psyche of having a much younger wife and family. Diana had also benefited from this union, not merely in financial terms but in the psychology of her person. Motherhood suited her well and as she gave birth to their second child, a little girl they named Jacinta, Helen realised that their happiness was complete. It was wrong to be envious but Helen more than once found herself wondering whether marriage and motherhood were unattainable to some.

The rigours of the work continued. As Helen worked harder she began to sense that she was being watched. There was no positive evidence but the sensation was unnerving. On more than one occasion when leaving Horton House and Tetlow's factory she had the distinct impression that there was somebody watching and even following her. The experience unnerved her even more when she recalled Lizzy's disappearance and death and the detectives' advice 'to keep what you know to yourself'. Her mind began to race ahead and she imagined American assassins were tailing her. Such thoughts she kept to herself for fear of being condemned as a laughing stock or unduly alarming the Tetlow household.

Unforeseen circumstances of a different nature were suddenly about to alter Helen's life. The arrival one morning of a solicitor's letter informed her that she was the main beneficiary in William Fawcett's will. He had left instructions that small gifts of money should be apportioned to his long serving, and no doubt longsuffering, staff but the majority of his wealth, including Mount Hall, would pass to Helen. Whilst being both generous and totally unexpected, the sanctioning of his wishes made her cry.

At the invitation of the solicitor the interested parties assembled for the reading of the will. Helen instantly recognised two familiar faces: those of William Fawcett's former staff, the chauffeur, Mr Clough, and the cook, Mrs Bentley, whose eyes seemed to continually gaze upon Helen. Both had long left Fawcett's employment and Helen had not seen them since that afternoon when Diana had persuaded her to participate in a little role-play. The recollection of the deception made her blush and she tried to turn her attention to the other four people who she did recognise as the current staff. The solicitor began by confirming that this was the last will and testament of William Fawcett and there was no other living relative absent from the room – an older sister had died in childhood.

'To Helen Tetlow, who has been a true and sincere friend and granddaughter, I bequeath Mount Hall estate and contents. To each of my listed loyal servants, both past and present, who have unquestionably served me and put up with my bad temper, the sum of 200 pounds.' There was a noticeable gasp of excitement following this last sentence.

'If we can please continue,' the solicitor intercepted. 'To the son of John Norton, or therein his direct descendents, I bequeath the sum of 10 000 pounds in recognition of a long and overdue payment.' The gasp of astonishment at this announcement was even more noticeable than the last and quite audibly questions were being raised as to who this person was. Helen was the only person present to understand why this bequest had been sanctioned. The man at least now had a name, although his identity was still an enigma to her, as it was so obviously to the solicitor.

'We have been unable to trace either this gentleman or his descendents but we will continue to search and ascertain their whereabouts and forthwith inform him, or them, of their good fortune,' the solicitor stated in his matter of fact way. The completion of the reading of the will had been reached and as the solicitor placed the papers on his desk a solitary voice questioned what everyone was thinking.

'What about his mill? Who has he left that to?' Mrs Clough enquired in her usual no nonsense way.

'Ah, yes the question of Fawcett's mill,' came the well rehearsed and no doubt expected explanation by the solicitor. 'A certain portion of unused buildings was given by William Fawcett to the Tetlows. However, more recently, I was instructed by William Fawcett to sell the remaining buildings and the business to an independent purchaser.'

'May we know the identity of that purchaser?' asked Helen.

'The name?' All eyes were now intently focussed upon the solicitor who found himself somewhat cornered by the assembled party. He momentarily cleared his throat before proceeding. 'His name is Petheridge, or to be precise, Lord Petheridge of Stansdale.'

A quizzical look appeared on the majority of the faces. Some repeated his name in a knowing way whilst others raised the question of why William had sold his business to him. Helen knew exactly why he had done so. She now knew the source of the 50 000 pounds. William Fawcett had indeed been the epitome of a doting and generous grandfather and by the time she reached Horton House she had already decided upon the future of her legacy.

****

'Are you absolutely certain that you want to sell?'

'Without a doubt.'

'Mount Hall is your birthright and you should remember that.' Richard had always been logical and prudent throughout his life, the exception being his marriage to Diana.

'I will never forget my family but I cannot live in a house which hosts such memories.'

'Quite. Of course we understand Helen and this will be your home for as long as you want. We are your family. Always remember that.'

'I will. Thank you.' Helen stepped forward and lightly kissed Richard upon the cheek. He was an exceptional man, kind, thoughtful and genuine. As she closed the study door she reflected upon one of his other qualities, that of discretion. He had not questioned what she intended to do with the exceedingly large sum of money which would be released upon the sale of the estate. Her mind had already settled that dilemma.

****

Mount Hall was swiftly put on the market for sale as the indication was that it would be sometime before a genuine buyer would be found for such a sizeable asset. A definite price had not been agreed upon, nor had Helen begun to consider how to dispose of the contents, when an attractive offer was proposed. It appeared that an unknown purchaser was willing to buy the house, estate and contents, without viewing, and match a price that Helen wished to accept. The offer was too good to believe and naturally curiosity reared its head. Helen refused to sell to an anonymous owner. She was prepared to wait, knowing that time would be her leverage as such desperation would surely force the unknown out into the open. The tactic was successful. At last the time had arrived to face the inevitable.

****

A definite numbness began to take a hold of her body as the car turned to enter the driveway. It felt as though nature was securing its own anaesthetic in order to ensure calm and logic. Throughout her life Helen had had to deal with a number of adversaries but instinctively she knew that he would be her worst. The opulence of the gatehouses straddling the imposing drive and the large ornamental iron gates at their sides signalled the grandness of the estate within. Wealth and power indeed could be unwelcome adversaries to those who questioned or opposed. Determined to be neither fazed nor frightened, she swallowed hard, staring at the infinite space around her. There were no visible boundaries or close neighbours, only land, his land.

Stansdale Hall stood with majestic pride and authority at the end of the long drive. Its stone turreted walls rose with a sense of foreboding purpose and a challenging warning to any potential perpetrators. For centuries it had been the home of a successive lineage of the Petheridge family and like its inhabitants had survived the vicissitudes of fortune. Originally dating from the 1500s, consecutive descendants had duly restored and altered the house adding their own originality to produce a sprawling building of monumental size. As the car neared the hall Helen could see that the upper portion of many of the windows were filled with stained glass and above one was a finely carved stone crest. The car drew to a halt at the entrance porch, a structure emulating the grandeur of the house with its three finely moulded stone arches, its battlemented parapet and cornicing. Visibly presiding over this was a carved shield complete with its own indecipherable Latin motto, at least indecipherable to Helen, as her education had failed to include

Latin on the timetable. A butler swiftly opened the car door and as she stepped out she turned and peered at the infinite open grounds in front, quietly contemplating her grandmother's actions and those of William Fawcett, neither one able to have foretold the eventual consequences. At that point she realised that she was about to meet the one person who had had the greatest influence upon her life.

The massive oak panelled entrance doors were staunch like the rest of the house and each one had been opened wide, enabling Helen to view the interior before even stepping inside. The walls were also oak panelled and she could also see an imposing arched entrance to the grand staircase which dominated the entrance hall. As they passed the many large oil paintings adorning the walls Helen stopped for a moment to view one of the largest canvases she had ever seen. Normally a work of art of such proportion would only be found in an art gallery or museum. The subject was of a group of deer and as Helen looked on with sheer curiosity the butler, obviously mistaking her inquisitiveness for artistic knowledge, was keen to inform her that it was none other than a Landseer. As she returned his look of eager anticipation with only a blank expression which in no way conveyed any form of recognition the butler declined to comment on other possible treasures and abstained from providing any further information. Helen realised how little she knew and how sadly lacking in education she was.

The house seemed to be a labyrinth of corridors, presumably the indirect result of centuries of transformation by idealistic owners. There were walls lined with portrait paintings of men, women and children, the latter having been depicted as miniature adults in both manner and clothing. It appeared that childhood had not existed, only the avid need for generations of descendants to maintain the Petheridge line. She wondered how many countless ancestors were staring down at her, their eyes following her intensely. Helen made a concerted effort to maintain the same pace as the butler as his footsteps appeared to quicken. They passed along corridors lined with gigantic French tapestries, bordered with antique medallion work representing fruits and game birds which were regularly interfused by the radiant shots of colour from the Chinese vases standing proudly in front of them. On and on they passed through rooms where light rarely touched the interior to those where it flooded in through mullion, garden view windows which allowed the visitor to appreciate the acres of grounds surrounding the house. Landscaped gardens with tree lined waterside walks captured the eye through every window. Tall statuesque trees, including the chestnut, lime, oak and sycamore, artistically provided height to a vast panoramic view as well as offering vistas with seclusion and privacy; secluded areas where intrigue could flourish for lovers and assassins alike.

Finally they turned into quite a dark and sombre looking corridor which by its appearance made Helen feel that this was possibly the oldest part of the house. Intimating for her to wait, the butler entered a room and disappeared from view before returning to invite her to follow him.

'Lord Petheridge will see you now.' At that moment Helen needed all the resolve she could find to continue.

The room inside, like the corridor outside, was dark and gloomy which immediately conveyed an atmosphere of unpredictability. The embers of a fire gave a glow to the interior, drawing Helen towards the large imposing stone fireplace that appeared to dominate the room. There was something about the scene which was familiar but at the same time disturbing. Instinctively she realised why. There was a presence in the room, albeit the darkness was preventing her from discerning her companion, she could see from the build and outline that it was a man huddled in a large fireside chair.

'Come closer Helen. Let me see your face.'
The whole scene was uncannily reminiscent of that dream and as she tried to see his face the darkness still impeded and presented nothing more than a faceless shape. Fear prevented her from moving any closer.

'Closer girl! I cannot see you.' The request had now turned into a summons.

She approached slowly until the flickering light caught his profile and then his guise. He was a very old man, judging from his sparsely combed grey hair, which framed an equally craggy but lingering face sitting at the head of a contorted body frame. Faint, almost colourless, opaque eyes peered back, unwilling to reveal the thoughts of the inner soul.

'I knew one day you would come back.' The comment unnerved and slightly shocked Helen.

'Come back? I've never been here before in my life!'

'But you have through Helena. Come closer. I want to look at your face.' A skeletal hand slowly rose and touched Helen's face as she crouched at his side. Repulsed she looked away.

'Beautiful, beautiful. You look so like her. You even react to me as she did.' This last comment caused Helen to turn abruptly to face him.

'Don't you care for what you see? Neither did she. As a small boy I had the misfortune to be afflicted with polio which at first made her pity me but ultimately it led to aversion. I may not have been blessed with looks but she could have been my wife and mistress of all of this.' The look on Helen's face was enough to show how shocked she was.

'She was your sister. How can you speak of her like this?'

'We were cousins. Her parents had both died in a railway accident, the carriage having dismounted from the tracks. Fortunately Helena, who was only a small baby, had remained behind in the care of her nurse. She came to live here and we grew up as brother and sister. The only trouble was that as I became older I felt a little more for her than just brotherly love and she did not reciprocate my feelings. Instead she preferred the rough and roguish charms of one of the estate workers, a man with nothing more to his name than a tied cottage and a wife and child.' At this point his voice became raised as he clenched his bony fist and slammed it down hard onto the arm of his chair.

'Can you imagine how it felt for me to find them together that day in the barn? Their pleasure was my misery. How could she do that to the family? Her father had been the younger brother to mine and therefore she was a Petheridge in her own right. With her breeding and her beauty, her destiny was here by my side. A bastard child would of course have brought great shame upon the family name and I could not allow that. Therefore I did the only decent thing that I could do and arranged an acceptable marriage for her to Fawcett.'

'I take it by your manner towards him he was not your ideal choice?'

'He was a mill owner. What more can I say? Not exactly in my league but with soiled goods to dispose of I was not in any position to choose. He had sufficient means to provide for her, especially with the sizeable dowry that I provided, and like most men was besotted from the first moment he saw her. I had had business dealings with him, supplying the wool from my estate farms. He had met Helena when he had visited me here and I could clearly see from his reaction that he was deeply attracted.'

'However, the same could not be said for my grandmother,' Helen quietly reminded him.

'That was of no concern to me. She had made it abundantly clear that she did not wish to become my wife and I certainly was not going to allow her the indiscretion of becoming his wife, either through bigamy or divorce. Therefore I did the next best thing.'

'Which was?'

'To allow Fawcett to marry her.'

'What exactly did he have to do to gain that privilege?' Helen enquired.

'Do? Marry her of course!'

'The proposition was a little more complicated than that I believe.'

'Then you believe wrong,' snapped Petheridge.

'I don't think so. A dying man's confession relies upon the truth as he faces his Maker.' For the first time Petheridge began to look uneasy and attempted to move in his chair.

'Damn the man! I do not know what lies he has told you but without my intervention Helena would never have even looked at him, let alone marry him.'

'Your intervention? Did that concern disposing of the child's father? Did you give any thought to the man's wife and child?' Helen continued to maintain her stare as she watched the reaction upon his face and felt the penetration of anger being emitted from those insidious eyes. Her confidence was at last beginning to build.

The dramatic moment was interrupted by a faint knock at the door as the butler entered with a tea tray. Not a word was uttered as he placed the tray down and poured the tea before leaving his master and visitor alone to add their own milk or lemon and continue their conversation. Following the click of the door some time elapsed before the next word was uttered.

'He deserved to die. Being the animal that he was I would have enjoyed feeding him to the pigs on the estate, but Fawcett would have none of that. Fire was seen to be the great cleanser, the only true way to dispose of unsavoury evidence. It had to look like an accident.' The long bony hand reached out and slowly took hold of the cup and saucer as silence once more prevailed. Helen abstained from any refreshment, nauseated by her host's revelations.

'Drink Helen or your tea will be cold.'

'I don't have the stomach for anything from you.'

'There you are wrong my girl. I suspect you'll accept my more than generous offer for Mount Hall. That is of course why you have come here today.'

'I am sorry to have to disappoint you but my reason for coming here is to find out why the lives of my family have been cursed with misfortune. My mother and my grandparents all suffered directly or indirectly as a result of your actions. You ruined their lives but you'll not ruin mine!'

'Strong words Helen. But that is all they are. Your mother and grandmother chose their own destiny and were responsible for their own actions through foolish, misguided notions of the heart. Mixing with inferiors, their so-called love affairs were at the expense of their family duties. A conflict of class will always end in disaster. But you, Helen, you are different. I've had you watched for some time. Albeit you've survived a lower status marriage, but as a young and beautiful widow you are in an enviable position and will attract a suitable match. I will make sure of that for the sake of this estate and the family name. You are my heir to all of this.'

The emotions seething within Helen began to bubble with anger. Audacious and pompous he may be but he had no right to assume that he could control her. He was the one who had had her followed. For that at least she had to be grateful being genuinely relieved that the imagined American assassins were nothing more than a figment of her imagination. However his expectations could not be allowed to fester any longer.

Drawing herself to her fullest height Helen stood in front of the deformed shell of manhood who stared back with a smile of self-imposed conjecture.

'I'm pleased that I came here today because now I totally understand what is important in my life. I will never make the mistake that my grandmother made. Family and friends are very important to me. By that I mean those who have always been there for me. My family consists of true and genuine friends, not vast estates. I will never sell Mount Hall to you and I want nothing more to do with you.'

'Foolish words Helen. You are the sole heir to a vast fortune. I will forgive you for your ingratitude and insolence but you must not marry beneath you. Do that and I'll disinherit you! The gutter is an unforgiving place Helen. Easy to fall into but difficult to climb out of.'

His final words continued to resound through her head long after she had lost sight of Stansdale Hall.

CHAPTER TWENTY-FIVE

The sale of Mount Hall attracted far more interest than anyone had anticipated. Large mansions rarely came onto the market as there were always family members to inherit and occupy them. Publicly this was seen as the reason for the heightened interest but privately a ghoulish and frankly morbid fascination was producing mounting speculation as to where the deaths had occurred. Questions abounded as to which rooms the acts had taken place in; if there been much blood and whether there were still visible remains of any bloodstains. Overwhelming interest, not in the transaction of a sale but in hearsay, intrigue, and publicity, demanded that an auction was out of the question. It would be a private sale and only genuine and legitimately interested parties were encouraged to apply; thrill seekers could look elsewhere. It was also decided that the house would be emptied and the contents sent for auction far away from Beckston.

It had been accepted that finding a suitable purchaser would not be an easy feat but an unexpected offer arrived within days of Helen's visit to Stansdale Hall. Cautiously she enquired as to the name of the interested party but the disclosure was not enlightening. She had to be sure that Petheridge was not behind this offer and demanded that she met the prospective purchaser.

Mr Elsworth was a middle-aged gentleman who had made his fortune in the automobile industry. Single until now, his wealth had attracted the attention of one of the daughters of the Ickringill's Textile Empire. The moment that Helen was introduced to the couple she instantly knew that the offer was genuine and in no way related to Petheridge. The meeting filled her with an innate sense of pride and, if the truth were told, a slight touch of retribution as she remembered the last time that she had been in the company of Constance Ickringill.

There was still evidence of Constance's haughty manner as she pre-empted an introduction with, 'Have we met somewhere before?' Helen avoided the momentary temptation to answer with a direct affirmative and instead allowed a period of time to elapse before replying. The eyes of the two women bore into each other, permitting sufficient time for memories of that evening to be recalled. When the woman began to blush and look slightly ill at ease Helen knew the desired effect had been achieved.

'Perhaps it was in another life?' ventured Helen.

'Perhaps it was,' came the slightly dispirited reply.

Helen was not naturally a vindictive person but the circumstances of her past had shaped her personality and she was determined that from now no one would forget that.

****

Disposing of Mount Hall to Mr Elsworth and his future wife provided a dramatic turning point in the lives of Helen and those closest to her. She had known for a long time the designation of the proceeds. One third she would give to Diana and Richard, no doubt to ease the financial worries of the Tetlow business and any further worries about providing for their growing family. Another third she would give to Arnie and Sarah, no doubt to provide a suitable home for the newly married couple. The remaining capital was the most difficult as Helen had never before experienced having money. She felt guilty, particularly when she recalled the times she had seen Annie trying to produce a dish for the family with little more than root vegetables or darn holes in clothes that had been repeatedly darned before. If only she was still alive Helen could have given her a different lifestyle. That was the problem; life could be so unfair, especially to those who abused it the least.

Helen waited for Arnie and Sarah to return from their honeymoon before explaining to each of the couples her financial intentions. Protestations abounded with absolute defiance but Helen was equally defiant. The true value of money lay in its ability to provide pleasure and in Helen's eyes helping her friends was without doubt the best way of contentment. She did not want gratitude, just the acceptance of her wishes.

That evening was spent in the rich company of alcohol and whimsical conversation. Forgetfulness had almost intervened when Arnie and Sarah exchanged furtive glances before disappearing and returning with Cornish gifts of pottery for their friends. The anxiety upon their faces became intense as they handed Helen an additional parcel wrapped in brown paper. Intrigued she untied the string binding it and unwrapped it to find a portrait of her own face staring back at her. A small card fell onto the floor from the watercolour canvas. Silence pervaded as Helen picked it up and read the message:

Helen,
    If you would like to keep the painting just let me see the original again.
Yours,
Thomas.

Arnie punctured the stunned silence by relating their initial meeting with Puck Evans who had been responsible for bringing them to Thomas's cottage. To Helen his tales of boyhood encounters with Thomas Ledgard became mere ramblings as her mind began to wander. She was, however, grateful that Arnie conspicuously made no reference to Harry. She continued to stare at his writing, contemplating both the message and her fated response. Again and again she read the same words, finding it unbelievable that something that she had desired for so long was now in her grasp. It had all seemed so impossible and even Annie's wise words of 'if you believe in something long enough, it will come true,' had consistently failed to materialise over the years. Now at last she appeared to have been dealt life's winning card except warily she knew that life was never totally free of danger.

'Danger? What are you talking about Helen? The only danger you'll suffer will be from us if you don't go.' Diana was resolute that her friend was not going to throw away Cupid's arrow.

'I'm frightened that because I've wanted to see him for so long, we may both have changed and...'

'And what?' snapped Sarah. 'You may just find your soul mate. If life offers you a chance of happiness, grab it with both hands. I certainly did as we all have in this room.' The sentiments were so uncharacteristic of Sarah who was normally not given to emotional outbursts but they had been delivered so fervently that Richard, Diana, Arnie and Sarah nodded in total agreement before embracing one another. Helen fully appreciated the meaning of this message.

'Well I won't know unless I take a chance, will I?' Helen pondered softly.

'That's all we're asking,' came the collective response.

****

The gentle brushstrokes of the watercolour had been applied deftly in an attempt to perfectly capture both the beauty and pensiveness of her face. Every detail of light and shade, of colour and texture, had been utilised to reproduce a faithful likeness of her; now no longer confined in his head but tangibly presented on paper. The image staring back was the memory he held of her which she hoped she would not jeopardise when they were reunited.

Although the painting had initially been a little unsettling to view, in part because it was an excellent representation, Helen found it far more bizarre that a painting attributed to her grandmother should bear such a striking resemblance to herself. Helen had sent the entire contents of Mount Hall to auction with the exception of two items, the oil painting of her grandmother Helena and her jewellery box. These she retained as her only family heirlooms and personal reminders of the past.

The oil painting was both large and striking. It had been commissioned by William before their wedding and was an exceedingly fine piece of artwork by a well-known portrait painter of the time. The value of it, like those of Helena's jewels, was immaterial to Helen. Being neither a connoisseur nor collector of creative works, Helen had no experience of what constituted artistic ability. She accepted that the oil painting was accredited as such by experts but, returning her gaze to the watercolour, appreciated that Thomas, like his father, had undisputed talent. Each had been born with a gift which working in a mill had never allowed the nurturing of. Against the odds of a humdrum existence both father and son held artistic promise which until now had been stifled through an excess of work and exhaustion.

****

The air journey had been calm and tranquil unlike the turbulence in her mind and stomach which had whirled with misgivings from the start of the flight. Travelling alone did not trouble her but the prospect of the outcome did. Now more than ever before she candidly admitted that her deception and actions following that night had resulted in dire consequences for everyone. She had duped one man into marriage and possible fatherhood, as well as much maligning an innocent one and now she expected to find happiness with him. She did not deserve a good and honest man and continued to torture herself with that thought. That was until she stepped out of the plane and breathed in the Cornish air. Its instant hallucinatory qualities freed her from troublesome thoughts with its refreshing breezy charms. This was the land that Tennyson had drawn inspiration from for his Arthurian romances. She instantly understood why artistic souls sought satisfaction amidst its charms.

The little car trundled slowly to a halt as Mousehole Harbour came into distant view. Helen had initially failed to give the taxi driver any specific details of her intended destination other than the place name itself.

'Which way?'

'Down to the harbour please.' Helen could not account for this impromptu decision except that this entire picturesque fishing village clearly owed its existence to the harbour and the sea. It seemed a natural choice to begin with. It also afforded her some time.

Travelling with only a small suitcase at her side, not dissimilar to that day when she had first accompanied Annie down Paradise Street, she quietly made her way along the narrow, twisting streets lined with sturdy cottages built from Lamorna granite. The buildings themselves seemed to provide not only character but also collective strength as they huddled together around the inner edge of this bustling port. Men and women hurriedly engaged themselves with the work of the day. Local fishing boats now returned from their early morning journeys, bouncing together buoyantly, having once more safely and successfully delivered their crews and daily quotas of pilchards. The two sturdy breakwaters seemed to curve almost maternally around the harbour, protecting the area and its inhabitants from the force of the sea, whilst large bodied gulls raucously screamed like fishwives for their own fishy treats. Against all of this activity the magnificence of the Atlantic provided its own uninterrupted panorama with the inherent pounding force of its waves. Every sense of the body could be touched, mesmerised and even aroused by the surrounding stimuli.

He had noticed her first. Oblivious to his fixed gaze she continued to walk towards him preoccupied by the surrounding sights of harbour life. Amidst the throng of activity, unfamiliar accents, noises and pungent odours, she noticed the stillness of one man. The dark eyes burned into her very soul and like the rest of his dark features were unmistakable. Strong and swarthy, distant and seemingly unattainable, he remained silhouetted in his fixed stance as people moved around him. Helen would have behaved likewise but the bustle of fishermen and their baskets prevented her from remaining stationary. As she drew nearer to him he recognised the beautiful girl that he had always been in love with but he also witnessed a degree of refinement and sophistication that had not previously existed. The elegance of her walk, her clothing and her manner, served only to intensify his embarrassment. By contrast the roughness of his clothing and the ubiquitous, lingering smell of fish which he carried about his person, were hardly conducive to romance. Helen noticed nothing other than a man who possessed everything that she wanted.

They embraced and politely kissed, oblivious to the public stares of surprise and envy. Neither recalled walking from the quay through the narrow streets, up a steep winding lane to a small stone cottage overlooking the waters of Mount Bay. Thomas opened the door and she immediately saw a small simple room which hosted a gallery of talent, his talent. The portrait of her had shown that but the proliferation of local scenes would have convinced even the most sceptical expert. Unassuming by nature, Thomas appeared to be uncomfortable by her praiseworthy comments. At times an awkward silence would intervene and both Thomas and Helen admitted to themselves that they needed to become familiar with each other again.

'You must stay here with me.'

'I had intended to stay in a hotel, nearby obviously,' explained Helen.

'Why nearby when we can be as near to each other as possible?' Thomas seemed to momentarily blush as he made his comment. 'Obviously I will sleep in here and you can have my room.' The insistence upon the correctness of etiquette made Helen smile in response.

'Obviously,' came Helen's reply. Their eyes met and each understood perfectly the boundary of decency. Haste now would only result in regret later. There was no reason to rush back to Beckston; everyone at Horton House had made that very clear.

The weeks that followed were unquestionably the happiest that Helen had ever known. She unburdened herself and told him everything. Far better to be honest now and let him judge for himself the necessity for her scheming manipulation. She hated herself and dreaded his reaction. To her relief he listened patiently and embraced her more tenderly than before. No detail was omitted as she afforded him graphic descriptions of her relationships with all who had affected her life and indeed those before her. As the hours passed Thomas sat and listened and following her eyes watched the numerous emotional expressions which accompanied her revelations. He remained silent in the hope that she would continue to unburden the legacy of pain which had deeply buried itself into her soul. The only exception was her reference to Petheridge. There was still something which distressed her about him; he was her only living tormentor and for that reason she chose to refer to him sparingly. She had already decided that she had no intention of ever seeing him again.

They filled their time both apart and together in simple ways. When Thomas went out fishing, Helen busied herself around the cottage with domestic chores. This was the first time that she had ever done so and quite surprisingly found that she enjoyed preparing meals and the home for his return. Thomas still seemed uncomfortable with this division of workload and would happily have done everything for her himself. That was the problem between them; he had always recognised that she was descended from a different stock to him. There was still a charged sexual tension between them which each felt distinctly and poignantly whilst sharing the other's company. Evening time was always the worst when a kiss or an embrace led to nothing more. Thomas would not transcend the boundary. He wanted to and fought hard to maintain this conviction. He ached to make love to her but he had ached for years and had learned to live with it.

****

As the sun shone down onto Mousehole Harbour early that Sunday morning Thomas decided it would be an ideal day to capture the scene upon canvas. They clambered up to the ancient hilltop village of Paul before selecting a suitable vantage point. Thomas began to lightly sketch the surroundings out in pencil whilst Helen watched, both impressed and beguiled. A few strokes of his pencil rapidly captured the landscape in minutes. She lay back on the rug in relaxation and welcomed the feeling of warmth penetrating her skin from the sun's rays. Following a picnic lunch she once more lay back and knew it would only be a matter of time before sleep intervened. Everything was so perfect on that day as Thomas painted and Helen dozed. There was nothing to interrupt or distract them.

As Helen drifted into a drowsy slumber Thomas remained completely preoccupied in his painting. He was so intent upon capturing the initial scene that he refused to allow himself to notice that the welcoming light breeze was steadily in the path of a prevailing south-westerly wind. He had also failed to notice that the fluffy higher lying cumulus clouds were being joined with lower lying cloud layers. The cloud sheet spread rapidly across the skyline of the sea until it reached the land and dislodged its sudden raindrops unmercifully. Within seconds the painting and the couple were pelted with the deluge until the saturated droplets ran down them. They tried unsuccessfully to find shelter and decided eventually that, as wet as they were, the best solution would be to return to the cottage. Once inside they looked at one another, each drenched to the skin. No longer sweating from the running they were now beginning to shiver.

Helen quickly disrobed in the bedroom, bathed, and looked for some dry clothing. Most of her changes were still drying following laundering. Thomas had changed into clean trousers but his chest was bare as she entered the front room. She remembered how as a little girl she had often seen him without a shirt as Annie had struggled to quickly iron one for him. His torso and upper arms now were muscular and developed, no doubt as a result of the physical effort imparted from daily fishing. The definitive peak of his masculinity was unquestionably evident in the thick black mass of body hair that covered his chest. Helen had never before experienced the intensity of such pleasure and pain as she felt now.

Thomas returned her gaze with a conviction that he knew he was steadily surrendering. She looked so different wearing one of his oversized shirts. Her hair was wet and everything about her lacked the sophisticated elegance he had grown to know. Simple and unadorned she radiated purity and innocence. He remembered his feelings for her as a boy and knew that they had remained the same. She reminded him of that night and his resolve began to break.

Holding one another's gaze in silence they simultaneously began to close the space between them. As Thomas touched her he trembled with anticipation, his fingers gently caressing her soft complexion before tracing the gentle contours of her lips. Lightly he pressed his own lips to hers before wrapping his arms around her and drawing her body against his. He felt her response by the way she thrust her body towards him and in the fervent heat of the kiss. The rounded contours of her body pressed against his most noticeably and, as his fingers travelled down her back, she pulled away allowing them to travel down her front, lingering at her covered breasts until such impetus made him unfasten the buttons so that the clothing barrier was removed. He used his lips to kiss every soft and gentle area of her naked body. As they lay on the floor he looked into her eyes tenderly and quietly asked if she was certain. The affirmative response was far from ambiguous for both had waited so long for this. At the moment they became one, individually and jointly, they experienced an intensity of pleasure previously unknown to either.

They lay in one another's arms for some time afterwards. There seemed no need for spoken communication, each preferring to affectionately kiss and nestle into the other's body. To Helen it appeared as though she had reached her Utopia and could not possibly want anything else in life. Thomas, however, felt differently. He suddenly sat up and looked quite pensive.

'Are you alright?' Helen enquired.

'Yes, but I could still be happier.' Thomas's response slightly unnerved Helen. She knew from life's past experiences that happiness was often marred with ensuing problems.

'Happier. How?'

'Helen, will you marry me?'

'Yes.'

'You may want time to think about it.'

'I've had many years to do just that.'

He beamed with delight at her before enveloping her with kisses. Neither had ever experienced such happiness.

****

The coronation of King George VI and Queen Elizabeth was celebrated throughout the land with a plethora of patriotic rosettes and bunting. Although shy, afflicted with a stammer, and called quite unexpectedly to the throne, George VI was greeted warmly by his people. He was universally liked because he appeared kind, unassuming and accepting of the duties that fate had consigned to him. He had inherited his father's sense of duty and with a staunch resolve of determination and the strong support of his wife, Queen Elizabeth, the Duke of York ascended the throne on that dull and rainy day in May 1937. The public now looked forward to an era of hopeful certainty under a new monarch trying to dispel the uncertain worries of Hitler and Mussolini's ambitions as well as the turmoil of the Spanish Civil War. Mousehole, like numerous other settlements, rejoiced with intrinsic celebrations and drew inwardly for neighbourly sustenance. The worries of Europe, after all were not close at hand but far away.

****

More immediate matters were now on Thomas's mind. They had both agreed to a small and early wedding and had booked the first available date at Penzance's Registry Office. Helen had never once broached the subject of an engagement ring but it constantly plagued Thomas's mind. The problem was that jewellery, however small, came with a price tag that necessitated surplus funds which Thomas did not possess. He resolved to do the one thing he liked least: portrait painting.

Wealthy tourists would pay handsomely for a vision of themselves or their loved ones in pencil, charcoal, ink or watercolour. Thomas had always preferred the beauty of landscapes and had never concerned himself with commercial enterprise but now he needed assistance.

'I've told you before, boy, that you've got talent and people will pay for that. Your only trouble is that you don't seem bothered about selling your pieces.'

'Well I am now,' came the definitive reply. Thomas had contacted his old associate, Puck Evans. A photographer of some renown he also had wide connections with the artistic market. The sparkling emerald green eyes resplendently twinkled as Helen entered the room. He instantly recognised her.

'I totally understand. I'd work day and night for you. The painting and photograph were beautiful but there is nothing to match the original. Hello Helen, I'm Puck Evans and I'm about to market this young man's talent. It's time I did.'

'Thank you for coming.' Thomas reached out and shook his hand. 'There's just one other thing.'

'Yes,' came the melodious Welsh accent. 'Ask me anything,' his eyes still mesmerised by the young woman in front of them.

'Would you and your wife be witnesses at our wedding?'

'I'd be insulted if you didn't ask us. Of course we will. I'll take the liberty of bringing the camera along too!'

The boyish charms of this impish Welshman infected everyone with good humour. Helen and Thomas were still smiling, long after the Welsh Wizard had left.

****

Mrs Evans seemed a perfect soulmate for her husband. Small and square and in possession of an extremely agreeable temperament, she wore a continuous smile on her face throughout the ceremony. Helen and Thomas had agreed that their civil ceremony would be informal, small and intimate and with only two witnesses present. They exchanged their vows for the benefit of one another, simply, but with significance. There had been moments of regret that they had neither invited nor informed family and friends of their wedding arrangements, particularly for Helen as the Tetlows and the Barracloughs were in her eyes true family. She hoped that they would understand their need to marry quickly and looked forward to taking her new husband back to them.

Dressed in a simple lilac two piece, a suit which she had taken with her to Cornwall, Helen looked radiant as the registrar pronounced them man and wife. Thomas kissed her passionately whilst clutching her to him with excessive contentment. The Evans accorded them a little time before approaching them to offer their own congratulations. It was such a happy scene, as weddings should be, but this one possessed something more than just a future promise, it had closure from the past. The event that had just occurred had always been destined to happen and finally it had.

They returned to Mousehole and celebrated with a meal and drinks at a local inn. Puck and his wife insisted upon paying for the bill as a wedding present.

'We absolutely insist. Furthermore, when I get these little beauties developed, you're also going to have a wonderful reminder of your day with an album of photographs.'

'What can we say, but thank you?' Helen and Thomas were unanimous in their gratitude.

'Ssh… You deserve it. In fact, I have something else to tell you. You don't need to worry about doing any more portrait drawings Thomas, I know you don't enjoy them much. I've found a very interested buyer for two of your watercolours who has agreed to pay handsomely for them. At last your talent is beginning to pay off.'

'You shouldn't say that in front of my wife. Oh my goodness, that does sound unusual but very nice.' Thomas reached out and took Helen's left hand in both of his. 'She may decide that the engagement ring that I did those portrait drawings for ought to be replaced with something larger.'

'Certainly not! It was the one that I wanted and the one that you bought for me.' The sentiment was truthful on Helen's part as she knew how hard Thomas had worked to afford to buy that ring. She could not help but wonder whether Thomas's pride would accept the fact that he was now married to a wealthy woman. She had not completely divulged how much her grandfather had left her in case it made Thomas feel inadequate as a man and provider. That revelation could wait until they reached Beckston.

CHAPTER TWENTY-SIX

As Whitsuntide approached Helen realised that the time had come to return to Beckston. She had the freedom to stay longer as there had been no persuasion on anyone's part for her to go back, but go back she knew she must. Telephone calls and letters had been kept deliberately short so as to avoid disclosure of her news; she longed to see the reactions of those closest to her when she returned with her husband and for that reason only had chosen to remain silent.

It was not long before the news travelled through the twisting streets of their own Cornish community. Although not a true Cornishman by birth Thomas had been truly accepted by his neighbours, as one had pointed out, 'the next best thing to a Cornishman is a Yorkshire man.' Not surprisingly Helen likewise had been accepted and the villagers were keen to continue the celebrations with their own brand of homespun hospitality. For days the newly weds were visited and left with generous donations of homemade food, drinks and crafts, all testament to the extreme kindness of the people around. They themselves possessed very little but were only too willing to share it, even with a stranger such as Helen. These actions made her reflective of her own pecuniary position and she resolved that she would find a way to use her fortune to the benefit of others. She was determined that her money would be put to some good use. What that would be, she needed to consider.

It was difficult to leave the happy, settled life behind, even for a short time span. Married life would eventually continue in Mousehole but, as Helen was aware, she firstly had to finalise her arrangements in Beckston. Thomas had never flown before and his apprehension for once allowed Helen the chance to be the strong one. It seemed strange that she did not share his fear but previous flying experience had acclimatised her to this mode of transport.

The flight passed without incident and once airborne Thomas began to relax and finally enjoy his travelling. There was no doubt that this fear had been superseded by an equally daunting one: that of meeting the family. Thomas's fear of failing to live up to expectation was vanquished within moments of the initial introduction. It appeared that Helen's unexpected announcement had been an expected conclusion.

'Helen, we all knew that you were the only person who hadn't seen the signs,' Diana laughed teasingly. 'They've always been there but you just needed a little help along the way.' Diana then turned to Thomas and laughingly but politely chided him, 'And you're no better. It took these two, who were on their own honeymoon, to bring you together.'

Horton House rang with laughter and happiness that evening. A special dinner had been arranged for the celebrations and, once Jack and his young sister Jacinta had reluctantly agreed to go to bed, the three couples enjoyed a wealth of effortless conversation, fine cuisine and copious liquid refreshments.

As was customary the men withdrew to enjoy their port and allow Richard to smoke his cigar outside on the terrace.

'You have two beautiful children,' Thomas remarked.

'Yes, I am extremely lucky, particularly at my time of life to have found a beautiful, young woman who agreed to marry me and give such happiness with a family of our own,' Richard replied. 'You never know what is round the corner, do you?'

'Certainly not,' Arnie said. 'Do you know that Sarah and I think the same? I think we are like two peas from the same pod.' Richard and Thomas smiled briefly but whimsically at one another before Richard replied, 'I think you might just be right there. There is no one else quite like you two.'

'Is that a compliment Richard or are you making merry with me?' Arnie enquired.

'Just put it down to the fact that Diana's sense of humour has finally rubbed off on me,' replied Richard.

'Well, I won't argue with that,' Arnie said. 'A good woman can only change a man for the better.' All three men nodded in agreement, each one aware that they had been fortunate enough to marry a good woman.

****

Diana and Sarah had long been reconciled to the fact that Helen would no longer be an active partner at the firm. The sight of the newlyweds together had rapidly quashed any vague hopes or suspicions of anything else. It may have taken some time for these two people to be joined together but there was no question as to their mutual suitability. Everyone around them recognised and respected that.

A few days before they were due to leave Beckston for Cornwall Helen received an unexpected telephone call.

'May I ask if I am speaking to Mrs Helen Tetlow?' came the enquiry.

'Yes, speaking.' Helen was still familiar with her old title rather than her more recent one.

'My name is Roberts, personal butler to Lord Petheridge.'
'I'm sorry but I do not wish to pursue this conversation any further.' Helen was quite adamant that she did not want any future contact with this man.

'Please, I can understand your reluctance in this matter, but he has instructed me to contact you. In truth he wishes to see you just once more.'

'Absolutely not! I thought that I had made it extremely clear to him at that first and last meeting that I wanted nothing more to do with him.'

'Apparently you did. However he wishes to see you. I'm afraid he is dying and according to his doctor unlikely to see the week out. He is most anxious to speak with you. If you can come, please make it as soon as possible. Thank you Mrs Tetlow.' The line went dead and Helen became reconciled as to the next course of action.

****

This time the journey was slightly more bearable, presumably because having undertaken it once before it appeared a little more familiar and her husband was also at her side. Thomas appeared a little uneasy as the car followed the long driveway before allowing the majestic hall to become visible.

Helen grasped his hand and squeezed it. 'What are you thinking?'

'I cannot believe that all this is home to just one man,' came Thomas's reply.

'And to his servants.'

'Of course those as well. How can one man own all of this? Just think of the good that it could be put to. A school, a hospital, the possibilities are endless.'

'I know they are,' Helen murmured quietly. The problem was that Petheridge was far from being a benefactor. At that precise moment Helen suddenly wondered if his insistence upon her visiting him was linked to her previous meeting. 'You are the sole heir to a vast fortune.' Those words, his words, suddenly struck her. She really did not want anything from this man except to be left alone to enjoy a simple life with her new husband.

By the time the car had stopped at the entrance porch Helen was feeling distinctly sick. Her emotions were causing her to feel both hot and cold simultaneously. She had only told Thomas the basis of her connection to Petheridge, through her grandmother's ancestry, and had purposefully omitted to mention anything more. Now she glanced upwards to the carved stone shield, reading the still incomprehensible Latin motto: 'Nulli Secundus'; sighed and resigned herself to the fact that she had to meet with him once more.

Presumably the butler opening the car door and uttering gratitude was Roberts, the man who had persuaded her to put aside her rationale for staying away. A decided look of surprise filtered across his face as Thomas followed his wife from the car. Helen declined to enlighten the butler as to who this stranger was and instead, taking hold of her husband's hand, led him through the massive oak panelled doors and into the grand entrance beyond. Casting a glance only once at him she was surprised and relieved by the calmness upon his face. She had expected a traumatised look but instead found one of astonishment as his eyes swept fleetingly across the numerous canvases of oil paintings. Not a word passed between them as he surveyed the artistic gallery, appreciating not their value but their quality.

This time the butler intimated for them to follow him to the imposing arched entrance before ascending the great black oak staircase. Lining the walls were portraits whose eyes peered out of the darkness with an unnerving persistence at the visitors. Helen resisted staring back for fear of making eye contact with the hall's previous inhabitants. Reaching the first floor they continued to follow the butler along a wide corridor or gallery passing many finely carved oak chests which were situated at intervals between doors leading to numerous bedchambers. They eventually turned into a darkened corridor where the walls and floor were lined in oak that through the years had mellowed to a rich brown tint. There was little light here as there were only two small windows, situated at opposite ends of this corridor, which were allowing ineffective shafts of light to penetrate through. The butler stopped outside one of the doors and intimated for them to wait as he entered, closing the door behind him. Within seconds he returned and Helen, grasping Thomas's hand quite tightly, entered the chamber.

The dark oak lined walls in this room were dominated by an elaborate plaster ceiling whose ornamentation in high relief consisted of birds and small animals' heads set amidst convoluted tree branches that wound around the curious collections before tapering to indistinguishable ends of entwined leaves, flowers and fruits. The ornate details were continued in a striking mantelpiece which reached the height of the room and eventually drew Helen's eyes to the centrepiece of the chamber, a dominant four poster, resplendent with red silken drapes. Helen had never seen a bed like this before and, releasing Thomas's hand, she slowly walked towards it where the butler was motioning for her to attend. There its occupant lay, still and motionless, white in pallor and lifeless in body. As the butler stooped low and spoke to his master, Petheridge opened his eyes and a faint grimace crossed his countenance.

'Helen. I knew you would not fail me.'

'No.'

'Come close. You must be close.' The invitation caused revulsion as she peered down at him. The skeletal frame now had even less flesh covering it than before.
'I don't have long left. This will soon be yours. Helen, I want you to promise me something.' His speech trailed off to an almost inaudible utterance. Helen made no reply. Fearfully she waited for the request.

'Will you give me your promise?'

'It depends what you want from me,' came her reply.

At this he appeared amused and once more a faint grimace passed across his face.

'You are so like her in both looks and gestures. When I look at you, I see only her and do you know that is worth going to my grave for.' For a few moments he lay back on the pillow and studied her face.

'You can afford to be choosy Helen. The family motto, 'Nulli Secundus, Inferior to None,' is a clear indication that only money and breeding will do. So Helen, you must give me your promise that you will not make an unsuitable marriage. You need to carry the line on.'

'Yes, I give you my promise that I have not made an inferior match. My husband is certainly not inferior to me. If anything I question whether I am good enough for him.' A perplexed look ran across Petheridge's face.

'Let me introduce my husband, Mr Thomas Ledgard.' Helen turned, stretched out her hand in an effort to offer encouragement and waited until he walked slowly across to join her. He was clearly uncomfortable and would have preferred to remain concealed in the darkness of the corner. Thomas found on closer inspection that Petheridge was a weakened and extremely infirm old man whose remaining vestige of life was rapidly deteriorating. It appeared that he was dying before their very eyes. The sight of Thomas suddenly changed everything.

'Why have you come here?' demanded Petheridge. Neither Thomas nor Helen could understand the note of recognition that had hit Petheridge. He began to stir in an agitated and confused way.

'Why now? Why have you brought him to me now Helena?' The look of fear in his eyes was disturbing.

'You are mistaken. This is Thomas Ledgard, my husband.' Helen tried to calm him.

'No. You are lying to me. It is John Norton, the man that you have always loved and the man that I sent to the grave.' A moment elapsed before Petheridge continued. 'So it is just. You have come to take me to mine now. Well, I'll not go with you!'

'You need to rest. You are just a little confused. It may be the medication.' Helen tried to reassure and comfort him.

Without warning, Petheridge suddenly sat upright in bed and pointed his finger accusingly towards Helen.

'Helena, I'm not so confused to know that you carry his seed in your belly. You cannot deny that.' The accusation seemed totally absurd and was but proof of Petheridge's failing mind.

'No I cannot,' came her stunned reply.

The admission gave closure as Petheridge simply expired and fell back upon his pillows.

****

The final cessation of life had been expected. However the moments leading up to it had not. Afterwards Helen and Thomas had remained at Stansdale Hall until the doctor had arrived and pronounced him dead. They remained out of duty, self imposed, but nevertheless a necessary obligation. There were neither tears shed nor any visual display of emotion. It was only when they were safely travelling back to Horton House that Thomas ventured to ask.

'Why did he call you Helena?'

'That was my grandmother's name and I have been told that I look very much like her.'

A moment elapsed before Thomas spoke again.

'Who was John Norton and why did he think I was him?'

'That is a mystery on both counts. I've heard the name somewhere before but I don't know why he thought you were him.'

'Perhaps there is some truth in what old Mrs Shackleton used to say.'

'About what?' Helen looked at him with some intrigue.

'She always used to say that when someone was dying often a loved one who had already died would return to them in the guise of the living, in order to help them into the next world.'

'I don't think that John Norton was a loved one. In fact by the description, just the opposite.'

Helen suddenly remembered where she had heard the name. The solicitor who had read William Fawcett's will had astonished everyone present by announcing the bequest of 10 000 pounds to the son or descendents of John Norton. Her mind now began to whirl with possibilities until Thomas interrupted with a further question.

'What did you mean when you said that you could not deny Petheridge's accusation?'

'Ah, now that is something I can answer. I was going to tell you tonight. I've just found out that I'm pregnant, Thomas. You're going to be a father.'

This announcement was something that they both mutually desired. Each one was ecstatic with happiness and as they embraced and kissed the previous encounter with Petheridge and Stansdale Hall was momentarily blocked from their memories. However, common sense once more prevailed.

'How could Petheridge have known that you were pregnant? You hadn't told him.'

'Call it a dying man's intuition,' Helen remarked lightly.

As they laughed at the unearthly notion Helen seriously wondered how Petheridge could have known. A shiver ran down her back with that mortal thought.

* *

The natural cycle of life always seemed to miraculously replenish unexpectedly; as death followed birth in life, birth would follow death. Horton House was abuzz with excitement and celebration. Champagne corks popped, glasses chinked and Helen steadfastly toasted with orange juice, as Diana selflessly teased that she would be only too happy to help Helen dispose of her alcohol. Amidst all of these celebrations the prospective parents felt that they still had one obligation to carry out: that of visiting Tom. Neither Thomas nor Helen looked forward to the prospect but each one agreed that he should know of their marriage and of the opportunity to be a grandparent. How he would react to each piece of news no one could predict.

Helen's insistence upon accompanying Thomas upon the visit had been so strongly imparted that he had been unable to refuse her. It stemmed not from the urge to see him once more but from the innate sense of duty that she felt as Thomas's wife. This time, with Thomas at her side, she felt less apprehensive as the old front door opened. With some surprise they gazed upon a gentle caring face, one not dissimilar to Annie's. The greeting they received from this lady was totally different to the one that Helen had previously received. A benevolent soul, Mrs Barker was a neighbour who had voluntarily agreed to keep an eye upon Tom since his previous 'housekeeper' had left. Helen suspected that the term 'housekeeper' was an enthusiastic use of the euphemism which referred to the unpleasant old crone. Mrs Barker was a true philanthropist in every way; having a husband of her own she did not live in the house and received no monetary rewards for her diligence. However her efforts were clearly visible as the house now looked clean and tidy.

'He refuses to go to his bed,' Mrs Barker remarked disapprovingly.

'Bed! That's where you bloody die woman.' The objection was followed by a convulsion of uncontrollable wheezing and coughing. As the outburst finally cleared Tom recognised that he had visitors.

'Good God! Look what the wind 'as blown in. I'm surprised to see you 'ere.' Tom was as always predictable, leaving no room for niceties. Slumped in his chair he listened to their news impassively and made no comment.

Finally as they said farewell and turned to leave, he spoke.

'I don't know why you've bothered to come and see me. What is it to me that you're 'aving a child? I'll never see it. I'll be long dead before then.'

The words were indeed a premonitory warning. Within the week Tom was dead.

****

They paid their respects at the meanly attended funeral. Judging by those present around his grave, Tom had been far from popular. He had lived his life without sentimentality and could now expect nothing more. With their duty behind them Helen and Thomas used their emotions instead to bid farewell to their friends in Beckston before returning to Cornwall.

The Cornish charms never failed but to rejuvenate the stresses of modern day life. Whether it was the landscape, the water, the people or the air that magically healed the careworn, everyone testified to the elixir of Cornish life. Thomas returned jubilantly to his simplistic life of being a fisherman and an artist, leaving Helen time to contemplate her future as a wife and a mother. It was everything that Helen had ever wanted but now she realised that it was no longer enough. The turmoil throughout her life had resulted in the creation of a resilient woman who unknowingly feasted off challenge. There was now neither challenge nor adversity of any kind but Helen had a craving for more than just pregnancy.

The timing of Puck Evans's visit could not have been better. He was genuinely pleased to see them, hear of their news and to impart that he had sold more of Thomas's paintings.

'I tell you both, Thomas here is in demand. Give up the day job boy and concentrate on what you're really good at. Get yourself a studio and exhibit your work. With someone to push your sales you could be really successful.'

'That's all very well but you need money to do that and we cannot afford it at the moment,' Thomas replied.

The conversation made Helen realise that she needed to talk to her husband quickly. He still had no knowledge of her wealth. He also did not know that she now more than ever required a challenge and that she had just recognised what that would be.

Thomas's pride held a staunch resolve against Helen's suggestion of using her considerable inheritance to purchase somewhere which could be used to exhibit his paintings. He continued to oppose the idea until she presented another scenario.

'The money is not just mine. It's ours Thomas and should be used as such. It is also there for our children. Instead of living in a rented cottage, which will soon prove to be too small for us, why don't we buy our own home and develop a studio there? In other words we could live and work together. Just think of it, you could paint and I could be responsible for the selling of your work. I've had enough experience from my work at Tetlows to be able to do that. The products may be different but the process is the same.'

His resolve weakened as Thomas watched the animated glow of excitement which emulated from his wife's eyes. This was a side of her that he had never witnessed before. As he began to smile she knew that her words had been effective and was now more determined than ever to succeed.

'You are exceedingly talented Thomas. You could spend your life doing a job which you really love and live well from it. But if people don't know about your work they won't be able to buy it. That's why we need to do this properly. And before your masculine pride kicks in, just consider that if you take this chance, you'll be the one who is earning good money to keep his family. I'm only setting us up; you'll be doing the rest.'

Thomas nodded slowly in agreement. He was determined that this mutual business venture would succeed and prosper, not just because of his masculine pride and desire to provide for his family, but because of the satisfaction he knew it would give Helen. Anxious to secure these dreams they began to look around for suitable property but neither had envisaged that they would be interrupted in their search by the arrival of a letter.

The contents of the letter were not entirely unforeseen but Helen wished that Lord Petheridge had not named her as his main beneficiary. Her feelings for him now remained the same; she loathed both the man and any connection to him. The letter however was most specific that Helen was required to attend the reading of the will at the solicitor's office in Beckston. It was a considerable estate and Helen reluctantly agreed to be present. What was a little less clear was that Thomas was also required to accompany her.

The oldest solicitors practice in Beckston, Clarksons, had been duly selected to handle the affairs of so eminent a person as Lord Petheridge of Stansdale. By coincidence Mr Clarkson had also dealt with William Fawcett's estate and therefore clearly recognised Helen.

'You are indeed a most fortunate young woman. By that I do not of course refer to your sad losses, but to the fact that you have now been cited in two substantial estates as the main beneficiary.' As Mr Clarkson continued Helen began to feel decidedly uncomfortable.

'With the exception of but a few token amounts of money to loyal servants I am happy to inform you that Lord Petheridge has bequeathed all of his assets to you, Mrs Ledgard. The said assets of course include Stansdale Hall, its contents, which are conderable and unquestionably valuable, all of the surrounding land in which the hall is situated, substantial bank accounts and ownership of Fawcett's mill, which of course also includes both the business and the buildings themselves. You may recall that at the reading of William Fawcett's will it was disclosed that the aforesaid had sold the majority of his business to Lord Petheridge.' The solicitor paused, allowing Helen some time to reflect, contemplate her future and pose questions. Her face was grave and she made no attempt to speak. Her thoughts were clearly distant as her eyes showed no acknowledgement or indeed astonishment at the disclosures.

'Mrs Ledgard, are you alright?' came the concerned query.

'Yes, perfectly. Thank you.' Helen reached out to take hold of her husband's hand and as she did so, threw him a smile, which he returned.

'Well, thank you for your time, Mr Clarkson. Obviously we need some time to think about all of this. Before we leave, may I just ask whether you have been able to trace John Norton who was mentioned in William Fawcett's will?' Helen felt that as Mr Clarkson had referred to her grandfather it would not be inappropriate now to make this enquiry.

'By a strange quirk of fate I have managed to identify his descendents. John Norton himself disappeared approximately fifty years ago whilst in the employment of Lord Petheridge. The coincidence here is remarkable. He has never been sighted and by now, without question, must be assumed dead. He left a young wife and baby son. It appears that with her husband missing the wife returned to Beckston to live with her own parents. Presumably, this was due to financial necessity. It appears that the marriage may not have been a happy one as the wife then resorted to using her maiden name for both herself and baby son. As you can imagine this factor alone has caused unprecedented difficulties with trying to trace the family line. The wife died many years ago and the son, a father himself, died recently. Mr Ledgard, I requested your presence here today, not because of anything that your father has left you for there were no assets at all, but because you are the direct and only living descendent of John Norton, who was your grandfather. By the terms of William Fawcett's will, you are to receive 10 000 pounds which was left and I quote, "in recognition of a long and overdue payment".'

CHAPTER TWENTY-SEVEN

The conversation that night repeatedly focussed upon the New Look. Everyone was in agreement that those long mid calf, swirling skirts initiated by Christian Dior in Paris would sweep away the post-war blues in England. Material may still have been rationed but they all recognised an opportunity which would finally bring wartime austerity to an end and allow consumerism to be reborn. There was nothing like fashion to do just that.

It was true that the extravagant use of material would create disapproval in a nation that had had to resort to frugality. Supplies of raw materials were difficult to obtain and mills were still in the transition period between wartime and peacetime production. Even Tetlows had proved to be versatile for the war effort having been requisitioned to produce utilitarian military garments instead of the desires of fashion. All were in agreement, however, that 1947 would be the year to offer change and that is when they instigated the idea which would do just that.

They knew it would succeed because it had done so previously. Cornwall had the best backdrops of stunning scenery for fashion shoots: wild, desirable and romantic. Diana and Sarah worked tirelessly with their workforce to create the illusions from design into reality whilst Arnie eagerly agreed to produce the fashion photographs which would capture the retail market.

The Second World War had had unprecedented effects upon the lives of everyone in Britain. For some these had been more demanding than others. Diana and Sarah had continued to run the business amidst the uncertainties of the time by fulfilling the necessary requirements of the armed forces for hardwearing worsted serge uniforms. Conformity to practicality rather than desirability became the order of the day. However with the advent of peacetime and the promising return of indulgent human consumerism, Sarah's creativity was easily ignited into a frenzy of couturier designs. This, coupled with the dawning of the New Look, provided sufficient impetus to relaunch the name of Tetlows in the fashion world. For Diana the additional workload demands and dimensions of the project became a welcome relief and diversification from the memory of the war years. Like many women these years had seen her lose a husband but not as a result of active service as Richard's age had been a barrier to that. A heart attack had quietly and unexpectedly removed him from her life. The once incorrigible Diana now grieved for the man that against all likelihood in the eyes of many she had truly loved and now sorely missed. Her consolation increasingly became her work and her son and daughter.

Sarah's creativity also benefited from the fact that she had now been reunited with Arnie. They were a couple that functioned as one; never having felt the need for a family of their own they revelled in each other's company. Therefore the strain of separation imposed by war had proved exceedingly difficult. Arnie was keen to join the air force and they were keen to accept him. They recognised that his photography skills could be of enormous advantage, especially in reconnaissance work in surveying regions, in order to locate the enemy or ascertain strategic features. A freelance photographer should certainly never be turned away.

****

The driveway to the house was neither grand nor pretentious. Surrounded with rhododendrons and camellias a Georgian house of sufficient size presided over carefully tended grounds which swept down towards the sea and the cliffs beyond. In the distance one could glimpse the little harbour of Mousehole with its curved stone quays offering protection to the little coastal village. Before the car had stopped their hosts were waiting to greet them. The scene was one of highly charged emotions as everyone crushed one another with affectionate kisses and tightly held hugs. There were squeals of delight and gasps of astonishment as each member intermingled with those they knew and those they had just met. Almost ten years had passed and there was a great deal of catching up to do.

Helen and Thomas had found their ideal home; one which possessed outbuildings where Thomas could both paint and exhibit his artwork in a modern studio. Helen had been the driving force behind this as she was in the marketing of his paintings. His name was well-known and well respected to the extent that his paintings were regularly commissioned, often from different parts of the world, thereby securing large fees. If ever Thomas had worried about the threat of his wife's inheritance he could now feel secure in the marked profits of his achievements. Puck Evans had indeed been astute and correct in encouraging such talent.

Thomas had of course insisted that the legacy he received from William Fawcett had to be used with Helen's money in purchasing their home. The revelation that he was truly a Norton had been unexpected. The fact that both Helen and he were true cousins was, without question, a bewildering surprise to each of them. His father Tom had left him nothing except his own pen and ink drawings which were a clear indication of his talent. Perhaps there had been some truth in his words that the gift could be passed down from generation to generation. This had certainly been substantiated when Helen had found a small piece of paper carefully folded and hidden in her grandmother's jewellery box. Without question it was a simple ink drawing of Helena, her grandmother. The identity of the artist would remain a secret no longer for it held as its inscription the letters 'JN' in the bottom right hand corner. The finding of this proved to be a decisive turning point in the identity of the family name. They were neither Ledgard nor Norton and therefore it somehow seemed fitting to finally become the Norton-Ledgards.

There had been considerable changes in Helen's life throughout the last decade. Her personal life had altered greatly but she was now totally content. The war was at an end, Thomas had returned safe and well from service in the navy, and she was content in the knowledge that she had not touched a penny of Petheridge's money for herself. Instead she had simply given the entire estate and accumulative wealth to be used as a hospital. The timing of her gift to the nation could not have been better as numerous servicemen found to their advantage.

The days that passed with their friends were simple and happy. There were now no further skeletons to emerge or unwanted guests to appear. The only extra visitors were those they were eager to see. Puck Evans and his most agreeable wife arrived and were encouraged to stay with the house party. They particularly enjoyed the company of the youngsters, Jack, Jacinta and Anne.

At twelve years old Jack Tetlow had his mother's twinkle in his eye and a measure of her self-assurance. Everyone agreed within a few years the girls would prove to be putty in his hands. Jacinta was two years junior to her brother and appeared more reticent, rather like Richard had been. Everyone agreed that they were a credit to Diana. Anne played well with both of them considering she was an only child. Her dark eyes and raven black hair were distinctive and definitely a result of her father's colouring. Thomas's dark features had always been unmistakeable. At nine years old she already possessed her mother's full sensuous mouth and captivating dimples and was indeed becoming a beauty. Although the blue eyes and blond hair were absent there was something in her demeanour that caused Puck Evans to remark upon the resemblance to her great grandmother. The oil painting of Helena hung in the dining room and following his comment Helen acknowledged it with just a smile. Anne, whom they had named after gentle and caring Annie, possessed a feisty spirit which if Helen wasn't mistaken would, with her looks, trap the hearts of many men in the future.

At 35 years old both Helen and Diana considered themselves too old to be models for the photo shoot. Arnie and Sarah vehemently disagreed and ultimately persuaded them to pose with their individual degree of elegance which the New Look demanded. The whole adventure brought back memories and together they giggled and somehow began to recall past memories and long forgotten anecdotes. They were still talking of these as they returned home.

Later Diana joined Helen in the garden for a glass of wine.

'I want you to have this,' Diana said, holding out an old book.
'What is it?'

'It belonged to Richard. I know he would have wanted you to have it. Do you remember you often used to go into his library and read his books?'

'Yes, I do. Richard was always very kind to me and it was he who introduced me to many different poets and authors. I found that I could always solve my problems by reading. This was one of his favourite books. A book of poetry.'

Upon opening the book fell open at a well-used page and Helen read the lines out loud:

"Oh, what a tangled web we weave,
When first we practise to deceive."
Sir Walter Scott (1771-1832).

Helen fell silent and stared towards a nearby bush where a spider had just been repairing its own intricately woven web.

'How strange! I've just been watching a spider here, marvelling at his creativity. I've never before considered how life can be likened to a spider's web. Oh Diana, I've deceived and those before me have also deceived, little realising the consequences of those actions. Do I now deserve to be this happy with Thomas? If I had my life over again...'

'You'd do the same. We all would. It's all down to fate,' remarked Diana.

'Yes, that's what Annie once said. Perhaps your life is all mapped out for you at the time of birth.'

'Anyway, you shouldn't be concerned with the past. What's done is done. Forget the past, live for the present and look forward to the future. That has always been my motto. In fact the future is just in front of us.'

Both women glanced away from the spider and focussed their attention upon the three children playing happily on the lawns in front of them. Jack seemed oblivious to anything around him, appearing quite mesmerised by Anne who was happily dictating orders to her two companions who were agreeably complying.

The moment was broken as Thomas and the others joined them.

'We've come to join you with some drinks. More wine anyone?' As Thomas filled the glasses everyone looked at Diana as she gestured and took centre stage. They raised their glasses in anticipation.

'Let's have a toast. Here's to friendship,' said Diana.

'To friendship and to the future,' said Helen.

Lightning Source UK Ltd.
Milton Keynes UK
UKOW04f0946041214

242643UK00001B/48/P